THE BRIDE OF LOWTHER FELL

We passed Miss Cowdie almost at once, standing under the signpost, beaming foolishly up the road that led to Uldale. Unless one knew why she stood there, there was nothing intrinsically pathetic in her stance. Agreed, nobody stands in the middle of a lonely country road in pouring rain like that unless there is something wrong with them, but nobody passing, as I went by in my mini, would have thought anything of it. She looked so cheerful and expectant and quite confident. Any motorist could have been forgiven for imagining that she was about to be picked up any second and that the waiting was pre-arranged. She stood slightly on tip-toe, one hand at the collar of her coat and the other half raised as if in greeting – it was quite feasible that she could already see who was coming and was about to wave. I slowed down slightly, not wanting to spray her with rain from the large puddle I was about to go through in order to turn the corner to Caldbeck, and as I did so she stopped staring up the road for a minute and the smile left her face. She bent down, her face contorted, and shook her fist at me . . .

By the same author

FICTION
Dame's Delight
Georgy Girl
The Bogeyman
The Travels of Maudie Tipstaff
The Park
Miss Owen-Owen is At Home
Fenella Phizackerley
Mr Bone's Retreat
The Seduction of Mrs Pendlebury
Mother Can You Hear Me?

BIOGRAPHY
The Rash Adventurer:
The Rise and Fall of Charles Edward Stuart
William Makepeace Thackeray
Memoirs of a Victorian Gentleman

THE BRIDE OF LOWTHER FELL

A Romance

Margaret Forster

Hamlyn Paperbacks

THE BRIDE OF LOWTHER FELL

ISBN 0 600 20448 0

First published in Great Britain 1980
by Secker & Warburg Ltd
Hamlyn Paperbacks edition 1982

Hamlyn Paperbacks are published by
The Hamlyn Publishing Group Ltd,
Astronaut House, Feltham.
Middlesex, England

Printed and bound in Great Britain by
Cox & Wyman Ltd, Reading

For my fellow Cumbrian
Melvyn Bragg

Prologue

Last night there was a storm. It rained torrentially, drumming with steel fingers on the slate roof of this cottage, but this morning all was blue and calm. I walked into Caldbeck, perhaps for the last time. I walked along the track, avoiding the potholes filled to the brim with dark brown water, and down past the turning to the Crosthwaites' farm – there was no smoke coming from their chimney in the distance – and onto the beginnings of the hard-core path which led to the road. As I came out from the shelter of the hill, the wind suddenly got up, blowing hard across the fell from the north-west, bringing the scent and sting of the far-off sea, but the sun shone and softened its bitter whiplash. I reached Greenhead and crossed the bridge and took a short cut across the rough grass to the mud path leading down to Parkend. It hugs the dry stone wall, dipping into marshy pastures, swerving between thick gorse bushes, which I remember as pretty yellow things when I arrived, and comes out at two cottages, set back from the road. I don't know who lives in them. I have never seen anyone go in or out.

I stood for a while looking into Parkend Beck. The water frothed and foamed and here and there carried with it broken lumps of ice. I wondered, a little dismally, if it could ever be hot enough here to want to throw oneself into that icy torrent. Perhaps summer did come, but I could not imagine it. This seems a part of the world doomed to be always cold. I could not believe, as I looked about me, that those brown hills looming behind me could ever look gentle in the full heat of a blazing June day. Even then, they must surely threaten rain and mist and that raw sleet we have had so much of all winter. Nothing grew on those hills except grass. I had never seen a flower anywhere in mile after mile of wet, dark green ground and even the trees were poor battered things to whom the glories of blossom or autumn leaves were largely unknown. Snow still lay on the top of Skiddaw and on the slopes of High Pike white fingers cruelly scarred the outcrops of rock.

The beck was in full spate with all the snow that had already melted and in the sudden sun, as likely to go as soon as it had come, it sparkled and flashed. It was a noisy stream at all times, but this morning it seemed more boisterous than ever, spluttering and choking over the stones and threatening to flood the smooth green banks on the road side. I followed it with pleasure, glad to be down from the fells, glad to let it guide me to civilisation of a sort. At Whelpo the geese chased me, pecking at my boots and arching their necks in triumph. At the top of the hill that dropped down into Caldbeck, I turned left and crossed the stile and took the field path that led to the Howk, a strange, deserted place where once there had been a thriving mill. All that was left was a ruined building beside the water and a sense of darkness and decay. Even in winter the trees kept out the light and as I went carefully down the slippery steps – clinging to the iron rail – the gloom came up to meet me.

The door into the village street was open – one of those doors within a door, a huge wooden door that kept in all the farm animals. There never seemed to be anyone about, although I had used that path ever since I discovered it three months before. There were cows and hens in the yard often enough, and sometimes a sheep dog would appear and bark, but never a single person. I was always careful to close the smaller door properly, though the step to get through it was too high for most animals to attempt without encouragement. On the green, I paused to look at the duckpond – murky and full of weeds with only two extremely dirty brown ducks upon it – and at the pretty houses that edged it. These houses were different from the fell houses. They had painted doors and window frames and though they were built of the same stone they seemed altogether more mellow. Perhaps their sheltered position preserves the colours. These houses are visibly cared for and yet I do not know who cares for them any more than I know who neglects those other places on the fell. I have never seen anyone coming out of them to ask any questions of – questions quite harmless in nature. I imagine them to be inhabited by local gentry, solicitors and magistrates, who go into Carlisle once a week to change their library books and shop at Bulloughs, who wear nicely faded tweed clothes and drive ancient but well maintained Morris Minors. But I don't know.

I went the back way into the churchyard, crossing the beck yet again, now a subdued trickle at this point. The church, St Kentigern's, is sixteenth century, small, with a spire that seems rather short and blunt. I have never been inside, not even out of curiosity. The insides of churches depress me and I try to keep out of them. Churchyards – graveyards – on the other hand console me and I am fond of them. I like to study the tombstones and work out the degree of grief the bereaved might safely be assumed to have felt, given the facts upon them. Silly, I know, when Mary Harrison may have felt more prolonged distress than can possibly be imagined over the death of Her Husband, aged eighty three, whereas the parents of Thomas, aged two months, may since have reared such a large healthy family that all they remember is a momentary numbness.

John Peel is buried in Caldbeck churchyard, which brings a few tourists to it. All I know about Mr Peel is that he was a huntsman and breeder of hounds, which makes him singularly uninteresting in my eyes. Almost everywhere around here has connections with him and the craftshop fairly bursts with souvenirs, but actual facts about his life are hard to come by. A legend has crystallised round a song, written much later, and the man himself hardly deserves it. But his white gravestone next to a large holly tree is large and impressive and I never pass it without reading the inscription yet again, and giving him a nod. The new graves are over at the other side, as ugly as the old ones are beautiful. The stones are too white, the graves too neat, the flowers upon them too bright. Since I had not been at the funeral, I did not know where to look for the unmarked grave, but of course it was easy to find. The sods on top of it were still cut in squares and had not had time to grow together. I stood and looked down at the hump shaped mound, poking the wet earth with the squat toe of my Wellington boot. I ought to have been more affected than I was. No tears came, nor did I feel particularly sad. What was there to cry about? It was all over and done with – finished. I would only be crying for myself and I had too much self-respect to do that. But as I turned away, pausing only to turn over the single wreath – from me, of course – which had fallen flowers downwards, I felt suddenly nauseous. I found myself standing clutching at the iron gate of the churchyard, head spinning, and my limbs weak and shaking. I crouched down behind the stone wall and forced myself to overcome the sensation of falling, of unsteadiness and sickness, that had seemed to strike me, as soon as I left the grave, with all the force of a well aimed stone. Simply reaction, that was all. I am very good in disasters – calm, sensible, level headed – and then, when it is all over, sometimes weeks after it is all over, I collapse trembling, as though whatever iron will had enabled me to be brave had been worn away without my knowing it and had at last snapped.

Five minutes later I was striding through the village, past the shop and the pub, past the craftshop on the corner where already – though it was still winter – there were people stopping in their cars to poke and pry and satisfy their urge to collect some pointless memento of "a nice run". And I do stride, I know that. I turn every walk into a race. I like to stick my hands deep into the pockets of my jacket and huddle into myself and eat up the ground with my feet as though I were the possessor of seven-league boots. There is no fun in meandering along. I like to feel all my limbs moving vigorously and if people say I walk like a man I choose to take it as a compliment. If I were taller, if I did not have thick long hair, if I were altogether broader and squarer then I might also look like a man and nobody would remark upon my stride.

The way back to Lowther Fell has always been tiring. The road climbs steeply out of the village and even when it appears to straighten and flatten itself this is an illusion – it still climbs relentlessly. At Whelpo bridge you can see the road ahead stretching across and upwards towards Uldale and it looks inviting until you are upon it. Then, once over the cattle grid that marks the beginning of the fell proper, it becomes exhausting to follow. It climbs in fits and starts, in twists and bends, to the signpost that says Caldbeck 3½ miles, Uldale 2, open on both sides to the winds that rage with such violence that trees are bent double with the force. At the signpost, I turned left for Brae Fell, not a car to be seen anywhere on the long stretch ahead. The road here is so exposed that not a creature could hide on it, should they wish to do so. There is no shelter, no possibility of protection. Were it not so narrow and winding, it would be like a Roman Road, taking the easiest way in rough terrain and going for its destination with a sure eye.

I left it at Brae Fell and walked along the broad grassy track towards Longlands. It is a beautiful path – on a fine day, looking to the right, one can see the Solway Firth and Criffel across the sea. I am always reluctant to leave it for the rougher way to Lowther Fell. The break is abrupt. There is a stream which comes pouring down from Lowther Fell – it runs behind my cottage – and where it so rudely cuts the Longlands path in half the bumpy track home begins. It leads into the folds of the fell itself, following the lowest contour in a great arc, and there is a certain excitement in scrambling along it. Nothing ahead can be seen for half a mile and then suddenly it opens out and there, rising ahead, is the smooth domed top of the fell with my cottage underneath it.

I slowed down, reluctant to make the final climb. I have always felt reluctant. The events of the last few weeks, startling and horrible though they have been, have done no more than confirm my original sense of unease. I knew I should never have come.

I should never have come and then none of this would have happened – a fatal line of thought to pursue. I excuse myself on the grounds that I never remember choosing to come – it was all thrust upon me. I behaved at the time as though I had been given a set of instructions I must at all costs carry out. I simply obeyed a strong instinct and I shall have to wonder all the rest of my life whether it was wrong. As I began on that last gruelling climb up to my cottage, my steps much slower and shorter now, I tried hard to remember exactly how I had felt that awful day in September last year when my whole life abruptly changed its course.

One

There was no gradual build up to the tragedy – it came upon us all in the way of tragedies, full pelt out of a clear blue sky. I remember that sky particularly well. I came out of my basement flat in a house in Church Row, Hampstead, and looked up and thought what an absurd kind of life I lived when I could, I knew, have got a much larger flat – light, airy – in a different part of London. I could have had a flat in which I could lie in bed and *see* that sky before I even got up. I marched across the street full of resentment, resolving that I would move – and that, I suppose, was the beginning, before anything had really happened.

I had my car parked in a lock-up garage in Holly Walk – absurdly inconvenient but there was no alternative, living where I did. It cost me a fortune in rent but I could not bear to be without a car – it was, if you like, my independence. From the moment I bought my first car – a mini, when I was twenty – I felt free. I was at nobody's beck and call. I could go wherever I liked on my own terms and not be stranded. It became a symbol of the kind of life I wished to lead and I cannot overstress its importance to me. Not that the machine itself had any sort of power over me – I did not invest metal with meaning – I was not in the least sentimental about my MGB sports car. Well, not very. I did not polish it lovingly (or unlovingly) or anything like that. But, once at the wheel, I felt happy and secure and very confident.

My happiness on the morning that the brilliant blue sky had put me in such a bad mood was debatable. I drove round the Heath towards Highgate Art College where I worked, thinking how stale everything was. I did not normally find my existence stale. At thirty-two years old I had things organised as I liked them. I taught art because I liked to teach art – I like simply to teach. I went for exciting holidays twice a year and whenever the spirit moved me I went to the theatre, to films, to a variety of interesting events. Housework bores me and I had therefore long since cut it out – my two roomed flat was so arranged that it hardly needed to be cleaned and when it did I hired someone from an agency to give it a thorough going over. Cooking was no problem. I ate out a lot and when I was in I preferred fresh fruit, salads and cheese to any more elaborate concoctions.

I lived alone, through choice. People still find it hard to believe that a single woman can wish to live alone but those who knew me had accepted it was obviously true. My relatives had stopped worrying about me. They hoped, of course, that I would marry Edward one day but I think Antonia at least knew I would not. Edward had come and gone – come and been sent away, he would have said – in my life for more than ten years. One of the reasons for buying such a small flat was that Edward would no longer be able to live with me for months on end. "The flat is too small," I had begun to say triumphantly and he had seen this was unhappily for him true. Friends stayed, at the most, for the weekend and however nice I was glad to see them go. I am not tolerant. I find everyone maddening after half an hour – I simply cannot stand all those mannerisms to which everyone is entitled but which become so wearing to observe. Quite simply things like the unnecessary vigour with which a person butters their toast can make me wince if I have to witness it more than once. I know the fault lies in me but I no longer fight it – I just get rid of the source of the annoyance as quickly as possible. I am better on my own and if that is selfish then I am selfish.

My mother always said I would have to live on my own and how dreadful it would be to pay the penalty of my temperament. There was nothing to be proud of, she said, in not being able to stand other people – but I was not proud of it. It worried me and I tried for many years to swallow my irritation but it only made things worse. I am lucky that I was born at the beginning of an era in which women were becoming liberated from the kind of image to which I would have found it painful to conform. Nineteen forty eight was a good year for an independent minded girl to be born: ninety sixty nine, an excellent year in which to become of age. I like to think of myself as a creature of my times, most certainly not born to blush unseen but with every prospect of flowering into exactly what I wanted.

But what I wanted was always the trouble. I wanted freedom and I got it – freedom from the restrictions imposed by a strict and domineering mother and an over-anxious father; freedom from an absurdly old fashioned school; freedom from the economic necessity of having to earn my living. Not, of course, that I did not have to work – I do not wish to imply that I was rich, or had a substantial private income, but the death of my parents had given both Antonia and me a degree of independence, financially, which normally does not come to people until late middle age. My car and my flat came out of what I inherited at the tender age of twenty and they set me up for life. The money was a surprise. It came from the sale of my parents' house in north Oxford – a large, Edwardian mansion which inside resembled an Oxfam shop. They had bought it many years ago, knowing they could not maintain it as it needed maintaining. They could not afford to heat it even half adequately. They could not even afford to furnish it. It was full of junk – not antique-type junk, simply junk. The idea had been that they would let the top two floors as flats and live on the income but instead they housed a variety of undergraduates, who made bed-sitting-rooms of the proposed flats and could never pay much in rent. How my mother, who was an extremely sensible and practical person in all other respects, could have allowed this to happen is a mystery. At least she had seen to it that the house was purchased freehold and not leasehold from one of the colleges who owned most of that area. That proved a masterstroke. In 1970, when Antonia and I sold the house, it was snapped up for an absurdly large sum of money.

I may have sounded too enthusiastic about that inheritance, as though I thought it well worth a couple of deaths. This is not true. My parents and I had many fights during my adolescence, but I loved them. How to define that sort of love? Unlike Antonia, I am not demonstrative. "This is the cuddly one," people used to say of Antonia when we were both young, but then with identical twins there is a great urge to find distinguishing features. Rather more cruelly, Antonia was also "the happy one". Even my mother slipped into that appalling habit. "Which is Alexandra?" people would ask, and she would reply, "The one not smiling." It was no compensation that later I was also "the clever one", and even – as Antonia developed some form of eczema – "the pretty one", though this was never said aloud. Antonia remained the one who kissed and embraced our parents while I held back and satirised my own peck-on-the-cheek. I envied her that spontaneity, particularly in that terrible interval between Father's sudden death and Mother's suicide.

Father died of a heart attack, aged fifty one. I have read of this sort of completely unexpected coronary often enough – he even died in bed, without waking Mother up – but I suppose I had never quite believed there could be no symptoms to a discerning eye. Father was fit and healthy. He exercised frequently – tennis and golf and long daily walks to and from the Ashmolean – and ate and drank sensibly. He was not a worrier and under no sort of stress. Antonia and I, his only children, were safely launched on respectable careers. We wondered if we should discover later, during the investigation of his papers and affairs in general, whether he would turn out to have incurred some secret debt – but all was in order. He had very little money in the bank but absolutely no debts and a house virtually mortgage free. Mother was completely bewildered, her normal common sense brutally assaulted, and it was then that Antonia's ability to simply take her in her arms and comfort her caused me great anguish. I could not do it. I longed to help, and I saw physical contact did help, but I did not seem to be able to do what Antonia could so easily do. My role was to see to the funeral and the business side of Father's death – dreary, depressing work. Mother was grateful – she knew how essential but how unrewarding taking things over in that sense was – but I felt I had let her down. This feeling of failure made her own death six months later even more of a nightmare. Would Mother have taken her own life if I had been able, like Antonia, to love her openly? Would the love of two of us have saved her when the love of one did not? It is nonsense to talk like that but then suicides stimulate that kind of maudlin rubbish. Mother killed herself because she did not *want* to bear life without Father, to discover that time heals all and other platitudes. I admired her for it. It was desperately sad to think of her state of mind but I had a feeling of rightness about her conscious decision which Antonia did not share.

At thirty years old, then, I had achieved most of the things I wanted, even if in the most tragic way. And I was happy. For ten years I had enjoyed my position in life and pitied others who were obliged to settle for less, who hungered after what I had, or who had made decisions which later had turned out to be wrong. Invariably, these mistakes hinged on marriage and maternity – too many of my contemporaries had married too quickly and found themselves at thirty trapped in an arrangement they had never wanted. Children complicated what might still have been a simple issue. God knows I have seen enough of those sort of situations – friends with three or even four young children, realising how they hate their own lives. I have never ceased to be grateful that I did not share that same fate and I say that without smugness. I know I could have done. When first I fell in love with Edward – well, yes, I could have married him, and as for having his children, I would have found nothing more enticing at a certain stage.

Edward had just spent the weekend with me, that Monday morning I drove so sourly to work. He had come on Friday evening and left on Sunday afternoon after our row. He was, he said, bored with my pretence that I was the happiest girl in the world – happiest *woman*, he had corrected himself with a sneer. At thirty, I was no longer a girl. It was time, he said, to stop pissing about and settle down – to life with him. If, he said, he truly believed I liked things as they were between us then he would leave me alone but the truth was I lied to myself. My car, my flat, my job – what did I think they all added up to? My life was empty and I knew it. I really wanted to live with him, married or unmarried, and I would not admit it. I was hung up on ridiculous notions about freedom and liberty and meanwhile I was wasting the best years of our life. Then he said, at the end of this familiar tirade, that he loved me, that he had always loved me and that he knew – he knew – that I loved him.

Afterwards, when he had gone, I felt disturbed and weary. There was nothing new in what he had said – it might have been more interesting if there had been – but there was something different in my reaction to it. Usually, I laughed at him. He always looked so absurd, so comical in his determination to convert me to his point of view. Almost always I soothed him with a kiss and ruffled his hair in an insulting way and asked him teasingly who had stolen his scone. Then I would be gentle and tolerant with him and we would make love and he would groan at my evident pleasure in this and yet my continued refusal to interpret our closeness as a sign that I ought to marry him and give up my solitary existence. But that particular time I had not responded like that. Whether Edward was more strident than normal – whether he was harsher and more convincing – I do not know, but Monday morning found me still unsettled and annoyed. He had begun a train of thought that did not go in the direction I wished it to take.

I did my work with less enthusiasm than usual. All morning, while outside that blue, blue sky remained unclouded, I fussed and fidgeted with a new consignment of clay, deploring its texture. I had a class of first-year students, none of whom had any talent whatsoever – or at least, not where pottery was concerned. I had tried to teach them the basic skills but not one of them could even control a wheel with any appearance of confidence. Then they giggled and were silly and more like a nursery class than art college students – oh, I could not tolerate their levity. When I complained of it to another member of staff he smiled, rather unkindly I thought, and said, "You're getting middle aged, Alexandra – it's a sure sign." I thought about his judgement all lunch hour. Perhaps Edward had merely touched a nerve which was already throbbing – perhaps there was a basic discontent in me which I was only just beginning to notice. I waited for my afternoon class to arrive, turning over in my mind the startling hypothesis *that I was not as happy as I seemed*. Yet what else did I want? Not domesticity – certainly not that. I would run a million miles from the picture of myself wearing an apron and warming slippers by the fire. Not company – I still wanted it only on my own terms. What, then? What did I want that I did not have? Simply a change? Of job, routine, friends? Could I possibly be stuck in a rut and secretly resenting it?

I thought, at that precise moment when it must have happened, of Antonia. There was nothing weird about it – I very often think of Antonia – it was perfectly logical that, considering ruts, I should think of my twin sister. Antonia had been in a rut for years, a rut which never varied in the slightest. It made me wild to see how boring her life was, lacking any excitement at all. At eighteen she had married the dullest man you are ever likely to find in this world – he is so dull, Antonia's Gerald, that the mere sight of his bland face makes me yawn. I literally feel the yawns starting in my throat when confronted with him and I am powerless to prevent them emerging. "Tired again, Alexandra?" he always says, kindly, without malice, and when I smile weakly rather than risk a reply he shakes his head and says I lead too fast a life. Any life, in comparison with Gerald and Antonia's, would seem fast. They live – they lived – on the Holly Lodge Estate in Highgate, a strangely suburban enclave in the midst of an area of mostly Victorian elegance. I was quite appalled when first I went to their house. At the time I did not know London at all well but when Antonia said, "off Highgate West Hill," I had a vision in my head of a certain sort of house – circa 1870 perhaps, three storeyed, with sash windows and one of those iron balconies outside the sitting room windows, upon which there would be window boxes full of geraniums. There would be a pretty fanlight above the heavy wooden front door and the number painted beautifully in the middle of it. I remember driving through the scruffy high streets of Camden and Kentish Town – those depressing rows of ugly shops – and thinking, as I passed the bus terminus at Parliament Hill Fields and began to drive up the hill, that Antonia had done well to seek the greenery and fresher air of Highgate. I drove slowly, the A–Z map of London open on my knee, looking for Cranleigh Gardens. I thought it must be a left turning, leading down to Hampstead Heath, but after I had gone up and down the hill twice I realised it must be on the right and therefore part of the semi-detached sprawl I had been ignoring. At least, it was not a sprawl – the estate, when finally I found my way into it through Swains Lane – was extremely regimented. The houses were in rigid tidy rows, rising one upon the other in ever increasing grandeur. A road ran straight up the middle and all the other roads opened at regular spaced-out intervals all the way up. There were trees and well tended gardens and a broad band of grass in front of the houses on the main road.

Cranleigh Gardens was the second turning on the left, between Langbourne Avenue and Makepeace Avenue. It was a quite hideous row of post-First World War villas. Antonia's house was on the right, which meant it looked down the hill and had rather a steep ascent to the front door. I parked my car and sat outside for ten full minutes, just staring and refusing to believe my eyes. It was such a mean little house, though I suppose it was not so very little. The windows had nasty little panes and curved outwards in a pathetic attempt at a Georgian bow window. The door was mostly frosted glass with embellishments. The front of this horror was covered in stucco, painted a revolting insipid cream, and I knew without going inside that not a single room would have any proportions whatsoever – it would be two boxes to the right of the slot-of-a-hall and, directly above, two more. At the back there would be a square kitchen, armour plated in Formica.

It was exactly like that. There had been nothing at all that Antonia's sense of colour and style could do about it – in fact, it hurt to see her taste so powerless. Though there were no three piece suites or sideboards to compound the architectural crime, though the walls did not sport flowered wallpapers or the windows pelmets and fancy draped muslin curtains, the feeling was the same. But Antonia glowed. "You don't need to say a word, Alexandra," she said at once. "I know exactly what you think but I don't care. Gerald wanted to live here and I want what he wants." Gerald, it emerged, hated old houses. He hated dirty streets too. What Gerald liked was a nice, clean place to live with no cars or lorries or buses hurtling about. The Holly Lodge Estate was closed to all but private traffic. It was closed to Hawkers and Pedlars. It had large white gates closing it in from the contaminated other world outside. Everything within it was orderly and organised –

like Gerald. "You might at least," I said, "have gone for something completely new." But Gerald did not like new buildings any more than he liked old ones. He liked something in between.

I did not go to see Antonia very often at her home simply because I loathed that house. She came to see me, or we met in some restaurant. After Casper was born, we often met on Hampstead Heath and walked him along the ponds or round Kenwood, where we sat in the garden drinking their rather good coffee, our backs to the brick wall which got all the sun that was going. Casper, as far as I was concerned, completed Antonia's servitude but she adored him – he was the final seal on her happiness. When first she saw him the look on her face almost frightened me – such longing, such joy – I felt it could never be preserved, that she had laid herself open to be terribly hurt. I was there when Casper was born. I was with her. We were in a nursing home in the country and Gerald – the baby was a month premature – was on a business trip. I didn't stay to see Gerald's face – I left so that they could be together – but later, when I saw them both, he had the same vulnerable expression.

They had no more children. I once heard Casper ask Antonia why he had no brothers and sisters and Antonia said, "We were afraid to have any more in case they were not as nice as you, darling." That was how she brought him up. It made me feel slightly sick. It was hardly the child's fault that he grew into an extremely precious little boy, horribly knowing and precocious – not my idea of a boy at all. He collected stamps – railway stamps – and played the violin and never kicked a ball in his life. I tried to do something about it but failed. Casper did not like me much. I suppose I was too critical and my disapproval of him showed. I tried taking him on outings – to museums and films, that sort of thing – but we never got on well. Quite often we would spend the whole time together in total silence – I could never think of anything to say to him. As he grew older the constraint between us grew more marked, so it was fortunate we rarely met. He was sent to Highgate Public School, a step I greatly opposed, but then, I had no rights in the matter – absurd to think his parents cared what I thought. Gerald naturally thought a public school education essential for a boy – state schools were all right until seven but, after that, they suddenly became taboo. I suppose what I particularly detested about Gerald on this subject was his hypocrisy. I would have respected him far more if he had stated his prejudices clearly but he did not – he pretended to give the local state school a go (I think it was called Brookfield) and then, when Casper approached seven, he began talking about the child not being stretched and having no alternative but to do the right thing by him. Such a mockery.

At any rate, it all fitted in to the pattern. Gerald flourished as a business man and Antonia faded as a business man's wife. I tried to get her to see how boring she was becoming but she only smiled complacently. She shopped, she cooked, she did a little voluntary work and sat on the odd committee and hung on Casper's and Gerald's every word. Twice a year they went abroad for holidays – once taking Casper and once on their own. I used to offer to come and look after Casper but Gerald's mother always wanted him and I gracefully, and gratefully, gave way. She was a widow who lived in Hampstead Garden Suburb, very handy for Casper's school, and her grandson was the light of her life. So like dear Gerald, she said all the time – Gerald's mouth, Gerald's eyes, Gerald's quiet, sweet disposition. It made me smile. The boy, of course, had not a single gene of Gerald's in him – nobody could have been less like his father, if examined by a dispassionate observer.

It was Gerald's mother, Mrs Matlock, who rang me during that afternoon. I had just put a tray of pots in the kiln, feeling a little more cheerful than I had done in the morning, when a message was brought to say I was wanted on the telephone. I thought it was Edward. When I went into the staff room someone said no, the call for me was in the secretary's office and it was some hysterical old woman. Even then, I had no inkling of who it could be. I remember taking the telephone in my hand, feeling nothing but puzzled – I simply did not know any hysterical old women. Mrs Matlock was incoherent. "There's been a dreadful accident," she said, over and over again, but it took me some time to make out the words. I naturally thought something had happened to Casper, since I knew Antonia and Gerald had left that morning for Greece.

Envy of them – so rare an emotion on my part towards them – had made me resent the blueness of the sky even more. "I'll come right over," I said, all brisk and businesslike. And I put the telephone down without attempting to sort anything out.

I therefore met Casper on the doorstep of his grandmother's home without knowing his parents had both been killed.

Two

If there is one person to whom I would not have wished my fate to be linked, it is Casper James Matlock. I doubt very much whether anyone could take on a thirteen-year-old boy and, in the sort of circumstances I have described, make a success of the relationship. My feelings, when eventually I realised the implications of the deaths of Antonia and Gerald in that appalling aircrash – you will have read of it, the crash of the Boeing 707 in September 1979, when 242 passengers and all eight crew were killed – were of total horror. It was the one thing I had done everything to avoid. There was no need to wait for any last will and testament to be read – I knew I was Casper's guardian. Antonia had insisted, much against my wishes, and though Gerald had been less insistent it was he who had pointed out that there was no one else, a fact so obvious I could not dispute it. Gerald was an only child with an elderly ailing mother and Antonia had only me. And so I had been compelled to agree. I had never been asked to sign anything and knew nothing of any conditions that might be included in my guardianship, and I had little curiosity about their possible existence. It was enough that Casper was now my responsibility.

When I saw him on the doorstep of his grandmother's house that day I thought only that he seemed to be in one piece and that whatever had caused Mrs Matlock's hysteria must be as trivial as I had suspected. In fact, I said so. "You look all right," I said to Casper. "What's all the fuss about?" He gave a little smirk and looked into the distance over my right shoulder and I thought how unattractive he was. He had grown enormously in the few months since I had seen him – four or five, I suppose, I knew I had not met Antonia at her own house all summer. He was now tall and painfully thin, with the beginnings of acne on his pallid face. It was a face that always looked furtive, narrow and tight and always hanging down – one saw the top of Casper's head more than any other part of him. He moved towards people with his chin tucked into his collar and only lifted his head if told to do so. I could not say he was extra pale – he was always pale – or that he betrayed any signs of emotion, but then I was unfamiliar with Casper's distress signals. I would now, for example, notice immediately that his fists were so tightly bunched together in his pockets that the material threatened to split and that he whistled without making any actual noise in a maddening, deliberate way. But then, I saw nothing unusual.

In the background, I could hear Mrs Matlock wailing and I strode into the hall, seeking the direction the awful noise came from. Casper stayed on the doorstep. "Whatever is wrong?" I said, as I walked into the sitting room where Mrs Matlock lay on the sofa, her arm hanging down on one side and a large box of pink Kleenex tissues perched on her stomach. Every few seconds she took a handful of them, blotted her face and threw them aside, so that she appeared to be lying in candyfloss. I was, I confess, both amused and exasperated. I sat down and waited, scornfully refusing to pander to the silly woman's histrionics. Then I saw there was a telegram on the coffee table beside the sofa. As the disgusting wailing went on, I picked it up. It said, "REGRET NO SURVIVORS." I turned it over. I sought the envelope it had come in. I examined every inch of the sheet of paper minutely. Gradually, without needing to compel Mrs Matlock to stop, I pieced the whole thing together.

I should not have been so contemptuous of Gerald's mother, who had in fact behaved with commendable intelligence. She had heard on *The World at One* that a plane flying to Greece had crashed over the Italian Alps, and had instantly realised from the details given that it must be the plane her son was on. She had rung the travel agency she knew he always used and they had confirmed her suspicions. Then she sent a reply paid telegram to the BEA desk at Heathrow – a thing I would never have thought of doing – and was therefore one of the first relatives to know the truth. Even then, she had not immediately broken down but had telephoned Highgate School and had Casper brought home. The tears began when she set eyes upon him – "looking so like Gerald" (which, as I have told you, he did not) – and after she had rung me she had simply given way to the grief she had managed to control for two whole hours.

If I could not at that time see Casper was distressed, no more could he have told how shocked and sick I was feeling. I did not cry either. I sat still for a few minutes and then I said, "Gerald and Antonia's plane crashed?" and Mrs Matlock nodded her head. "Are you absolutely certain they were on it," I said. She nodded again. "Have you told Casper?" The weeping redoubled in strength. I got up and walked back into the hall, where Casper still stood with his back to me on the steps of the house. "Casper," I said, "come inside. Close the door." I wanted to sound gentle but the order came out abrupt and clipped. He did as he was told but stood with his back against the closed door, that foolish smile still on his face, his gaze still looking past me. I ought to have taken him in my arms but it was impossible – I think he would have struck me. There we stood, both wretched and numb, no use to each other at all. I saw him sneak a look at himself in the rather grand hall mirror – one of those huge gilt affairs that hung above a long shelf upon which stood green trailing plants – and adjust his hair. I found myself backing away from him until my heels hit the foot of the stairs, carpeted lavishly in red Wilton. I sat down on the bottom stair and put my head down on my knees. Casper didn't move. Mrs Matlock screeched and hiccupped on. "I'm just going to get my dog," Casper said and walked past me, down the hall corridor and out into the garden. I heard his dog, Rufus, a golden retriever to whom he was devoted, bark and I felt instantly relieved. At least the child had something – something to hold and hug and cry with. "Thank God," I kept saying, aloud, "thank *God* for that."

I did not thank God quite so fervently for Rufus in the weeks that followed. He was a nuisance. Large and energetic, he bounded round the flat like a maniac and had to be taken on the heath all day long. Casper was perfectly willing to be the one to take him but since he was at school until four – I insisted at once that he went to school, whatever he felt like – the job fell to me. I do not dislike dogs but neither do I positively like them. In particular, I found it tiresome to give Rufus all the affection he craved. Every time I sat down the stupid animal came to offer me his paw and if I accepted it and patted him then he half knocked me over to climb on my knee. And he stank. I tried to make Casper bath him but Casper said the job could only safely be done in the summer in a garden with a hosepipe – did I want my bathroom wrecked? No, I did not, so I had to put up with Rufus's revolting smell. I tried throwing a stick into the pond on the heath but though he swam eagerly the water did nothing to remove the stench. And he covered the heath in shit. I felt I was using the place as one giant lavatory and was ashamed. The only pleasure I got out of Rufus was watching him race away along the ridge leading along the backbone of the heath from Parliament Hill to Kenwood – then, as he ran so fast, a blur of golden russet brown fur, I felt quite proud of him. At least he was no prissy little lap dog, nor an ugly, ungainly hound – in action, Rufus pleased my aesthetic senses. But that was about all he pleased and if it had not been for Casper I would have had no hesitation in getting rid of him. Later, I promised myself, I would have a rational conversation with Casper about his dog and we would make some decisions (but I never did).

Rufus was low on my list of things I wanted to talk about with Casper – there were many, many more important topics to discuss. We discussed none of them. Casper, I quickly learned, was allergic to any kind of talk. Sentences more than six words long appeared to be too much for him to cope with. He was the most silent youth it has ever been my misfortune to know. He volunteered no opinions of any kind and if they were demanded of him he said he "didn't know". I thought his extreme reluctance to open his mouth might be a form of shock – obviously, a child like that would be capable of withdrawing into himself and must be allowed time to come out of the emotional trauma to which he had so mercilessly been subjected. But time made no difference, and when in desperation I talked to Casper's teachers they said this behaviour was normal – for Casper. It was, they said, nothing to worry about. But I found it extremely worrying. If there was to be no communication between Casper and me, how could I possibly hope to make any headway with him? As it was, I made enormous changes in his life and he uttered neither one word of protest nor one of agreement – I had no way of knowing if I was hurting him or not.

Our conversation would go something like this. "Casper," I said, "I am going to sell your parents' house – your home – do you mind?" He would shrug, pick at his teeth, lower his gaze even further. "Casper," I said, "tell me if you would rather go on living there – would it be a comfort to you to be still in your old surroundings, or do you find the idea of it awful?" Another shrug, a slight turning away. "Casper, I would like you to help me to decide – and it's something that does have to be decided – you can't expect me to know automatically what you think and feel." Finally, he said, "I don't care. Do what you like." It was always pointless pressing him further – indeed, it quickly seemed cruel. Soon, I was merely informing him of momentous decisions *after* I had made them and though this filled me with guilt I saw no other way of acting.

The truth was, I wished to change Casper totally. If it had not seemed too insulting to my dead sister, I would first of all have changed his name. Casper was such a ridiculously fancy name – I hated it. It seemed affected and silly to me. I would have like him to have a plain name, a name so ordinary that he would have to make it his own – John or David or Richard. I thought of beginning to call him by his middle name of James but could not quite bring myself to suggest that we drop the Casper. But in other respects I was more bold. For the moment I left him at Highgate School but I gave notice instantly that, at the end of term, if not sooner, he would be leaving. No ward of mine was going to go to a public school – about that I was definite. I laid the blame for at least half of Casper's personality at the door of his school, which was exactly the wrong kind of place for him. Left there, he would go through life unable to get on with the vast majority of human beings. His own kind would call to him and that would be that. The public school emphasis on duty and obedience and team spirit and playing the game was quite disastrous for a loner like Casper. I had no clear idea at first of where I would send him but it would not be to that type of school. I told him this but got no reaction. I asked him if he liked school and managed to drag out of him the grudging admission, "Don't mind it." I asked him if he would rather stay there and he said he didn't mind either way. So I took him at his word.

I gave away all his clothes, with the exception of his school uniform, which I was obliged to let him keep temporarily. Casper's clothes were terrible – and please do not tell me clothes do not matter. They matter a great deal, not as social landmarks but as disguises. Clothes change people outwardly, and that outward change can affect them inwardly. Casper's appalling prissy shirts and ties and velvet jacket and Terylene trousers and velour overcoat enraged me. There was no need for him to go around looking like some sort of cut-down adult in his father's terrible style. I took him with me to Colts in Hampstead High Street and there I bought him some well cut jeans and several Levi sweatshirts and an anorak and a couple of polo neck sweaters and some tough looking Kicker type shoes. He looked better immediately. "There," I said, "doesn't that feel better? Didn't you hate those ghastly clothes you had?" He would not admit that he liked his new image but it is one of the few things I am positive about – he *did* feel happier. I saw him relax inside them and they even changed his physique – he looked suddenly slim instead of weedy and his height appeared an advantage whereas formerly, his horrible loose shirts and trousers flapping on his spare frame, it had seemed almost a deformity. Once his hair grew – as I intended to let it – he would no longer look such an owlish idiot.

These alterations were nevertheless insignificant beside those that I slowly began to plan. When the first chaos was over – and it *was* chaotic, taking over someone else's life – it came to me in a moment of calm, pondering Casper's inheritance, that something drastic would have to be done. I could not take over from Antonia on Antonia's own ground. I could not provide another home for her son and give him any kind of future unless I started again, in some different environment, free of all those shadows that my sister would cast. I must lock up my flat and leave my job and remove Casper from everything he had ever known. I must take on the job of being his mother – a role I detested the thought of – away from all reminders of the life I had once led. It would not, after all, be forever. Casper was thirteen. In five years he would surely be launched on some career and no longer in need of me *in loco parentis* – or not in the same way.

But I do not wish to pretend that what I did was entirely Casper's fault, or entirely on his account. Throughout those turbulent first few days after the air crash, and in the middle of all the to-ing and fro-ing, I gradually began to feel that something irrevocable had been decided. Those vague feelings of unrest, that sensation of everything not being as it should be in my life, lifted. I felt as though the violence of my change in status had given me a sense of direction I had unconsciously lacked – no, which I had deliberately chosen to be without. It was without any pain that I gave in my notice at Highgate. I had been perfectly happy there but leaving caused me no regrets.

Leaving London was not so easily done, and I trembled on the brink of that momentous step for several weeks. I had come to believe that it had to be, and yet I hesitated. Might it not be sufficient merely to move districts? Why not find a flat or house on the other side of the river, almost another world, and be content with that? Was it necessary totally to uproot myself? I like London. My affection for it is real and deep. Never for one moment would I be stubborn enough to deny that living in London has many drawbacks – that the traffic is insufferable, for example – but in spite of the problems I love the city itself. And, unlike many people who live there, I used it. I used every amenity London had to offer and never grew tired of them. And I loved the streets and buildings. I love the Mall, and Westminster Bridge and Mayfair squares and all those Nash terraces – I love the excitement which the grandeur of those places provokes. When I walk down those older London streets I feel exhilarated, not just by their beauty but by the sense of life lived in them. If I moved to Greenwich or some such place I could still orientate myself towards the centre of London and in so many ways that mattered not lose by the change. When I reached in my mind for any other city to which I could go they all seemed intolerable. Manchester I loathed, Birmingham I hated so much I could not spend more than a day there, Liverpool was too ugly, Newcastle too dreary – I was a Londoner through and through. Smaller cities or towns were too much like Oxford, and I had no wish to return to the scenes of my childhood.

This process of elimination, together with the conviction which remained that I must leave London completely, led me to a startling idea. Why not go abroad? There could be nothing more therapeutic than a literal pulling away from England and flying off into the unknown. We could go, Casper and I, to California, rent an apartment in San Francisco and – and what? Try as I might, I could not envisage the kind of life we would lead there. What would I *do* with Casper abroad? He was so unbelievably English that I could not imagine him anywhere else. The thought of taking the risk, of embarking upon quite such a large adventure, scared me. For a while I wondered about somewhere more modest – the South of France, say – but again I lacked confidence in my ability to survive there with an awkward adolescent. I wanted drastic change but I wanted to feel reasonably secure too. The only other choice was the country, and I shrank from that. I am not a country person – or rather, I had always imagined I was not. I like the speed and bustle of cities and, most of all, the anonymity to be found within them. The English countryside is in my opinion inhabited by a still largely feudal society, and it repelled me. I had spent many weekends with friends at their blessed cottages and been amazed at the complicated hierarchies they felt obliged to fit in with. I could never live in a village. People talk so loosely about the friendliness of villages but I do not wish everyone to know me and everything about me – I do not want friendliness on those terms. The sheer necessity of having to recognise neighbours all the time would bore me to death – I like to greet people as and when I feel like it, without any thought of offending them. A village, in short, would threaten that independence I hold so dear.

Yet more and more I began to think of the country – somewhere wild and remote, somewhere isolated. I could see

Casper and me holing up in some cottage miles from anywhere and being forced to get on with each other. Torn out of our customary habitat, we would be like new people, able to react differently to each other. The idea had a strange fascination for me which I could not properly explain – it defied analysis. I thought I would try it out on Casper, half hoping to shock him into protest. "I am thinking of leaving London," I said to him. "You and I – we would go off to the mountains somewhere and lead a completely different life. What do you think?" He raised his eyebrows and stared at me, quite sharply for him. "It doesn't make much difference," he said. "Don't be stupid," I snapped back, "it makes the most enormous difference. If you haven't the imagination to see that I despair of you." He smiled, that insulting smirk I so hated. "Despair, then," he said, and went into his room with Rufus trotting at his heels.

He spent a great deal of time in that small room – he and his great animal squashed in there for hours on end doing God knows what. At first I used to listen outside, dreading the thought of perhaps hearing him cry, but there was absolute silence, which was much more unnerving. Casper did not play records or listen to Capital Radio like other teenagers – it would have been a relief if he had done so. Indeed, I had taken care to put up my stereo in his room, and a transistor radio, but when, after a month, both had been ignored, I removed them. Nor did he read, so far as I could tell. He brought no books with him from his house and when I offered to give him some – when I sorted out a few I thought a thirteen-year-old boy might enjoy – he declined without thanks. He did not draw, he did not paint, he did not even play the violin any longer. All he appeared to do was stare at his stamp collection and stroke Rufus.

I worried that by bringing him to my flat in Church Row, and pushing him into that small room which did not get much light, I might have depressed him still further. It was not the sort of place a teenage boy would enjoy living in. Casper might reasonably have claimed he felt cramped and crowded, that his quarters were prison-like, but he expressed no such opinion. When I said, that evening at his grandmother's, that I was taking him straight home with me, he did not demur.

In fact, when Mrs Matlock said, "There is more room here, darling – there is the room you have always stayed in, waiting for you," he said at once, "No thanks." Not much of a speech – certainly not enough to either flatter me or console his grandmother – but at least an indication that my company was not absolutely intolerable. If, in the poor child's brain, I was Scylla and his grandmother Charybdis, then he chose me as his particular doom.

It meant, of course, that I was immediately restricted in my freedom but I accepted that. Edward did not. When he turned up, some ten days after the tragedy, I would not let him in. I stood at the bottom of the steps leading up to street level and said he must go away. I simply did not want him to meet Casper, or rather, Casper to meet Edward. The thought was embarrassing. I envisaged the ghastliness of our stilted conversation and could not bear it. Briefly I told Edward what had happened and how things now stood and asked him to go away. He laughed and tried to push past me but I barred his way and said I was determined to keep him out. Then he grew exasperated, said I was being absurd and that he was interested in the boy and would get on with him a damn sight better than he knew I would. That I did not doubt – as I told him. Edward was good with children. He liked to do most of the things children like to do – things like playing board games, which I detested, or having snowball fights, or helping them make camps and swings. People said it was such a waste that he had no children of his own and he himself, at his most pathetic, would confess there was a part of him not being used – he was a father *manqué*.

But I did not want Edward to meet Casper. I felt so strongly about this – my reaction to the thought of them meeting was instinctive – that I did not stop to ask myself the reason why. I just wanted Edward to go. I said I would ring him when I knew what I was going to do and he had to be satisfied with that. He looked so dismal, trailing off up the steps.

Edward does not realise how hard I find it to let him go. Never once have I looked at his departing figure without wanting to hurl myself at him, and yet I never do. I keep this difficulty secret. When he leaves, I am nonchalant, hardly appearing to notice he is going, and, once his body is out of sight, I am safe. I feel happy. I know I have made the right decision.

I had no intention of telling Edward where I was going, when that was settled. He would follow me as he has always followed me and begin all over again his persistent pleading that I should marry him. So many times Edward has flushed me out – it has become a kind of joke, a not very funny joke. I suppose if, each time he discovered me in some new hideout, I firmly refused to have anything to do with him then he would eventually give up. But I am always so pleased to see him and I can never pretend otherwise. He always arrives just at that point in some new existence when I have decided every man I know is both boring and unattractive – then I open a door and there is Edward, both interesting and extremely attractive. At least, I think so. Antonia, whose friend he first was, did not think so. She found him exhausting. When I spoke of Edward's amazing vitality she groaned and condemned it as overwhelming, suffocating. When I said I thought he was handsome, she said she did not see how I could find a man with such a lot of wild black hair attractive. She hated his thick beard and eyebrows and his general rough, untidy, dark appearance – swarthy men were not to Antonia's taste, hence the pink-and-white Gerald. Edward was too quick, too energetic, too abrupt for Antonia, but for me he was perfect – in some ways, that is. And I never concealed my delight. We hugged each other passionately at each new discovery and I would feel that *rightness* about us that I felt with no one else.

But I would at least attempt to escape again. I would leave no forwarding address. Edward would curse and rave and then settle down to the hunt, for that was what it became. One day I knew he might tire of my obstinacy. He would not bother to track me down. He would find someone else and that would be that. Often, thinking of this possibility, I would find myself shivering. How long would I wait for Edward to find me before I came back, remorseful? And if, in those circumstances, I did come back – if I were the discoverer on the door – would Edward greet me as I always found myself greeting him? Impossible to say. I could not do without him, but I could not be with him all the time. Casper, far from complicating this already complicated and ridiculous situation, simplified it. Casper was my new alibi. He made it easier for me to behave irrationally. I convinced myself that I must protect him and devote myself entirely to him and that escape was the only possible way of doing so.

I began to study personal columns of newspapers, looking for a cottage. There were a surprising number of people advertising remote cottages for sale or to rent – each day I marked at least one, however unsuitable it was. It was quickly apparent that either Wales or the Lake District would provide what I wanted – plenty of cottages in the Cotswolds and East Anglia, but I could tell at a glance that they were not for me. The words used to describe them were "charming" and "picturesque" and "comfortable", and the attractions stressed were those of being near main-line trains, and shopping facilities two miles. The Welsh and Lake District places, on the other hand, made much of remoteness and inaccessibility and spoke proudly of no running water. I was not so sure that I was prepared to go as far as no running water but otherwise the descriptions suited me.

Once, the summer before my father died so suddenly, we had a family holiday in the Lake District, near Ullswater. Antonia and I were eighteen and had long since given up traditional family holidays with our parents but that summer, for a month, we went all together to a place called Sandwick, a mere scattering of cottages below Hallin Fell. We went to please my father, who had never quite given up hope that one of us would eventually turn out to share his passion for fell walking and climbing. He had been very good, that year, to us both – very understanding about our refusal to go to university. My mother raged at our stupidity, our shortsightedness, our wilful refusal to make the most of opportunities she had never had. She could never quite face up to the fact that not all people who are clever and able necessarily want to go to university. I, in particular, exasperated her. At 'A' level I had taken Art, Russian, French and English, and my three 'A's and one 'B' (in English) had delighted her. She was convinced that I would now see sense and follow the path to academic glory that she had mapped out for me. It hurt her terribly when instead I went to the Central School to study Art – "the waste, the waste," she cried all day long, like some plaintive bird that has had its young snatched from the nest. Father made not a murmur of protest. He said I must follow my inclinations and that he was happy to finance them. I loved him very much for his generosity. He was equally generous to Antonia, who said she simply wanted to marry Gerald. That, in my mother's eyes, was a heinous crime, far worse than failing to go to university. Her hopes for Antonia had not been as high as they had been for me – she was not so obviously clever, though with three 'B's had acquitted herself very creditably in 'A' levels, quite creditably enough to get a place almost anywhere she might choose, short of Oxbridge – but nevertheless she had had aspirations of an intellectual nature for her. Marriage was pure folly at such a tender age. Marriage without any training for a career beforehand was wicked beyond Mother's belief. Privately, I agreed, but Father smiled and said Antonia was eminently suited to be a wife and mother and Gerald was a lucky fellow. So Antonia was to marry in the September, with Father's blessing, and we both went for the whole of July to Ullswater to demonstrate our gratitude to Father.

And it was then I met Edward, or rather, Antonia met Edward. In spite of my athletic frame I detest all sports but Antonia loved to ride and swim and play every boring game you might mention. She had always longed to sail and joined, at vast expense, the Ullswater Sailing Club – a temporary membership only obtained after a great deal of persistence on her part. Every day she went to Howtown and put on a great many ridiculous waterproof clothes and learned to sail. Edward taught her. She came home at the end of the first day and said she had met the most absurdly conceited young man, through being teamed up with his sister. He was just down from Cambridge, working for three months at a local hotel as a waiter before beginning to teach at a school near Keswick. She brought him back to the cottage (we never met the sister, who went back early to her nursing career) we rented – a pretty place, literally with roses round the door – and I suppose I fell in love with him at once. I came down from Martindale, where I had spent all day walking with Father, and as I walked into the cottage, feeling utterly exhausted, I saw Edward standing in the corner beside the small, many paned window and felt a thrill of recognition. That is all I can call it. I did not, of course, know him, or anyone like him, but as he moved towards me in the semi-gloom of the small, claustrophobic room I felt my tiredness leave me instantly and I was suddenly alert and excited and could hardly bear to take his outstretched hand in case some sort of current should pass from me to him and reveal my agitation. We shook hands, looked into each other's eyes and all schoolgirlish fears that I would never find any man attractive fled. Within three days we were lovers, my virginity a happy loss.

I was not silly enough to think of going back to Sandwick – though nostalgia for that summer regularly tortured me – but the more I thought about it the more the thought of the Lake District appealed. Not Sandwick, or indeed anywhere near there, but somewhere on the northern fells, where I had been with Father. Those fells I remembered as bleaker and more sparsely populated than the crowded shores of any of the Lakes. I smiled a little maliciously to myself as I imagined Edward's confusion. He would never in a million years think that I would to to that place – he would think of it as the last place on earth I would choose to take Casper, basing his calculations on the distress as well as the joy he would know I associated with it. And even if he discovered I had gone there, he himself would be reluctant to follow me. Edward was a rolling stone, who had rarely stayed in one place more than two years – he always wanted to move on as soon as he had settled in. The year he had spent near Keswick he had often told me was the unhappiest in his life, and his desire to move on stronger than at any other time. He would not lightly return, even to search for me. Memories of tears, of pain, of inexpressible longing would haunt him and he would lack courage to face them.

I soon gave up searching the columns of the national newspapers. It was obvious I must be in the area to know what was on the market and pick accordingly. I sent for the local newspapers – from Penrith, Kendal and Carlisle – and made a list of local agents from them. I rang them all and had their lists sent and quickly discovered that all the interesting properties were for sale, not to rent, and that the sales took place at auctions. Was I bold enough to buy? The thought made me nervous but the more I confronted it, the more it appealed. It would amount to burning my boats and I wanted to burn them. It would get rid of any idea lingering on in my head that I was playing at starting again. I put my Church Row flat into the hands of Benham & Reeves and had an offer in twenty-four hours. That decided me. I took Casper to his grandmother's – she had still not forgiven me for taking him away and was delighted to have a chance to reclaim him – and said I was obliged to go away for a few days. I badly wanted Casper to ask me where I was going and why, but he did not. He took the news in his usual infuriatingly calm way and so I did not volunteer any information. When I am on my own with him, I vowed, I will change all this.

Mrs Matlock had a great deal to say to me when I dropped Casper off but I did not stay to listen. She pulled me into a little study which opened off the hall and closed the door on Casper, who was told to take Rufus into the garden and "run about", and said, "You are ruining that boy's life."

"I can't stop now, Mrs Matlock," I said, "but I promise to come and discuss everything with you when I return."

She was trembling and laid a restraining hand on my arm. "I won't let you do it," she said. "He is Gerald's son. Already you've tried to make him different – those terrible clothes – his hair – but it shines through – he is *still* Gerald's son, and he must be treated as such."

"Please, Mrs Matlock," I said, "don't upset yourself. I will come and talk to you next week." She had begun to cry and I felt cruel and brutal in my haste. "Casper will be upset if you cry," I said – a lie, Casper was never upset by anyone's tears. "Go and find him and feed him up. I'm afraid I've been giving him all the wrong kind of food – I'm not much interested in it myself and young boys have healthy appetites."

She stopped snivelling at once and I left. I drove very fast up the M1 and across to the M6 and was in Penrith by midday.

Three

Driving fast is what a sports car is for but I never had much opportunity, in London, to do this. I don't mean that I would have enjoyed simply roaring up and down race tracks but that I liked to put my car through its paces on a long run and glory in the response of the machine. It is the sort of thing people say of horses – that they like to feel the animal become part of them as together they jump and gallop and learn to move as one. I feel that way about cars, however impossible you may find it to believe. I like to have my foot on the accelerator and a long empty road ahead, curving and climbing just a little, and then under my hands on the steering wheel I feel all the power of the engine and there is a beauty in that force of which I am a part.

The M1, as doubtless you know, provides none of these thrills. It is gruelling, clocking up the miles in an ever increasing rage at the heaviness of the traffic and the poor standards of driving. But then, after I turned off to cross to Birmingham and the M6, things slowly improved – once through Spaghetti Junction the motorway was emptier and not quite so flat and dull and I made good time.

The last hour of my journey – the seventy miles or so before Penrith – was beautiful. Here, the motorway cuts through the mountains, following their curves and contours, in such a smooth, effortless way that to drive along it is like a gymnastic exercise – the body twists and turns with the road, gracefully bending and straightening, and all around are views of distant peaks that seem to pull one onwards. I have rarely enjoyed a drive so much and arrived in Penrith exhilarated by it. The feeling of excitement survived even my attempts to park in the crowded little market town and instead of finding a place to eat after five hours on the road I felt lively enough to go straight to the estate agents in the main street – Queens & Co. Ltd., they were called – where the man behind the desk did his utmost to bring me down to earth with a bump.

It ought to have been a depressing experience – being told they had nothing suitable – but I survived it well. Met with that kind of stubborn unhelpfulness I respond with an equally stubborn determination to prove I can find a way to get what I want, in spite of evidence to the contrary. Thank God I possess that ability or I would not have survived in Cumbria for more than five minutes – which is not to say that Cumbrians are not kind and generous but that they are nevertheless distinctly unwilling to please, at least at first. They try and test people. They like to summer them and winter them and then, this strange test of time passed, they are perhaps ready to help. Mr Graham in Queens & Co. Ltd. was a case in point. I said I was Alexandra Grove, who had corresponded with his firm about purchasing a cottage in Cumbria. I said I had just driven up from London and was anxious to look at as many properties as I could fit into two days. He smiled, slyly I thought, though later I interpreted that Cumbrian way of smiling as embarrassment, and said, "Well now, we've nothing suitable really. You'd be better to go home and wait for something to turn up." Was it honesty – an overwhelming basic honesty – or plain idleness or dislike that made him so off-putting? I stared at him in amazement, trying to work this approach out, and he stared back, not at all nonplussed, quite relishing my discomfiture.

Eventually, I said "How do you know what I think would be suitable?"

"Folk from London usually want the same things," he said. "Not too big, not too small, nicely converted, quiet, nice views, near some sort of village – I know the kind of thing. There's nothing doing at the moment."

"I can't believe," I said, and I know I said it haughtily but that only seemed to amuse him more, "I can't believe you have no properties whatsoever for sale on your books."

"Oh, we've got properties," he said, reaching into a drawer and producing a few foolscap sheets of paper, "but nothing suitable, nothing you'd like. I'd have told you if you'd rung up before coming."

"I've got places to see from advertisements in the local newspapers," I said. "I have several appointments already." I lied. I had none. I had replied to several and they had all been under offer or proved on further questioning to be impossible.

"You go off and see them, then," Mr Graham said, "because we've got nothing."

His complacency annoyed me so much I could barely read the printed sheets he pushed across his desk towards me – but I did, with what I hoped was maddening slowness. I read every word, down to the utterly incomprehensible details about drainage and so forth. There was only one that I could even pretend might be worth looking at.

"What about this?" I asked, pointing at the last sheet. "Lowther Fell Cottage – what about that? It sounds the sort of place I want."

"It isn't," Mr Graham said, pushing his hands into the pockets of his very hairy, aggressively countrified tweed sports jacket. "Anyway, it's going under the hammer in two hours' time. You've missed it."

I got up and held out my hand. "Can I have the keys?" I asked. "I'll go and look at it at once."

If I had hoped to dent Mr Graham's smugness I was disappointed. He smiled even more broadly, went into another room, and came back with a rather rusty set of keys. With perfect good humour – rather as one might allow a victim to feel the blade of the axe that it going to decapitate him – he took me over the route I must follow to get to Lowther Fell. He was most particular about making sure I had understood him – he even provided me with his own sketch of the final part of my road – and told me various landmarks to look out for. The auction, he said, started at two-thirty, but it would be after three before Lowther Fell Cottage was open to offers. He said he would keep me a seat.

I got into my car again, a little flushed after my encounter with Mr Grinning Graham. I hated being thought a joke, which was childish of me – I hated being categorised as a certain type and duly labelled and in this case, or so I felt, condemned to contempt. I reflected, as I drove onto the B2297, that if I was going to come and live in Cumbria I would come up against such branding all the time. It could hardly be helped. Nobody in London would look twice at me but in the Lake District area I was considering I would inevitably be a curiosity, and as for Casper – I could hardly bear the thought of what he might have to endure, with the burden of his public school education still resting so heavily on his back.

There was no fast driving on the roads I was now following but I enjoyed it all the same. I met no traffic, except for a tractor passing Rose Castle, and there was plenty of time to admire the slopes of the northern fells, as I drove towards them. It surprised me to find that all the way to the village of Caldbeck, the nearest village to the house I was looking for, the land was so rich and heavily grazed upon by cows and sheep. I had thought somehow that it would be more barren, less pastoral, and had not realised the difference between fells and fields was as abruptly marked as I saw it was – at Parkend, a mile or so out of the village, there was a cattle grid and after that unfenced roads with fields, quickly giving way to rough grassland higher up. I could see, looking to the left, exactly where the fields ended.

A signpost directed me to Greenhead but after turning right at the little bridge Mr Graham had marked across the stream there, I almost thought I had made a mistake. I passed a whitewashed cottage on the right and then the narrow road stopped. I stopped too and consulted Mr Graham's sketch and saw that in fact there was a break in the road, which was resumed half a mile on. Carefully – I do not like to mistreat my low-slung sports car, with its vulnerable exhaust pipe – I drove along the track and sure enough it did widen again into a road, or at least a kind of road. It was not tarmaced but covered roughly in cinders and broken rubble of one sort and another. It turned a sharp corner after another half mile into the very fold of the fell and then gave way to more beaten down mud, before ending in front of a stone house that looked straight onto the dark and forbidding side of the hill opposite.

It was not an attractive house. Not only did my heart not leap with joy, it sank with disappointment. I saw Mr Graham's grin. But I got out of the car – I had come so far and must look at it – and closed the door. The slam echoed loudly in the total silence (there is never, of course, total silence on the fells but my city ears were not then attuned to country noises).

There was a dry stone wall round the area of ground which surrounded the house – I cannot call it a garden, for nothing grew there – with a broken old gate in the middle, tied up with a heavy chain. It looked easier to climb over but I laboriously undid the chain and pushed the gate open, wondering if I would ever manage to get such an ill fitting thing closed again. I stood for a moment and looked critically at the house. The colour of the stone – a grey/brown colour – melded in with the fell behind, and so did the slate roof. The only patches of colour were the dirty cream surrounds of the windows and the green of the wooden latched door. Someone, sometime, had tried to brighten the building up and failed. But the windows were attractive – square, with nine panes of glass in each – the two lower ones exactly beneath the two upstairs ones. And the door was an old, solid one, very low and wide.

I walked right round the house before I tried to go inside. The back wall had been rendered, the concrete dirty and chipped, but the two end walls were stone, each with a tiny window high up. The whole house had been cut into the ground at the back – literally cut, a foot or so, into the side of the fell which rose steeply behind. A few sheep grazed nearby. There was a hole where the top stones had fallen off and I could see where the sheep had scrambled over to eat the few shrubs growing underneath the mountain ash which marked the boundary between garden and fell. Someone had dug up a patch or two of ground but nothing grew there. The only sign of cultivation was an uneven line of gooseberry bushes running along the inside of the left-hand wall.

The door opened with difficulty and I propped it wide with a stone, almost afraid that I might be trapped inside. It was hard to see in the gloom but then I saw there were heavy wooden shutters over the windows and when I had lifted these down – they were mere boards, fitted inside – I was able to see my way around. There was not much to see. One living room with an open fire – a very basic fireplace, not an inglenook – and a small scullery opening off it with a sink and absolutely nothing else. There was no furniture, except for a rag rug on the floor, barely covering a quarter of the stone paving flags, and a hideously modern black leather couch. The nicest thing in the room was the window sills – broad and wedge shaped and dark oak in colour. The room was low ceilinged, with one big beam running across the cracked white plaster.

I climbed the irregular, steep stone stairs to the bedrooms, holding on to the wooden rail to pull myself up. At least two of the steps were more than eighteen inches high, followed by others of a much shallower height. It made going upstairs the most disconcerting experience. There were two bedrooms and an attic where there was barely room to stand. Both rooms had views out onto the fell at the back and down to the track at the front which made them feel on a slant – pushed from behind, falling away at the front. There was nothing at all in either room. The floors were covered with ugly flowered linoleum. I bent down and picked up a corner and saw that underneath were beautiful broad wooden boards.

There was no bathroom. I went back downstairs and outside and found an outside shed where there was an evil smelling lavatory, but at least it was not of the Elsan type. I could not believe such a remote neglected house would have a proper lavatory but when I pulled the chain the cistern worked and it was obviously connected to some sewage system. I walked round the house again, opening all the doors of the various sheds I had ignored before. One was surprisingly large and clean – it was even whitewashed – and had a sink in it and an old tin tub and what looked like a primitive washing machine. This particular shed joined onto the end of the house and I saw that the wall between was not thick stone but brick, as though once there had been a door there and then the shed had been added and it had been bricked up. It could very easily be unbricked. There was a barn, a little distance from the house, which I could not get into.

The house inside seemed dry and though it was without any heating it did not seem cold. I did not know how to look for any sort of rot, but there were no suspicious patches anywhere, no stains on the ceilings or mould in the corners. I walked up and down the main room, thinking. In many ways, I was slowly beginning to like the place, against all first impressions. I thought, with a mocking smile to myself in the small square mirror hanging above the mottled brown sink, that it could certainly be described as very genuine. Nothing at all had been done to it – nobody had got there first and ravaged it. I could start from scratch, I could make what I liked of it. And the situation was very much what I had had in mind – cut off, but in reality only five miles from civilisation, along a quickly accessible road. There were no neighbours that I could see (in fact, there were, but the slope of the fell hid the other two houses from sight).

I looked at my watch. It was almost two thirty. If I was going to bid for this house I had to leave at once. Still not knowing what I wanted to do, still battling with my own indecision, I locked the door and walked quickly to my car. I reversed and turned and drove slowly back towards the road, imagining what a quagmire this path would be in the winter (though I never realised it would make any vehicle except a tractor unusable). Just before I reached the tarmac, I saw a figure walking towards me – a woman, wearing a blue head-scarf and a black raincoat and carrying a leather shopping basket. She had passed the whitewashed cottage – which suddenly looked sparkling and immensely comfortable, compared to what I had just left – and could only be going to Lowther Fell. I slowed down even further, curious and eager to find out any information she could give me. When I was almost abreast of her I stopped and waited and put my head through the window. "Excuse me," I said, "I've just been looking at Lowther Fell Cottage and I wondered if you could tell me anything about it?" Her hand flew to her mouth and concealed it and her eyes stared at me in terror, as though my innocent words were the most frightening she had ever heard. "Sorry," I said, "did I startle you?" – though I did not see how I could have done when she must have seen and heard my car approaching for the last five minutes.

"Oh," she said, clutching at the neck of her coat, which I saw was a man's, double breasted and much too wide for her. "I'm getting married in the morning – I can't help you, you see."

"I only wondered if–" I began, but she stepped backwards, shaking her head, and with a sort of ducking movement ran past my car.

Mr Graham had indeed kept me a seat. It was at the front of the saleroom with a card saying 'Reserved' on it and he made a great performance of pointing towards it when he saw me enter.

I sat in my position of unlooked-for prominence, feeling furtive. What business did I have among these people? Though none of the little groups talked to each other they were all relaxed in each other's company, whereas I felt isolated. They looked at me from time to time with what I felt was bright-eyed amusement – an amusement not as blatant as Mr Graham's, but there, all the same. The men wore flat checked caps and many had old fashioned stiffened collars and their clothes were very neat and clean with a sense of occasion about them – not church clothes exactly, but not working ones. The women seemed overshadowed by the men, though there was nothing in the least insubstantial about their persons – they were almost without exception stout and had ample laps upon which rested a wide variety of baskets and bags. The noise was astonishing – twice the auctioneer banged on the table and was not even heard and had to shout, "*NOW* ladies and gentlemen – *IF* you please," very loudly. He looked very stern, standing there in his best suit, the line of the jacket marred by the great number of pens clipped into the breast pocket, like a headmaster addressing an unruly assembly of children. "I'll thank you," he said, when silence had been obtained to a satisfactory degree, "to make your bids plain and above board." Even the coughing and rustling stopped. My heart began to pound with a sudden excitement – it was, I supposed, how people felt when they gambled and became caught up in the turn of the wheel or the show of a card. Nor was I the only one showing signs of a childish thrill – all round me, people tensed and sat forward, eyes fixed on the auctioneer. The men standing all round the edges of the hall stood as if transfixed, many with arms folded in an attitude of judgement.

"The first lot is at Caldbeck," the auctioneer said. "An interesting fellside property, six miles past Caldbeck on

Lowther Fell, between Brae Fell and Longlands. A cottage and barn and one acre garden is the first lot and thirteen acres of land the second. We'll try them separate and together." I had no idea what that meant. "First the land," he said. "Now, what am I bid for thirteen acres first rate land? It's been let for grassings the last twelvemonth at fifty pound an acre and likely to go up. Who'll start me at £13,000 now?" I waited anxiously – I did not want any land and would not bid but whoever did might also want the cottage and would be my rival. Nobody bid at all. I had the feeling that some well known ritual was being gone through, to which everyone except me was a party. Finally, someone bid £10,000 – I could not see who – but the auctioneer did not try to raise it. "We'll have them together," he said, and everyone seemed to relax.

"The cottage needs modernising," the auctioneer went on, "but it's solid, with a good roof. There's a cold water tap and a water closet with a septic tank. It could be turned into a very nice property with a bit of attention. Now, who'll start off?" A man standing half way back on my left shouted, "£12,000", and the auctioneer said, "I've a rival this afternoon. Very well, sir, £12,000 it is – now who'll give me £13,000?" Very slowly, the price rose, with the man standing competing with some unknown person at the back of the hall. There was a young couple standing beside the first bidder, whose faces were tense and worried, though their champion – a small, rather tubby little bespectacled man in brown – was perfectly at ease. He smiled every time his offer was topped.

The cottage cost me £19,950, and my rival in brown never knew how near he had come to gaining what he wanted. If it had been raised once more I should have dropped out and even felt relieved. I saw that he left the hall at once and that the young woman beside him had the young man's arm round her in a consoling way and she held a handkerchief to her face. I thought how popular I would be in the district if, as it appeared, I had robbed a young local couple of a home. Certainly, I felt no leap of triumph, no elation or joy – only a slightly sick feeling that I had been carried away and ought to have had more sense. How could I live in that hovel? How could I take Casper to it and feel I had done the right thing?

A couple stood in front of me, nodding as though I must

know who they were. The man was big – tall and heavy – with rich blond hair and bleached eyebrows in a florid face, and the woman was small, thin and insipid looking, with a hesitant, eager expression on her face. She spoke first. "Pleased to meet you," she said, smiling rather wanly. "Yes, pleased to meet you," the man said. He had a hoarse, deep voice that rumbled somewhere in his barrel-like chest. He seemed, I thought, wary – he watched me all the time during our conversation, his eyes narrowed as though to concentrate his vision better. I suppose he could have been called a handsome man if it had not been for the richness of his colouring, which made him seem overblown, a little too loud. "We're your nearest neighbours," he said. "Crosthwaite's the name. We've got your grassings. Will you be wanting them yourself?"

"No," I said. "Will you keep them on? The same terms?" He nodded and for the first time smiled and exchanged a quick conspiratorial look with his wife. So great was my relief to be rid of that particular problem straight away that I failed to interpret it for what it was – triumph that he had got the thirteen acres at the same rent when they both knew I would have been entitled to put it up to bring it into line with everyone else's.

"Will you be using Lowther Fell Cottage as a holiday home?" Mrs Crosthwaite asked.

"No, I'll be moving in to live there as soon as possible," I said.

"Never!" she exclaimed, and seemed excited.

All the way to Lowther Fell next day it rained torrentially. One of my windscreen wipers broke and I had to crouch forward and peer ahead all the time as I navigated the narrow country roads. I hardly had the heart to get out when I stopped before the cottage I had just bought but sat, slumped and defeated, staring with dislike at the broken windows and the cracked drainpipe where the rainwater gushed out in a shower under the eaves. It would have to be seen to – *I* would have to see to it.

I had brought with me pencil and paper to make notes on what should be done. I was determined there should be no major alterations – I wanted to move north as soon as possible but I was not so naïve as to suppose building work was speedy. When I came to consider it, even the minimum amount of work which needed doing was daunting. I stood in the middle of the main room and wondered how safe the ceiling was, and I was overcome with despair at the sight of the kitchen, or rather the non-kitchen. I might despise Antonia's formidable Formica units but, on the other hand, a blotchy brown sink with one cold water tap was not enough. I must have hot water and I must have a bath and I must have warmth. I walked many times round and round the cottage and up and down the stairs, trying to work out a possible bathroom, before I remembered the outhouse connected to the end wall, which could very easily be knocked through into and properly roofed and would solve the most pressing problem. All the time I was investigating this possibility – not really knowing what it might depend on, in the way of structural changes – the rain continued to thunder on the roof and there was a mist enveloping the fell that seemed to come nearer every time I looked out of a window. My shoes sounded like heavy boots as I paced the floors – the sound of each step magnified ten times by the utter stillness inside the house. The drumming rain, the heavy thudding footsteps – I felt quite panicky and was in a hurry to leave.

I was anxious before I left the fell to see where the Crosthwaites lived. Standing at the gate in the wall, the house behind me, there was no sign of any other habitation. My eyes searched the mist but saw only sheep, grey shapes clinging to the sodden ground like lumps of clay. There was no house anywhere. I began to walk further up the valley, along the mud path that was now so flooded that it seemed a tributary of the stream which ran along the back of the garden wall, unable to believe that there could be anything further on. My shoes and coat were totally inadequate – I was soaked quite literally to the skin after a hundred yards – but I was determined to at least turn the corner where the fellside folded into itself again. There, if I saw more open mountainside, I should retreat, knowing that wherever my neighbours were it was not there. But before I reached that point I saw, rising through the mist, a thin column of smoke, coming from above the line of the ground where it swept down to my path. I pressed on eagerly, glad that I had persevered. Round the hump of the fell I saw a very tiny cottage, much smaller than my own, with no wall round it and no sheds or outhouses near it. It was stuck under a giant sycamore tree, the only tree of any size that I had seen since I had left Greenhead. The size of the tree, which had an immense trunk and a great tangle of strong grey branches creaking in the wind that was beginning to rise, entirely dwarfed the humble little house. The end wall faced me as I approached. It had been whitewashed at one time and looked like a blank face – there were no windows in it, only a small door, strangely positioned in the extreme bottom right-hand corner. It was as if I had come upon the house that the witch lived in, in the story of Hansel and Gretel. At the top of this oddly pathetic wall was the chimney, black and squat, with wire over the top, from which the smoke came that I had seen. It looked a very small house for a family to live in.

I knocked at the door but there was no answer. I walked round the house and peered into the two windows but I could only make out the shape of a stool and a table. "Hello," I called, "anyone in?" I jumped when an upstairs window opened and a women leaned out. "What do you want?" she shouted rudely. "I don't know anything." I did not at first recognise her as the woman I had met on the road the day before. "Does Mr Crosthwaite live here?" I called, my voice squeaky and thin with disuse. I knew perfectly well that he could not but I wanted to use his name to prove I knew the area. "No," she shouted back, and started to close the window.

"Wait – please," I yelled up at her. "I am your new neighbour – Alexandra Grove is my name – I've bought Lowther Fell Cottage – I'm coming to live here."

"I don't know anything," she said. "I shall be gone when you come – I'm getting married in the morning – I'm only waiting." And she shut the window and drew the curtains. Angrily, I marched back to my car – it was unpleasant to be treated so badly. I suppose what made it worse was my belief that when I turned the corner I would see a snug farmhouse belonging to the Crosthwaites and be welcomed in and given a hot drink. My disappointment made me rage. I would be very glad to find my neighbour gone when I came to live beside her.

I passed the Crosthwaites' farmhouse on the way back – it

was up a track about half a mile from my cottage, on the way down to the road. There was only a stone, half covered with grass, with their name on it, easy to miss if not specifically looked for. It was too late to call upon them – I intended to drive back to London that day, knowing it would be impossible to do anything until I had contacted an architect or a surveyor, let alone a builder – but I regretted passing the end of their track without seeing them. They would, I was sure, have made me feel better – though later I reflected that at that time of day I would have been more likely to get their daughter, Eileen, who would not have made anyone feel better, at any time, about anything. At any rate, I drove straight on to London.

Mrs Matlock gave me tea in her "lounge" with every appearance of cordiality and after a long drag round the North Circular, coming after that last fifty miles of crowded, ugly motorway, I was glad to be sitting on one of her supremely vulgar but undeniably comfortable brocade-covered sofas. She had set the tea on one of those trolleys – tea things on the top layer, where the silver teapot gleamed among the Royal Worcester cups and saucers, and sandwiches and cake on the bottom – which she had pushed with difficulty through the ankle high shaggy white carpet. She clearly enjoyed the ritualistic pouring and sugaring and milking of the tea. I thought, however, that there was more than pleasure in the action that day – there was also power. She was looking very regal. Her white hair was pinned to the top of her head with a tortoiseshell comb and the effect, which ought to have been absurd on an old woman, was instead impressive. Grief at Gerald's death had stripped some of the fat from her face and the bone structure revealed made her look much more attractive. She had taken great care with her dress – a terrifyingly violent purple silk affair – and had put on all her rings. She looked what she was – a very rich widow, who toiled not neither did she spin.

"You're looking very well," I said, sipping the weak, fragrant tea (she had once told Antonia there were two things her son Gerald must always be given – good tea and good butter). "Having Casper must agree with you."

"Of course it agrees with me," she said, "he is my only grandchild. It is like having Gerald home again." But she said it without the usual sob in the voice, quite calmly and matter-of-factly.

"I'm sorry to be taking him away," I said, "but he can come regularly on holidays. I'm sure he will be glad to have a base in London when we're living in Cumbria." I knew I was very clipped and sharp in my speech but Mrs Matlock did not flinch.

"You're quite determined, then?" she said, refilling my cup and handing me the sandwiches with perfect poise.

"I am. I've bought a fellside cottage near Caldbeck. As soon as it's ready, we'll move up."

"I can't," Mrs Matlock said, carefully putting her cup down, "see the sense in it. You've never even tried to explain to me why you are dragging my grandson off to the wilds, in direct opposition to the life his parents had chosen for him, and so soon after this awful tragedy. I would have thought I was entitled to some discussion on the subject. Apart from anything else, Casper is my heir, now Gerald is gone. I would have thought that alone would give me some say in his future, even if you are not moved by more humane considerations. We, together, are the child's only relatives. We ought to be pulling together, for his sake."

It was quite a speech. Throughout it, Mrs Matlock's colour deepened slightly – her cheeks grew a little flushed and her forehead hot looking – but she never faltered. It occurred to me that she had practised saying all this many times, perhaps even in front of a mirror. She had set the scene and had some secret ending in mind with which she proposed to astound me. Rapidly, I went over in my head the legal document making me Casper's guardian. The solicitor had said it was quite unequivocal – I was sole guardian and trustee, in whom all rights were incontestably invested. Had Mrs Matlock perhaps found another will, making her joint guardian too? Or even – though it was quite impossible to imagine – making her Casper's sole guardian? I was amazed to discover that at the very thought I was promising myself to fight for Casper tooth and nail.

"I'm sorry if I haven't been very communicative," I said,

trying hard to soften my voice. "It wasn't intentional. I've just been so busy, trying to sort everything out, and I'm used to making decisions on my own. And anyway, there isn't really any rational explanation for this move north – I agree it seems silly and unnecessary – but I have an instinctive feeling that it is the right thing to do. I think Casper will benefit from it – it will be a total, complete change and that will help him readjust – it will be less painful than staying here and being constantly reminded of the past."

"That is arguable," Mrs Matlock said.

"Of course, but I have to do what I think best."

"There will only be you and Casper in this cottage – just the two of you – no extra?"

"No extra," I said, understanding exactly her drift. "No men friends to place your grandson in any immoral situation – he won't witness any disgusting scenes of carnal love, I promise you."

"It seems most unnatural for a young woman to coop herself up with a thirteen-year-old boy like that – especially an unmarried woman, who has never known what it is to be a mother."

I smiled, I hope unpleasantly, and with great sweetness said, "And what is it to be a mother, Mrs Matlock?"

"It is the greatest experience in one's life."

"Oh dear. And I have apparently missed it."

"The point is," Mrs Matlock said, her composure slipping just a little, "you don't know how to deal with a young boy. You don't even like him much, do you? I've always known that. I love him like his mother loved him, but you – you don't even like him."

"You're very confident," I said.

"Anyone can see it. He's just a nuisance to you, isn't he? You're taking him on out of a sense of duty and nothing else. I don't know why you don't admit it."

"Why do you want me to admit it?"

"You're a woman on your own without even a husband – you don't want to be tied down – Casper will simply ruin your life."

Echoes of so many painful conversations came back to me as I sat there among the knick-knacks and opulent furnishings which so exactly summed up the old lady in front of me. I saw other rooms, plain and poor, and heard other voices speaking with equal passion, and my skin crawled at the memory . . .

I stood up. "Mrs Matlock," I said, "I must go now. I don't want to upset you but you ought to be able to see we could never work together. I promise you that if, after a year, Casper is unhappy, then we will return to London. We may return anyway. I shall encourage him to write to you and to visit you – I very much want him to keep in contact – and I shan't touch a penny of his money, rest assured. Is he in the garden?"

She sat quite still. I saw her hands trembled a little.

"He isn't here," she said.

"Then where is he?"

"A friend of yours came to call and he has taken him on an outing – I thought it would be good for him."

"A friend? But who? Who could possibly take Casper out – do you know this person?"

"I have met him. I always thought he was a pleasant young man and I know Gerald thought highly of him and always hoped, eventually, that in time – you might – you – "

I flare up into anger easily – age has hardly brought the self control I expected and looked for – but rarely have I exploded so suddenly. I suppose I ought to be ashamed of the exhibition of myself that I made. I am afraid I swore, and stood up – jumped up – so swiftly that I set the tea trolley tinkling and then in my fury I kicked the brass fender viciously and turned on Mrs Matlock with rage. I expect my face was ugly and purple and that I shouted and probably waved my arms about – oh, I am not proud of my reaction, but I nevertheless thought it forgivable. I still do. Mrs Matlock's assumptions were so crass, her line of thought deeply insulting, her pathetic air of having outmanoeuvred me offensive. All her little mind could think of was getting me married so that Casper would have a new Daddy as quickly as possible.

And Edward – my feelings towards him were equally strong. How dare he be so sneaky, creeping into this area of my life, which he knew I wanted to myself? I had never known him to be so devious – I would have said his nature was to be excessively open – but now I suspected him of spying and other deceitful practices I hated to think about. He must have gone to some considerable lengths to track down where Casper was and to ingratiate himself with Mrs Matlock to the extent of being allowed to take her beloved grandson out while he was under her care and protection. Why had he wanted to do it? What was he now saying to Casper? What was the point of it all? I felt afraid.

Mrs Matlock was clearly astonished at my temper. She passed very quickly from being pleased at her stratagem to being bewildered by its effect. "I'm sorry," she said, as soon as I paused in my stream of abuse.

"So you should be – the stupidity," I yelled.

"I had no idea you would mind so much. I thought Edward Airlie an extremely respectable young man – am I mistaken? I thought he had been a friend of your family for many years – he was at Gerald and Antonia's wedding, was he not? And Casper knows him – he seemed to get on so well with him – I thought you would be delighted that he should enjoy some male company for a change – I thought I was being noble giving up some of my precious time with Casper so that he could take advantage of the opportunity."

"You're lying," I said.

"I *beg* your pardon –"

"I'm sorry if that upsets you, but you *are* lying – you never for one minute thought I would be delighted. You hoped to embarrass me, and what is even worse you are still hoping that at this very minute Casper and Edward will get along famously and it will help your silly little plot to work. But it won't. I have no intention of ever marrying anyone . . ."

"Oh, how can you say that, how can you *know* – ?"

"Of course I know. You – women like you – cannot ever get it into their heads that some people may actually want to stay single – that there may be other women, quite different from yourself, who value their independence and enjoy their unattached state. It has nothing to do with the 'being left on the shelf' attitude of your generation."

"How horrid," Mrs Matlock said, shuddering with distaste.

"Only to you – your world began and ended with being

a wife and mother – you can't comprehend anything beyond it."

"There isn't anything worthwhile beyond it," Mrs Matlock said, her voice quavering slightly. "They are the two glories of womanhood."

"Oh, what rubbish."

"Show me anything that is better."

"Freedom."

"From what?"

"Servitude – constantly giving in to other people's demands – having all the time to suppress your own instincts – "

"But mothering *was* my instinct – loving my husband and looking after him was all I ever wanted to do – and now I have no husband and no son all my instincts as a woman are thwarted."

"How contemptible," I said, and instantly regretted it. I knew Mrs Matlock spoke the truth and it was wrong of me to despise her because she was different.

"I apologise," I said quickly. "I ought not to have said that – I've been very rude – it's just that I am so distressed."

"I can see that," Mrs Matlock said, "and I fail still to understand why. Annoyed, yes, but to be so very angry for such a little thing – I thought you at least liked Edward?"

"I do like him."

"Then why object to him taking Casper out quite so strongly? Even if you won't believe my motives were entirely innocent – why should you be so upset?"

"Edward and Casper belong to different departments in my life," I said. "I don't wish them to mix."

"I find that extraordinary, almost as if – as if you were frightened of them liking each other too much and pushing you out, which of course is impossible."

"Impossible," I said emphatically.

Mrs Matlock was perhaps not the fool I had always taken her for, and I began to feel I ought to step more carefully. I tried to calm down and keep my voice level as I said, "It is almost five o'clock. What time do you expect Edward to bring Casper back?"

"He isn't bringing him back here." She went a little pink as I stared at her. "He thought it would be better if he took him home as he expected to be quite late – to your flat, you know. I said I thought that would be perfectly all right, so I said goodbye to Casper and he took his bag and of course the dog. Edward seemed most fond of the dog. I suppose that is one of the reasons Casper likes him."

"I suppose it is," I said, coldly. "Well, I will go home and wait. Thank you for having Casper. I'm sure he enjoyed being here, though I don't suppose he had the grace to say so."

"He doesn't need to say so. I don't look for thanks. People who do things out of love don't need it. If you were a wife or a mother you would know that."

We had spent half an hour hurting each other and still there was no quarter given. I got into my car, feeling I had fought a battle and lost it. I had used all my energy on Mrs Matlock, quite pointlessly, when I ought to have saved it to confront Edward. Now I was drained – all I wanted to do was go home and sleep. The flat, when I finally reached it, was hot and airless and smelled of the wretched Rufus. At least, when we were living on Lowther Fell, Rufus could have his own place in one of the outhouses – I should insist on that. I sat in the narrow garden, trying to collect together my thoughts before Edward appeared, determined to be rational and logical and give him no chance to accuse me of hysteria.

There was no opportunity to be either. Edward dropped Casper off, bag, dog and all, in Heath Street, opposite the antique market, and he came in on his own.

"Where's Edward?" I said, looking past him as he came into the kitchen.

"He's gone home."

"You mean he didn't bring you?"

"He dropped me off. He was in a hurry."

I gave a great sigh of exasperation – I had worked out such a masterly campaign and could not bear to be robbed of the carrying out. The things I had been going to say would now rattle around in my head all night.

"Edward is going to Argentina," Casper suddenly said.

I could not conceal my alarm. Edward had gone off many times but never so far. He had moved from teaching to educational psychology and now flitted from one university to another, lecturing in a subject he claimed was still in its infancy and would grow with him. I had always made fun of it – such a non-subject, somehow – but Edward was deadly serious. He lectured and even wrote books on his subject and had recently, since he had started to specialise in the growth of violence, taken to being on high-sounding committees, which I suspected simply gave him the chance to listen to his own voice. That is unkind, but Edward did like to talk and pontificate about his beliefs and I often found it very boring. Nothing, it seemed to me, could ever be proved one way or the other about what he said – none of his so-called "evidence" was evidence at all.

"Are you sure?" I asked, startled. He nodded. To my own alarm, I cried. Casper went to his room hastily. The tears poured down my face and I made no effort to stop them. On and on they cascaded, as I stood helplessly looking out of the window. Instinctively, I felt this was the point of no return – all the other times he had walked out, when I had driven him too far, were practices for this final moment. I wept for myself, high on my own daring, excited by the terrible promise of total freedom. I really would never see Edward again. He would become a memory to which I would cling when my body ached with longing for him. He would be everywhere in the Lakes – striding the fells before me, twenty one years old and bursting with energy and vitality, zig-zagging across Ullswater every time I passed along that shore road – he would be in my head wherever I went. And with him I would see myself, adoring, his devoted slave, sure we would be inseparable forever. I would not remember the bad times. When had they begun? Not that summer we met. The summer had been unsullied by doubt or argument. Then I had come to London and started at the Central School and Edward had begun teaching near Keswick. The quarrels started on those stolen weekends. All week we wrote each other fevered letters of longing and then, when I went to the Lake District or Edward came to London, we wasted our time fighting. I do not remember what we fought about but I remember the shouting – my shouting – and the exhaustion of the reconciliations. We seemed incapable of being happily together any more. Edward blamed the constant separations. I blamed something lacking in myself. We spent all our holidays together in Edward's rented cottage near Threlkeld and then – if we had long enough – we seemed to overcome our difficulties and be as we were that first summer – loving, passionate, as one. But always I had to return and mixed with the agony of separation there was always the joy and relief of once more being on my own. I hardly dared admit it. Backwards and forwards I went, all year, constantly tugged in both directions.

But I would not remember that time, or the aftermath. I knew I would never see us trudging through the rain, cold and miserable on Jenkins Hill as we struggled to resolve our dilemma by climbing Skiddaw. I would never see Edward's face, impassive and still as I looked at it that night in the small mirror I held so shakily in my hand, to prove to myself by gazing at my reflection that I was *there* and not the numb shadow I feared I had become. I was so convincing, that was the trouble. Antonia said I had missed my vocation. I acted out my mythical love-affair-with-another so well that Edward – clever, sensitive, clear sighted Edward – never guessed the truth. I disappeared for a year and he did not even try to find me. But I would have none of those agonising visions before me – I would see us happy, before the tempests, and I would grieve. I would see us cleaving to each other, giving ourselves freely and fully, before the deceits.

Eventually, I dried my tears. I went to Casper's room and knocked on the door and called through it, "Casper, I'm starving – come out and have a pizza with me – please – I'm perfectly all right now and I won't disgrace myself. Five minutes and I'll be ready – OK?" There was no reply. I washed my face, changed my blouse, collected some money and went to the door. I was nervous in case Casper would not be there, but he was, and I gave him what I hoped was a grateful smile and we went up Heath Street to the Pizza Express, where we sat in the window eating and staring out at passers-by. I felt I ought to offer some explanation for my behaviour an hour ago but for once we were comfortable together and I was afraid of spoiling such a precious atmosphere. Casper ate heartily, head lowered, and I picked at my food, trying to force it down. I felt like saying totally unacceptable things like "at least we have each other" but resisted the temptation. Instead, I said, "Would you like a bicycle when we move to the Lake District?" and was gratified to see Casper's startled expression before he could stop himself. We both laughed. "You could," I said, "ride to school. How about that?" For the briefest instant, before that shuttered expression came over his face again, there was a look of such pure delight in the boy's eyes that he gave me hope.

Four

I tried very hard to make our first expedition to Lowther Fell together a real adventure. I don't say that in any sarcastic way – I really did attempt to capture Casper's imagination. It was, if you like, a challenge for me and a test for him. I think we both were surprised at the degree of success attained.

We camped. I had woken up, the next day, purged of my immediate distress. I had of course wept again, the moment I was on my own in bed, but the tears were a relief and I let them come without trying to suppress them. I thought I would waken with a blinding headache and a stiff face and red rimmed eyes. I thought I would feel so dull and dreary and depressed that I would barely be able to move – but the reverse was true. All that bawling had a cathartic effect. I in fact woke up refreshed and alert. I pulled up the blind and peering out saw that the bottom end of my gloomy garden was brilliantly green with strong sunshine. I sang as I dressed, rejoicing in my physical well being, and as I brushed my hair I congratulated myself on my own buoyancy. I sat over a cup of coffee with a pad of paper and a pencil in my hand and made lists of what I had to do before the following weekend and as I scribbled I suddenly thought how much time it would save if we could stay at the cottage itself. In its existing state that was not an attractive prospect, but then I thought what fun it would be to camp.

I dashed about like a mad thing that week, buying a tent and sleeping bags and the minimum kit we would need. It quickly became obvious that my little sports car was not going to be much good for this sort of venture and I felt a pang of fear at the thought of having to give it up. My mind ran on new lines – I saw myself carting stuff about endlessly in the country – and I wondered what car I should buy. There was some fun in considering the rival merits of a Range Rover or a jeep or a more conventional estate car like a Volvo, but as I crammed more and more things into the narrow seat at the back of my MGB I thought how I would hate to sacrifice it, however imperative the need.

It was a glorious evening as we drove through Caldbeck on our way up to Lowther Fell and my spirits soared. The response the sight of the fells bathed in pink sunshine drew from me made me think I had been wrong to say I did not like the country. Aesthetically, surely, I loved it. Nobody, seeing that great expanse of land so beautifully lit, could fail to feel moved. The beauty was not prettiness but a deep, satisfying thing, permanent and solid, above all mere man made perfections. Perhaps it was age, but I began at last to feel as my father had felt when he walked those long distances along the Lakeland mountainsides – a feeling of himself not mattering, of somehow plugging himself into the continuity of the landscape. That is a clumsy, ugly way of expressing his views, as I remembered them, but I know that is roughly what he meant. It was nothing so false as thinking himself "at one" with nature, but simply that his worries seemed small and his faith in life stronger.

Casper said not a word. He had been abroad, often, with Antonia and Gerald, to frightful holiday hotels in awful seaside resorts such as the Mediterranean specialises in, but of his own country he knew very little. Gerald did not like roughing it, nor was he energetic. He never walked if he could drive, and the thought of climbing a mountain would have been an anathema to him. A little gentlemanly tennis was about the only sport he ever indulged in and Antonia had, as in everything, followed his lead. Whether Casper would like the open-air life was yet to be discovered – certainly, the signs were not encouraging. He took Rufus for walks only because it was necessary and I had not seen him play any game. But I intended to give him no option. We would not be car bound. Once on Lowther Fell, we would walk.

If I had been expecting any miracles while I was in London I was disappointed – the cottage looked exactly the same, dark and dilapidated. But Lowther Fell did not look the same. The sunset made the most astonishing difference. Every blade of grass seemed streaked with brilliant light and the green all around was dazzling. I wanted to reach out and stroke the hump back of the fell itself – it looked, in that glowing warmth of evening light, like an animal whose coat is silky and smooth. Even the rocks, last time so black and sinister in the dripping rain, seemed changed into soft, shadowy statues which nobody could fear. The sheep stood stock still, washed white in the sun and set apart from each other in what seemed carefully chosen positions. Birds cawing and swooping took my gaze high up to the top of the few trees and the leaves against the darkening blue sky were like mosaics.

Casper, I could see, felt a strange being. He got out of the car awkwardly and stood looking dazed for several minutes. Uneasily, he turned and looked about him, his hand over his mouth and his feet grinding a stone into the mud. I gave him no time for reflection. We unpacked the car and I helped him put up the tent, leaving him to hammer in the pegs that held the ropes. He was careful and methodical whereas I was slap-dash and hurried and he would make a much better job of making sure the tent did not blow away in the night. I got water from inside the house and even found some kindling that was completely dry in the shed and managed to make a campfire. Casper smiled as I put an iron grating over the fire and a frying pan on top and sausages into the pan. He shot me a quick look – cheeky, quite unlike himself – and I turned away to slice tomatoes, convinced it would be a mistake to smile back in case it was interpreted as condescending.

As the sun finally set, it grew colder. I thought (though knowing nothing about it) that there might even be frost next morning. We sat round the fire eating the rather burned and burst sausages and drinking cocoa. Both of us had thick jeans and sweaters on and anoraks on top and we were not cold, though aware that the temperature had rapidly dropped. I fed the fire with more wood, miraculously preserved in the shed, and it flared up again and again, warming and lighting the small patch of ground in front of the cottage. When the supply was finished I said we must go to bed. We crept inside the tent and into our sleeping bags just as we were and I turned off the huge torch I had brought.

Neither of us slept for a long time but we did not speak. Casper's head was very near my own – I could see his eyes open, staring at the roof of the tent, where the moon had made pale patches in the dark fabric. It would have been good to reach out and touch him, friendly to hold his hand, but I dared to do neither. What surprised me was that I felt the urge to make some sort of physical gesture – and I did. I felt tender towards him as we lay there side by side – we had been silent but extraordinarily close sitting round our campfire and I felt strangely compassionate towards my young charge. The touch of a hand would convey so much and yet I was afraid to follow my instinct. So I lay there instead with my arms securely in my sleeping bag, remembering Edward and other campfires and tents, not so very far from where we now lay. Edward loved camping and everything to do with it. He often slept out in the open in a sleeping bag and said there was nothing better than opening his eyes to the stars. Making love in the open air was his delight. Hot sun on a bare body was, he said, the greatest aphrodisiac in the world. I closed my eyes tightly at the memory but the dark only sharpened the images. Casper coughed, a clearing-of-the-throat sort of cough, and I wondered if he was going to say something, but he turned on his side and in a short while the regular breathing told me he had gone to sleep. I began to feel very slightly cold but even though Casper slept I did not dare to cuddle against his sleeping bag for warmth. Cautiously, I sat up and dragged on top of us a thick blanket I had providently laid across our feet, and then I settled down, knowing the light would waken us very early in the morning.

In fact, we both wakened long before that. I go from deep sleep to alert wakefulness in an instant – no intervening sleepiness at all – and so when the noise woke me up I was sharp and tense straight away. Casper, I think, was more dozy – more like Antonia, who, every morning of her life, took half an hour to get even one eye half open – but I was aware that he too was listening. It was a very light noise of someone or something walking round our tent. Because it was so dark, the moon heavily clouded over, there were no shadows. Casper sat up and leaned back on the palms of his hands. For a second time the whispering sound of the sides of the tent being brushed against disturbed the night-time silence. "It's only a sheep, Casper," I said. He jumped slightly and said, "I know," crossly, and snuggled back down into his bag. The noise had stopped, but I could not return to sleeping as easily as Casper. I lay there, quite still, listening. I had said it was a sheep, but I did not believe it – the movement had been too delicate for a sheep. Sheep blunder against things, and if they hear a voice near them they jump away. Whatever had gone round and round our tent had done so stealthily, and my voice, talking to Casper, had not frightened it. It might, I thought, as I strained to hear any movement, be a fox. Foxes were not dangerous – or so I told myself. It occurred to me rather late that we were quite unprotected and that this might prove foolish. Perhaps, as a woman living on my own with a child, I ought to have a gun, but then I remembered we would have Rufus, who this time we had left behind in London with Mrs Matlock, and that although his abilities as a guard dog had never been seriously put to the test, he was convincing enough to look at. Casper would be pleased that I considered Rufus an asset.

I suppose I had succeeded in falling into a light doze when the noise started again and brought me fully to consciousness. Casper did not move. I leaned over to see if he was awake but he was soundly asleep this time. Round and round the tent the footsteps went, very close to the sides and yet not falling over the guide ropes. I did not know what to do, if anything. I was not exactly afraid but I felt anxious – I did not want whatever it was to burst into the tent. If it was an animal – as it surely was – then the best thing to do was keep still and eventually it would go away. Then there was a distinct sound of a sneeze. It was quite unmistakable. I sat up and felt for my big, heavy torch, half thinking I could use it as a weapon. Should I waken Casper? If there was any struggle he would be wakened anyway and be much more frightened than if he had been prepared. But then, as I hesitated, despising myself for the way in which my hand had gone clammy round the torch, the footsteps stopped. I waited. When they started again they sounded further away – the tent was being given a wider berth. I realised that in fact it was no longer being circled, that the footsteps were receding. With relief came curiosity of a bolder kind. I crept to the flap of the tent and undid enough of the string to peer out. I did not expect to be able to see anything in the absolute blackness of that place, but as my eyes became accustomed to the dark I made out a figure walking – tiptoeing, I thought – away towards the path. I could tell very little from the blurred outline but I was convinced of one thing. The visitor had been a woman.

It was not quite so sunny the next morning – the air felt very cold and there was a wind that snaked in through the flap I had carelessly left open. I said nothing to Casper about our visitation. He remarked on the open flap – it had been his job to tie it up and he was concerned that perhaps he had not done it properly – and I told him I had wanted to let some air in. He went outside first and I could hear him looking round the tent. I knew he would be looking for marks and would be relieved to find none, and that, seeing sheep so near on the fell, he would conclude I had been right. Before I had gone back to sleep I had decided the only person it could possibly have been was the woman in the cottage further up the fell – the woman who had shouted down so rudely from her window that I was to go away because she was getting married in the morning.

There was no time for me to brood about the meaning of her prowling. As soon as I had got up and washed in freezing water, the agony of making hot coffee consumed my thoughts. Agony because making a fire in the morning was as maddening as it had been fun in the evening; it took hours for the wretched water to boil and we were both shivering, waiting for it. I did not want to talk and luckily Casper kept out of my way – not that he would have broken his own silence but any little thing he did was likely to irritate me. The minute we had drunk the coffee the first of a series of callers arrived and I was straight into discussions on alterations of every kind.

The most important consideration, as I stressed again and again, was speed. They all smiled at that – a Mr Graham of Queens & Co., Penrith smile – tolerant, slightly derisive, very annoying. The builder whose name I had got from Mr Crosthwaite, smiled most of all and said, "We don't rush things in this part of the world. You'll have to take us as you find us." He was a rough looking man, broad and heavy, but with no trace of a tradesman's subservience about him. It was clear, indeed, that he saw himself as far superior to any tradesman. His building firm, a family concern of himself, two sons and a son-in-law, was his empire and he was an emperor with all an emperor's arrogance (since I am arrogant myself I quickly identify it in others). He looked me boldly in the eye and was not, in his demeanour, above a certain sexual challenge. I did not like him at all but I had been told he was indisputably the best builder for miles around. And he had come, promptly, at the arranged time, and brought with him the District Planning Officer and a local surveyor, who was going to do the plans. They were also-rans. The meeting was dominated by Mr Rigg. He stuck his hands in his pockets and walked round the cottage, kicking walls experimentally and prodding ceilings with a stick. He laughed openly at all my ideas. "A bathroom in the shed, eh," he said. "You're asking for trouble." Having made this sort of pronouncement he never enlarged upon it – it was apparently his prerogative to make unsubstantiated statements. I tried hard to control my dislike but I know he sensed it and that it amused him even more. "You'll never get that fire to draw," he said, when I thought we had finished. "You won't be cosy of an evening when you're sitting there, doing your knitting." He laughed uproariously at his own wit. "It wants a new canopy," he said, "and that opening made bigger at the back, then it'll draw strong, sweet and warm your slippers." Evidently he thought it very good of him to explain, for he looked around for applause and the other two gentlemen nodded sagely.

Outside, we examined the barn which I wanted converted into a pottery. Mr Rigg saw no problems, for once. We all four stood for a minute before they got into their cars. Casper was sitting outside the tent, whittling away at a stick with a knife. He looked, for Casper, remarkably content. "That your lad?" Mr Rigg asked, giving him a critical once over. "No," I said, "It is my sister's boy. She was killed in an air crash this month – his father too." It was fortunate Casper was too far off to hear – he hated that sort of explanation of our relationship but I thought it best to be blunt to avoid speculation and the misunderstandings which so often follow. "An orphan, eh," Mr Rigg said. He seemed surprisingly moved. "Well," he said, "he'll do well up here – Wigton's a little jewel of a place and the school is grand." We walked to the gate and he looked at me sharply as he said, "And what'll you do, stuck out here?" I could not tell him not to be impertinent or that it was none of his business – his directness commanded an equal directness. "I make pottery, as I told you," I said. "I'm going to build a kiln and make pots and I hope to sell them."

"Well, good luck to you," he said. "There's no harm in that."

There was a last pause before he actually climbed into his car. The other two had driven off but Mr Rigg seemed in no hurry. "I like it up here you know," he said. "Used to come when I was a lad – used to run, one time, a regular Joss Naylor, like – he's the fell runner – but then I got married." He stood in the sunshine looking up at the fell and I saw his eye catch the thin line of smoke rising from behind the hump, where I knew the tiny whitewashed cottage lay. "Spoke to Miss Cowdie yet?" he asked, nodding his head in its direction. "Yes," I said, "but I caught her at a bad time – she was getting married the next morning and naturally didn't want to be disturbed." He laughed so loud that his face grew quite purple. "Oh yes," he said finally, gasping for breath, "you caught her at a bad time all right – oh, I'll say you did, you did that – oh dear me – " and he was off again in paroxysms of laughter. The sound of that laughter echoed down the track as he drove off along it, rising even above the noises of the car's engine and the stones flying up to hit its wheels.

We went, Casper and I, down to the Crosthwaites' farm, equipped with a basket to carry back the eggs and milk I expected to get. I was looking forward to meeting that couple again, so I was disappointed when our knock on the back door of the farmhouse – I was not so stupid as to knock on the front door – was answered by a girl. She did not open the door very far, merely a crack through which I could see her face and little else. "Good morning," I said. She said nothing. "Is Mrs Crosthwaite in?" She shook her head. "Will she be back soon, do you know?" Another dumb shake of the head. "I'm Alexandra Grove, your new neighbour," I said. "We're just here for the weekend, camping, trying to arrange to get the cottage put right." Still no reaction whatsoever. "Do you think you could sell us eggs and milk?" I said. "Don't sell milk," the girl said, "not allowed. But we've got eggs. 55p a dozen."

It might have been a ventriloquist operating her – the mouth hardly moved at all. As she opened the door to take the basket I saw that she was older than I had first thought. Her face was a very old face, the sort of face on a woman of sixty that makes you wonder how it could ever be young and here it was, young, on a girl of twenty or so, already inscrutably aged. It was a medieval face, narrow, with a long pointed nose and high forehead. The hair surrounding it was lank and pale gold in colour, and hung in unattractive clumps round the ears. But it was the hard, watchful, suspicious eyes that shocked me. They were full of some unspoken resentment towards the world and they repelled me. I wondered if the girl was some sort of servant – she was so different from the Crosthwaites that I could not believe she was in any way related to them. She went somewhere into the back of the house, leaving Casper and me standing uneasily at the open door, trying not to look inquisitively inside.

The girl came back with a dozen eggs and I paid the money. She stood watching us go, her arms folded across her thin chest. There was something insolent in her stance as she leaned against the wall and yet it was innocent enough – perhaps she was simply bored with the kind of life she must lead on that isolated farm. I was still thinking about her, still feeling those eyes that I felt could see for miles boring into my back, when we saw a man leaning on a gate we were obliged to pass. He was watching us too, but in a different sort of way. As we came abreast of him, almost at the end of the Crosthwaites' lane, he waved and said cheerfully, "Morning – nice day." We stopped and put down the eggs. "Morning," I said, not consciously imitating him but anxious to be as casual and friendly. "I came to see Mr and Mrs Crosthwaite," I said, "but they don't seem to be in and the girl who opened the door didn't seem to know when they would be back."

"It's a sale," he said. "They've got to Keswick, won't be back till evening. And you'll be the Londoner that's bought Lowther Fell Cottage, eh?"

"That's right."

"Real mess it is an' all, eh?"

"Yes, it is."

"It'll cost summat to put it right, but Rigg's a good man – he'll do a good job."

"Do you live here?" I asked, emboldened by his own questioning.

"I do that. I'm Geoff Crosthwaite, pleased to meet you," and he stuck out his large dirty hand which I took eagerly.

"This your lad, then?" he said, nodding at Casper.

"No, my nephew. He's going to live up here with me." I did not wish to go into details in front of Casper, who was already turning away with embarrassment.

"It'll put some hair on his chest," Geoff said, and laughed. "Colour in his cheeks, too. Wind never stops blowing up here." There was a wind blowing his fair, rather long hair into his mischievous eyes as he spoke. I suppose, as he pushed it away, I saw that he was a handsome young man – tall, strong, tough looking, like his father, and yet not coarse. His skin was brown with the open air and he had his father's bright pink cheeks. Indeed, his face was all colour, for as well as the brown and pink – odd on a young man – he had startlingly blue eyes. The blond hair completed the impression of a kind of Viking, yet there was only a physical impression of strength. I felt, straight away, that Geoff Crosthwaite was a weak young man in an extraordinarily strong body. There was a softness about him immediately apparent. Nor was it simply a case of his easy manner and ready smile making him seem soft – an absolute lack of determination came off him. I felt people must be able to do what they liked with Geoff. It is hard, looking back, to believe that I thought this, but I did. Geoff was so nice – sweet, even, standing there in his stained jeans and dirty sweater, chatting away so amicably. I felt protective and must confess that I did, however ludicrous it seems now.

"See you've got a car," he said. "Nice little job."

"Do you have a car?"

"Ay, but nowt like yours – a Riley, I've got, grand old car

but eats petrol. I'm overhauling it right now, but I'll give you a ride after."

I was careful not to smile. I am solemn about my car. Geoff was solemn about his. It was as if he had offered me a lick of his ice-cream.

"Well, I'd best get on," he said. "A farmer's work is never done."

As he got down from the gate, we both saw a woman pass the end of the track. It was the woman from the little cottage beyond mine, the woman whom I suspected of visiting our tent in the night, the woman who had told me she was getting married in the morning, the woman whom Mr Rigg had found so amusing.

"Who's that?" I said to Geoff, pointing.

"That's Miss Cowdie," he said, and smiled.

"She told me she was getting married."

"Ay, she's off to wait for her bridegroom now," Geoff said, "down there – at that signpost, back on the Caldbeck road – she sits there all morning, every morning, rain or shine, and when he doesn't come she goes home. Mad as a hatter."

"Mad?" I said. "But she doesn't seem mad – she seems perfectly coherent – and if she's mad, why isn't she looked after?"

"Won't let anyone near, and she doesn't bother folk so what's the harm? We've got worse loonies than that round here."

He was perfectly cheerful about it. Madness was a run-of-the-mill sort of complaint in Geoff's eyes, not nearly as serious as foot-and-mouth disease. He had no conception of the pain his so-called madness could entail for the person said to be suffering from it. Miss Cowdie was a joke, that was all. He told me, that morning, with absolute matter-of-factness that she was jilted ten years ago and she'd never been right since. She'd started acting funny. Nothing in trousers was safe from her – she thought every male in the area might be her bridegroom. As he related all this, before he went back to his tractor, Geoff Crosthwaite never once expressed any regret or pity for Miss Cowdie. He enjoyed giving me the details and when my expression must have told him how cruel I found it all he told me not to fret, she wouldn't bother me, she kept herself to herself, and then, as his parting shot, he pointed at Casper and winked and said I would have to watch out for the young lad.

Luckily, Casper had moved on during our conversation and did not hear. It was ridiculous anyway and I hated Geoff's cheap joke. We went back to our cottage and I set Casper to gathering wood, which he seemed to enjoy enough for me to think there actually were signs that he might turn out to be a country boy.

Five

We did not stray far afield that weekend – it was hectic enough fending for ourselves with so many difficulties against us. Foolish, I know, to moan about hardship when we had running water and a lavatory that worked but everything is relative and to us, used to a very spoiled existence, it felt like deprivation. I get no thrill, unlike Edward, out of living rough. It was just as I suspected – I soon grew tired of the enormous effort necessary to get so much as a mug of hot water and on the second night, when the temperature dropped quite alarmingly, I hated being cold. Casper, on the other hand, did not seem to mind. I saw that in these situations his stoical disposition was a great asset. It was clear that, whatever happened to us, he would not turn out to be a whiner.

The lady, Miss Cowdie, did not trouble us again. We never saw her during the day and, so far as I know, nobody prowled around our tent at night. We did pass her cottage on the way up to the top of Lowther Fell – where there was a stunning view all the way to the Solway Firth – but there was no sound or sight of anyone being there. Perhaps, as Geoff had told us, she was at the crossroads, waiting for her bridegroom, a thought which horrified me. For someone to have their life wrecked by a man like that – for someone's sanity to be unhinged by the loss of marital expectations – was too terrible for me to contemplate with any degree of equanimity. I felt angry as well as appalled – angry with Miss Cowdie herself for being so craven, for subscribing so readily to a nineteenth century idea of womanhood. She could have had no pride to go under so easily. As we climbed the fell, Casper and I, my head was full of the scene as I thought it must have been. I saw Miss Cowdie, young and smiling, standing in a traditional white dress, long and flowing, outside the church. I heard the bells pealing and felt the chill of the old building as she went inside and walked up the aisle on the arm of some shadowy father figure. I stood with her at the altar and waited. My heart thudded – I was climbing a steep fell, remember – and a sweat broke out of my flower-wreathed brow, and then as it finally came to me that there was no bridegroom I turned dizzily towards the congregation – silent, nervous – and sank to the ground.

"I must rest," I said to Casper, gasping, holding my side, "I'm dizzy." I groaned in an exaggerated fashion and lay down on the rough ground. He stood above me, not even the faintest flush on his thin cheeks, arms resting lightly on his hips. He wasn't even breathing hard. "You aren't such a weakling after all," I said. He turned away, pretending to look at the view. "Go ahead," I said, "I'll catch you up."

He was off instantly, straight up the steepest way, his back bent in a determined arc. I followed much more slowly, clutching at handfuls of grass to help me along, and leaning against any boulder kindly offering its shoulder. Miss Cowdie's father offered his, but she refused it. She refused to leave the church. Everyone went home until she was left on her own, resistant to all persuasion. Night came and at last, sobbing, she was led away and told – what? I could not imagine any message – the cruelty of the communication was beyond me. With Miss Cowdie, I refused to believe in its existence. The man I loved could never write that message. It must all be a mistake and tomorrow he could come.

Casper was on the top, waving. I dragged myself up towards him. Father was always shocked at how unfit I was – "A great girl like you," he would rage, "young and healthy, and puffed out after a few hundred feet." I did not look unfit – quite the reverse – but he would annually reveal to me that he had the superior physique. I took no exercise once I was London based – played no games, got very little fresh air. He said I would regret it but until that day, toiling up behind Casper, I never had, and of course there was always the dreadful irony of Father having died, in spite of his fitness, at such a tender age. But I resolved there and then to get myself into shape – nothing so vulgar as jogging or running around in one of those frightful track suits, but more a steady programme of toughening up. Perhaps part of that ennui I had been experiencing was due to years of slothful living catching up with me. I hate inefficiency, and suddenly my own body felt extremely inefficient.

We did none of the important things I meant to do, beyond meeting the builder and discussing what had to be done. Before we left, however, we called again on the Crosthwaites. I was relieved to find the parents in and no sign of the resentful girl, whom I now found was Mrs Crosthwaite's daughter, Eileen. Mrs Crosthwaite even apologised for her, and said she was "funny" with strangers. She was, Mrs Crosthwaite said, fed up, with no job ever since she had left school, and then she alarmed me by asking me if I would need anyone to help, because Eileen was a good worker once she got started. I asked at what, and her mother said at anything, provided it was simple. She said she'd heard tell I was an artist and going to make pots and Eileen would be a dab hand at any of the rough work involved. She was strong as a lad and could carry really heavy weights. I said I hadn't thought out what I was going to do yet but that certainly I would bear Eileen in mind, and then we left, with more of the delicious eggs.

Nor had I thought it out – what I was going to do, I mean. I squirmed slightly at the idea of making pots to sell locally. God knows, there are potteries every few miles in the Lake District, all turning out much the same sort of amateurish stuff, and I did not want to add to their number. Besides, opening a pottery on a commercial scale is not lightly undertaken. On the other hand, what else could I do? I wanted a change from teaching and even if I had not it would probably have been difficult for me to get a job. I could do nothing – but the thought was intolerable. Not even in London, surrounded by every kind of opportunity for diversion, could I do nothing. Work was essential to my well being. Prompted by Mrs

Crosthwaite's enquiry, I thought about it all the long way back and came to the obvious conclusion. Pottery of some sort it would have to be – but good, useful pottery, not fiddly rubbish, not ornaments. Handsome cups and saucers, generous mugs, strong graceful jugs, and all, I thought, in the same colour, so that Lowther Fell Pottery would be instantly recognisable. It would not be clumsy and crude, the way so much local pottery is, but on the contrary rather fine, though not fragile, with great attention paid to the moulding of handles and rims and all those parts of a pot which reveal instantly to the experienced eye some level of sophistication. The glaze, I thought, might be grey – shades of grey, dark and light, like so much of the sky in that part of the world, with perhaps a pattern in black or white. I would not sell my pots at the door, as it were – no notices saying "STUDIO" or arrows pointing to "POTTERY FOR SALE". I really could not bear tourists coming in and fingering my work – not that I feared disparaging remarks so much as that awful apathetic attitude displayed by those who do not know what they are looking for. I would try to sell my wares wholesale, to shops or even restaurants, and stand or fall on that. My income, after all, did not need to be large, not yet, not until I found out if this move was to be permanent. I had promised Mrs Matlock that I would not touch any of Casper's money – though under the terms of Gerald and Antonia's will I was entitled to – and I would keep that promise. We would live on the profit from the sale of my Church Row flat. I intended to invest that money in such a way as to produce a small income, though already I was doubtful if that would be possible when the renovations at the cottage were bound to be expensive.

At any rate, I refused – as I have always been able to refuse – to worry about money. We would manage with ease. But I must see that Mr Rigg installed a kiln while he was there. I would order all the equipment I would need in London, to be sure of getting exactly what I wanted and was used to, and I would try to be ready to start production just as soon as we arrived there. We would not hang about, Casper and I, targets for boredom – I was resolved that from the very first day we would be busy and industrious.

Meanwhile we went back to London and waited. We got on

better, but the truth was, being alone with Casper had one major disadvantage and that was the complete cessation of my sex life. I hate to refer to love-making in that cold way, but on the other hand it was sex, the lack of, and not love that concerned me. It was weeks since Edward had made love to me and since then – since the deaths of Gerald and Antonia – there had been no one. Normally, there would have been. I am not in the least promiscuous but I have several male friends whom I find attractive and with whom I had long been in the habit of going to bed. There is no need for me to tell you anything about them – they are not relevant to this story. They were all men I had known and liked and had fun with for a very long time. Two were married, three were not. I belonged to that part of their lives they reserved for affairs and I was happy that it should be so. Unlike Edward, I had not run from our love to another love – I had simply run from consuming love of any kind. I seemed to have a built-in detector of men friends who, at no price, wished to have their existing lives interfered with. You might suspect from what I have said that these sexual couplings were therefore sordid and disgusting in their lack of romantic love but it was not at all so. My lovers were friends. I went to the theatre with them, I ate with them, and most of all I talked and argued with them and going to bed was an extension of all these other pleasant activities. We did not always go to bed either – quite often we simply enjoyed each other's companionship and the flirtation was no more than verbal. Sometimes, a new man would come into my life and then I admit I was more wary, less sure of what I was doing, less confident than I was with my tried and trusty escorts. There was danger in that sudden strong physical attraction. The passion which it gave rise to was not easily controlled, and indulging in it invariably brought a feeling of sadness at the memory of that great passion that had been mine and Edward's. But I survived these brief storms, though often at some cost. If these liaisons did not quickly settle down into enjoyable affairs I gave them up – brutally, with no explanation. Edward told me once, in a moment of great distress, that he was always searching for another me. He said there had been two women with whom he thought he had found the same rapture we had shared but that eventually, he had realised his mistake. I, on the other hand, neither looked for nor found another Edward.

But since I had become Casper's guardian there had been no lovers and I felt the lack of them. I write that with some measure of distaste for the vulgarity of the sentiment but it is none the less true. Women *do* feel desire in a limbo. Some evenings in particular I would be overcome by a sensual sleepiness in which my limbs felt pliant and soft and yearned to be stroked and fondled. I would be lying on the sofa in front of the small fire which was my great luxury – a really small, two-tiny-wooden-logs-at-a-time fire in a miniscule grate left over from the year in which the house was built – feeling the extra pleasant heat and watching the flames flicker in the half light, and the book I was reading would drop out of my hand and I would be suddenly in great need of some man's arms round me and his body on mine. The telephone was at hand. I had only to pick it up and ring one of my friends and I had little doubt that within half an hour he would come. If that sounds very much like a bitch on heat then I cannot help it – it was true. But I did not call a lover. I did nothing, and the reason I did nothing was Casper. I could not bring men into that small flat with a thirteen-year-old boy watching every move I made. I could not consider lying to him – he would know this man was my lover – and yet I did not have the courage to expose myself so completely before him. I thought it might frighten him. He had known only Gerald and Antonia, locked in conjugal bliss, and to show him the reverse side of that coin – sex without marriage, passion without love – was too risky. I knew nothing of Casper's moral outlook – do thirteen-year-olds have moral outlooks? – but it was bound to be utterly conventional. Without being able to analyse the reasons for it, I felt obscurely ashamed before him of my desire. I wanted to be virtuous for Casper's sake. If I had brought him up from birth he could gradually have absorbed my own sexual philosophy but at thirteen, a stranger, at a delicate stage in his own development, he could not.

Nevertheless, this attitude was robbing me of one of the pleasures of my life and the deprivation disturbed me. Casper had been used to going to his grandmother's every third weekend, a tradition I had continued, but in October, just as I was plotting a pleasant weekend with a lover after so great a length of time, Mrs Matlock fell and broke her leg and was admitted to the Royal Free Hospital. It was obvious she would have to convalesce afterwards and that it would be a long job and that that convenient refuge for Casper was closed for some months. There was no one else I could ask to take him – no other relative, no friend. As I have told you, he had no close friends, nobody he went anywhere with, nobody he mentioned regularly. He was a loner, not exactly cut off from the society of his contemporaries but choosing to ignore it. Perhaps that was not as significant as I thought it was – I have since learned that it is quite normal for thirteen-year-old boys not to have particular friends, where it is unusual for a girl – but it made the outlook for me rather bleak. I supposed it would get even bleaker in Cumbria. The thought, gloomy enough in origin, soon made me smile. The choice of prospective lovers was ludicrous. Mr Crosthwaite? Mr Rigg? Geoff? Such a selection! And should I find some young blood in that remote place, how very unlikely it was that we could have a successful affair. I knew the country – the scandal would be spread everywhere and make things difficult. I might as well be sending myself to a nunnery. The thought of Miss Cowdie stuck uncomfortably at the back of my mind at the idea. How long had she lived there, waiting for her bridegroom to come, her femininity withering away among the damp and gloomy fells? But of course that could not happen to me and I threw off the notion impatiently. There was no need to give myself nightmares, or to scare myself with the image of a foolish, half-crazed woman.

I overcame these physical longings in the weeks that followed by sheer hard work. Once we had received the long awaited news that, against all the odds, the essential alterations had been completed in record time – "warm as a Turkish bath," Mr Rigg boasted and only laughed when I said I hoped not as wet – we fixed a date for our departure. It was Sunday, October 28th, a most stupid time to go. I would have preferred to wait until after Christmas when, the shortest day past, the promise of lighter nights within weeks would shorten the winter, but Casper argued so persuasively that I gave in, and was glad to do so – it was cheering to find he could produce a strength of mind before which I found myself yielding. He could not have done it three months before and I took some credit for nursing a deeply buried sense of rebellion in him. Gerald and Antonia, I felt, would not have known him – slowly but surely my personality was affecting him and the result was gratifying. But I was not blind to the other reasons why he wished to hasten our departure. To start with, school would be cut short. It was unlikely he would be able to start at a new school before January and like all boys he thought he would relish an extended holiday. Then there was the question of Christmas. Casper and his parents had always spent Christmas with Mrs Matlock and I had promised that if we were still in London he would do so again. The prospect depressed him, and though he did not enlarge on his dislike of this plan it did not take much imagination to see the horrors it held. Mrs Matlock was a ritualist. She would go through the motions of a traditional family Christmas even when there was only poor Casper there and the result would be pathetic. He went so far as to ask me if I would be there too and when I said no, his grandmother would not wish me to be, that my presence would interfere with her memories, he was visibly upset. So he wanted us out of London, away from all possible chance of a reunion with his grandmother, who would be newly home after her convalescence and looking to him for warmth and cheer.

I will not bore you with a recital of all the tasks it is necessary to accomplish before one can move anywhere, but I assure you it is a procedure fraught with problems. I was leaving the Art College in the lurch – they were very good allowing me to go so abruptly when technically I should have given a term's notice, so I worked till the last minute. I went to bed each evening much too exhausted with packing up, on top of a hard day's work, to want any lover. My body ached with dragging furniture about and manhandling things into packing cases and the sole thrill I wanted was a hot bath. Casper, on the other hand, grew daily more lively. He was immensely helpful. That same methodical nature I had noted in him when we were camping came into its own. I was efficient in a hurried, slap-dash sort of way but Casper was thorough and painstaking. He saw the value of labelling every item as it was wrapped, whereas I depended on my memory. I don't think that my memory would have let me down which was why I smiled at

Casper's precious labelling, but there was no denying that theoretically his system was preferable. He took such care wrapping things that I could not watch – sheets and sheets of newspaper for something that was hardly likely to smash anyway and even if it had it wouldn't have mattered.

We did not have a furniture van – I was not taking any furniture. Nothing I had was in the least suitable for a fellside cottage. My treasured chaise-longue, covered in pale green silk, would have looked quite ludicrous in the tiny living-room and was not the sort of thing upon which to flop in muddy jeans and Wellingtons. Mrs Matlock kindly let me put it into an upstairs room in her house, together with several other items with which I did not wish to part and yet would have no use for. I thought about taking the beds but they hardly seemed worth their transport. I was sure I could pick beds up cheaply enough at a sale. I intended to pick everything up at a sale. As the day for our departure approached, I began cutting out notices of furniture auctions in the *Cumberland News* and felt confident that for very little money I could furnish the cottage with second-hand stuff that would be in keeping. A cooker I had already ordered from the local electricity board, and also the cheapest refrigerator – they were the only two articles I wanted new and there when I arrived, except for blankets and sheets. But that still left four large packing cases, which fitted into my new car with difficulty.

Ah, my new car! Tearfully I had parted with my MGB, hating the day it was driven away and with it a glorious decade of my young life. In its place I had bought a brilliant scarlet Range Rover, which Casper thought was superb. I felt grudging towards it, though I had chosen it after great and lengthy deliberation. A large estate car would in many ways have made more sense but the Range Rover had such panache – the estate cars were lacking, all of them, in excitement or glamour. I could in time, I thought, come to love it, and there was no doubt that with its huge strong wheels and a chassis lifted so far off the ground it was eminently suited to negotiating that muddy track to my cottage.

There were no touching farewells to the empty flat. I did not allow them. When Antonia and I had sold the Oxford house we were awash with sentiment – literally sobbing from deserted room to deserted room, hardly able to bear it, sick to the stomach at the finality of it all. But a flat was a flat. It had been a base, a refuge, and that was all. I locked all the doors very briskly and popped the keys across the road to Benham & Reeves and started the car without a backward look. I felt a great surge of energy as we soared up Heath Street and a great eagerness to be gone. The whole of the autumn had been a preparation for this final setting-off into the unknown – unknown in every sense – and I was greedy for the adventure ahead. But then I did not know what sort of adventure it was to turn out to be. "Adventure" meant, to me, excitement, change, variety. I did not realise that excitement could be dangerous, change devastating, the variety only between different kinds of pain. Adventure, in my eyes, had connotations of pleasure and none at all of disaster.

Six

I woke in the early hours of the morning to the sound of torrential rain lashing against the bedroom window – rain driven by a wind so violent that it was as if a steamroller was trying to crush the whole cottage. It swept down from the open fellside with nothing in its way, no trees or hedges, and blasted the defenceless windows. I lay in my sleeping bag in a corner of the room and wondered if the new glass would stand it. "Storm proof," Mr Rigg had said when I queried the cost, "and you'll be glad of it." There were, as yet, no curtains up and though it was still dark there was enough light, as dawn approached, to see the white painted frame of the window and against it the blackness of the rain. I wondered if Casper had woken too – how could he be asleep in this? – but he had chosen the attic as his room and I could hear no movement from it. Like me, he would be cowering in a sleeping bag, eyes flickering round the empty room full of barely formed shadows.

It had rained ever since we arrived, a week ago, on the last good day of the autumn. One brief glimpse of tawny browns and reds and then the colour was extinguished by clouds so thick and darkly grey that nothing below them could have any brightness. With the clouds, most mornings, came a mist, swirling and fine, whirling in continuous motion around our cottage, clearing at midday, only to return with the dark around four in the afternoon. The ground outside was deep in mud, the track that led to the road swimming again, and it was impossible to step outside without immediately sinking into it. We must have a gravel path and a paved area round the cottage or one day we would be swept along in the storm like Noah's ark. Some days there was more than a foot of water all around us, doing untold damage to the foundations, but when I voiced my fears to Mr Rigg he smiled in a patronising way and said the little cot had stood for two hundred years and was likely to survive another good few.

I thought about the people who had lain in this room before me, listening to such rain and wind. A child had been born in the room in which I lay, only five years before – Mrs Crosthwaite had told me. In the middle of just such a storm, a farm worker's wife had given birth to a little girl all on her own, without doctor or midwife or even her husband. He had set off to fetch help and his car had stuck half a mile down the track and he had run all the way to the Crosthwaites' to telephone and by the time he got back the baby was born, dead, strangled by its own cord. I thought of the woman lying where I lay in pain and terror, and of the small, still warm corpse between her bloodied legs. The fells were full of such stories – people in desperate plights, trapped and tricked by the elements in a way impossible for a city dweller to understand. And they accepted their lot or got out.

Except Eileen. She did not accept her lot, nor did she get out. She stayed on her parents' farm, hating the life she led, loathing the day-to-day routine, sunk in gloom and misery at the prospect of nothing else. Each morning she now trudged up the track to my cottage and at the sight of her coming my heart sank. I knew I should never have agreed to her coming – I did not need her – but her mother was so desperately anxious that I should. She walked with her hands thrust into the torn pockets of a dreadful violet and pink tweed coat with a fur collar, which reached barely to the knees, and her whole thin body was hunched with the effort of putting one foot in front of another. Slowly, slowly, she came, a string bag suspended from her wrist. In it she carried an apron – a pinny, as she called it – and a pair of sandals which she wore inside, and rubber gloves to protect her hands, of which she was very proud. Her hands were the only thing about her with any pretention to beauty and they were so incongruous at the end of muscular, rather red and hairy arms that they were easily overlooked. She had long nails and perfect half-moon cuticles and delicate fingers with a silver ring on each. She spent a lot of time admiring her hands – splaying them out in front of her and turning them over and over before thrusting them into their plastic coverings. I saw her do it and admired them and she took my admiration as her due, without embarrassment. In a low monotone she regaled me with the history of each tawdry ring – where she had got it, how much it had cost, what it represented. She said she never took them off and had given instructions that she was to be buried in them. I did not laugh – nobody laughed in front of Eileen. Indeed, I felt chilled by her morbid thought and could see her instantly in her coffin with the famous hands clasped on her thin chest and each cheap ring glistening.

Eileen, when she arrived at nine o'clock, would have some tale of woe – some piece of dreadful information about a mishap in the middle of the downpour. Six sheep drowned, a boy killed by a falling tree, a family flooded out by the river bursting its banks. She related all the local disasters without ever betraying the slightest emotion. Sometimes the thinnest of smiles would flicker for a moment across her slit of a mouth as she described a happening particularly distressing, as though the tragedy was worthy of a show of mirth at the ludicrous nature of the universe. "Do you think that funny, Eileen?" I would ask, stung to objection, and she would say, "Oh no, not funny." But the smile had been there.

She found Miss Cowdie endlessly funny, however. All the miserable week she had stood washing dishes at the kitchen window – her first job – and said, "There she goes – nine thirty on the dot." I watched with her. Miss Cowdie passed our cottage, some fifty yards away on the track, walking purposefully, arms swinging and head erect. She even hurried, sometimes stumbling as she broke into a little run for a moment, clutching at her hat in case it fell off. The hat was a straw bonnet, originally cream but faded and dirtied with age, with three pink roses bouncing in a tattered cluster to one side. "She wore that hat to go away in," Eileen informed me, "only she never went," and she laughed. "Wears it every morning to go and wait for him." At midday, when Miss Cowdie passed on her return journey, dragging her feet as she ploughed her way home, Eileen was usually sweeping the floor and had the door open to let out the stour which rose from the paving stones. "No luck today," Eileen would say, and lean on her broom and chuckle in the most unpleasant manner. I stopped her on the third day. "That's enough, Eileen," I said sharply. Eileen was not at all put out. She stopped chuckling and went on sweeping without comment. The daily spectacle of Miss Cowdie going to meet her bridegroom was one of her few treats and there was nothing I could do to spoil her enjoyment.

By the time morning had properly come, the rain had lessened. It was impossible to see out of the window because of it but the wind had died down and it was no longer blown against our walls. Instead, it simply fell steadily, straight down in an unremitting stream. I could hardly force myself up. The central heating had clicked on and the warmth already filled the room but it was little consolation. In the evening, with a great log fire blazing underneath the new copper canopy and two oil lamps burning in each dark corner, the cottage living-room had great charm and Casper and I had slumped there, perfectly content, feeling snug and hidden away and somehow cheerful because of it. But the mornings were terrible. The cottage was incredibly dark when the rain fell outside. It seemed sinister and cold and claustrophobic and we felt oppressed by the gloom. We put on lamps and even re-lit a small fire on the last night's ashes, but it was no use – we still shivered and longed to be out, anywhere, just so long as we could escape. I sighed and got dressed and went mournfully downstairs. It was like descending into a submarine. I put the kettle on and peered out, ashamed that the weather should so affect my mood. I felt utterly dismal and low. Not only had it rained without ceasing but all sorts of small things had gone wrong. The Range Rover, hardly out of the showroom, had developed engine trouble and I discovered straight away the disadvantages of living in such a remote place. The nearest Rover dealer was in Carlisle and so off to Carlisle we had to go, the engine hiccupping in the most alarming way. Naturally, it had to be left there and because we could not therefore get back

I had to hire a car. I hired a mini and hated it. We could hardly struggle up Warnell in third gear and I felt as if I was pedalling it. It was impossible to attempt the waterlogged track in such a car and so we had to leave it on the road and soak ourselves getting to the cottage. Then the kiln I had had built at some expense would not fire. Twice I had gone to the Crosthwaites' and phoned for the specialist firm who had supplied the parts, and twice they failed to turn up. Without a kiln in operation I could hardly begin work and in any case the stuff I had asked to be sent from London – glazes, imported from Germany, and various essential tools – still had not arrived.

Things were against us – all small, but profoundly irritating. And I hated being in charge. Casper was very good but he naturally looked to me to solve difficulties and I unfairly resented this. He never actually said, "What shall we do?" but he *looked* it and I snapped at him. We were not playing at living in the country any more – we were there, and having to struggle against the sort of predictable odds I had wilfully chosen to ignore in my calculations of three months ago. Originally we had decided Casper should start school on January 7th, the first day of the new term, but already I had changed my mind. That morning I intended to visit Nelson Thomlinson School in Wigton and ask the headmaster if he could begin on Monday. It would be difficult for Casper but better than hanging about in a rain marooned cottage. My visions of us striding the fells and having picnics on tops of mountains and sailing on lakes as we acclimatised ourselves had not materialised. It was better to admit defeat before the weather. With Casper at school, a routine would be imposed upon our miserable day and we would both benefit from it. And I could not stand being with him all day long.

How *do* people stand being with children all day long? My feelings were no real reflection on poor Casper, who might not yet be the most fascinating of individuals but who had improved beyond all recognition – I am sure that even if I was bequeathed a paragon of a child I should still be mentally exhausted at the end of a day with it. Small children can, I suppose, be put to bed occasionally and the day thereby shortened but teenagers cannot. Their lumpen presence is there all the time and that aimlessness, which is the affliction of the age, distracts anyone near them. Perhaps boarding schools are the answer but then they must simply complicate the problem of communication and if you care about your children at all, and your future with them, boarding schools must represent an act of *hara-kiri* . . .

A knock at the door broke into my inane musings. It was so entirely unexpected that the shock paralysed me for an instant – nobody had knocked at our door since we had arrived. Those few visitors we had had were seen arriving – seen coming up the track from half a mile away, seen walking across the grass from the gate in the dry stone wall some two hundreds yards away – and the door was opened long before they got there. But I had seen no one, though I had stood gazing out on the rain for fully five minutes, waiting for the kettle to boil. Whoever it was could not have come up the track from the road, and whoever it was, calling upon us at seven in the morning in this weather, must be needing us urgently. There flashed into my head the thought of Miss Cowdie – for some reason, now that I knew something of her history, I dreaded an encounter with her. I pulled my dressing-gown more tightly round me – it was a dark red towelling bathrobe, belted in the middle – and went to open the door, wishing that Casper was up and dressed and behind me.

I was so unprepared for the sight of a man that I suppose I looked what I was, startled and even frightened. It showed me how much I had already been affected by my short taste of isolation. Isolation withdraws you so completely from society that all human contact is an effort – you soon learn not to want it, to resent it and treat it when it comes your way with suspicion. It could have been Eileen, opening my door so grudgingly and peering out apprehensively.

"Sorry to disturb you," the man said, and I felt instantly relieved by his voice, which was low and, though regional, not exactly local dialect. "I'm horribly lost and I wondered if you could put me right?" I saw that he had an ordnance survey map in his hand and that he was dressed in hiker's gear – dark blue waterproof trousers and anorak and heavy climbing boots. "I thought I came down from High Pike and ought to be at Nether Row but I can't find the mine or any other landmark."

"You went too far along," I said. "This is Lowther Fell."

"Good God," he muttered. "I can't imagine how I did that – it must have been the mist. So if I follow your track I'll come to the road at Greenhead?"

"That's right."

"Thank you. I'm sorry to have bothered you." He bent down and I saw for the first time that he had a small pack on the ground, with a tent strapped underneath.

"Come in and have a cup of coffee," I suddenly said. "I've just got up and I'm making some."

"No – oh no, thank you," he said, looking absolutely terrified, and immediately rushed off.

I watched him make his way laboriously to the track and begin to plod along it. At least I would have given him something to think about. Doubtless I would figure in his dreams, a hard, designing, predatory female, out of whose clutches he had only just escaped. Pity, really, that he had not knocked on Miss Cowdie's door, further up the fell – I found myself smiling in that nasty way Eileen smiled when I thought of the possible consequences. The bridegroom himself come to claim her, and her without her bonnet on. What a fright he would have got and how I would have liked to see her terrify him. What would she have wanted from him? Sex? It seemed impossible – she was over fifty and surely trapped into virginal ways. Yet her mind had stopped at that abortive wedding and then, surely, she must have entertained thoughts of her wedding night, or was her love chaste? I suppose the love of many women is, though it is less likely today. Perhaps all poor Miss Cowdie had wanted was that elusive title, Mrs something or other, and nothing else.

By the time Eileen arrived I was in an extremely bad temper. Casper had at last got up – children "sleeping in" disgusts me – and was sulking at my abrupt announcement that he was to go to school on Monday. Immediately, with that threatening look I thought he had given up, he had said, "You *said* I could cycle to school – you *said* you would buy me a bike." I hated that. I knew perfectly well what I had promised and did not need reminding. We were going to collect the car that very day and I intended to buy his bicycle then, but the unreasonable way in which he demanded it enraged me. I had an awful urge to say, "For that, you can do without one." I controlled it but did not reassure him – with some malicious pleasure I let him continue to think I had forgotten. I told him to get ready quickly because I wanted to be gone as soon as Eileen arrived.

She was smirking as she took off her wet coat and solemnly fastened her apron. Slyly, she looked sideways at me as I gave her instructions about what I wanted her to do.

"Had a visitor last night?" she said, pulling on her revolting gloves over her beloved hands.

"Certainly not," I said, taken aback. "Whatever are you talking about?"

"A visitor was seen," she said, not at all abashed, "leaving this morning. A man, they say."

"What do you mean, 'they'?" I said scornfully. "You mean *you* saw a man leaving and put two and two together and as usual made five. The man was a lost hiker, that's all."

Eileen was not ashamed but said, unabashed, "You want to watch men like that – we're always getting them – saying they're lost and really they're just seeing if you're on your own, likely. You didn't let him in, did you?"

"Of course I did. I gave him some coffee too and didn't even get raped for my pains."

It was a great mistake to attempt to be satirical with Eileen. She took everything I said absolutely at face value. Her narrow little eyes opened wider than they were ever meant to with shock and she literally drew in her breath.

"Oh for *God's* sake, Eileen," I said, "I was joking."

"You didn't let him in, then?"

"No."

Eileen sighed. "Never let men in in these parts – you don't know who strangers might be. Miss Cowdie let one in once and got her clock stole and her silver wedding spoons and he hit her. You want to be careful."

"Her wedding spoons?" I said, stupidly.

"What someone give her for her wedding present. This fellow – *he* said he was a lost hiker too – he took them. The police never caught him but they found the spoons in the beck, all tarnished – not even real silver, just tin, and there she was screaming the place down something chronic about her valuables. Mind you, she can look after herself. Has a shotgun, like our Geoff's. Knows how to shoot a rabbit an' all."

The same loathsome smirk. "Eileen," I said, "I hate the way you tell those stories." Shakily, I picked up the car keys and told Casper to come. We walked down the track to the road, where the car was pulled into a clearing beside the Crosthwaites' gate. By the time we got there, our coats were soaked through with rain. Thankfully, we got into the horrid little mini but the wretched thing would not start – I supposed the leads were waterlogged. Cursing fluently, I got out again, not bothering to don my waterproof armour, and lifted the bonnet and fiddled about trying to dry the leads, which was pretty hopeless, considering more rain poured in than I could get out. I slammed the bonnet shut and got back into the car and tried again. No luck. "Now what do we do?" I said aloud. "I don't know," Casper said, "it isn't my fault." "Oh you stupid little idiot," I said, "nobody suggested it was."

I sat there, silently raging, staring out at the bloody rain and hating everything. Edward always used to say cars were funny things and their temperament ought to be respected – he said you should always have patience in cases like this and wait and then try again and sometimes, miraculously, that was enough. I used to say that was merely a convenient philosophy he had evolved to hide his lack of mechanical expertise but there I was, sitting in the rain, doing just that. Casper only had to say one more unhelpful thing or move a muscle and I would hit him. And then Miss Cowdie passed us, rushing down the track on to the road, the flowers on her bonnet stuck damply to the side of her head. She had put a scarf over the bonnet in a pathetic attempt to protect it but might as well not have bothered. Under her raincoat the grey-white tulle of her wedding dress hung lank and wet, dripping into her Wellingtons. She did not acknowledge us at all, but rushed past, eyes fixed on the crossroads some half a mile away. I sat and watched her. I saw the clumsy figure recede in the distance until it became indistinct but because I knew it was there I could still trace its progress. I saw it stop at the signpost and stand there, motionless, and I knew she would be putting her hand to her eyes and peering down the road. There were tears in my eyes.

I jumped out again, furious, and wrenched open the bonnet. Out of the boot I took a large umbrella and rigged it up over the open engine and worked away with a dry cloth at everything in sight. "What you want is a polythene bag," a voice said suddenly, and I turned to find Geoff Crosthwaite on a horse behind me. The horse was a great black stallion which he exercised for some local trainer and, mounted on it, the affable Geoff looked altogether less amiable and more forceful.

"Do I?" I said, shortly. "Thanks very much for telling me. I haven't got one."

He dismounted and tethered the horse to the gatepost. He was wearing no sort of coat or anorak, only a thick pullover and a leather jerkin, shining with rain. "Give over," he said, shoving slightly, "let's look."

I stood aside, humbly, and watched him. His fingers were deft and quick. He went from wire to wire, tightening and screwing, and though I wanted to learn what he was doing I was distracted by the arc of his body as it bent over my car. I realised I very much wanted to touch Geoff – he seemed unbearably attractive, so tough and rough and strong. I moved away slightly and stood in the rain, waiting. Finally, he removed the umbrella and closed the bonnet and said, "Give it a go now." I got back in. The engine started at once. Geoff smiled and bent down to speak to me through the window. I saw his eyes flicker over my white shirt, which was stuck, soaking wet, to my breasts and I returned his look steadily.

"Should get you to Carlisle," he said, enunciating the words with difficulty, "with care."

"Thank you," I said and then added boldly, "Thank goodness you came along – I needed someone like you."

"Any time," he said and I was glad to see his open friendly face was quite expressionless. Just as I was about to start the car moving, he said quickly, "I hear you had a visitor last night, eh?"

"No," I said, "no such luck. I had a lost hiker, who enquired his way at seven o'clock this morning."

"You want to be careful."

"Eileen's already lectured me on that. I gather she never lets anyone in."

He laughed. "Our Eileen's got nothing to worry about," he

said, "she'd frighten anyone away. But you," – and again he ran his eyes over me – "you want to watch out."

"I will," I said. "I'll only let in friends."

Then I revved up and shot off, leaving Geoff staring after me. Casper, ignored all this time, was hunched and tense beside me.

"Well, that was fortunate," I said loudly. He did not reply. "What's wrong?" I challenged him. "You look as miserable as if we were still sitting in the rain." He still made no comment. "Oh, for heaven's sake, Casper," I said, "I know perfectly well why you're not speaking to me. You thought I flirted with Geoff Crosthwaite, didn't you? Why don't you say so, instead of bottling everything up inside you? We can't go on forever with you expecting me to behave like some screwed up old maiden aunt. There's nothing wrong with that sort of teasing chat I had with Geoff."

Still I could not goad him into speaking. His resentment stayed inside, burning away in his silly head, and I thought how very tiresome prudish adolescents were. I knew if I went on pressing him to blurt out his disgust of me we would end up worse off than when we had started off, back in September, and so I pressed my lips firmly together and, with a great effort, kept quiet.

We passed Miss Cowdie almost at once, standing under the signpost, beaming foolishly up the road that led to Uldale. Unless one knew why she stood there, there was nothing intrinsically pathetic in her stance. Agreed, nobody stands in the middle of a lonely country road in pouring rain like that unless there is something wrong with them, but nobody passing, as I went by in my mini, would have thought anything of it. She looked so cheerful and expectant and quite confident. Any motorist could have been forgiven for imagining that she was about to be picked up any second and that the waiting was pre-arranged. She stood slightly on tip-toe, one hand at the collar of her coat and the other half raised as if in greeting – it was quite feasible that she could already see who was coming and was about to wave. I slowed down slightly, not wanting to spray her with rain from the large puddle I was about to go through in order to turn the corner to Caldbeck, and as I did so she stopped staring up the road for a minute and the smile left her face. She bent down, her face contorted, and shook her fist at me and I found myself so alarmed and frightened that I almost stalled the car. Gathering speed, I did not look back.

"What was that for?" Casper said, shocked out of his sulking.

"I don't know," I said.

But as we drove on through Caldbeck and down from the fells towards Carlisle, I thought I did. Miss Cowdie was coming to see me as a rival, someone who would take her bridegroom away – someone who had perhaps already, in her feverish imagination, done so. It was not too far-fetched. The more I thought of it, the more likely it seemed, and I knew I could not afford to ignore my presentiment. If I did, Miss Cowdie would become convinced that I was a threat to her – I must act at once to stop such an absurd situation developing. No matter how distasteful I found the suggestion, I must make friends with my solitary neighbour – I must not accept the judgement of the locals that she was half mad and best left alone. Firmly, I must approach her and, little by little, convince her that she need fear nothing from me. I must show her that I did not ridicule her as others did, that I understood her state of permanent distress and wished to help. It was simply ridiculous of me to be already half terrified of a harmless woman, going along with unsubstantiated tales about her, accepting as gospel truth all the rumours I had been fed. I would not fall into that trap. As soon as we returned to the cottage I would begin my campaign.

But in fact I did not. We got back from Carlisle late, after an exhausting day. The Range Rover was ready, mercifully, but I had scores of jobs to do in the town, as well as letting Casper buy his bicycle. We bought it at T.P. Bell's in Castle Street – a proper bicycle shop, with the authentic smells of tyres and puncture repairing glue, and an assistant in an old fashioned brown overall, who knew everything there was to know about his trade. The bicycle Casper chose was a Raleigh Sports with eight gears, bright red in colour. I was amazed he chose anything so flash, and glad of it – perhaps it revealed a more frivolous side to his nature, that eventually I would uncover. The bicycle safely in the Range Rover, we then shopped in the market, where I was surprised to find both a cheese and a coffee stall among all the cabbages and potatoes, and afterwards we went from shop to shop, stocking up on the hundred and one items I had discovered I needed, from buckets to rope, and step-ladders to hosepipes. I checked at the post office in Warwick Road for mail – I had a Poste Restante arrangement there, not wanting to give a forwarding address in London because of Edward – and at the railway station for the arrival of my lost equipment (it had not yet arrived but they promised to send it in a van as soon as it did.)

So it was late when we returned and we were both tired and hungry. The rain still poured down and carrying all the stuff inside we quickly got soaked again. Nor was the cottage inviting to return to – the first furniture auction in Wigton since we had arrived was not until the next day and the rooms were still empty. It was Casper who saw the rabbit first, lying at the bottom of the stone stairs. It was dead. Its throat had been cut and the severed head placed neatly between its paws, resting on its genitals.

Seven

We spent rather too long staring at that pathetic bloody bundle of fur. We stood, both of us, looking down at it without saying a word. With anyone else I am sure I would have instinctively launched into a string of platitudes – "How did that get there?" and that sort of thing – but because I was with Casper I said nothing. He had a habit of making me measure my words. But the result of not getting rid of such pointless yet natural questions in a quick burst of talk was that I thought all the harder about them. Rabbits do not get into locked cottages and decapitate themselves. They do not pick up their own heads and arrange them neatly between their paws.

"I suppose we'd better clear it up," I said eventually. "No good gawping at it. Will you do it or shall I?"

"Where will we put it?" Casper said, frowning.

"Out on the fell. There must be hundreds of dead rabbits out there. A fox will eat it."

"You don't think we should bury it?" he asked. I thought for a moment that he was imagining a little funeral ceremony, as a younger child might, and I was startled at this sudden show of sentimentality, but then he added, "I mean, a dog might – you know – be attracted to it – pull it apart – it might be horrible."

"Well then, bury it," I said.

The burial fully occupied Casper for the next hour. He fiddled about cutting a piece of cardboard from a box and sliding it under the mess, and then he ceremoniously carried it outside, out of the door and up behind the cottage onto the fell. He had already taken out a spade and trowel, rusty with disuse, left behind by the previous owners in the shed, and I could see him from the window, struggling to make an impression on the tough grass. Meanwhile, I attacked the bloodstained paving stone with a scrubbing brush and hot water laced with strong disinfectant. Blood on stone is stubborn. Though I scrubbed vigorously and applied copious amounts of Vim, the sticky blood seemed to have seeped indelibly into the stone. When it dried out, much later, there was still visible to the discerning, knowing eye a faint dark stain – a shadow on the stone which I noticed every time I set foot upon it.

There were windows open upstairs, of course. I had locked the door through force of London habit, rather than because I thought it necessary, but I had never considered closing any of the upstairs windows. The landing window at the top of the short staircase was wide open, for example, and since it was the sort of window which opens on a latch it was extremely easy to climb through. Nor was the distance from the ground very great – no more than ten feet at the most. A drainpipe conveniently ran up the wall past it and moreover the stones of the wall itself, on this non-rendered side, were not exactly even – some jutted out a fraction of an inch, making a perfect niche for a toe-hold. I looked for footmarks but could see none. It proved nothing. The stairs were stone, the small amount of wall beneath the window was stone – there was no surface which would readily have shown prints of any kind.

Casper had achieved his objective. I saw him leaning on his spade and looking down at his work. Any other child would have besieged me with questions, if not at first then certainly later, when we had eaten and were sitting in front of the fire, but Casper as usual unnerved me by his silence. We did not discuss the rabbit, neither its manner of dying nor how it had got there. Since neither of us could possibly know the answer to either conundrum, there may be grounds for thinking this showed a certain maturity on Casper's part – he simply saw no point in idle chatter. But I am afraid I did not interpret his reticence so flatteringly. It seemed to me hostile – it was Casper deliberately disassociating himself from all human fellowship and I resented it. He spent the evening reading leaflets and booklets about his new bicycle and did not address a single word to me.

I found myself unable to sleep. I sat up a long time staring into the fire – which still smoked, in spite of Mr Rigg's new canopy – full of gloomy thoughts about what that miserable rabbit represented. It was exactly the sort of incident Eileen loved – exactly the sort of small melodramatic happening she loved to relate. She would see in it a sinister omen. I resolved not to tell her, unable to bear her delighted reaction. It seemed to me in any case that only one person had given any sign of enmity and that was Miss Cowdie. For an elderly woman to kill a rabbit, sever its head, and climb up a drainpipe with the carcase in order to deposit it at the foot of someone's staircase was absurd, but then Miss Cowdie *was* absurd. There was no one else who might consider such an absurdity. My depression increased the more I pondered the problem. Should Miss Cowdie continue in her ridiculous attitude, life would be intolerable. Eileen, I knew, would counsel me to "leave well alone". She would give this piece of advice with all the force of her local experience – psychologically and temperamentally, Eileen believed in being negative. She endured. However discontented, I knew already that she never, ever, did anything about the source of her discontent. She just resigned herself to her fate and I believed I saw in her the archetypal country girl – despairing of change, acknowledging no options, grimly determined to put up with the rotten deal life had dealt her. But I was no Eileen. I refused to contemplate putting up with such a ludicrous situation. There was no doubt whatsoever in my mind that I would confront Miss Cowdie the next day, my only regret that I had not been able to do so sooner, before the rabbit scare.

In the event, I delayed even longer. Though I was impatient to march along to Miss Cowdie and insist she spoke to me properly, the next day was the sale of furniture at Hope's in Wigton and I could not afford to miss it since I intended to furnish the cottage from it. Casper and I were there half an hour before the auction began but already the hall was packed. I confess I was slightly appalled by the rubbish there seemed to be for sale – visions of wonderful antiques, to be bought for a song, vanished at once. The entire hall was packed round the sides with all manner of horrible utility furniture – frightful sideboards and easy chairs covered in moquette and awful dressing tables with blurred triple mirrors. The trestle tables at the front were piled high with ugly clocks and hideous ornaments and garish gilt framed pictures. I almost left at once, but having made the effort I thought we should stay and of course I was glad within a very short time that I had. My disdain had only revealed my inexperience, for underneath all the debris were the very things I was looking for – all it needed, as any country sale expert will tell you, was patience. I sat with all the old women – flasks at the ready, and a keen eye out for anything plastic and unbroken – and gradually I relaxed and became, like them, almost cow-like in my acceptance of the slowness of the transactions. Soon I was in a trance, breathless to see who wanted a broken carpet sweeper at forty pence, or a battered dustbin for twenty. There was maniac bidding for what looked like heaps of rags and shoddy bedding, mostly pink. Mops, bedraggled beyond belief, went for amazing sums and calor gas heaters in any condition were a prize. But I bought a twenty-two piece dinner service for five pounds – I could hardly credit it. The tureens I would leave behind, but there were seventeen plates in a lovely cream colour with a delicate green patterned border that would be perfect. Even a plastic plate at Woolworth's would have cost more than the amount I had paid. I bought, with equal excitement, two wrought iron bedsteads and a magnificent blanket box and a heavy mahogany chest of drawers and an oval mirror on a stand. A small sofa with a dirty cretonne cover cost a mere four pounds, a large deal table with a drawer ten pounds. The only time my enthusiasm was checked was over a wooden Windsor chair. It went for thirty-five pounds and was hotly contested. "Dealers," the woman next to me murmured, and I craned to see who it was and saw she was right. There were, in the hall, a sprinkling of professional buyers among all the amateurs. One in particular began to catch my attention, and I his.

He was young, not more than thirty I thought, with a foreign look about him – perhaps half Spanish or Italian. Dark complexioned rather than swarthy, by which I mean his colouring was olive rather than deep brown, he had tightly curled black hair which he wore quite long with thick sideboards. Lean, tall and long legged, he sat with his elbows on his knees, chin cupped in hands covered with rings, an expression of acute boredom on his gypsy features. There was nothing gypsy-ish about his clothes except the colours. His boots were the sort that you can tell at a glance are made of the most expensive, soft, supple leather and his trousers were narrow and well cut and an unusual shade of maroon such as Wigton must never have seen in its life before. There was a silk scarf knotted round his neck – not a cravat, just a length of brilliant purple silk – and he had his white canvas jacket slung over his shoulder on top of a vivid pink satin shirt. He looked a little ridiculous in that setting – like a peacock caught among crows – and yet one would not apply the word effeminate to him. In spite of all the showy clothes and the rings, he had an air of strength – even cruelty – that made one hesitate to criticise him. Not, of course, that anyone was likely to do so. Those around him stared at him in that frank, open, Cumbrian way, half amused and half fascinated, but not in the least hostile. He ignored them, spoke to no one, returned no looks. He seemed sunk in gloom, raising his hand wearily whenever he made a bid and showing no animation if it was successful.

The auctioneer knew him by name. "Chair to Mr Garibaldi for thirty-five pounds," he said. I laughed out loud – Garibaldi indeed. The idea of my dandified opponent being called Garibaldi amused me no end. How, I wondered, could a man with a name like that, with a style of dress like that, function in a place like Wigton? He bought several more chairs, most of which I would have liked but for which I was not prepared to pay so much just to grace a fellside cottage, and then he bid for a hanging corner cupboard which I had decided on sight I really did both need and want. There was very little room in our cottage. Once the sofa was along one wall, and the table under the window along the other, there was really no sizeable floor space left. The fireplace took up virtually all the third wall and since the door opened straight into the living room the fourth wall could not be blocked. A corner cupboard was just the thing. We could put glasses and bottles in it – I wanted it. Bidding began at twenty pounds "for this very nice oak corner cupboard". I put my hand up straight away, I suppose stupidly. Mr Garibaldi bid twenty-five, I bid thirty, and before I knew what was happening we were somehow up to £100. The incessant noise in the hall – endless comings and goings – suddenly stopped as everyone realised there was a battle in progress. The fact that it was between two outlandish protagonists lent it extra glamour. I felt the lady next to me stiffen with excitement – she even murmured, "You carry on, pet," when I showed signs of faltering – and it was as though a spotlight had been trained on me, so exposed did I feel. I was absolutely determined to get that cupboard. I fixed no ceiling in my head – I would simply carry on until Mr Garibaldi's business sense told him to stop, as it was bound to do once we reached whatever the market price was. I paid £150 for it but felt flushed with triumph at my success. "Well done," my neighbour said, with not a hint of horror at the price. I got up at once and went to look at the cupboard, which had been immediately shunted to the side of the hall, away from the auctioneer's desk. I got out my cheque book and paid one of the girls for everything I had bought. She sat at a table with a cashbox in front of her and a wooden box affair with different compartments in it, into which she popped tickets of sale. She seemed permanently flustered but had time to smile and say, "London address?" For some reason it gave me great pleasure to reply, "No, local."

"Setting up in business?" a voice said behind me. It was Mr Garibaldi. I smiled, hoping he did not sense I was laughing at him in his absurd gear. He returned my smile quite pleasantly but with no warmth whatsoever.

"No," I said, at my most haughty all of a sudden, "I'll leave that to you."

"Did I hear you say local address?"

"I think you must have done."

"Perhaps you've just moved up here?"

"Yes, as a matter of fact I have."

"Then you must be furnishing a house?"

"You're awfully bright," I murmured sarcastically.

"I thought you might like to come and look round my place, see if there is anything you want."

His voice was rather deep and resonant but the vowels were nearer Geoff's than my own – flat 'a's and long 'o's showing he had been bred in Cumbria. He handed me a card, which said, "David Garibaldi, Antique Dealer", followed by the address.

"What a pity," I said, "about the David. Seems a waste, doesn't it?"

"Yes," he said, very sharp, "but then Giuseppe is a little unmanageable for a Carlisle-born Italian, don't you think?"

I blushed slightly and put the card in my pocket, though I had meant to hand it back. I can never resist that sort of showing off – that testing of somebody's knowledge. I had thought him a hick, incapable even of knowing Garibaldi's Christian name, and I had hoped he would be mystified by my bogus regret over the David. Now he knew what a loathsome little pedant I set myself up to be. I owed him an apology but was certainly not going to give him one. I only said, "Yes, I suppose so," as offhandedly as possible, as though I had intended no slight. But he tried to get his own back. "You know about corner cupboards, do you?" he asked. I was not to be caught. "No," I said, "I know nothing at all. I simply liked it and needed it."

"A determined lady."

"Absolutely."

"How lucky it was worth what you paid."

"Was it? I couldn't really care less – I'm not really interested in what it is worth. It's pretty, that's all I care about, and useful."

"It's a George III oak cupboard, as a matter of fact. Any time you want rid of it, I'll buy it from you for ten pounds more than you paid."

"If it's worth ten pounds more, why didn't you pay it?"

"I spotted a determined lady when I saw one. I just thought I'd give you a run for your money, as you gave me for mine. You made me rather cross, making me pay thirty-five pounds for that Windsor chair."

"Why, wasn't it worth it?"

"Oh yes – it's nineteenth century, high backed, in good

condition – I'll sell it for seventy pounds but the point is I would have got it for a tenner without you."

"I'm sorry."

"So you should be. And as for that yew and elm Georgian effort – I resented paying thirty for that, even though it's worth four times the price."

"How greedy you are."

"Very greedy."

His boldness came as a surprise. We had, during this repartee, moved out of the hall and into the car park at the back. Two decrepit grey overalled men accompanied us, carrying the cupboard, and Casper trailed behind with the plates. All the time we were scoring points I was busy – unlocking the car, directing the men where to put the cupboard – and that helped. I did not want this rather crude but after all not ignorant young man to see how much I was enjoying the verbal fencing. He might think, and think rightly, that I was attracted to him, and I could not allow that. It was purely physical attraction – not that I admired either his looks or his style but there was a magnetism about him that I could not help but respond to. I suppose men always know this. No matter how disdainful one looks, how abstracted, they can after all sense the pull and that is what makes them persistent in the face of apparent discouragement. I detest the disgusting word "sexy" but nevertheless it is sometimes apt. Mr Garibaldi was sexy, and if there was one thing I wished to make clear to him it was that I was not a cheap lay.

"Get in, Casper," I said briskly when everything we could manage to take had been packed into the car, "we're off." Mr Garibaldi was sharp as the proverbial needle. "You bought two iron bedsteads, I believe," he said. "I'll follow behind you and drop them off, if you like."

"Good gracious, no," I said – schoolma'amish, impatient with his chivalry, "that's far too kind and completely unnecessary."

"I have a van – it's no problem," he persisted. "What I've bought today won't nearly fill it. Charlie!" he shouted after one of the disappearing grey coated men. "I'll take the lady's bedsteads. I might just as well go to Carlisle by Caldbeck," he said, turning back to me.

I admire cheek. I hate to see a man servile and hesitant. But the ridiculous Mr Garibaldi's cheek went beyond being acceptable – his cockiness was an affront. I climbed into my car without saying another word and then, as insolently as possible, leant out of the window and said, "If you are determined to bring those bedsteads then I can't stop you, but I've already paid to have them delivered and there is absolutely no need. Anyway, I can't wait so you can't follow me. The address is Lowther Fell Cottage, near Caldbeck. See if you can find it and if you can't you'll just have to keep the stuff."

It was very rude of me, and also a little silly when in fact I needed the bedsteads, but Mr Garibaldi could not be allowed to steam-roller over me. I could be as dictatorial as he could and twice as arrogant. Off I drove, unable to see out of the back because we were so loaded down with furniture, and we were out of Wigton in two minutes, before Mr Garibaldi had even a chance to fill his own van, wherever it was. I smiled to myself, imagining how he would curse me. He might not turn up for hours, by which time Casper and I would have gone again, leaving an insulting note on the door.

"Wasn't he extraordinary?" I said to Casper, sitting beside me clutching the plates. He did not reply. "He had such a high opinion of himself," I said, "and he looked so stupid in those clothes. I wonder what people think of him. I wonder how he came to be born in Carlisle. I bet his family sell ice-cream or something." Still Casper said nothing. "Have you no thoughts at all on Mr Garibaldi, Casper?" I asked, an edge to my voice.

"No," Casper said, quite violently.

"You looked at him and heard him and absolutely nothing went through your head?"

"Nothing."

"What a very empty little head you must have."

But I could not sting him into a reply. He sat tense and disapproving, furious with me again for engaging in human discourse. How had Antonia stood it? Antonia, who could talk for hours with me about people, who loved to analyse and dissect our entire acquaintanceship. What a bore Casper was – the glimmer of light I had seen had not been light after all, merely a mirage. He remained dull. Two weeks of his company, marooned in our cottage, had brought me near to hating him, which is a most wicked thing to admit. I longed for him to be at school, to relieve me of his presence, and any sympathy I had felt for him vanished in a wave of pity for myself.

We went back through the village to pick up some milk, which I had forgotten to get in Wigton, but that only added five minutes to our journey. As I turned off the Greenhead track I laughed to think of Mr Garibaldi's fury at being unable to find us – he would have to get out of his car several times and knock on cottage doors and ask the way and all his lovely clothes would get very wet indeed in the heavy rain. Probably his van would get stuck in the mud and he would have to suffer the indignity of being pulled out by Geoff Crosthwaite's tractor – if he could persuade Geoff.

It was a shock to find the man I was deriding and pitying already there. I admit to a total loss of composure. Dumbfounded, I stared at the white van parked outside my cottage – a large, battered dirty white van with no lettering on it. I stalled the Range Rover and had trouble starting it again to cover the last fifty yards. As I crawled up to the gate, Mr Garibaldi got out. He was wearing a black raincoat – one of those PVC ones – which covered him completely. He came up to my car before I could get out and I braced myself for the obvious crack – "What kept you?" or suchlike – but all he said was, "You aren't a very trusting lady, locking doors. Give me the key and I'll carry the stuff in. You don't need to bother. Make some coffee and your son and I will do it."

There was no possibility of not obeying – I was utterly beholden to Mr Garibaldi. He and Casper trudged backwards and forwards in torrential rain, making at least half a dozen trips, until they had manhandled all the furniture into the cottage. When they had done, Mr Garibaldi took off his raincoat and hung it on a nail and sat himself down very firmly on one of the new chairs. He folded his arms and looked about him with unabashed interest. "Well well well," he said, as I handed him coffee, "not at all what I expected – not at all."

"You shouldn't judge by appearances," I said.

"Unlike you?" he said swiftly. "No, indeed one should not." He sipped the coffee. "So, what brings a lady like you to a place like this? Unhappy love affair? Divorce? Wanted to get away from it all?"

"Only three alternatives?" I said.

Casper went out as we spoke, banging the door hard so that it rattled on its latch. I took a quick look out of the window. He had gone off down the track, Rufus at his heels. I hoped he had gone to the Crosthwaites' to take up an offer Geoff had made to let him help with his car, but I doubted it.

"Not a happy looking youth," Mr Garibaldi said.

"No. His parents were killed recently – in a plane crash."

"Ah, it begins to fit. You're the aunt – guardian – and you thought you'd make a completely new home – new environment, everything – for him. But why here? So very out of the way?"

"Why not?"

"Several reasons. It's dull, unbelievably dull. It's inconvenient. It has very little to offer a beautiful young lady on her own. Unless she's hiding."

"I'm hiding then."

"Who from?"

"A big bad wolf."

"Then I wouldn't stay here or he'll flush you out – you're far too obvious – and he'll come and huff and puff and blow your house down. I shall have to stay here and protect you, no doubt about it."

"I can protect myself, thank you."

"Not in these parts you can't. You need somebody who knows their way around, like me. I know all the most secret hiding places – man and boy I've walked these fells, know them like the back of my hand."

"I don't believe you. You don't look as if you have ever gone for a walk in your life."

"Appearances again?"

"More coffee?"

I had started all this and now I did not like where it was leading, which was undoubtedly to bed. I felt extremely nervous as I chatted to my visitor, telling him about my intended pottery, unable to relax or be casual. Nor could I keep up my contemptuous attitude towards Mr Garibaldi – he was far too interesting after all. And yet my dignity was at stake, if not my self-respect – I could not simply go to bed with him. Why not? As ever, that nasty little question popped up at the back of my mind – why, *why* not? What was wrong with it? My body was not a holy vessel which it was my duty to protect. Mr Garibaldi was the first attractive man who had come my way in two months and why should I pass up the chance of a good fuck? For that was precisely what I wanted, without any strings attached. Only yesterday I had sat here, in the same chair, holding the same mug of coffee, despising that spineless lost walker, who had gone off, so terrified of me. Now, I had a cultivated man, who had pursued me with some skill, sitting opposite me, wanting me as much as I wanted him. Casper would be gone at least an hour. There was no reason at all why I should not indulge myself with the waiting Mr Garibaldi.

Yet I held back, uncharacteristically worrying over the consequences. Should I be as matter-of-fact about sex here as I was in London, I would instantly be misunderstood. Nobody, in London, had ever accused me of being a nymphomaniac but here, where standards were different, I would run that risk. And I did not know anything about Mr Garibaldi – I had never quite gone to bed with such an unknown quantity. I did not like the idea, either, of being so easy for him to locate. He could come to the cottage and I would have no means of escape – I would be trapped, obliged literally to board myself in if I did not want to see him. I was thinking before he had even touched me that he could become a nuisance – flattering myself that once he found he was on to a good thing he would not want to keep away. And then, most of all, there was the wretched Casper, sullen and disapproving if I so much as spoke to any man.

"You're going to get lonely here," Mr Garibaldi was saying. "The winter hasn't started yet. It goes on a long time – dark mornings, long dark evenings."

"I'm never lonely, Mr Garibaldi."

"You've had enough fun with the Garibaldi," he said, tapping his enamel coffee mug with a spoon softly, "good job I'm used to it. David is the name. And you?"

"Alexandra Grove."

"Nice."

I got up, scraping my chair on the stone floor. "Awful to

turn you out when you've done so much for me," I said, sweetly, "but I've got such a lot to do."

"Anything I can help with? I'm very handy."

"No, thank you. It's been a great pleasure meeting you." I held out my hand, dismissively. He took it and slowly, very slowly, shook it. His hand was dry, strong, warm. Mine was cold and limp. I wondered what he would say, envying as ever the male prerogative of taking the initiative. It is a strange fact that though I am utterly liberated I still do not like to take the initiative openly, that I cling in an annoyingly pathetic way to the rituals evolved over the centuries for the pursuit of men by women.

"I'll come again," he said. "We could go for a walk, or even a drive. There aren't a lot of opportunities for meeting in this neck of the woods."

"I may be out."

"I'll take my chance. Good luck with the pots. I might have some contacts you could use when you're ready."

He took a long time buttoning himself into his black oilskin coat – long enough for me to regret that he was going. A long boring afternoon with the miserable Casper stretched ahead and all the things I might find to do did not tempt me. I could polish the furniture I had bought. I could hang up the corner cupboard. I could – would have to – erect the bedsteads and paint them. I could drive to Penrith or Carlisle and choose material to recover the sofa. There were jobs in plenty and none of them tempted as much as the ludicrously named David Garibaldi. It struck me, as I opened the door for him and the rain blew inside in a great gust, that he could not even ring me because I had no telephone. I watched him go out to his van – without, I may say, a backward look – with a dismal sensation of loss. He might not come again and it would serve me right for subscribing to that wretched traditional doctrine which has said since time began that a woman must not throw herself at a man.

Edward was the only man I had thrown myself at, instantly. I stood with my back against the heavy wooden door, the latch digging into me, remembering with pleasure, not shame, how eager I had been. On the very first day we walked together, along the shore of Ullswater on Place Fell, I had stopped at the top of the steepest part of the path and, turning myself towards him, had said, "Kiss me." Five seconds later we were in the undergrowth to the side of the path making love, a case of uncontrollable passion. I never hesitated, though Edward did – "You might become . . ." he began, and I put a hand over his mouth, not wanting the air contaminated by those awful words. Pregnancy was not something I worried about, not because I was so infatuated that I had never considered it, nor because I was on the pill or anything so fortuitous, but because I saw it as quite simple – I would take my chance. I did not want my first lovemaking sullied by precautions – I did not want Edward even to think about it. I took command and never regretted it.

But then, of course, I was sure I was in love. Passion was only part of what I felt for Edward. There was no humiliation possible when I adored everything about him – no calculations of cause and effect to be made. I could be abandoned because I had no doubts and if there is one thing I look back to with pride, it is my ardent fearlessness. Good, I say to myself now, good, good, you had the courage to over-ride convention and take what you wanted with both hands. I discovered that day what being voluptuous meant – not having a perfect body, not being fleshy and soft, but being capable of relishing pleasure endlessly. I was half insane with pleasure – often sobbing and wild with it, every tiny particle of my body and brain suffused with gratified lust. And I thought, at each orgasmic height, that I understood the universe – in brilliant flashes of insight everything seemed possible – and when, afterwards, I lay there peacefully, the glimpses gone, I still retained the memory of those visitations. Nobody can ever take that away from me – though layers and layers of lesser experiences have overlaid that vivid day, it is still there, untarnished, for me to unearth any time I like and take comfort from, as I did that day.

I tried to be brisk. I raced upstairs and began putting up the bedsteads, humming loudly and making as much noise as possible. David Garibaldi was not important – he could not be considered in the same category as Edward, nor even half a dozen others. Now that he had gone, and that dreadfully pressing physical temptation had been removed, I saw how shoddy the whole thing would have been, quite terrible, worse than casting my eye over Geoff Crosthwaite, though God knows poor innocent Geoff had never even offered himself. I was supposed to be breaking with my past and testing myself anew – sordid sexual encounters were no part of my plan. The bedsteads up, I began going over the wrought iron headboards with wire wool, removing the rust and chipped paint. When Casper came back I would hand the beastly task over to him and watch him making an excellent job of it. Meanwhile, I would go to the Crosthwaites' and ring Carlisle station and see if the equipment I expected had yet arrived. Work, real work, was what I needed, and no amount of bustling about doing household jobs would make up for it.

Properly equipped – knee-high, heavy Wellington boots, oilskin with collar turned up, close-fitting thick woollen cap – I set off to the Crosthwaites' farm, not minding the rain so much. Already, though it was early afternoon, there was a darkness about the mist and the sky was black with low, dense cloud. I thought of what David Garibaldi had said about the winter and shuddered. In London, winter was nothing. Every year I was astonished by the number of mild sunny days – only a certain bleakness around the end of January, when already the spring was not far off, was hard to enjoy. But here, under the lee of the mountains, winter meant something altogether different. It would be an endurance test of another sort from the one I had anticipated and as I trudged down the track, every pothole overflowing with water, I was not sure that I could stand it. Head down, hands in pockets – a mistake, for it opened them to the rain – I almost bumped into Miss Cowdie, returning early from her vigil. I saw her feet before I heard any noise – into my lowered range of vision came her cracked old shoes and the stockings full of holes and ladders, and I hardly dared look up but knew that I must. Miss Cowdie must be made to realise that I was not an enemy, that I was not going to treat her as others treated her, that she could trust me. Like her, I was a woman on my own – Casper hardly counted – and like her I resented interference. I stopped, and looked up.

"Hello, Miss Cowdie," I said very clearly, standing smack in front of her, so that I was blocking her way along the only bit of the track not submerged by rain. Her hand flew to her mouth, as ever, and she side-stepped quickly into a puddle, and made to dash off. I put a restraining hand on her arm. "Don't go," I said, "I'd like to talk to you." I was quite unprepared for the fury with which she rounded on me, knocking my hand violently away and sending me flying with an almighty shove in the chest before she ran off, splashing mud and rain all over me, stumbling and staggering in a weaving race to her home.

Eight

Geoff Crosthwaite found me there, floundering in the mud at the side of the track, collapsed in an undignified heap on the sodden grass. "What's up w'you?" he shouted from a hundred yards away as he cantered back from exercising his horse. I shook my head and got up. The fall had made me no wetter than I already was. Geoff, coming from behind the brow of Longlands, must just have missed seeing Miss Cowdie push me aside. "Nothing," I said, "I fell. Have you seen Casper and Rufus?"

"Ay, wet as the devil and a face as black as thunder an' all. What's wrong wi' the lad? He never even looks up or gives me the time of day."

"It's the age," I said. Geoff looked blank. Yet again I was in the position of standing looking up at him, all powerful on his gleaming black steed. I suspected that were I ever to see him on his own two feet, dressed in his Sunday best, I would be appalled by the disappearance of any charisma.

"I don't know about that," he said, "you can speak to folk at any age, should have thought. Hear you were at Wigton this morning – bought a lot of junk, so they say."

"Oh, 'they' do, do they?" I said, smiling.

"Ay, an' you got off wi' that Garibaldi from Carlisle. You want to watch him. He's a bit of a lad."

I could not tell Geoff to stop being so impertinent – he didn't know what the word meant and, should I attempt to teach him, I would offend him to the point of being shunned forever after. There was no chance of drawing myself up to my full height and withering him with a look – on his horse he was much taller than I and twice as impressive. Besides, the brutal honesty of his words should not be run away from. I ought to meet them head on. So I said, as casually as possible, "Thanks for the warning, though I don't think I needed it."

"I don't know about that," Geoff said very seriously, "there's queer folk about these days and everyone for miles around knows you're on your own with just that lad. You want to be careful – anything could happen."

"So Eileen tells me all the time. Where was she today, anyway? She seems to have left early – she didn't do the fire."

"She was took badly."

"Oh. Anything serious?"

"No, shouldn't think so. She'll be back tomorrow, her usual sparkling self," and he burst out laughing. "Where you off to in this, anyway? Hasn't stopped for a week, has it?" and he looked at the sky admiringly.

"I was coming to use your telephone, if you don't mind."

"I don't mind," he said, and suddenly swung down from his horse in one quick leap. I was startled and jumped. "My, you're nervous," he said, grinning, his great wet face peering into mine. I was so irritated I could have slapped it. But we plodded on together towards his farmhouse, the horse snorting and tossing its head at our side. "You go in," he said, "door's open. I'll just rub down this animal. Shan't be two ticks."

I went into the kitchen, removing my boots at the door. There was no one there. I moved about rather nervously, unsure whether I would be invading the Crosthwaites' privacy if I went further into the house in search of the telephone. The kitchen was tidy and clean but as far from the popular image of a farmhouse kitchen as it was possible to get. No quarry tiles or stone flags on the floor – only a highly coloured, cheap, flowered linoleum. No splendid oak dresser running along the stone wall – only a utility cupboard with lace mats on top and china ornaments. No giant pine table – only a yellow topped spindly Formica effort, with a leaf to let out on either side. No Aga – only an electric stove. No rows and rows of preserves –

just bottles of HP Sauce and tomato ketchup along the working surface.

"Haven't you put the kettle on?" Geoff said.

I protested I only wanted to make my phone call and go but he was adamant that I must have a cup of tea because he was having one and wouldn't take no for an answer. "Go on," he urged, "put the kettle on. It's a shame to get Eileen down to do it. Teapot's over there and tea's in the caddy near the stove and milk and sugar is in that cupboard with the cups." He gestured here and there as he instructed me and I realised I was meant to make the tea – his invitation did not extend to actually doing so himself. I obeyed, with reluctance, but said, as I plonked the teapot down in front of him. "Don't you make your own tea?"

"Dear me, no," he said, "that's woman's work in this house," and he laughed again, that great roar which so set my teeth on edge. Geoff was so lacking in any kind of sensitivity – his laugh betrayed the vacant mind of Matthew Arnold's poem.

"Doesn't say much for your women, does it?" I said as lightly as possible.

"They've nowt better to do," Geoff said, slurping away at his heavily sugared tea. "Dad and I keep them wi' our work and they look after the house. Seems fair enough to me."

"Oh, it's fair enough to *you*," I said "but not to Eileen or your mother."

"But what else would they do?"

"That's what isn't," I said, "they have no choice."

"Neither do I. I have to work, don't I? Going out all weathers, rain or snow, freezing cold and wet while they're snug in the kitchen. Isn't fair to me. I haven't any choice that I can see."

"Can't you see the difference?" I said, exasperated, and then as I looked at Geoff's open, bland face I saw that indeed he could not. "Women are just servants to you, aren't they, Geoff?" I said. "Just people to look after you, that's all."

"It isn't my fault," Geoff said, "blame Nature. Nothing to do with me. Women are made that way, aren't they?"

"I'm not."

"You're different," Geoff said, "you're educated an' that.

But even you, when you get married and have babies, you'll fall the same, you'll see."

"I'm not going to get married and have babies."

"Oh, they all say that, but they all do – unless nobody asks them, like our Eileen, or they go crazy, like Miss Cowdie. All women want to get married and have babies and you won't convince me otherwise, any more tea?" I poured it, not even angry. There was no hope of converting Geoff to even the mildest feminism. " 'Course," he said, "that's what's wrong wi' Eileen. She needs a man. First man who took an interest and she'd throw herself at him."

"Poor Eileen."

"Poor man," Geoff said, and roared again. "By God, I'd like to see it."

"Where's the telephone?" I said.

He took me into the hall, where the telephone had an unhappy look among the coats near the door. Clearly, business calls, direct and to the point, were the only ones ever made on this instrument. I rang the railway station while Geoff went politely back into the kitchen. I spoke very loudly so that he would be able to hear every word without straining. There were three crates awaiting me but they could not be delivered until the van next went in my direction, in five days' time. I said I would pick them up myself the next day – five days was too long to wait in my present gloomy, restless mood. I thanked Geoff and made for the door.

"Wait a bit," he said, "I was going to ask you if you'd like a run to Windermere, to test the car out, like, show you what it can do."

"I think I'm too busy at the moment," I said, knowing he had heard about my stuff having arrived. "I'm anxious to get to work as soon as I can. Maybe another time?"

Turning down a man's invitation is never easy – Geoff in particular was dangerous to rebuff, with his exaggerated notions of male supremacy – but I thought I sounded convincing. "Later on, then, when weather's better," he said, quite agreeably, and then, in a sudden burst, "I'm going to the pictures in Carlisle tonight, with Mildred Johnstone. But you don't want to listen to anything anyone tells you about me and Mildred – there's nowt in it."

"Liar," said Eileen, coming in silently behind him and moving in her usual zombie fashion towards the teapot. She shook it, put it down in disgust, went to put the kettle on again and said, in her monotone voice, "He's been chasing Mildred Johnstone ever since he was out of short pants but she won't have him. She just gets him to take her to Carlisle when all her other fellas are busy and then she makes fun of him wi' them something cruel."

"Shut your bloody mouth," Geoff said, flushing deep crimson. "You're just jealous because nobody's ever taken you to the pictures in your life."

"Wouldn't want to go," Eileen said. "You can get better on the tele, without spending all that money. You should stay in and watch it, instead of being made a mug of."

"Are you better, Eileen?" I said, intervening quickly before Geoff's humiliation became too great for him to bear.

"Had a bad back," she said, avoiding my eyes. "I'll be in tomorrow, likely."

"Good. I'm collecting the stuff I need to work tomorrow, so I may have gone – just do the usual."

She nodded and I left, smiling at Geoff, who stayed behind looking furious. Before I had gone ten yards I heard a crash and Eileen's scream. I suppose I had half expected it or else I would have been shocked into stopping. As it was, I hardly slackened my pace, though I felt a little sick in the stomach. I didn't for one minute think Geoff would really hurt Eileen – I was sure a hard slap was all that had happened – but the thought of his mortification was as painful as the thought of Eileen's injury. He had so wanted me to think him a devil of a fellow on his black horse, the sort of man who, with his car and blond good looks, only had to click his fingers and the girls came running. He wanted me to see him as masterful and exciting and though I had not for a second been deceived he would imagine it was Eileen's taunting that had revealed the truth. I thought it highly probable that poor Geoff was a virgin, haunted night and day by sexual fantasies about the divine Mildred. If I was not very careful, I would become another candidate for speculation and what a bore that would be.

No way home could have been less cheering than the one I took along the flooded track. Visibility was down to twenty yards with the combination of heavy rain and black sky. Mostly, I had my head down, focusing on each perilous step I was taking, but occasionally I would look up, in desperation, searching for a break in the dark sky. There was never even a suspicion of such a thing. The fells closed in on me, menacing in the gloom, and I hardly wanted to go further into their threatening folds. My own cottage, when it loomed into view, was almost invisible. I had noticed before how the stone exactly blended into the landscape on a grey day and yet I was astonished all over again at the way so solid an edifice could disappear. My father used to tell me how Wordsworth raged against the whitewashing of Lakeland houses because the glare ruined the harmonious greys and greens and browns of the hills but I longed at that moment for a burst of light – I would have taken Mr Wordsworth by the hand and pleaded my cause, stressing how much more welcoming a white wall is than an indistinguishable murky mass of stone. No smoke came from the chimney – we had not yet cleaned out the fire from the evening before – and there was no friendly lamp burning in any window. Casper must still be out, and at the thought, the brief elation I had felt at the news of my materials having arrived in Carlisle disappeared. It was awful to imagine Casper's mood and the responsibility for at least in part causing it. This was no life for a thirteen-year-old boy. Miserable, unbearably conscious of the mistake I had made, I was in the very lowest state possible to face the sight that greeted me as I opened the door of the cottage.

I had not this time locked it – it had never even occurred to me. I was only going to the Crosthwaites' farm to use the telephone and knew I would not be gone very long. Even though my planned ten minute visit had stretched into an hour I had still not been gone very long, but it was enough time for someone to enter and leave just inside the door – so positioned that I was bound to stumble over it – the decaying head of a sheep. I screamed out loud – it was a most disgusting sight. Half the head, the right-hand side, had decomposed completely into a pulpy mess of gangrenous green and black, but the other half still had flesh upon it, with dirty grey matted wool hanging limply from it. The smell was appalling and even though I had heavy rubber boots on, the feel of the object

– the squelch as the rotten part gave at a touch – revolted me. I gazed down at it in a panic. There was no Casper, before whom it was essential to maintain a dignified calm, and I could not stop myself shivering. But then, the longer I stood there, anger began to replace fear and soon I was running to the shed where I seized a long handled stiff brush and, rushing back to the loathsome object, I began thrusting it outside. Half sobbing with fury now, I pushed and pummelled the oozing head along the ground, where it collected mud and grime until it was a grotesque lump of filth. We reached the beck and with one sweep I brushed the thing into the water – fast flowing and brown with rain – where it sank immediately. The current was so strong that I was sure it would be carried miles downstream and that I need have no nightmares of it sticking on the stones at the bottom, only to emerge to frighten me in the summer, when the bed of the beck was revealed.

There was no doubt in my mind that it must be Miss Cowdie. She had pushed me to the ground and then done this silly, ugly thing in revenge for my imagined crimes. I had no intention of allowing such wilful malice to continue and I straightaway returned to the cottage, washed my hands – though they had not come anywhere near the sheep's carcase – and dashed out again, running clumsily through the rain, which appeared to have redoubled in its prodigious strength yet again, I made for Miss Cowdie's cottage, determined to face her at once, while my rage still gave me courage. Quite what I would say I did not know – until confronted with this woman so longing to be my enemy I could not think of how I would defend myself, but I clearly could not allow such a distressing state of affairs to continue.

There was a light on inside her little house. I was relieved to see it, fearing that she might have stayed outside in order to escape any visit from me. But of course she did not need to do that – she only had to lock the door, and when I had knocked and shouted and there was no reply I tried to open it and discovered that was just what she had done. Defeated, I leaned against it, my head full of rebellious ideas about staying there forever, until my captive was forced to come out. That would not work – even in my excitable state I new Miss Cowdie could easily win at any game of patience. I must employ my brains.

Since hers were addled I ought to have the advantage there. I prowled round the cottage, examining the windows, but though these were old, the frames breaking off in splinters, there were none so weak that they would cave in at my exploratory touch. Next I gazed up at the roof, thinking how easy it would be to scale such a small height and hoping to find a skylight, but I could see none. The drainpipes in any case looked much too frail to bear my weight. So I sat down, in full view of anyone secretly watching me from the house, on a large boulder resting beneath the giant sycamore which dwarfed it. I sat there, horribly wet and cold, with my knees drawn up and my chin resting upon them. And I stared hard at every window, watching for the merest shadow of a movement. Quite apart from my position, I knew that the violent yellow of my oilskin would make me unmistakably prominent and, I hoped, unbearable to Miss Cowdie. She would see me and go on seeing me and I would irritate her into some reaction and once I got that reaction I could work upon it.

I sat huddled on that boulder for a long time and though I hated every minute of my uncomfortable siege I was in the end glad that I had had to endure it. It gave me time to return to my original position on Miss Cowdie. I had come to Lowther Fell distressed that any woman could have so tragic a past and disgusted at the derision this past inspired in the people among whom she lived, but gradually, as I sank more and more into my own gloom, I had fallen victim to their disease. I too had come to regard poor Miss Cowdie with contempt. My previous compassion, my refusal to accept their judgement that she was "mad" and to be despised, had been replaced by an unbalanced anger towards her. I sat there, reminding myself that I had no proof that Miss Cowdie was responsible for either the rabbit or the sheep's head – though there was in fact no doubt that she *was* to blame – and that apart from spitting at my car and pushing me into the mud she had not harmed me. I reminded myself of how my coming must appear to her, and I admitted to myself that I had perhaps set about approaching her in the wrong way. I had exercised neither tact nor caution. All resentment towards Miss Cowdie slowly left me and I began to feel again that strange sympathy which had at first overwhelmed me.

By the time she appeared at the top window, I had reached the stage of being resigned to going away and starting again some other way, some other day. I wished I had not either banged on the door or tried the windows – both actions could only have made her feel more persecuted. I was about to get up and go home and have a hot bath before taking the unfortunate Casper down to Parkend for a sumptuous dinner, which I hoped might in part compensate for the horror of the whole dreary day – and then I saw Miss Cowdie, at the top window, half behind the curtain. I kept quite still, lowering my head further onto my knees. I did not want her to be afraid of me. I hoped that if I looked sufficiently abject and harmless she might come closer, as an animal would. When I looked she had gone but the dirty rag of net curtain still moved. In a few minutes she was at the other window, a little bolder now, peering out without hiding herself. Still I sat there, hunched and miserable. Curiosity began to get the better of her. She stood slap in the middle of the window, looking at me, and I lifted my head and looked back, steadily. The distance was much too far for either of us to see with any degree of certainty into each other's eyes but we both held each other's gaze as though we were no more than a yard apart. Slowly, she opened the window to its full extent. I stood up, making the movement as smooth as I could, taking my time over rising. Then I stayed still again. "Go away," Miss Cowdie shouted. "You out there all this time, bothering me – go away." I didn't reply or go any nearer the cottage. "I can't help you," she called, hand hovering over the latch of the window, ready to slam it shut at the slightest hint of reaction. "I'm getting married in the morning – you'll just have to go away. I don't want you here when the Earl comes – go away – shoo," – and she made flapping gestures with her hands, as though I were a bird she was trying to scare into flying. I took a small step nearer and then stopped. Dare I go nearer? Dare I speak? Miss Cowdie disappeared, leaving the window open, and then I heard the distinct sound of a bolt being drawn and to my surprise the door opened.

We were now face to face, though still twenty yards apart. Without her hat she looked smaller than I had reckoned. Her hair was an unusual auburn colour, streaked with grey but still pretty and plentiful. She had it parted in the centre and caught in a bun at the back but half of it had escaped its moorings and hung in untidy wisps round her face and neck. It was quite easy to visualise how beautiful it had been ten years ago, how luxuriant and rich, as it cascaded down her back. I imagined it instantly like Rapunzel's hair, brushed until it sparkled with red lights, falling dramatically to below her waist. But the rest of her did not lend itself to such a romantic transformation. Her face was weather-beaten and greatly wrinkled – only the sharpness of the blue eyes indicated Miss Cowdie's comparative youth. She wore an odd collection of old and shapeless garments – a man's cardigan with the buttons missing over a filthy white lacy jumper, through which peeped some kind of checked blouse, caught at the neck with a safety pin. Her yellow skirt was covered in stains and torn at the side, revealing several inches of blue nylon underskirt. On her feet she still had her Wellingtons.

She stared at me hard and I hung my head, hoping to look beaten. "You must *not* be here when the Earl comes," she said severely, "he wouldn't like it – it would look bad. He's very shy, you know." I nodded and whispered, "I know." "Speak up," she said sharply, "I can't hear what you are saying, mumbling like that."

"I'm sorry," I said.

"What do you want, hanging about? I don't like you, you know, not a bit."

"Why not?" I kept my voice down, in spite of her instructions.

"Anyone can see why not – I can see what you're after, sneaking up like this. It won't work, you know – the Earl thinks only of me, he would never look at another woman."

"No," I said, "I know he wouldn't."

"Do you know him?"

It was tempting to say I did but something about Miss Cowdie's voice, as she asked, checked my lie. For that question it had subtly changed – it was level and direct, the voice of a normal person asking a normal question, whereas before there had been something sing-song and high pitched about her dialogue, as though she were acting in a play. I thought it possible that every now and again she would be capable of sudden moments of sanity – if indeed she was mad, as it appeared – and that during them she would be able to discern instantly who was fooling around with her and who was not. So I said, "No."

"Then what are you talking about?"

"I meant the Earl, whoever he is, would not be interested in me, just as I am not interested in him."

"Are you married?"

"No." I took a deep breath and said, daringly, "I was going to be married once but then I didn't. I like to be on my own, with my nephew. I've come here to make pots and sell them – I mean no harm to you or anyone."

"So you say."

"You will see it is the truth. There is no need to try to scare me away."

"I haven't tried."

I thought it would be asking for trouble to accuse her of dumping the rabbit and the sheep's head and so I said, "I'm glad you haven't. I thought you had. You spat at my car and pushed me down on the track."

"No," she said firmly, "I did not. It wasn't me."

"Oh. Well – I'm glad."

"What do you want?"

"Nothing."

"Then why did you come?"

"I was angry. When I came home there was a rotting sheep's head in my cottage. I thought you might know something about it."

"I don't." But I noticed she seemed neither indignant nor surprised.

"Then I'm sorry I bothered you. I'll go home."

"I can't ask you in. I'm very busy. I'm getting married tomorrow."

"How lovely. Good luck."

"Luck?" Her hand flew to her throat and an expression of great terror passed over her thin face.

"Yes – for your wedding day."

To my consternation, tears began to pour down her cheeks. She clung to the doorposts for support and I ran the short distance that still separated us to comfort her. No sound came from her mouth but her brow was furrowed in pain and the tears went on and on. I looked around for a chair but there appeared to be no such object – all I could see was a small three-legged stool, in front of the fireplace. I sat her down upon it, with difficulty, and she put her hands over her head and crouched there, shaking with silent sobs.

I wanted to make her some tea but I could find none. The kitchen was a mere hole with a cold water tap and a terrible rusted cooker and a broken glass-fronted cupboard taking up the rest of the tiny space. I opened the cupboard but it was more bare than Mother Hubbard's, nothing in it but cobwebs and mouse droppings. I took hold of a cracked mug and washed it out and filled it with cold water, for want of anything else. But I could not get Miss Cowdie to remove her hands from her head. Diffidently, knowing I would hate it myself, I patted her back and made what I hoped were comforting noises – not quite "there, there," but not much more effective. All the time I was looking round the living-room, hardly able to credit the degree of poverty it spoke of. It was dark and bitterly cold but I could see after a while that I had not been mistaken – there were no chairs except for that absurdly small hard wooden stool. All there was was a table covered with oilcloth, a treadle sewing machine, a basket for wood (empty), a small bench beside the table and a bookcase in one corner with two rows full of quite solid looking hardbacked books, and the other two packed with magazines. On the table was a plate with an apple core on it, and an empty glass, and a can of Heinz baked beans with a spoon sticking out of the top. There was a rag rug on the floor near the fireplace, black with age. I could see no lights, but since I had seen lights on in the house I presumed there must be electricity somewhere, even though in that room the ceiling had no electric lead dangling from it.

I would have liked to light a fire but there was neither kindling nor wood. Some paper had been burnt in the grate quite recently – the light black ash was still floating about – and though I hated to think of it, I thought it likely that was all Miss Cowdie had to burn, at least at the moment. Yet such feck-lessness was strange – her fire must be a great comfort and she was surrounded by the fells, where it was easy to gather sticks, even if there were no real logs. My eye caught her bonnet and coat, hanging behind the door on a peg, dripping onto the stone flags with a persistent tip-tapping. There was no other sound except for the rain on the window panes and a banging from upstairs, rhythmic and harsh, as though a door was blowing against some metal surface. I could feel on my cheek spots of rain swept through the broken pane near the door and each icy spot stung as it landed.

I very much dreaded Miss Cowdie coming out of her grief – I was sure she would have forgotten who I was, or what had happened to bring me into her cottage, and she would see me as an intruder. She would either be frightened or angry and become violent as a result. So I stood there, tense with anticipation, helplessly watching her with that stupid mug of water in my hand, unable to decide what I should say or do when eventually she looked up. But I need not have worried. Miss Cowdie was not in the least alarmed. She simply rubbed her eyes and sighed and looked, vaguely, round the room, as though her surroundings were the surprise and not me. Clearly, she was waiting for me to explain myself, looking up helplessly at me in a trusting fashion.

"I wanted to make you some tea," I said, "but I couldn't find where you kept the tea."

"There isn't any tea," she said, "there hasn't been any tea for a long time now. I don't know where it has gone. I used to have plenty of tea, plenty of it, I was fond of tea. But there you are. Everything comes to an end."

"I'll bring you some tea," I said impulsively, "tomorrow. Will you let me bring you some?"

She nodded eagerly, quite delighted by the idea, and I thought that was a good moment to leave, when she still thought of me as a friend.

She saw me to the door and stood framed in the doorway, watching me make my way down to the bend that hid my own cottage. I waved when I reached the point after which she would no longer be able to see me. Ahead, I saw friendly lights on in my cottage, so I knew Casper was back. He had even cleaned out the grate and lit another fire because I could see smoke rising from the chimney. Drawn by the brightness of the window downstairs – squares of orange and yellow, darkly set in the black wet stone wall – I did not go in at once but stood looking into my own room, fascinated by the warmth of the image. A great log fire leapt and blazed in the stone fireplace and the lamp I had brought with me from Church Row – an old, heavy based stone lamp with an apricot shade which cast a beautiful soft light – lit the small sofa we had bought that day so kindly that the shabby cretonne looked charming. Then I started, suddenly catching sight of Casper, who was sitting at the table with his head in his hands, his shoulders slumped, his neck craning back as though his head was too weighty to be held up. He looked abject, defeated, even more so than Miss Cowdie, and I went quickly to the door, resolved to break a lifetime's habit by taking him in my arm and comforting him for whatever was wrong.

But when I opened the door, Casper was no longer sitting at the table. I was sure he had not seen me. The click of the latch had given him only a second's warning and yet in that time he must have leapt up and gone into the kitchen beside which he had been sitting, a matter of a yard only. I hesitated. "Casper?" I called. I could hear him moving very, very quietly up the stairs – not until he got to the top of that short flight did he shout back, "Yes?"

"Nothing – just wanted to make sure you were in." He did not reply, no pleasantry to greet mine.

"Casper?"

"Yes?"

"I thought we might go out and eat at Parkend – what do you think?"

"Not hungry."

"But we haven't eaten all day. Are you all right? You're not feeling sick or anything?"

"No."

"Don't you want anything at all?"

"No."

"Aren't you going to come down?"

"No. I'm going to bed."

"But it isn't even six o'clock yet. Are you *sure* you're all right? Let me look at you."

I began to climb the stairs but he went ahead and shut and bolted the door to his attic. There was no point in making a scene. I reminded myself, as I went reluctantly back down again, that I had loathed my mother when she had fussed about meals and fresh air and sleep – I was simply inflicting my own standards on Casper and I should not. He was healthy (I thought) and strong and normally ate enormous quantities – it did not matter in the slightest if he gave his stomach a rest for twenty-four hours. And as for going to bed so early in the evening, well, I had done that often enough myself, deliberately using my retreat as a weapon to disturb adults. I told myself I ought to be glad but I found that though it meant I could be on my own, which normally I would have welcomed, I was upset. He rejected me at every turn – I was allowed to share neither the child's sorrows nor his joys. I was useless to him and he had no one else, no confidante to take the place of the mother I ought to have been and was not. I wished that I had taken more notice of Antonia's burblings about him – his idiosyncracies and moods – but they had bored me and I had not.

Another evening by the fire, eating toast and drinking red wine, defiantly, wanting it to console me. But drinking of any sort never does – comfort me, I mean. The point in drinking for me lies in being happy already and putting the seal on that happiness – drinking when I am depressed never works. In fact, it was a harmless indulgence. I drank half a bottle and did feel a little better for it – at least the edges of my gloom became a little fuzzed and there was some pleasure in the memories induced of other evenings in front of a log fire like this, though there was danger in those memories too, for they were all of Edward. I suppose that original Lakeland cottage was not more than twenty miles away – I would find it easily, should I care to look. There had been the same sort of furniture – the minimum, and all second-hand – but I remembered thick crimson curtains hanging from rings slung onto a wooden pole which had strangely carved knobs on the end. I still had no curtains. Anyone could look in – ghosts, witches, werewolves. I stared boldly out of the window, glass in hand, daring them all to come and mock me. I might get some crimson curtains and shut out the sodden, pitch black fell.

We had made love in front of that fire, often – after sunshine, the romantic Edward liked firelight – anything but the conventional bed with the light out. He used to annoy me slightly later on by setting the scene too carefully – we were meant to lie naturally, easily, in front of the fire, a place we just found ourselves, and we ought to have made love without any contriving. But long after total spontaneity had gone, Edward arranged it, like a film director positioning his actors. I would be three jumps ahead of him, sneering, mocking his artistic eye. But not then, in that other cottage – then, I had been only too eager to fall in with whatever he had in mind and I was as in love with us in love as he was. "Forever and ever," Edward had said, and I had echoed him, pledging myself to eternity before I knew what it meant.

I put the lamp out and crouched in front of the embers of the fire with a poker in my hand, prodding the last piece of wood still burning, trying not to think of Miss Cowdie in her cold room or Casper in his tiny attic. It was too easy to become like Eileen – I saw how it could happen, the beginnings were all there, and I must stamp on them. The rain, the dark, the cold, the isolation – they all lent themselves to the kind of introspection which ended in despair, if not madness. I saw I must take my chances, that I must not shun what was offered in the mistaken belief that being alone meant cutting myself off from all human contact. I could be alone and yet among others, surely. It was mortifying, perhaps, to discover so early that I needed the company I affected to despise but better a small measure of mortification than being drowned in self-pity. And I needed men – another humiliation. Never before had I removed myself so decisively from the sort of men with whom I could be friends, and now I was seeing the consequences. I missed Edward unbearably.

Nine

A small miracle took place the following day – the sun shone. I awoke dazzled by the light, unaccustomed to the day beginning with such certainty. And then I lay there, filled with pleasure as the room filled with sunshine, even smiling, lazily, and stretching out under the bedcovers like a cat rejoicing in the warmth. When I got up and went to the window I could hardly believe that colour had been restored to the landscape – it made me dizzy to see green and blue again after weeks of black and grey. The sun caught the many pools of water lying on the ground and flashed off the silver spots impatiently, giving the air a shimmering that made it move before my eyes. Far away the fell stretched to the horizon, soft and smooth, the sheep calmly grazing, undisturbed by the violence of the change.

I dressed and rushed downstairs and flung open the door and stood raising my face to the sun like a pit pony. It was in fact bitterly cold – only the sun on glass had made my bedroom warm – but I refused to acknowledge the chill. I was intoxicated by the day, suddenly rejuvenated, alive and alert in every limb, ready to go out into it and stay there, greedy for the very air itself. My instinct was to get my jacket and put on my boots and go off with an apple in my pocket and walk until exhaustion forced a halt, but I had my crates to pick up in Carlisle and the sooner I did so, the sooner I could start work and benefit from the great rush of energy I now felt sweeping through me. I called up to Casper, "Casper – get up – it's a fantastic day – we're leaving for Carlisle in ten minutes." A small part of me was terrified he would carry forward his resentment from the day before into this morning, but I heard his feet on the floor immediately and within seconds he was beside me in the kitchen, dishevelled but ready, and though not exactly smiling, distinctly more cheerful than usual.

We were in Carlisle before nine o'clock, parked outside the wonderfully Gothic station. Before I went into the parcels office Casper asked if he could go to some stamp centre he'd read about in Lowther Street. I was not keen for him to do this – I wanted to be home within an hour from start to finish in order to capitalise on the weather – but he so rarely asked to do anything I could not refuse, so I arranged to meet him in an hour, thinking I could go to the post office to check if there was any mail after I had loaded the crates. Or rather, supervised the loading of them, for they were much too heavy for me to handle. I fumed and fussed while two porters were found to do the job – they seemed so slow and reluctant to believe the crates would ever go in. It took them all of half an hour and even then they pronounced the tyres of my Range Rover would be irreparably damaged by the weight inflicted upon them. I said I'd take the chance and tipped them heavily and then dashed off towards the Warwick Road post office, knowing that they were leaning on their trolleys and watching me with that by now familiar Cumbrian air of tolerant amusement. They would be saying to each other that I was "daft" and that I couldn't be told anything.

Such was my haste that I almost knocked down David Garibaldi on the corner of the crescent, where it meets Warwick Road. "Whoa!" he said, flinging both his arms wide, so that it was impossible for me not to go straight into them. The impact stunned me – smack I went into his body and felt his arms swiftly come down to encircle me, so that for a moment we were locked together in an accidental embrace. I struggled to be free and he let me go at once. "Where are you going on such a lovely day?" he said.

"To the post office, to see if there is any mail for me."

"You must be expecting an exciting letter to be running like this for it."

"No, I'm hurrying because I want to get home as soon as possible and unpack my stuff – I've just collected glazes and some special clay and that sort of thing – I want to get back and get started while this weather lasts and makes me feel keen."

"It won't last," he said. "Sorry to be depressing, but it won't, I promise you. It was too bright too early – a common trick in these parts. Look," – and he pointed west over the rooftops – "that thin white looking line is cloud. By midday it will have grown to cover the sun and by evening it will be raining."

"Well then, I'll have to hurry all the more," I said, annoyed, side-stepping him smartly. "Good-bye."

But when I got back to the car, he was standing there looking critically at the tyres. Quickly, I put the three letters I had collected into my pocket, damning Casper for not yet having appeared, so that I was obliged, in waiting for him, to endure David's company. He smiled and pointed at the back of the car. "It's an expensive bit of machinery to ruin," he said, "seems a pity, when it's new. If you drive this load up Warnell, with the weight on the back axle, you'll bugger it up completely."

"Oh, it will be all right," I said airily, and looked at my watch impatiently.

"You know about cars, do you?" he said, still smiling – smirking, I should say.

"No. But it looks all right to me. I'll take the chance."

"Ah," he said, "not only a determined lady but one who relishes unnecessary risks. I learn something exciting about you every time we meet."

"It isn't unnecessary," I said, stung by his tone of mocking contempt. "I want it back in Caldbeck today so I have to take them with me – there is no delivery until next Wednesday."

"I'll deliver one of them," he said, quick as a flash, so much so that I realised he had planned the entire duologue. "I'm going to Keswick in half an hour, to a sale at Thornthwaite. I'm going with an empty van and I literally pass your road end."

"Thank you," I said, "but I really do not want – "

"– me arriving to spend the day with you, using my kindness as an excuse," he finished for me. "Do not worry. I want to be at Thornthwaite before eleven. I won't even have time for a cup of coffee. It will take me five seconds to dump the crate and you won't see me for dust – positively no strings attached. I just don't want to see a new car wrecked. Right? Now I'll go and get my van and meanwhile you will decide not to be so foolish as to pass up such an opportunity out of a mistaken belief that you will then be obliged to me. You won't. I never exact payment for services rendered."

He walked off, waving as he went, before I could protest. I got into the car with an uneasy feeling that I had been bested, if that is the word. The crates probably *were* too heavy for the car – the porters had already said so. And if David was really going on to a sale, which seemed both possible and probable, I had nothing to fear, just as he had said. I sat and looked out on the station square, wondering at my mixed feelings – I did not like being organised by anyone else but, on the other hand, I revelled in the show of a strong hand, whoever's it was. It was nothing so silly as wanting to be subservient or made to feel the little woman but all the same a decisive man did appeal to me. Edward, once so decisive, had in the end not appealed enough but I had plenty of theories about why I had grown out of admiring his apparent masterfulness. That was the point – it was more apparent than real. It was to do with things that did not matter – deciding which film to see, which restaurant to patronise, which town to visit – and failed in deeper matters. When I wanted Edward to order me, he left me to make my own decision and never once tried to force me.

This frightful habit of relating every man I came into contact with to Edward had to stop. David was not in the least like Edward and I must not continually make the comparison. The relationship, if there was to be one, had to be on a different footing and as I saw his van come up from the crescent I knew I had to treat David more naturally – I was making a fool of myself with my haughty suspicious behaviour. I greeted him with a smile and thanked him with feeling as he heaved one of the crates into his van. "You may get there before me," I said. "I've let Casper go off to look at stamps." I watched him closely but no flicker of disappointment crossed his face. "No problem," he said briskly. "I'll leave it at that broken gate. 'Bye," and he was into his van and off before I could thank him again. Casper came five minutes later – immensely pleased at having purchased a set of two Chilean railway stamps commemorating some centenary – and we followed not far behind David over the viaduct and through Nelson Street to Dalston Road. As we passed the cemetery I saw his white van ahead but we stopped for petrol at Bridgend past Dalston and never picked him up again. I drove slowly and carefully up Warnell – the car felt extremely heavy and I knew everyone had been right about that third crate. By the time we got to the top road above Caldbeck, the clouds were beginning to break up from behind Skiddaw. They were slowly spreading across that brilliant blue and would soon reach and begin to obscure the sun. I drove down the Faulds road and as we began to descend the steep hill, driving with care between the two farm-houses, I saw David Garibaldi's van coming away from the Greenhead turning. He had kept his word and, though I was glad, I was also sorry. There would be no opportunity to put my new resolution to the test.

We tried very hard, Casper and I, to lug the three crates into the barn but we failed. They were impossible to move without some sort of trolley and we had nothing suitable. It almost killed us getting the two we had brought out of the car – it was lucky I had no future plans for my childbearing organs because the immense weight I took as Casper pushed each crate towards me must have ruined them for life. After half an hour of heaving and straining I conceded defeat. "We will have to get Geoff Crosthwaite's help," I said. "He's bound to have something to lift these with." I was going to ask Casper to go down to the farm to get him but then I thought this might become too embarrassing, and instead I went in to ask Eileen when might be the best time to ask Geoff for his assistance.

All the time that we had struggled, Eileen had been watching us from the window, her face as usual impassive. I could tell from the movements of her arms that she was washing the dishes, slopping them through the water without looking at them, making of a simple job a laborious ritual. At no time did she come out, either to offer help or to share in our general consternation. I knew she was enjoying the spectacle – it was just the kind of scene that appealed to her. Mirth, in Eileen's book, was reserved for difficulties and misfortunes of all kinds. If, as seemed likely at one point, a crate had dropped on my toe and broken it, she would have laughed soundlessly to herself. As it was, the sight of my hands, red raw and covered in scratches from manhandling the rough wooden edges of the huge crate, would go a long way towards satisfying her baser instincts. She would see the long scratches where the iron bands fastened round the crates had rubbed against my arms and she would smile. Knowing this, I was deliberately extra cheerful. "Well, Eileen," I said, "you're better, I'm glad to see." She didn't bother to reply.

"It's a lovely day, anyway," I said.

"Won't last," she said quickly.

"No, I've already been told that. That's why I'm anxious to get these bloody crates into the barn. Do you think Geoff would help?"

" 'Spect so," Eileen said grudgingly.

"Is he at home?"

"He's in the top field, with the tractor, getting swedes."

"Would he be able to come if I went for him?"

"You'll have to ask."

"Thanks, Eileen," I said sarcastically, but sarcasm was lost on her – she saw it as a sign of weakness, which indeed it was. I ran through a list of jobs she was to do that morning and then set off to find Geoff. As I was going out of the door she called after, "That Garibaldi left a message."

"Oh yes?"

"Said he'd look in some time."

"Oh, right. Thank you."

"You don't want to tell our Geoff that," Eileen said, her back to me but her tone revealing her malicious pleasure far more effectively than her face would have done.

"There isn't anything to tell," I said. "Mr Garibaldi, as you can see, merely dropped a crate off. That's all."

"Wouldn't do it for nothing," Eileen muttered. "Our Geoff'll say that, if he's seen him."

"Your Geoff can say what he likes," I said, and walked out.

It was just as I told you I had expected – it was impossible to move a finger in the country without everyone knowing and jumping to conclusions. I was watched like a hawk by a dozen pairs of eyes. I could not go anywhere or be visited by anyone without giving rise to the most intense speculation and there was no way in which I could stop it. Hiding away in a lonely cottage on a lonely fell was the surest method of exposing myself that I could have invented and I saw all over again how basically unsuited I was to the way of life. In my London street my independence and anonymity were real. Here, they were both seriously imperilled, and I had to take the irritating consequences.

I left Casper brushing out the barn in readiness for setting up the contents of the crates and went in search of Geoff. He was about half a mile beyond his farm, picking up swedes with a hoe and hurling them into a truck attached to the back of his tractor. I waved, but he did not stop – I concluded he could not see me, though I was very prominent, walking along the broad ridge behind his fields. The engine of the tractor was still running, making it pointless to shout, so I had to plod my way through the wet muddy field until I was right up to him. Even then, he neither stopped nor turned off the engine, but went steadily on, working in a smooth swinging motion which made everything look easy. The sleeves of his pullover were rolled up so that the muscles in his strong brown arms stood out as he heaved and swung with his hoe, and his legs in their dirty jeans were braced apart, showing a similar strength about the tightly covered thighs. His hair was dishevelled and his face stubbly with a day's growth of beard. I stood humbly watching him, waiting until he would spare the time to notice me.

"Can't stop," he shouted eventually, over the racket of the tractor. "Want this lot under cover before the rain starts."

"I've got some heavy crates with pottery stuff in," I shouted back. "I've just picked them up from Carlisle and they're too heavy for me to get into my barn. Will you help me, when you can spare the time?"

"What's it worth?" he yelled, grinning.

"What?" I had heard but wanted to pretend I had not.

He put down his hoe and wiping his grimy hands on his even filthier jeans went over to his tractor and switched off the engine. The field went suddenly quiet, except for the cries of seagulls swooping over the turned up earth. Leaning against the side of the truck, which was now almost full of the strong smelling swedes, Geoff put his hands into his pockets and looked at me. "What's it worth?" he said again, smiling, sure of himself. I blushed. "What do you charge?" I asked, abruptly, turning away and looking up at the sun, which was playing hide and seek with the first of the big white clouds.

"Dunno. Haven't done that sort of job before. What did that I-tie charge?"

"Do you mean Mr Garibaldi?"

"Ay. The poofy ice-cream man from Carlisle. I used to get a cornet from his Dad's shop when I was little – special treat, it was."

"I don't know anything about that," I said. "Mr Garibaldi just saw my car at the station with three crates in it and he insisted on helping me out by bringing one of them on the way to a sale."

"Insisted, eh? What does he get out of it? A kiss?"

There was no point in me walking off in disgust. In London, I could have done so and never seen the offender again but situated as I was it was childish. I could not avoid Geoff Crosthwaite. I had to live side by side with his family and feuds were pointless.

"Look, Geoff," I said, "I'm sorry I bothered you. I made a mistake. I thought you would be glad to help, out of ordinary friendship. I'm sorry I asked." I was careful to keep my voice quite level and without anger as I added, "I won't ask again," and then turned on my heel and began to walk away.

"Aw, come on," Geoff said, easily catching me up, one restraining hand on my shoulder, "I were only teasing. I'll come in a minute when I've finished this."

"Don't bother," I said, but I hope not petulantly.

"It's no bother."

"I'll pay you for your time."

"Give over. Only payment I want is what Garibaldi wants."

"And what do you imagine that is?"

"*You* know."

"No, I don't. But you seem to."

"Well, what every fellow wants. He doesn't just help you out for fun, does he? He isn't just being kind, is he? You can't think that."

"Why not? Why can't I?"

"It isn't human nature."

"Oh, back to human nature, are we? What is human nature then, Geoff, as you're so hot on it?"

We were by this time at the far end of the field, near the gate that opened onto the ridge track. I was walking faster, now that the mud-clinging field was almost left behind, and Geoff had to hurry to keep up with me. When I suddenly stopped without warning he shot past me and had to turn and come back. It was curious to see how all that confidence he had displayed while engaged on dealing with the swedes had disappeared – but then, that was Geoff. Words made him uncomfortable. He was a cheerfully physical person, only happy when he was obeying bodily rhythms, when he was letting his arms and legs do what they had been trained to do. Geoff making love would be like a bull in a china shop – no finesse, only a certain vigorous brutality and a conviction that as the sex urge was "human nature" all he had to do was follow it.

"Well?" I said, when finally he had turned back to face me, looking embarrassed and awkward.

"Oh, nothing," he said, "forget it." He was redder than ever in the face and sullen. "What time do you want me to come – before dinner or after? It's all the same to me."

"Before then," I said. "The sooner I get the crates in, the sooner I can unpack them and get started."

"As long as that I-tie isn't coming back, that's all, though I don't suppose he could even half lift anything heavy."

"He certainly isn't as strong as you," I said, pandering to his vanity.

"He wouldn't be, would he – he hasn't got a man's job, has he? Selling rubbish in a shop. That doesn't give you muscles."

"No, it doesn't," I agreed, "but there's more to a man than muscles."

Geoff looked, as he walked back to his hoeing, as if he doubted the truth of that statement. I could almost hear him saying to himself "*Is* there more to a man than muscles?" and worrying about it. All his life he had been brought up to believe men were big and strong and powerful and didn't do daft sissy things like read books or listen to music or talk. They hoed swedes and trained horses and drove tractors and ploughed fields and rounded up sheep. They were rough and tough and expected to be admired for it. I was turning poor Geoff's world upside down.

Eileen had finished and so had Casper. The barn was clean and empty of the odds and ends we had stored in it. The shelves Mr Rigg had put up were shining with varnish and the racks upon which the pots would dry gleamed with fresh paint. Casper grunted at my thanks for the good job he had done – he was too taken up with fixing a milometer to his new bicycle to be interested in my gratitude. Only one more day and he would be out of my sight at school, and then our days would be taken up with work of various sorts and the agony of marking time would be over – or I hoped it would. I think I was very near, then, to giving up before I had properly begun. Only the arrival of my materials and the sunshine in the morning and a basic stubbornness had stopped me getting the first train to London.

"Everything's done," Eileen said.

"Thank you. I'll see you on Monday then, Eileen. I hope I'll be working by then, so there might be more interesting things for you to do." Eileen did not ask what. She put on her coat and did it up. "What do you do on Sunday, Eileen?" I asked – God knows why. It was something to do with her obvious reluctance to go home – how slowly she always got ready to go, even though nothing at all had been said to make me think it was any more exciting in my cottage than it was in her own farmhouse.

"Nothing," she said. "Get the dinner, that's about all. Clear up. Maybe go out wi' the dog, maybes not. Depends."

"What does Geoff do?"

"Does the work, has his dinner, then he goes out after that Mildred in his car – hangs about Hesket at the pub. Goes drinking at night."

"Doesn't he ever take you with him?"

"Our Geoff?" she said, in disgust. "He hates me. I hate him. Wouldn't go, anyways." She turned her collar up. "I'd best go. Dad and Geoff'll be in for their dinners. They scream blue murder if it isn't on the table and Mam's doing the bedrooms this morning."

I watched her trail off, head bent, mournful and depressed. There was no doubt I would have to do something about

Eileen before very long, however much any interference might upset Geoff. I was thinking about her as I took my jacket off and made myself some coffee, filling in the hour until Geoff arrived. Her existence was hardly any better than Miss Cowdie's. Both imagined only a man could put their world right and neither had any prospects of getting one. I frowned as I sat down with my cup of coffee and thoughtfully poured in a little milk. I alone needed no man – and yet that proud assertion had been shown already not to be true. It maddened me, this flaw in myself. I drank the coffee, the silence around me heavy and menacing, as it always was in the daytime in that cottage – peace and quiet there was too convincing. I got up, scraping the chair on the floor, and as I did so I caught sight of the corners of my three letters, sticking out of my jacket pocket. One was for Casper and I knew from the stamp that it was from Edward.

One of mine was from Mrs Matlock.

Dear Alexandra,

It is now almost a month since you removed my darling Casper from my life, and I must confess it has given me great pain to discover that you evidently do not intend to keep your promise to keep in touch. I have looked for a letter – even a postcard – every day since you left. I am reluctant to believe, now, that there will ever be any communication from you, and I am too old and ill to pretend it does not matter.

Naturally, I have made allowances for the state of upheaval you must be in – I know very well how time-consuming moving can be. I gather from listening to weather forecasts on the wireless that the weather has not been good in your new part of the world and I expect that has complicated everything. But all the same I would have thought Casper could find five minutes to write to me a few lines, telling me how he is getting on. Has he started school? Is he happy? Does he like his new home?

You must remember, Alexandra, that you took on a sacred trust when you became Casper's guardian. You may not have wished to, but you did. It is your duty to keep up the standards Antonia and Gerald had for Casper and not to let him slide into apathy. He is his father's son and will need help to fulfil his expectations.

You will say none of this is any business of mine, but I believe it to be. In the name of common decency I ask you to write to me with some news of my only grandson. If it were not too insulting, I would enclose a stamped addressed envelope to encourage you – anything to make writing easy.

I hardly dare mention it, but at this time of the year one's thoughts turn naturally to Christmas. It will be the first Christmas since Gerald and Antonia's tragic deaths and I need hardly say I dread spending it alone. I feel it is a time for us to draw closer together and would like to welcome both you and Casper to my home for the festive season. Won't you come? God knows, in the state of health I am in at the moment, I do not expect to see many more Christmases. Even two or three days would be sufficient to assuage the pain I feel at the thought of an empty house on Christmas Day, full of memories and nothing else.

Please write to me, however briefly.

Yours sincerely,
Vera Matlock.

The letter may strike you as sad and pathetic but I am afraid it did not have that effect on me. The pathos struck me as extremely calculated and I found it unforgivable. Mrs Matlock was indulging in emotional blackmail of the variety I most despise. If she had written a kindly inquiring letter I should have flown to answer her but this self-righteous whining irritated me. It did not matter that the facts of the case were true – it was the way in which she presented them. She had thought only of herself, not of Casper. We had already discussed Christmas before we left London, and I knew he hated spending it at his grandmother's. I had no idea how we would celebrate that obligatory occasion but I was absolutely determined not to give into his grandmother's desire to have him with her, however pitiful her circumstances.

And as for the remark about "standards" – that enraged me. What, after all, had these so-called standards of Antonia and Gerald's produced? A child who was uncommunicative to the point of almost being autistic – a child so repressed that he was incapable of showing any emotion. Nor did I need to blame myself for his sad state – he had been like this long before his parents were killed. How dare Mrs Matlock imply I was not carrying on some golden tradition, that I was wilfully breaking with wonderful rules that Antonia and Gerald had followed? My instinct was to sit down there and then and dash off a furious reply but the sight of Geoff roaring up the track in his tractor fortunately prevented me from obeying it, and really I was glad because I always regret those terrible scrawls of mine, written in the heat of the moment. They have done me more harm that I care to remember.

Geoff left his tractor running and jumped off to look at the crates. I was relieved to see all signs of sullenness had vanished – unlike his sister Eileen, Geoff did not appear to harbour any grudges and had a disposition so basically cheerful that he could not subdue his natural good spirits for long. If he had only known it, this was much more attractive, though less manly, than the muscles of which he was so inordinately proud.

"Brutes, eh?" he shouted. Experimentally he lifted one of them while I watched anxiously. It had taken two porters to lift one crate onto a trolley and David Garibaldi had only managed it with the help of a jack he kept in his van. But Geoff lifted the crate clean off the ground and began staggering with it towards the barn, a distance of some fifty yards. He rested only once. In spite of myself I was impressed at such a show of immense strength in a man who was by no means a gorilla to look at. Geoff's power lay in his arms and legs but otherwise he was of moderate build. Before he lifted the second crate he stopped and pulled off his shirt and I saw how beautifully he was made. His shoulders were broad but his chest tapered to a slim waist and had none of the bull-like thickness I had guessed at. And his beloved muscles were indeed extraordinary – one did not need to feel them to realise how compact and hard they were in his upper arms. He looked like an illustration in some art book on how to draw the human figure – the sort that does cross-sections of sinews and tendons. From being in the open air all the time, his skin was as brown and healthy on his body as it was on his face, and curiously free of much hair – a smattering across the nipples and down the middle of his abdomen and that was all.

When he had finished, he stood wiping his brow, where the sweat ran into his eyes. He was scarlet in the face but still smiling. "Phew," he said, "some weight. I could drink the Solway dry." I don't think he was hinting, and even if he was, he was well within his rights – I ought to have offered him a drink before he mentioned his thirst. "What can I get you?" I said. "I've got canned lager and Guinness but no beer." "Water," he said firmly. "God's own drink'll do me grand." "Are you sure?" I said, not believing him but knowing sarcasm was not in his line. He nodded vigorously so I went into the cottage and filled a jug with water and ice cubes and brought it out to him. The sun had come out again for a moment, though it was flanked on either side by thick black clouds, and we stood bathed in its temporary warmth, both drinking water. Geoff drank four great glassfuls without stopping. "Just as well it isn't beer," I said, "if that's how you drink." "Never in the week," he said, "only on a Saturday, and that's my lot. Can't drink and work – it saps your strength."

"Well," I said, "I can't thank you enough. I don't know how I would have managed – it was very good of you. I hope I can do something for you sometime." Perhaps Geoff was not completely stupid. I felt that an hour or so ago, before our little scene in the field, he might well have replied that there certainly was something I could do for him, and that he would have leered as he said it. But he had learned already and said nothing. He got on his tractor and waved and lumbered off to Eileen and his dinner, leaving me with a vague aching feeling of excitement. Geoff, who had no lover's arts and was a novice in all sexual matters, would not believe the effect the sight of his bare chest had had. In his opinion, lust was an entirely male prerogative. He would not understand that, to a woman, a man's flesh can be as erotic as a woman's to a man. The discovery, if he ever made it, would both bewilder and appal him – he would quickly be convinced that any woman who confessed to such thoughts was a harlot and a hussy. Suppose I were to say to him (as I would like to have done), "Geoff, take all your clothes off and let me look at you" – how he would have run away. Geoff was a man for a quick humping in the dark and no worship of the body at all. He was a man to be made awkward by an erect penis – he would cover it with his hands and feel no pride, only shame. And unless he was very lucky that would suit whoever he took for his bride, and he would go through the act of copulation unaware of its finer points.

Smiling to think that as I entertained these visions of Geoff he would be sloshing through his potatoes and gravy, I went back into the cottage and put on the soup Eileen had made. I had discovered in the first few days that soup was one thing she could make well. It took her two hours of slow scraping and chopping of vegetables and simmering of bones but I was disposed to let her take as long as she liked. At least making soup was a little more creative than all the other dreary household tasks I was obliged to give her to do. Casper loved it and ate enormous bowlfuls, so it was also a great standby, especially as I was finding his normal appetite a strain. We had no bread so I sent him down to the village shop to buy some, stressing that he was not to come back with packaged white rolls, of which the shop was full. He was to persuade the shopkeeper to let him have anything at all not sliced or wrapped. It was ironic that in the county of Cumbria, which boasts such beautiful home-baked bread, I had to give him any such instructions, but the sad truth was that village shops throughout the entire area were serviced by large vans bringing them commercial pap – bread from the big bakeries packed to keep. I thought perhaps I might at some point overcome my hatred of cookery sufficiently to learn how to bake bread, but that day had not yet come (and never did). I thought I might ask Eileen if this was another hidden talent.

Casper went on his bicycle, pleased to have a genuine reason to use it. He walked down the track with it without my mentioning that this might be a good thing to do, in view of the ruts and potholes. I knew it would take him around forty five minutes and took out my second letter with a pleasant feeling of anticipation. In London, I rarely got letters – friends telephoned or visited – and even when I did they were rarely relished. I would rip them open on my way to the college, skimming the contents at each traffic light, and often doing no more. But already I could see what an event letters were bound to be, things to be savoured, things to become the focal point of the day. I could not think who it could be from, and took a childish delight in delaying the pleasure of knowing by examining the address and the postmark. They gave nothing away. The address was typewritten and of course simply had the Post Restante number on. The postmark was London WC1, the area of both my solicitor and my bank. One or the other had forwarded it – but why in a new envelope? Why not simply re-directed? Slowly, I opened the rather large square buff envelope, quite expecting to find it contained a collection of bills, but inside was a blue airmail envelope, bulky and heavily stamped. My first thought was "Edward," and I almost pushed the envelope back in and threw it into the fireplace – but I did not recognise the handwriting (large and flourishing) and the postmark was not South America. It was India. I knew nobody at all in India. Intensely curious, I began to open it.

Ten

I cannot tell you what was in that letter – not yet, not until I have finished my story – nor can I tell you who it was from. The name would mean nothing to you anyway, since I have not mentioned the lady in my narrative. But the shock it gave me to hear from her devastated me so completely that I cannot go on without recording it. Partly, it was the unpleasant associations the name had when I saw it at the end of the long letter, and partly it was the nature of the communication. My correspondent had written to me on her deathbed – there was a short note enclosed from the English doctor in the hospital in Calcutta where she had died. He (the doctor) said his patient had been delirious for days before she died but that for the brief spell during which she had dictated her letter to me, on the eve of her death, she had been perfectly lucid and coherent, and that the fever seemed to leave her as soon as she had finished it. She had died, plainly relieved, after he had promised on oath that the letter would be sent on to me as soon as possible. He was fulfilling that promise and hoped in doing so he was not causing me undue distress.

His hope was in vain. I was extremely distressed – not so much by the confession, or what amounted to a confession, as by the thought of this figure from my past carrying this burden through her short and unhappy life. If only she had known that her guilt existed only in her own imagination, how much unnecessary suffering she could have avoided. She said she felt her deceit – the wretched little bit of duplicity to which she confessed – had ruined my life, but she was quite, quite wrong. I would have made the same decision even if I had known she had guessed. I could not bear to think of her worrying and fretting for ten years over something so basically insignificant. She had carried what she thought of as a hideous secret all the way to India, and it had haunted her all those dutiful years she had spent nursing the sick and poor. From what I had been told, she was such a good person, the sort of person I had always admired from afar and known I could never in a million years emulate. And she had had so little out of life, it seemed to me – not much happiness, only the doubtful satisfaction of duty done. My capacity for pleasure and my inordinate self-interest must always have puzzled her – I suspect she half disapproved and half longed to be me, and I suppose there was that faint tinge of jealousy which had prompted the silence she now admitted. She said, in the course of her letter, that she had many times wanted to confront me but had not dared. She was frightened of my anger. She was afraid I would lay at her door fearful consequences which she could not face.

I felt slightly sick as I sat there at the table under the window. The sun had finally gone again and the familiar gloom stole down to envelop the cottage. In a minute it would rain, and the wind would rise and the cold, wet air seep through every crack. I fancied I could hear the voice of my correspondent as she unburdened herself to the Indian clerk brought in especially to transcribe the pages I held listlessly in my hand. It rose and fell in my head, light and breathless, with that faint hint of Scottish vowels that I remembered so well in the voice of her brother. She was frail, her thin voice had no strength, but I heard it clearly and its sweetness was painful. I wanted to stretch out across continents, to reach back in time, and put my hand over her mouth and tell her to hush, hush, there was no need to say anything. For once, I was glad of the chilling isolation of my cottage, glad that the elements outside seemed to mourn with me, and inevitably, as I sat, stunned and sad, I could not fail to re-live the past of which she had spoken. I went through those awful days, the worst period of my entire life, and I felt for a few brief moments the same anguish and misery I had felt then. Now that Antonia was dead, there was no one but this other dead woman who could bring back to me the peculiar quality of a protracted nightmare that had characterised those weeks and months. I had not known that she knew. Beside that, everything else was trivial.

I noticed, even in my dazed state, that I did not seem surprised by her revelation of how she had indeed known what was going on in my life – of what I had done. She had spared me so much by keeping quiet, though she could not imagine it. Afterwards, when it was all over and my equilibrium regained, I had been triumphant at the brilliance of my successful manoeuvre. Antonia had said I could not pull it off, that I was foolish to try, and I was gratified that my faith in myself had been vindicated. Everything had gone entirely to plan, and I did not even know of the slip which must have revealed my breathtaking audacity to a woman who had concealed her information right up to the moment she died.

I did not tear up and burn the letter, though I was tempted. It was written on thin, crisp rice paper, easy to crumple up, but I smoothed the sheets out – three of them, large and closely written, in a neat clear hand – and folded them and put them back into the envelope. I would never want to read it again. I would never want to show it to anyone. Yet all the same I found I could not lightly destroy something so important to the sender. I would keep it, tuck it away in the wooden box where I kept other letters that had meant something, and in that small way I would somehow preserve the intention of the sender. Someone else, after I was dead, could throw it away – so long as that person was not Casper it did not much matter and I could not see that my uninquisitive nephew would ever play that role.

It is hard, after one's world has been shaken on its axis, to go back to humdrum tasks which before had seemed important. The contents of the crates from London, only that morning so enticing, were now of little interest. The thought of being able to start work did not thrill me any longer. I felt apathetic and dull – I felt like going to sleep for a long time, as an escape from depression. But even as I entertained the idea I saw Casper wheeling his bike along the track, stopping every now and again to peer anxiously at the tyres.

"They only had malt bread," he said, coming in holding it, "with raisins."

"Never mind. Anything will do," I said in the sort of leaden, dolorous voice Eileen used. "I'll get the soup."

I had put the letter for Casper on the table, propped against the salt. I saw him hesitate, holding the thin airmail envelope in his hand, and I knew he wanted to keep the contents to himself, whatever they were. But with an obvious effort of will he opened it and I saw some stamps flutter out of the envelope. He seized them eagerly and could not contain his excitement. "Look," he said, "look – three Guatemalan railway stamps – I've got two already – I've nearly got half the set." "Is that good?" I said, bored – the stamps looked dull to me, faded and blurred with only the smallest train in the top left corner. Casper had many more spectacular ones in his album. "Good?" he echoed, "of course it's good – the set is worth fifty pounds. And one of these is yellow, the most expensive of the twelve. I'll have to write back and thank Edward." I wanted to ask if there was a letter but Casper pushed the envelope into his pocket and I took a pride in betraying no further interest. It was like Edward, of course – to remember a boy's passion for railway stamps and to go to the trouble of finding out which ones mattered. I could not for a minute pretend there was any other motive in his gesture.

We sat at the table and ate from our bowls, utterly silent. I looked out of the window to avoid looking at Casper. The only noise was the irritating sound of him blowing on the hot soup and slurping it up afterwards. To avoid going mad, I spoke. "Your grandmother has written," I said. "She wants you to spend Christmas with her, and me too. Do you want to?"

"No."

"Then you must write and tell her so yourself. If I do it, she will think I'm keeping you from her."

"I don't know what to say."

"Then you'll have to think it out."

"What *can* I say?"

"Well, why don't you want to go? Start with thinking about that."

"I just don't want to. It would be boring. She'd go on and on about – you know – other years. I'd hate it."

"Then there you are – say it would be too painful and you couldn't bear it, just as you're getting over your mother and father's death."

Did I speak callously? I don't think so. For one thing, I was much too low myself to be so energetic. But Casper flushed and put his spoon down and was visibly upset. "I'm sorry," I said quickly, "I keep forgetting you can't bear to have it mentioned." I held my breath, convinced he was going to push his chair back and rush upstairs, but he didn't – the lure of the soup was too great, perhaps, or, if that sounds horribly cynical, he realised I was genuinely penitent. "Casper," I said, cautiously, "*are* you getting over it, just a little? I know I mustn't ask, but I can't help it. There isn't any way I can tell, unless you admit it directly. Maybe I've made a terrible mistake anyway, going along with your not wanting it mentioned – maybe I should have forced you to mention it and that would have helped you more. But when I was young I hated adults thinking they knew what was best for me and I vowed I'd always remember that if I ever had children – "

"Well, you didn't," he said, quite rudely.

"It still applies, with you."

"It doesn't."

"All right," I shrugged, "if you want to be illogical I'm too fed up to argue. I won't inquire about your feelings any more – "

"Good."

" – that is, if you have any. Oh Christ, you goad me into such childishness. I didn't mean that. I just wanted to be spiteful because you'd hurt me." I paused. He had nearly finished all the soup that was left and would soon no longer be a semi-captive audience. "But of course you won't ask, 'how did I hurt you?' You don't give a damn about any troubles I might have. I'm amazed you want to stay with me at all."

"I don't," he said, "but I have to. My mother and father – " he choked over the words, "made you my guardian. And I have to do what they wanted until I'm eighteen."

I sat transfixed at the window, watching him go off up the fell, Rufus bounding joyously at his heels, his golden fur the only colour on the now dark green turf. With a sickening feeling of guilt, I saw the whole pathos of Casper's position and my heart turned over. Here he was, stuck with an aunt he did not like, in a place where any options were closed and no escape was possible, and all the time his attitudes and moods were challenged in a way he could not defend. I saw that my contempt came through to him – I may have thought I practised patience and tolerance, I may have imagined I was being forbearing, but all that came through to Casper was my innate dislike of what he was. And now I had bleated for sympathy and forced him to retaliate. It was as I had always known – I was not fit to be a mother. I had none of the qualities needed and was bound to make a poor job of it. I thanked God I had foreseen this and resisted the temptation to believe what others told me – that the act of birth in itself was sufficient to bring about a total change in my character. They said I only had to hold my baby in my arms and waves of tenderness would overwhelm me. They said I only had to suckle it and love would remove my fears. Wisely, I had not believed them, though I did not doubt the tenderness and love – it was my ability to continue with those maternal qualities, my capacity for surmounting the difficulties it led to, that had made me set my face upon embarking on that career. Now, with Casper, I saw how right I had been. I could not cope with his unhappiness and how much worse that sense of inadequacy would have been if I had been his mother from birth.

Self-pity is rightly held to be one of the most destructive of human emotions. I sat and sat, wallowing in it, feeling more miserable and desperate with every minute and quite unable to pull myself together and be brisk and do something constructive to dispel my introspective nightmare. There was no telephone to reach out for, no theatre to rush off to, no busy streets outside to lose myself in. There was no hubbub to drown my plaintive inner voice. I thought of jumping in my car and driving off somewhere – anywhere – but there was no comfort any longer in that tank-like creature – I could feel no release in sitting at the wheel of such a hulk when what I wanted was to zoom along roads in my beloved lost MGB. And Casper might return and think I had left him and feel more persecuted than ever. I wished someone would call – anyone – but the chances were zero. Wilfully, I had cut myself off. Wilfully, I now stared myself in the face and hated what I saw.

Eventually I drifted into the tiny kitchen and made myself some tea and in doing so remembered my promise to Miss Cowdie. I ignored the boiling kettle and took down from the cupboard two packets of tea, Twinings Darjeeling tea, which had a pleasant mild flavour, far superior to other brands. It was something to do, somewhere to go, however pathetic. Hurrying now, frantic to get out of that horrible room, I put on my jacket and boots and slipped the tea into my pockets. I scrawled a quick note to Casper, telling him where I had gone, and then set off up the track towards Miss Cowdie's hidden cottage, pleased to have a genuine errand to do, no matter how contrived, and pondering as I went upon the mystery of how she had come to live there in the first place. I wondered if it would be wise to ask anything at all about the past or whether that was an area to keep strictly away from.

The little whitewashed cottage had the same familiar shuttered look. It struck me that, though the inside was so poverty stricken and neglected, the outside was quite freshly painted, perhaps only a year or two old. Mr Rigg had already told me, when I had thought of whitewashing the whole of my own cottage, that if I did it would take some keeping up. He said the wind and rain were so fierce in these parts that in a single winter paint of any kind could be wiped off – literally flaked into holes by the elements. But Miss Cowdie's cottage exterior, though it lay in a much more exposed position than mine, was in good condition. I wondered who had done it, whether she had a landlord who attended to it for her. If he did, it was the only thing he cared about (painting the outside walls, I mean), because everywhere else were visible signs of long term neglect. The roof sagged, the chimney was bent at a crazy angle, and the windows and doors were in a dreadful state of repair.

I knocked at the door, expecting to have to go through the whole pantomime of getting in again, but to my surprise the door opened at once and a tidier, cleaner Miss Cowdie stood there with a smiling face. "You've brought the tea?"

she asked at once, and when I produced it from my pockets she literally clapped her hands. "I have had the kettle boiling all day," she said, almost snatching it from me and running into the kitchen. I closed the rackety old door carefully and followed her inside. The room was as cold and bleak as the day before, but I was relieved to see a fire set but not lit. It was piled high with sticks and on the hearth was another pile of larger branches from some tree, all broken into pieces to go on later.

She came in with a brown teapot full of tea and said with great dignity and a graceful gesture of the hand, "Shall we partake?" I sat down on the bench and she pulled out a stool that I had not noticed before, tucked under the table and covered by the overhanging oilcloth, and sat herself down. She poured the tea, almost purring over the amber colour. "I hope it is strong enough," I said, fearing that the delicacy of that particular brand might not please her. "I dislike strong tea," she said firmly. "Coffee, yes, but tea, no." She held her hands over the steaming cup and said, as she watched the steam rise through her outspread fingers, "without milk or sugar, I trust?" I do in fact take milk in my tea, though not sugar, but I thought she would not have any milk (I was quite right) and did not want to spoil her pleasure, so I said, "Quite right – no milk, no sugar."

Solemnly, we drank the tea as soon as it was bearable to the palate. Miss Cowdie closed her eyes in ecstasy and I looked away, embarrassed, knowing her exaggerated pleasure was not feigned. I drank my own thoughtfully, waiting to follow whatever lead she gave me. "I am so glad to have tea," she said, after she had drained the first cup, "not just for myself but to offer guests." I expected some reference to the Earl enjoying her hospitality but then she said, "I shall be able to entertain Mr Roger when he comes and that will be such a pleasure." I felt it safe to ask who Mr Roger was, and so I did. "My landlord," she said, "though of course he only administers the Earl's estate. It is the Earl who is really my landlord." "Does Mr Roger come here himself?" I asked. "Oh yes, on behalf of the Earl. He is a very kind young man, very well brought up. He went to preparatory school – to Lyme House and then St Bees. A most charming young man. I am quite resolved when

I am married to do something for him. Quite what, I don't know. I shall have to discuss it with the Earl."

The ritual of pouring and exclaiming over the second cup of tea gave me time to cover my confusion. As so often in life, I needed a guide to my companion's autobiography – I wanted someone to hand who could elucidate the finer points of her dialogue. What bothered me most was whether this Roger existed or whether he was yet another figment of Miss Cowdie's imagination, part of that rich tapestry she had embroidered in her madness. I realised I did not even know whether there was in fact a real Earl of Cumberland, upon whom Miss Cowdie had fortuitously alighted to console herself, or whether the whole title was a charade. This happens, of course, with everyone – how often have I wanted explained who someone is talking about and been unable to ask because my knowledge of them has been presumed – but with unbalanced people the problem is much more acute and direct interruption and inquiry not always the best method.

"He isn't handsome like the Earl," Miss Cowdie was saying, "he isn't tall, you know, and I do think height matters in a man – the Earl is very tall – and he has a moustache, which I have never liked in a man, and he is not always very tidy in his dress, but he has a pleasant face and a beautiful speaking voice. And he is so kind, so well mannered. He never fails to ask after my health and is most solicitous. I am quite surprised he is not married at thirty. Of course, for a man, thirty is nothing, whereas for a woman it is a considerable age. If one is not married by thirty then the chances are much less." She nodded her head significantly, as though to emphasise that she herself was well under thirty, and I found myself once again trying to work out her actual age. It was difficult. Her clothes and generally unkempt appearance aged her, most probably, and the rough life she led, standing for hours at that crossroads in rain and hail, had coarsened her face to make it look more ancient than it was. The lines on her forehead and around her eyes were deeply etched but there were not many of them. I estimated she was in her early forties, though I had at first assumed she was nearer sixty.

"But is marriage so important?" I asked her, wanting to say something in reply, wanting to please her by having a real conversation over the teacups. "Oh *yes*," she said, shocked, putting down her cup for the first time with quite a bang. "Oh indeed, *yes*. Why, a woman who has never been a bride has never known what it is to be a woman." She clasped her hands together and turned her head away from me and raised her closed eyes to the ceiling in an attitude of prayer. "When a man asks a woman for her hand in marriage the happiness she feels is almost insupportable – to be so loved, to be so honoured . . ." Her voice trailed off, choked with emotion. I said nothing at all, fearing to precipitate another breakdown. She seemed to come out of her reverie quite quickly and to have a new sharpness about her. "Now," she said, decisively, "let us finish this tea. Not a drop must be wasted." Obediently, I pushed my cup forwards and as I did so there swam into my head a vision of the last time I had drunk tea I did not want and been told marriage was a woman's destiny. Nothing could have been more different than the surroundings in Mrs Matlock's sitting room but her convictions were now being echoed by Miss Cowdie and my unspoken resentment grew in the same way.

"May I ask your name?" Miss Cowdie said. She was sitting up ramrod straight, the teacup held ever ready an inch or so from her lips. Her smile was very bright and yet false.

"Alexandra Grove," I said, and growing bold, "may I ask yours?"

"Elfrida Cowdie," she said, "but of course only until tomorrow, and then I shall change it forever. You have never married, yourself?"

"No," I said.

"Alas," Miss Cowdie said, sighing heavily, "we cannot all be blessed. And there is time still – you are very young and beautiful."

"I am over thirty," I said, wickedly, "the fatal age, the point of no return, as I understood you to say a few moments ago."

My levity was a mistake. She clutched her throat and looked distressed, so I added, "But I really do not want to marry. I am happy alone."

She looked at me slyly and said, "With your love-child?" I suppose my deep blush made me look guilty. "My sister's son," I said. "I am Casper's guardian. His parents were killed in a plane crash in September."

"How sad. The poor child. And now you will dedicate your life to him and find solace in motherhood."

"No, I won't," I said, getting up. "I'll provide a home for him for several years and then he will make his own way. I have things to do, Miss Cowdie – I must go. Do come and visit me – any time. I should like to give you a cup of tea in my own cottage."

"That is kind," she said, also rising. "I have things to do too. Thank you for the tea – it was most delicious," and she extended her hand graciously for me to shake. It felt dry and rough and I was glad to release it.

Eileen, the next morning she came, was glad to illuminate the darker mysteries of Miss Cowdie's saga. "She means Roger Markham," Eileen said, lips set even more fiercely than usual in a grim line of disapproval. "He's the Earl of Cumberland's factor."

"So there really is an Earl?"

"Oh ay, there's an Earl all right, but *she's* never seen him, never set eyes on him."

"Then why has she chosen him to be her bridegroom?"

"The fellow that jilted her, like, he was a guest at the Earl's house once – there's summat in the connection, anyways – and when she got stood up she just seemed to switch to the Earl. Daft."

"But this Roger visits her?"

"He comes for the rent. The Earl's the landlord for most folks round here. Most of them are only tenant farmers."

"Does Miss Cowdie pay her rent?"

"Not for a twelvemonth, so Roger says. The Earl lets her stay out of charity, likely. He doesn't want that hovel anyway, and there's no land till it."

"If she can't pay her rent, how can she pay her bills?"

"Can't. Electricity cut off long ago. Isn't any others."

"I've seen lights on."

"Paraffin lamps."

"How does she pay for paraffin?"

"Begs it."

"Who from?"

"Us. Turnbulls, over the hill."

"And do you give it to her?"

"Mam does. Geoff and I don't, and Dad doesn't. He'd play war with Mam if he found her giving it. Just encourages her, he says."

"Hasn't she a pension?"

"What for? She isn't old. Isn't a widow."

"From her work – "

"What work? She niver worked that anyone knows of."

"Social Security, then."

"She won't have anything to do with it. Says the Earl is coming for her in the morning – she only begs for the day then makes it last."

"What does she eat?"

"Scraps. Berries – she picks all sorts of queer things, seems to know what she's doing, anyways. Hasn't poisoned herself yet. She sells things to folk around here – bits of furniture and that – and it keeps her going. She had plenty till a year ago and then it ran out, likely. Used to be well off, Dad says, had a tidy bit put by, probably."

"Poor thing. What a life," I said, depressed by Eileen's bleak recital. "What will happen if she falls ill?"

"They'll cart her off to Garlands in Carlisle. Where she belongs."

"Is that a mental hospital?"

"Loony bin," Eileen agreed, smirking.

"Hasn't she ever had any treatment?"

"No. Won't let a doctor near her and she doesn't harm anyone so nobody can do owt. Doesn't interfere with anyone, does nothing wrong. Couldn't tell she was potty unless you knew. Doesn't do anything mad, like, except stand at them crossroads."

I thought briefly of the rabbit and the sheep's head – at all costs I resolved to keep those events from Eileen or anyone else. Both pathetic incidents were quite enough to get Miss Cowdie suspected of carrying her madness into a more positively mischievous stage, and to convince others she must be put away. I slightly regretted having asked Eileen all this but Sunday had passed in such endless idle speculation on my part that I could not bear not to have my curiosity satisfied. But in doing so I felt I had lost face with Eileen – I had reduced myself to her level, and shown myself no different from anyone else, whereas the whole basis of the relationship I was trying to build rested on Eileen thinking I *was* different.

"Mr Roger'll come today," Eileen said. "He'll come in his jeep, you'll see him go past after dinner. Has his dinner at the pub and then comes on up."

"She says he's nice to her."

"He's nice to anything in a skirt," Eileen said sourly, "even an old bag like her. All smiles, he is. Fancies hisself. And he's nothing, just jumped up farming folk with big ideas. Went to a swanky school an' all. My mam were at village school with his mam."

"Miss Cowdie is surprised he isn't married."

"Married? Oh no, he'll not marry when he can get what he wants easy enough. Got plenty in the family way round here, but he always gets out of being married. No flies on him. Our Geoff had a fight wi' him, one time. Knocked him out, flat on his back like a pancake."

"What about?" I reflected I was indulging in shameless gossip and that it was too late to stop. God knows, there was little enough spice in our daily life for me to be able to rise above it.

"A girl, of course. Madge Williams. Geoff fancied her before Mildred but Roger got in first and she fell for a baby. Wouldn't marry her. Said he knew for a fact she'd been with three others and one of them was our Geoff. Geoff told him to shut his filthy mouth and Roger said he was sorry, he hadn't known our Geoff couldn't get it up. Geoff murdered him nearly. Blood everywhere – had three stitches in corner of his mouth. Said he'd sue, but he never did."

Eileen paused, quite exhausted by the excessive length of her story. She was washing clothes for me at the sink and was up to her elbows in soap suds. I had wanted to laugh at the absurd image of Geoff stoutly defending his manhood but I had not dared – Eileen spoke with such pride, terse though she was. I could not wait to get a glimpse of the swaggering Mr Roger Markham.

As I might have guessed, that gentleman did not bear the least resemblence to Eileen's portrait. I had imagined a loud-mouthed Hurray Harry, complete with florid complexion and heavy jowls, but Roger Markham, when he passed by the open door of the barn where I was working that afternoon, could not have been more different. He was in fact rather small (as Miss Cowdie had said) and slight, and it was easy to see how one of Geoff's great fists could have smashed his face to bits and felled him to the ground – an unfair contest, if ever there was one. His moustache, which I had thought would be of the bristling military type, was rather sweet and poetic and though (like Miss Cowdie) I dislike moustaches, there was something appealing about it. That was it, of course – Roger Markham had great appeal altogether. One could not admire his body, as one could Geoff Crosthwaite's, one could not be attracted by his sensual quality, as one could be by David Garibaldi's, but he had a much more subtle attraction, which was hard to analyse. A certain diffidence about his walk – I saw him from a hundred yards away, as I was bound to see anyone who walked up the track after they had left their car – a shyness about his smile, a general pleasantness in his demeanour, and, most captivating of all, a smile far too warm and radiant for a man. (Horrid to fall into such a sexist cliché, but the thought sprang naturally to mind.)

He stopped in front of the open door, where I was on my knees, carefully washing out the inside of the cooling chamber in the kiln. "Good afternoon," he said, nodding and smiling. I liked the way he then squatted down to my level, in an unaffected manner, and said, "I know nothing about pottery. What's that you're cleaning?" I gave him a little lecture on the process of firing pots, watching all the time for those tell-tale signs of polite boredom which usually afflict those who ask that kind of question. There were none of them. He asked further intelligent questions and seemed genuinely interested. "Well," he said after ten minutes of this, "I must get on. I wish you luck with your venture."

"You're going to see Miss Cowdie, aren't you?" I said.

"Yes." He seemed surprised that I knew, though he must have been perfectly aware of how everyone knew everything in this part of the world within days of arriving there.

"She talked about you yesterday to me."

"She did?" He was clearly astonished. "I can hardly believe it. I mean, the poor old soul doesn't talk to anyone. She shuts herself in and won't have anything to do with anyone. How did she come to talk to you?"

"Oh, it's too long to explain," I said, "but I am her neighbour now, and I got tired of how she seemed to hate me for no reason, so I made an effort and finally she became quite friendly."

"Well, that's marvellous," he said, "perhaps you can do her a lot of good, if she comes to trust you. Howard will be very pleased – we might make some progress, get her out of that dump into somewhere better, or at least get her to let us modernise it."

"Howard is your employer?"

"Yes. The Earl of Cumberland. He farms most of his land himself and I help look after – "

"Yes, I know," I interrupted. "Eileen Crosthwaite helps me and she filled me in."

He made a face that was difficult to interpret – it could have meant, "you can't have heard anything good", or, "don't tell me any more", or even simpler, "I can't bear that girl."

"Look," he said, glancing at his wrist-watch, "I don't like to think of the gossip you've heard – I'd rather we started from scratch. I'd like to talk to you about Miss Cowdie when I've been up to see her – could you spare the time to come and have a chat and a sandwich or something, down at Parkend? We should just catch the end of their lunch hour."

"You've had your lunch at the Oddfellows Arms in Caldbeck," I said, teasingly. "Eileen said you always do, before you come up."

He blushed slightly. "Well Eileen's wrong," he said, "today I didn't. Will you come, in about half an hour?"

Should I have said no? Eileen would see me go. She would tell Geoff, if he did not pass us anyway on his tractor. Geoff would be furious. There was no reason whatsoever why I should care what Geoff thought, except I would feel mean because I had not gone out with him. How complicated this open country life was becoming – and yet I said yes to Roger because I wanted to and did not care who knew it. He struck me as the first civilised person I had come across since I had left London and I could not bring myself to forgo the sheer pleasure of his company. He had treated me as an interesting person and not, like Geoff, a sex symbol, or, like David, a challenge. I felt relaxed in his presence, unworried by either excitement or irritation. And we had something specific to discuss, there was a point to our meeting.

He went off further up the track to Miss Cowdie's, and I hurried inside to clean myself up a little. I am not a vain person but it seemed to me unnecessarily rude to go anywhere in my very stained and old work clothes. I went past Eileen, who of course had observed everything, and without a word took the steps two at a time to my bedroom, thankful that at last Casper was safely at school and I no longer had to run the gauntlet of his scorn too. I changed into clean trousers and I will admit took some time deciding which colour sweater suited me best, the vivid scarlet or the dark green. I chose the green. I brushed my hair and tied it up and then went back downstairs.

"I'm going out," I said to Eileen, still slumped over the sink – oh, how I longed to push her aside and do the whole thing in two minutes. "I won't be long, but if you get those clothes out before I get back you can go."

Eileen was quite silent. I wondered whether to volunteer the information that I was going to Parkend with Roger Markham to discuss Miss Cowdie but then I thought, why the hell should I? It would only sound like a justification and there was no need for that. Eileen and everyone else must learn that I did what I wanted to do and was beholden to no one.

Out I went, back to the barn, where I donned a large rubber apron I kept for the messy job of shifting clay, and got back to work on the kiln. I wanted to keep myself occupied, to seem busy and not obviously hanging about for Roger. It was absurd how much I was looking forward to the little event – I was quite ashamed of my anticipation. I felt so pleased when I saw him running down the hill – he had been a little longer than his estimated half an hour – and took my apron off quickly. "Sorry," he said, breathless, "took longer than I thought – let's go." We walked down to his jeep, parked where the track turned to mud, and got in. I did not dare look towards Eileen, still at the window as we passed, and tensed as we bumped slowly down to the road, my eyes searching fell-side and fields for any sign of Geoff Crosthwaite's approaching tractor. Only when we had safely passed Greenhead and turned onto the road that joined the Uldale one did I begin to enjoy myself. The ridiculous feeling of being watched and judged passed – an almost physical sensation of freedom as we came out of the fells and withdrew from their power. The land now was open, the horizons distant, and though there was no sun there was a brightness in the air which lightened the sombre colours of the surrounding landscape. The whitewashed farmhouse perched on the steep road that led to Wigton beckoned us cheerfully on, and when we turned and began to drive down to Parkend the distant trees gave a lushness to the grey sky behind. By the time we parked in front of the restaurant, all fear of swift retribution for this indulgence had left me, and I had convinced myself I had merely imagined the feelings of guilt and foreboding which had gripped me in the shadows of Lowther Fell. It was something atmospheric, I told myself as I followed Roger into the bar, and I must watch it.

Eleven

We sat outside, obviously thought of as quite mad by the people who ran the place, and had soup and paté and some delicious hot fruit pie. We sat side by side on a garden bench, looking at the restaurant garden, which had a look about it of having been reclaimed quite recently from the wilderness, and beyond that to the fells from which we had just escaped. From that distance they looked so soft and gentle that the very idea of needing to escape from them seemed absurd – how inviting they seemed, how friendly and even pretty in the weak afternoon sun. I could not imagine why I had felt such immense relief on leaving them behind.

Roger talked at length about Miss Cowdie and I listened, shooting occasional curious glances at the tiny scar in the corner of his mouth. Eileen must surely be right about the injury, at any rate. He said Miss Cowdie was a great worry to him and that he felt guilty every time he left her on her own. Each quarter, when he returned for the rent, he half expected to find a corpse. He said he had discussed with the various local authorities the matter of Miss Cowdie being eligible for some sort of social security payment but it had been explained to him that so long as she refused to sign any kind of form – and she emphatically did – then nothing could be done. Howard (the Earl) was not in the least bothered about any rent – it was a minute amount anyway – and sent him to collect it more to keep up contact with Miss Cowdie than anything else. She was (as she had told me) fond of him. Naturally, I asked him, as I had asked Eileen, what exactly had happened, but he was not really much wiser, telling the same basic story as Eileen, with only a few more details. He knew, for example, that Miss Cowdie was originally from Gloucester and had come north when the man she was engaged to had come to farm, the other side of Bassenthwaite. His name was Armstrong and he had inherited the farm from his grandfather. It was this grandfather who had known the Earl's family and through that connection the grandson and his fiancée (Miss Cowdie) had been, once only, to Hithop Hall, the Earl's country seat. The present Earl, Howard, had never met them. He was in France at the time and, as far as he knew, his mother had given Armstrong and his fiancée tea, and that was that. There had been an invitation to the wedding, which had been declined, and it was with some astonishment that the family had heard, not long afterwards, that not only had the wedding not taken place but that somehow Miss Cowdie had transferred her affections to the young Earl, who was quite in ignorance of her. It was surmised that the confusion had arisen because the Earl was also married the day Miss Cowdie was jilted. She had known of this other wedding – it had been the ostensible and perfectly natural excuse for the family declining her invitation – and it was supposed that, in her crazed state, she had substituted Howard for her real fiancé, as a direct compensation.

I asked Roger if he knew what had happened to Mr Armstrong but he didn't. He had disappeared and was thought to have married someone else. The farm had been sold. He had never been seen in these parts again. I asked if he knew the circumstances of the abortive wedding day – had Miss Cowdie ever reached the church? Had many people witnessed her humiliation? – but he knew nothing. He did not know if she had any family, back in Gloucester. She had arrived on her own and stayed on her own and was not known to have any human contact. I asked, cautiously, if she had ever shown any other signs of madness, apart from proclaiming constantly that she was going to marry the Earl of Cumberland next day, and going to wait at the crossroads in all weathers for him. He said no, and then corrected himself. She had occasionally, particularly over the last few years, taken an intense dislike to various women in the area – was known to have spat and cursed them in a way totally at variance with her real character. And she had fixed on other men as the Earl. But since everyone round about knew her and her history, no harm was done. Her jealousy towards her female victims soon vanished, and her fixation with the masculine ones passed as soon as they were able to establish their identity. Almost everyone round about had had their turn in her fantasies and were, to varying degrees, amused by it. Nobody was frightened of her.

I broke in to say nobody accepted her as in any way a communal responsibility either. Roger laughed out loud and said I must have a funny idea of what communities up here meant. He expounded the local philosophy of minding your own business at some length and resolutely defended it against my scornful attack. When I went on to say that what struck me as the most pathetic part about Miss Cowdie's story was the underlying assumption that unless a woman was married she was nothing, he was silent and thoughtful. "It was the shame that drove her insane," I finished, "I'm sure of it – she thought her life was over if she couldn't marry, and from what I've seen around here she wasn't far wrong. Women have no real place in this society. They're still chattels to the men up here – the ordinary women, I mean. No wonder Miss Cowdie couldn't face an existence, unmarried. All any girl ever thinks about here is getting married. They have no opportunities for anything else if they stay. The whole of this countryside" – and I waved my hand to include the fells – "is full of lonely cottages and farmhouses with women slaving away and thinking nothing of it. Look at Eileen Crosthwaite – "

"I'd rather not," Roger interrupted.

"Why? She's a perfect example of what I mean."

"She isn't typical. There are lots of perfectly happy girls around, nothing like Eileen. She's always been like that. It comes from being illegitimate."

"What? Eileen?"

"Her mother had her before she married John Crosthwaite. She was at school with my mother, so I know. She was only sixteen, didn't marry John till she was eighteen. He took the child as his own, but everyone knew. It was good of him, but he's a good man. But Eileen was always odd–sulky little thing–and she hated Geoff from the day he was born. You can't count Eileen. I could show you scores of other girls quite happy with what you think of as a dreadful lot. I don't see anything wrong in them wanting to marry. I expect a girl to want to marry. It wouldn't be natural if she didn't."

"My God," I said, showing my exasperation, "and I thought you were civilised."

"I like things as they are," he said, perfectly serious. "I don't want the old order changed."

"Well of course not – you're a man – it's to your advantage to keep the *status quo*."

We had finished our lunch long ago and had our coffee cups refilled twice. I had my jacket zipped up and the collar turned up and my hands thrust in my pockets – it really was far too cold to sit outside but I was not going to say so, showing myself as soft, when Roger was sitting there without a shiver, wearing only a shirt and a much darned pullover. I had rapidly reversed my original opinion of him and was in the process of damning him as, after all, a boring little man, who couldn't see further than the end of his nose. I suppose I glared at him, and frowned, and showed my contempt for his trite observations, and thoroughly unattractive I must have looked, but he did not appear in the least discomforted. He smiled, as pleasantly as ever, and said, "We'll see how you make out with your woman's liberation ideas. They won't go down well up here."

"I couldn't care less,' I said swiftly. "I'm answerable to nobody but myself. I'm no Eileen Crosthwaite, you know."

"I can see that."

"And I'm not looking to trap any man into marriage, like all the girls I hear you run away from. I don't see you in any way as a catch, so you needn't think I do. Men to me are just people. I have no designs for them."

"I'm sure you haven't," he said, quietly, "and I don't run away from girls, I run towards them. I like them. I actually want to find one to marry because, unlike you, I believe in marriage. I believe in finding one woman to love and cherish, to share a home with and have children by. I'll work hard to look after her and she'll work hard to look after me."

"How perfectly disgusting," I said, rudely.

"Some girl won't think so."

"Sir Galahad himself. Except I'm told you aren't quite the Knight Errant at all – I'm told you behave in a distinctly unknightly way to damsels in distress – distressed by you."

It was very petty and vulgar of me to resort to such a cheap jibe and I was instantly ashamed, but Roger just laughed and was not at all offended. "At least," he said, "you're not quite the cat who walks by herself, if you relish such gossip. It doesn't really fit in with the image you like to project."

"I don't try to project any image," I said.

"Not much – tucking yourself away up there with that child, having nothing to do with anyone, denying yourself even a telephone or a television, and talking about opening a pottery – isn't all that projecting an image?"

"It's doing what I want to do. I can't help what it looks like."

"It looks bloody silly," he said aggressively.

"It's none of your business – "

"I have a sense of communal responsibility."

"Touché," I said, sarcastically.

"No, I have," he said, "I honestly have. I'm that sort of person – "

"You worry about the old, the mad and the sick."

"I worry about the solitary. Man, woman too, was never meant to be solitary."

"Rubbish. I've always been solitary."

He toyed with his empty coffee cup and seemed to hesitate. Already, he looked quite different to me because of the things he had said – the smile was less engaging, the poetic moustache more threatening, as though it might hide a cruel mouth, and his whole outline seemed harder and sharper. "In fact," he said slowly, "I've heard you've been seen around here before, years ago, and that you were not solitary then." A distinct shock travelled from my brain to my stomach and I shivered, hiding my confusion in the cold I felt. "It's freezing," I said, standing up, "I must go." He stayed sitting. "They say there was a schoolmaster at Keswick Grammar School and that you were never seen without him. They say you walked the fells with him and sailed and you were inseparable. They say you hung on his every word. You were recognised, you see, right from the beginning. People up here have very long memories and they notice every little thing."

"I have never been in Caldbeck in my life until six weeks ago," I said. My voice sounded hoarse and strained. "I wasn't talking about Caldbeck," he said, "by 'round here' I mean an area of twenty miles. People travel about, you know, there's quite a close contact between villages that way. They have cousins and aunts and uncles all over the place and all sorts of interesting little histories get filed away. The least breath of scandal and someone always knows and remembers and can bring it out years after. You can't hide anything up here. It was around Skiddaw you were known – often there, they say, parking your car at Ormathwaite or Threlkeld or Dodd Wood – it was often seen, and you noted. I gather you haven't changed much – still beautiful and haughty. But they wonder what happened to the man? He left under some sort of cloud, they say, never seen in these parts again. They wonder if you've come back to look for him. They wonder if you're hiding from him. They wonder why you've come back at all like this, with that boy. How old is he? Thirteen, they say . . ."

I had begun to walk away, across the crunchy gravel to the wrought iron gate that led out onto the road. Panic surged through me, making my heart knock against my ribs and my head sing and mouth go dry. It was foolish to run away from Roger Markham but I had not been able to control my instinctive urge to run, even though I knew it would amount to a fatal mistake. But it had been so unexpected – one moment we had been chatting in an entirely sympathetic way about Miss Cowdie and her problems and then, without warning, we had moved into an area of conflict which had ended in this devastating recital of my past life. I could hardly believe he could know so much. He had begun so quietly, lazily, as though he was merely going to give me an amusing lecture on communications in Cumbria and I had been lulled into a false sense of detachment by his pleasant manner, yet all the time he had been planning to unload this vicious résumé of my affair with Edward. It was hard for me to credit that anyone had ever remarked upon us in the first place, never mind that they had remembered us so long. Surely nobody ever had seen us – my memories were of utterly empty bleak landscapes with a solitary walker a great event. We had never gone onto the crowded slopes of Skiddaw itself – we had always gone far into the interior of those fells, to the lonely wastes of Mungrisdale Common and the sharp sides of Great Calva. We had followed streams to their source – Roughten Gill and Sinen Gill and Salehow Beck – and never seen a soul. We had lain on Sale How above Skiddaw House and, looking down on the winding course of the river Caldew, we had been unable to see anything move at all. Nobody could have seen us. Nobody could have known who we were. We spoke to nobody, avoided even the occasional shepherd. And there were no habitations in the places we parked our car – we always drove as far as we could and then pulled onto the side of the track. Who knew us? Who had seen and speculated?

"Hey," Roger said, catching me at the bridge and walking beside me, "don't run off. I just thought you needed teased –"

"Teased?" I said, stopping abruptly.

"Yes – I thought you'd enjoy hearing what the locals say about you. You mustn't take such a lot of old tripe so seriously. They all make up the most amazing things – starts in the pub or the shop and goes on from there. I don't suppose they know you from Adam – Eve, then. You just have to get used to it, they have to fill the time in somehow and you're pretty good copy, you must admit. I can't imagine why you're so upset – unless they've accidentally hit the nail on the head?"

There was no mistaking the question mark in his voice, but I seemed incapable of answering – it was beyond my comprehension that he had not been serious. My brain worked sluggishly – I stood stupidly looking at him, trying desperately to work out all the ramifications of what he had said. So many of the details had been true – Edward had indeed been a teacher at Keswick School, we had certainly walked in the Skiddaw area – that I could not now believe Roger had told me so much, thinking it was only idle gossip. And now that he sought confirmation that it was, I was unsure again – was this a challenge, was it another trick? I was afraid to reply. I cleared my throat.

"I did know a master at Keswick school once," I said, "but I can't remember his name now. I spent a summer up here with my family when I was eighteen – we met then, and and I stayed on for a while. I can't credit we made any sort of impression on anyone – it was so long ago, and such a short period of time really. It seems extraordinary."

"There's usually a grain or two of truth in everything they get hold of," Roger said. I thought he sounded cautious. "Anyway, I wouldn't worry about it – just let them have their fun. It's harmless. Look, let me run you home – I'm going that way."

"Nobody goes that way," I said, flatly, "that's why I chose it. It's a dead end."

"I meant I'm going along the Uldale road –"

"I'll walk. I want to. Thank you for the lunch."

"We must do it again sometime properly. I hope I didn't upset you with my joking – I mean, all the anti-women's lib stuff. I'm not really a reactionary male chauvinist pig – you sort of provoked me, somehow." He smiled very nicely as he finished.

"I'll turn off here,' I said.

He tooted his horn at me a few minutes later, as he passed in his jeep. I was some distance from the road, cutting up the path that led along the front of Greenrigg and joined the Greenhead road later on. It was rough common ground, full of hidden holes, and I had to concentrate on my feet, so I had an excuse for my abstracted wave. But I watched his jeep all along the high, flat-looking unfenced road that led to Uldale, and wondered about his sincerity. He was smarter, more devious, than he had appeared. First impressions of general niceness had given way to suspicion. I did not know if I liked him or not, and I was dissapointed at the way things had turned out. I felt I had been made a fool of – in I had rushed to change my clothes at the suggestion of an outing with him, and off I had gone, as delighted as a child on a treat. He must have laughed at my eagerness. Then I had thought he was a kindred spirit – somebody, at last, to talk to – and it was annoying to have been so mistaken. I found myself passionately hoping that Eileen had gone, so that I would not have to hide my mortification. If she was there, I would have to put on some sort of convincingly debonair front – all smiles and jollity and yes, what a lovely time I had had. I feared Eileen's steady stare, that was perhaps capable of seeing through any subterfuge. I slowed down, trudging along without looking about me, and thinking what a waste it was not to have Rufus – I had left so quickly I had forgotten about him. Now that Casper was at school, taking Rufus for walks would be part of my responsibility too. Casper would come back tired after his long bike ride and be glad I had already taken Rufus for a walk, relieving him of the necessity.

I wondered, as I walked along over the rough grass, how Casper would survive a daily bike ride of four miles there, four miles back, throughout the winter. We had kitted him out in waterproof gear but, even so, he would often get soaked. But he was remarkably keen to do it, even though there were a great many steep hills between our cottage and Nelson Tomlinson School in Wigton. It was a gruelling ride. We had bought an old second-hand bike for me, and I had done a test ride with him to make sure it was feasible, and I must say I was exhausted before we were half way there. Of course, my ancient Hercules had no gears, whereas Casper's sparkling new Raleigh had ten, or something absurd, and that made quite a difference. He shot ahead of me and seemed to find it all effortless, but then we were in no hurry and it was the middle of a sunny day, and I thought things might be very different on cold, dark, wet days after school. Still, he was game and I must not discourage him, especially since the only alternative – going onto the top Faulds road and waiting for the minibus, which went round several villages – would be a nuisance. I had wanted to encourage independence and cycling was the independent way.

I heard Rufus's far-off barking before I had left the hard-core road for the track, and stopped for a moment in surprise, trying to remember where I had left him. Surely I had not shut him up? Casper had said he need never be shut up – he was much too obedient and trustworthy to go outside the bounds of the immediate fellside. Coming back from anywhere at all, Casper liked to get out of the car and whistle and wait for Rufus to bound out and meet him. No, I had no memory of shutting Rufus in and yet, as I hurried up the track, I could tell the noise came from inside. Eileen must have shut him in the outhouse before she left, not understanding that he could be left to roam. The dog sounded desperate – the barking was high pitched and frenzied – and I ran the last few yards to the newly painted door of what had been an old stable.

Rufus was in an appalling state, covered in lather and foaming at the mouth. He jumped up on me, paws on my shoulders, and whined and panted and then collapsed onto the ground, where he lay on his side, utterly exhausted, his sides heaving and his eyes almost colourless. I had not the slightest idea what to do, but I was glad that Casper, who would have known, was not there to be distressed by his friend's pitiful state. I knelt down and patted him and muttered vague words of comfort, and when he seemed a little easier I searched around the outhouse for his blanket and covered him with it and filled an old tin plate with water from the outside tap and gave him a drink. In a remarkably short time he seemed to recover completely – got up, shook his tail, licked my hand and trotted round the garden, sniffing anything interesting.

I went into the cottage, convinced it must have been the experience of being shut in that had alarmed the stupid dog, but it seemed an extravagant reaction. I think I was a little nervous that I might find an intruder had broken in and that this was the cause of Rufus's hysteria and I tried the door cautiously – it was still locked – and then peered through the window. Everything looked perfectly all right. I took the key out of my pocket and went in, eyes darting to right and left, and then I went upstairs and took a quick look there. Nothing had been disturbed. No gruesome visiting cards lay around to frighten me. Relieved, I went back downstairs and put the kettle on to make some more coffee, before I returned to the barn to continue my preparations for work. Eileen had pegged the clothes out at the back and I looked out on them blowing in the slight wind which had sprung up in the last hour. It was centuries since I had seen clothes hanging on a line to dry. We used to have a cleaning lady who put them out in Oxford during my childhood but then, once I left home, I used laundries and launderettes with their drying machines and such humble sights passed me by. It was strangely soothing to watch, the white billowing sheets filling with wind and arching out in huge bows, only to fade to limp rags as the air escaped.

Backwards and forwards they went, buffeted by the wind, and I found the movement hypnotic.

I put back on my old clothes and carried my coffee with me. Before I was half way to the barn – but clearly going there – Rufus dashed at me and began barking again. I cursed him for making me spill some of the hot coffee and told him to shut up and go away but he kept on with the same yelping. When I reached the closed door he suddenly stopped and crouched down, his hind legs straight but his front ones bent and his head lowered. He watched the door as a cat watches a mouse-hole and he made me nervous all over again. Suppose someone was hiding in there, the same someone who had shut Rufus up? It could be one of those prowlers Eileen was always warning me about, one of those itinerant vagrants, whose occasional thieving and violence she firmly believed in. It struck me that Rufus would not be much good as my defender if he had already been pushed into a shed and successfully locked up – indeed, fear made his fur bristle as he crouched there and I felt sure his only contribution would be to bark and then run away. Yet I could not bring myself to leave the barn alone and wait until Casper came home, or until I had sought out Geoff or John Crosthwaite. If I began to do that sort of thing, there would be no end to it. A hundred times a week I would be afraid of something or other – there were all sorts of sinister portents around my cottage. The climate, the situation, my solitary state – all were conducive to the unreasonable terror that disaster of some sort would strike.

Firmly, I pushed open the door. It swung on its hinges and crashed against the stone wall inside. There seemed to be nobody there. I said, "Silly dog," to Rufus, who still had not moved, and stepped inside, glad I had not given in to my craven instincts. In spite of the light from the new windows Mr Rigg had made – slits which looked as if they belonged to medieval battlements – it was still gloomy in there without the double doors open at the other end. The trouble was, if I had them open, the cold was so awful it numbed my fingers, but I intended, when the kiln was working, always to have them open and go backwards and forwards to it that way. I would have to learn to stand the cold, for heating the place would be absurdly expensive and impractical. I finished my coffee and put the mug down on the step and as I did so I saw on the whitewashed rim of the step a footprint, quite large and heavy. It stood out very clearly, as though traced in black paint. Hesitant again, I looked down at my shoes, the same shoes I had been wearing before I went to Parkend with Roger. Without matching the print, I knew it could not be mine, but all the same I placed my foot upon it. It was at least twice the size all round – a large man's footprint. I tried to remember Roger's shoes – I shut my eyes tight and worked downwards from his navy blue sweater to his faded grey corduroys, and then I saw his shoes, thick brogue types with leather soles. The footprint in front of me had ridges across it. I searched ahead in the semi-gloom and saw another, and then another. "Hello?" I shouted, my voice ludicrously weak. Slowly, I walked inside, holding the end of the broomstick with which I had, that morning, been sweeping out the barn. "Hello?" I shouted again, advancing further in. My voice echoed. Gaining confidence as each step showed no one there, I at last reached the big doors, unbolted them, flung them open and turned rapidly round.

The barn was still empty. Every corner of it stood clearly revealed. The packing cases stood against the wall and could conceal no one. The tools I had been using were still laid out in a neat line. The parts of the kiln I had been cleaning before assembling were still lying there, untouched. None of the glazes had been tampered with – the tops were still screwed firmly on the canisters. I stood with my hands on my hips, checking everything off, my eyes constantly searching every inch of the place and finding everything satisfactory. Rufus, at the door, still crouched and would not come, however much I called, but I was rapidly deciding the dog was mad. I took up the cloth I had been using and started polishing the round surface of the kiln. My hand, going round and round, gradually came to a halt. Seated as I was on a low stool, the line of the footprints I had been following was once more in my range of vision and I saw that they did not peter out, as I had thought – they continued, but this time were not so noticeable because the soft white dust on that side of the room – scattered from the straw in the packing cases – absorbed them. But they were there, once my eyes had got used to the change in the surface. They were there, and they went in a straight line to the foot of the open tread staircase that led to the loft. Whoever it was had hidden themselves up there. Rufus knew it. There were pieces of furniture up there – the corner cupboard, bought at such a price, which we still had not fixed, an old armchair I thought might be re-upholstered, and more packing cases and trunks and the torn dirty curtains that had been in the cottage, which I thought might do for rags in my pottery. There was plenty of junk to hide amongst, and I could no longer ignore the fact that someone was.

Slowly, I bent down and undid the laces of the heavy shoes I was wearing. I slipped them off, and the thick socks underneath too. There was always the possibility that whoever was up there was watching me and had seen what I had done and that creeping softly up the staircase, bare footed, would not surprise them, but I thought it might give me the smallest of advantages. Equally slowly, taking care not to let one tool clink against another, I took hold of a fettling knife, made from a hacksaw blade, a wicked looking instrument with a narrow but very sharp edge. I stood up, holding it firmly in my hand, and with extreme care edged my way from behind the kiln. I stole across the barn floor, the coldness of the quarry tiles pressing against my naked feet, with the hand holding the knife hidden behind my back, and when I got to the foot of the staircase I paused to listen. Outside, sheep bleated, that hoarse, rough little sound they make to each other every time they change position, and the noise was carried through the open doors by the wind, which also rattled in the roof above me. There was a very, very faint burring from the Crosthwaites' tractor – a mile away or more – and the louder rushing of the beck beyond the cottage. My ears, attuned to each disturbance in the overwhelming silence which prevailed all round, picked up no other interruptions. Cautiously, I climbed the stairs, on tip-toe, sweating with fear, and the perspiration making the handle of the knife stick to my nervous palm. I paused again, two stairs from the top. Another step and I would be able to see over the old armchair, shrouded in a blanket, and whoever was there would be able to see me. I hesitated, very afraid, wondering if perhaps I ought not to turn and go back down again and outside, and simply lock in the intruder before fetching help. Another half an hour and Casper would be home and could be despatched to the Crosthwaites' farm to telephone for the nearest police.

But yet again my unwillingness to become permanently prey to this sort of fear gave me courage to continue. I would *not* become known as a woman who could not look after herself. My foot trembled as I raised it to put it on that next step and the muscles in my arm holding the knife were taut with apprehension. It is so much easier for men. They may be as afraid in such a situation, but their greater physical strength is an unfair asset. I knew I was not strong. In any struggle I would be quite easily overpowered, knife or not. My only method of attack would have to be that of fooling any aggressor into believing I would do what in fact I suspected I was incapable of doing – sticking a knife into his guts. I intended to seem very fierce and furious, though the dryness at the back of my throat made me think not even a squeak would come forth at the right time.

I took a deep breath, gripping my knife as firmly as my wet hand would permit, and boldly raised myself to the top step, where I stood with my head held high, looking into the jumble of furniture ahead. It was dark up there, even in daylight, but the gloom was cut by a small fanlight in the far corner, which let in a thin shaft of watery sun. My pounding heart quietened and my knees began to shake with relief. There was no one at all there. A little laugh escaped me and I wiped my forehead with the back of my free hand. Leaning against the armchair, I put down the silly fettling knife and closed my eyes, feeling absurdly weak. Of course – an intruder probably had been in here – Rufus could probably smell him – but then he had rummaged through this dumping ground and left. The fact that there were no returning footprints bothered me, even though I could see nobody there, but I concluded there were some but that I had been unable to see them. It was the sort of thing that I began to realise might happen quite often – any old tramp could come off the fells and be attracted to the carefully restored barn – and I must either take greater precautions or learn to accept it philosophically. But for the moment the drama was over. I decided, while I was up there, to ferret out a pug-mill which I knew I had stored up there, together with a special plaster sink I would soon be needing, and I went over to the far corner, to the packing case I thought they were in, banging my shins as I blundered about on the corner of an old fashioned sea trunk with metal edges that had once been Edward's father's in his Indian days. How I had come to have it I did not know – it was a handsome object with brass handles and clasps, but so heavy that, even empty, it was difficult to lift, and when half filled I could not get it off the ground at all and was therefore unlikely to use it. It belonged to a bygone age when porters were plentiful and no gentleman, let alone any lady, would ever have had to reckon how he could cope with such a weight.

I knelt down on the floor and began struggling with the plywood, battened down on the top of the packing case. I needed a knife to prise open the tin tacks with which the lid had been too efficiently put on by a zealous Casper. Remembering the fettling knife I had put down on the armchair I got up to get it and as I did so a pair of hands came swiftly round my eyes. Instantly I was blind. The hands pressed hard into my eyeballs and the blackness was streaked with red and my own hands went up instinctively to meet a pair of thick, solid wrists. I did not scream, nor did I struggle. Had I *seen* my attacker I have no doubt I would have done both. Sight is always a greater shock to the system than anything else, or so I have found, and deprived of sight I was able to control my terror much more easily. I waited, almost weeping at the memory of the knife which I had so unwisely abandoned. My head was full of images, not of murder but of rape – it raced ahead to scenes of blood and I saw myself spread-eagled and mutilated on the dirty boards of the loft, while outside Rufus would uselessly bark. I stood very straight, dropping my hands to my side. I heard the tearing of material to my left and in another moment, in one quick movement, a thick band of dark cotton, torn off the edge of a musty, stained curtain, replaced the hands round my eyes. I ought to have chosen that second to move, but I was half paralysed, though not so much with fear as caution – I did not want to make a *wrong* move and concentrated all my energies on trying to think ahead. The makeshift scarf tied so tightly that it dug into my cheeks viciously, my assailant next got hold of my hands and tied them behind my back with the same rough strength. He have me a little push forward and I tottered a few steps towards the muddle of furniture, cringing in anticipation of walking slap into something hard. I came up against the post which went right through the loft onto the floor of the barn. It was a wooden post, a foot square, and held the roof up at a crucial point. As I walked into it, half knocking myself out, the man behind me turned me round and pressed me against it and I braced myself, legs apart, from what I thought would be his attack – but all that happened was that another length of cloth went round my waist, binding me to the post. There was a lot of pushing around of objects I could not see but which I could remember – the cases and boxes and odds and ends I have mentioned – and I could not think what was being done. The delay somehow gave me hope. This brute could not be a maniac – everything he had done showed more than a measure of control. He was in no hurry to do whatever he was going to do. I felt that the time had come for me to talk – to use my intelligence to stall for time. If he had wanted to overpower me at once and throw me to the ground and leap upon me there would have been nothing I could do, but this deliberate tying up suggested a mind to which I could perhaps appeal. "I don't know who you are," I said, glad to hear my voice sound cross instead of wavering, "but you would be very stupid to imagine you can get away with this." The moving around me went on. I heard a dragging movement and all at once remembered the spare mattress I had thrown at the back of the other rubbish. He was clearing a space for the mattress, and when he had made himself quite cosy, then – coldly and comfortably – he would untie me and hurl me upon it and I would be quite powerless.

Twelve

Then there was silence. The shuffling noises stopped. Whoever it was had finished their preparations. I had to press my bound hands into the wooden post, clawing at it until I broke off large splinters that stuck painfully in my nails, in order not to scream at the idea of some monstrous man standing in front of me, looking at me, plotting what he would do with me. Shivers ran up the inside of my neck and seemed to catch in my throat until I was gulping and swallowing the bile that collected all the time. Nausea turned my stomach to a shifting mass of water and, though it disgusts me to remember, waves of some horrible excitement swept through me. All resolution to speak and persuade had gone. I felt as if the rags that bound me to the post were all that held me up, that without them my slack and shuddering body would collapse. My ears, half muffled by the musty smelling material binding my eyes, strained to pick up every sound, but the moving of furniture had stopped and there was not even the shuffling of booted feet. I could not decide whether the intruder was very near me or some way off, and I waited all the time for the first approach to be made.

None came. I waited and waited, but none came. In the end, I *wanted* it to come – to get it over, to end this awful war of nerves, and yet still I was afraid to speak. The silence made me more afraid with every minute and yet, as it went on and on, my confidence grew again – whatever was going to be done would not be in the heat of the moment. There was thought here – perhaps even doubt – and I could benefit by both. But when those strong hands suddenly came together on my waist, closing upon it like a vice, the same terror surged through me as it had done in the beginning and once more I was panic-stricken. The hands moved up and down my body, feeling as a blind man feels, and now I heard rasping breathing, half like sobbing, and I began to lose all control as this madman's growing frenzy passed itself on to me. The hands were everywhere – on my neck, pushing my sweater down, on my arms, pushing the sleeves up, on my trousers, forcing the waistband open, on my face, in my hair, stroking and squeezing, taking my flesh between iron fingers, crawling everywhere like an invasive insect, until every tiny corner of me felt possessed, and all the time I struggled and turned this way and that, arching my neck, pulling myself away from the post and all the time anticipating the breaking of the bands that held me and the sickening smack with which I would be thrown on the ground. There was no doubt at all in my mind that I would be brutally assaulted – that the harder I fought, the more I goaded my attacker into a more brutal rape – and yet all my former intentions to keep still and use my brains had left me. "Keep your head," they tell women in those absurd articles on how to defend yourself against an attacker – but how? Do they know, those writers, what if feels like to be tied up and molested? Do they imagine anything so puny as a head can be kept in order, while below a body is ravished? I might as well have had no head, no brain at all – I was not aware of anything except a series of violent physical sensations, against which all reason was powerless. And I began to cry, helplessly, and to say, "No – please – no," over and over again. Rage left me, and in its place came an unbearable distress. I stopped struggling. I bowed my head and wept. The small, broken voice that came out of me was not my own. "Please," it whispered, "oh please – no – please." The hand slowed down. I felt the fingers touching my wet cheeks, slowly tracing patterns on my face. They slowed down entirely, they came to rest on my breasts and stopped, and then they were removed and when they returned they patted me, awkwardly. I had no difficulty redoubling my crying. Relief, a secret, triumphant recognition that pity was my assailant's undoing, made me sob even more heartbrokenly, and my cries became the mewings of the weakest kitten. I let myself hang drunkenly from my bonds and after a moment or two of suspense, so strong it felt tangible – thick and solid in the air around me – I heard footsteps retreating. The hands came no more. I cried all the harder, wildly, convulsed with sobs, and above my own wailing I heard the stairs being descended. I heard the barn door creak, and then Rufus's insane barking.

And now I struggled frantically, twisting and turning against the post, pulling at the cotton band until my wrists were bleeding with the friction, and still I could not untie myself. Any moment that creature might return – I by no means thought of my escape as permanent – and unless I had my hands free I would be as helpless as before, and inevitably less lucky. "Rufus!" I shouted. "Rufus! Come on! Good boy! Rufus – oh you bloody dog, *come on*." I shouted this over and over again until at last the wretched animal overcame his fear – or saw the attacker go – and came bounding up to me, licking me and whining. "Down Rufus." I said. "Down, down. Look, boy, look," and I pulled myself round on the post to the furthest limit I could go and showed him where I was tied. He was a stupid dog. I wanted him to bite through the material but all he did was bark excitedly and rush round and round the post. "Up Rufus," I said, thinking that all I could get him to do would be to scrape all the post with his claws, which were quite sharp. "Up, up." He jumped obediently but every swipe at the rope of material that held me was accidental – the dog did not have the slightest idea what I wanted him to do. It took a long time, hit and miss, over and over again, until by good luck a strand of material caught in his claws and he pulled to unloosen it and the material came away with the almighty tug he gave it.

At once I pulled off my blindfold and looked about me quickly. I knew the intruder had gone but I wanted the reassurance of seeing this was true. And then, though I wanted to run into the cottage and shut myself in, I collapsed on the ground. I put my head on my knees and locked my arms round them and stayed crouching for an age, and then I stretched out, aching and weak, and lay quite still, listening to my own still frantic heartbeat. I could hardly get to my feet. I stumbled eventually down the stairs, clinging to the rail, and out I staggered into the garden, blinded, though the fading afternoon light was dim. I took great, deep breaths of air, cold and sharp and cleansing, and then I went into the cottage, sick and shaking, and tried to think what I should do. I could call the police. Which police? I had no idea, but there must be someone to call. And what would I say? That I had been assaulted in my own home by some unknown person, who had tied me up and then left me? There were footprints, perhaps fingerprints, perhaps other clues I knew nothing about. But I would have to endure endless questions and at the end of it all nothing would be achieved. Nothing could compensate for the dreadful experience. I did not believe my assailant could be caught and even if he could I did not want to see him.

Calming down was hard. I ran a deep hot bath and lay in it for half an hour, soaking my injured wrists and covering my eyes with wet pads of cotton wool. I could not bring myself, when I got out, to dry myself properly – I could not bear to touch myself in any way, so appalled did I still feel at the memory of those fingers crawling round my body, and so I huddled in a big towel, wrapping it round and round myself protectively, until the damp was absorbed. I made strong coffee and drank some brandy and still I felt terribly ill. The need to spill out all that had happened to me pressed inside me until I wanted to run outside and yell at the sheep, simply to release the horror. I had no one to whom I could turn. I thought of the Crosthwaites, the only possible confidants, and shrank from disclosing such an attack to them. I could not tell Casper when he came – it would embarrass and frighten him. There was no father or mother or sister or lover to flee to and be comforted and sustained by, and as the truth of this came to me I saw for the first time the full penalties of being a woman on my own. I needed a protector and I had none. I needed a shoulder to weep upon and had carefully removed myself from all those who might offer it. I tried to control my self-pity but only managed to do so by imagining how much worse my situation could have been, and that only terrified me more. I could be dead, I could be lying mutilated on the floor of the loft for Casper to discover and at that thought I gasped and started to weep all over again. I was not brave. I could not shrug off the degradation that had befallen me. I did not know how I was going to cope, how I was going to keep up even an appearance of normal behaviour.

But I did. When Casper came in – quite late, as it happened, because he had stayed behind to watch a rehearsal for the Christmas play – I managed to make him some tea, though my hand shook so much when I poured it out that half of it missed his cup. He looked slightly surprised. He stared at the small puddle on the table and said, "Are you ill?" I said I was. I said I had a headache and felt shivery and expected it was just a cold coming on. He grunted and went on stuffing himself with biscuits. I said I thought I would have to go to bed, and then I filled a hot water bottle and went upstairs and got under the blankets, the hot water bottle hugged to my chest. Below, I could hear Casper in the kitchen, opening some baked beans, his great standby when he was ravenous. He seemed cheerful, whistling as he pottered about in a tuneless way that reminded me of my father. He did not mind my retiring to bed, was probably glad of it. He had Rufus for company – Rufus, who had given him such an exaggerated welcome that day, and yet he had seen nothing remarkable in the wildly extravagant show of affection.

I thought I would never sleep but in a very short time I had fallen into so deep a sleep it resembled a coma. Casper said, the next morning, that he had knocked on my door and asked me if I wanted a hot drink when he made his own before bed, but I never heard him. Nor did I hear the storm, which he told me had raged all night, making every window frame rattle and the tiles on the roof lift in places. I had not heard a branch of Miss Cowdie's huge sycamore tree break off – Casper said it was like a pistol shot – nor the old corrugated iron roof of the coal shed lift clean off and go crashing against the barn wall. I heard nothing. Casper had locked the barn up, he had locked the cottage door and put up all the shutters and secured them as soon as he heard the wind, which had been rising all afternoon, reach gale force. He had acted in a thoroughly responsible way and I was proud of him, but I had not heard a thing and nor had

I dreamed of my ordeal as I had expected. I had floated away on a haze of misery, numbed into total resignation, exhausted to the point of surrender. I suppose it was the very best thing that could have happened and yet I did not feel in the least refreshed when I woke up. I felt stiff and heavy eyed, and my wrists were still sore. Anyone but Casper would have remarked on the difficulty I had cutting bread – the slightest movement made the raw flesh hurt. But at least I was up and calm and able to function again, even if I felt drained and listless. "Are you better?" Casper said, mouth stuffed with toast. I nodded and he went off quite satisfied, loaded down with his waterproof clothing. He said he had enjoyed the bike ride, that it was better on the way there than on the way back. I managed to ask him if anyone else cycled and he said yes, lots, and there my interest flagged.

Eileen passed him as he set off. I watched the one going and the other coming, both with their heads down, barely acknowledging each other's existence. I remembered telling Eileen I wanted her to be early so that she could help me move clay into the barn and do all sorts of other jobs connected with starting work, but now I bitterly regretted my enthusiasm. I was not ready to start. I had not finished preparing my equipment, owing to the various interruptions of the day before, and even if I had forced myself to complete them I was in no mood to begin. I had no energy. I wanted to go back to bed and sleep and sleep. We had no food in the cottage and I had planned to go into Wigton first to shop, but I did not know if I had the strength. Eileen was the last person I wanted to see coming up the path – the last person to give me heart.

She did not speak as she came in. She never did. I sat and watched her hang up her awful coat on the nail on the back of the door and take her pinny out of her shopping bag and put it on. I was damned if I was even going to say good morning first. She came over to the table and began stacking the dishes. I wondered what she would do if I burst into tears and told her a man had tied me up in the barn yesterday and then gone away. I doubted if she would even have the wit to laugh at the absurdity of it, never mind to weep at the horror. I had a great desire to put her to the test but managed to resist the temptation. Confiding in Eileen would be fatal. So I got up and said, "I'm not feeling too good, Eileen. I think I will have to go back to bed. I don't think I'll be able to start work today, after all." She nodded, expressing neither surprise nor disappointment. Eileen just accepted all news. "If you just clean up generally," I said, "and perhaps make some more soup." I finished my cup of tea while she carried the few dishes to the sink and then I went upstairs. As I reached the top, her toneless voice pursued me. "Can't make soup t'day," she said, "isn't anything to mek it with." Of course, she was right. All the vegetables were finished, there was no meat or chicken left over, but I resented her lack of initiative. Couldn't she have looked around and found something without bothering me? This irrational rage fuelled my tired body. I wheeled round and stamped down the stairs. "Right," I said, while Eileen stared at me as though I were mad, "I'll go straight into Wigton and buy you something to make it with."

I drove far too fast into Wigton and parked in the main car park behind the market. By good luck – for I had not realised it – it was market day and there were several stalls inside, selling local vegetables. I bought a turnip, a cabbage, carrots, onions, and potatoes and leeks. None of the things I felt like were to be had. Not an aubergine in sight, no peppers, not even a courgette. Wigton was stocked with meat and bread shops, and greengrocers came nowhere in the pecking order. I took my bag straight back to the car because it was heavy and then I went in search of a chicken and some bones for Eileen's soup. I suppose I did not quite know where I was going – I had cut through one of the alleys into what I took to be the main street – and I was blundering along, looking vacantly into shop windows, when I met David Garibaldi. I stood stock still, making no move to dodge him as I had done before. I was dreadfully afraid my eyes were going to fill with tears, just at the sight of someone I knew, just at the thought of a friendly voice, and so I made a great performance of getting a non-existent speck out of them.

"Good morning, Pansy Potter," he said smiling. I smiled weakly back, barely able to get my mouth into the right position. "What's wrong?" he said, and took hold of my arm. "Have you exhausted yourself, moving all that stuff around?"

"No," I said, "I think I'm getting flu or something."

"You should be in bed."

"Yes. I'm going straight back. I just had to buy some food."

"What do you want? I'll buy it for you. I'm a very experienced shopper."

"Thanks, but – "

"No buts. Come on – what do you need? Bread? Meat? There's the fish van at the Memorial – how about a nice bit of Solway fish to put you in better health?"

I let him send me back to my car, where I slumped in my seat and closed my eyes. I still wanted to cry, and indeed a few tears did escape and wet my cheeks. I wiped them away hastily. A damsel in distres was David Garibaldi's line. When he returned with the few items I had listed I was more composed and able to thank him properly. "I don't like to think of you stuck out there on your own if you're ill," he said. I searched his face for signs of hypocrisy but he seemed perfectly sincere. "You haven't even a telephone, have you?"

"No, but there's Casper, and Eileen comes every day. I'm not really alone."

"Still. Look, I'll worry about you. I'm going to a sale on Thursday, near Ambleside. I'll pop in on my way back, just to check up on you." Before I could protest he had slammed the door shut and waved and was off, heading towards the Market Hall, where I presumed he had some business.

I was almost sad to see him go. All the way home, through a landscape bleakly preparing itself for winter, I thought how cheered I had been by his solicitude. Each time I met him I felt more deeply the full extent of my misjudgement. His dark, flashy, foreign look had made me think of him as on the make, shallow and lacking in any kind of sensitivity, and now I knew that facile first impression to be wrong. I knew I would look forward to his coming, that I might even feel able to tell him what had happened, or some of what had happened, and that I would welcome his advice. But by Thursday any advice would be a little superfluous – if I had not reported the assault to some sort of authority by then, it would seem ridiculous finally to do so. And it seemed I was not going to report it. The more I turned the idea over in my head, the more repugnant it seemed. I could not face some village bobby on his bicycle coming out to see me, and inevitably a couple of faded plain-clothes gentlemen, who had heard it all before and only wanted to enjoy the salacious details. They probably would not believe the attacker had not touched me in the end – they would imagine I was covering up because I was ashamed. It did not make sense that, having gone to such lengths, a maniac would then turn tail and go off.

He might, of course, come back, and it was this very obvious fear that made me unable to relax. He would not know that I had not called the police – any sensible person would have naturally done so – and this might act as a deterrent, but surely only for a time. It depended, really, upon whether the man was a local, or whether the whole thing had been pure chance – a madman, intent on burglary, who had been surprised into an action he had pulled back from, just in time. That, I thought, as I neared Greenhead, must be the explanation. I felt a little better at this guess. What I did not want to believe was that my enemy had planned his crime – that someone hereabouts had been watching me and had plotted the whole unpleasant incident. If that was true, then he would also know I had not reported the attack, and that would encourage him to return – and soon, while I was still frightened. It must, it *must*, I told myself over and over again, have been a chance encounter.

Geoff Crosthwaite was turning into the road from his farm as I drove along towards the track. He tooted his horn and waved cheerfully. I waved back. As I carried my bags into the cottage I said to Eileen, simply for something to say, to show I was in better spirits, "Geoff looks happy. I've just passed him on the road." "He always looks happy," Eileen said darkly, "that's our Geoff."

"Well, that's a nice trait," I said.

"He isn't happy with you, any road," Eileen said.

"Why not?"

"Saw you with that Roger Markham. Said he were surprised at you. Said he were disgusted."

"Well, he's got over his disgust very quickly. He gave me a wave."

"Doesn't mean anything," Eileen said stubbornly. "He smiles when he hits me. Often."

"You shouldn't let him hit you," I said, but unthinkingly,

carrying the bags to the table because there was nowhere to put them in the tiny kitchen.

"Can't stop him," Eileen said, beginning to take out the vegetables, "he's stronger than me. Can't do anything about it except tell Mam, and she's always on his side."

"Then get out of it," I said, impatiently. "You're over twenty one, aren't you? Just leave home. You don't have to put up with that kind of treatment."

"Where would I go?" Eileen said, staring at me, helpless and astonished, over the onions.

"Anywhere – get yourself a room in Carlisle or something, and a job – anything – I really don't know, but there must be something you could do."

"On me own?"

"Well of course, why not?"

"I've never been on me own."

"Then try it."

"Geoff 'ud be flaming mad."

"It isn't any of his business."

"And who'd help Mam? If she were took badly? She often is. Who'd look after her and the house?"

"Geoff and your father."

"Them? Oh no, that wouldn't be right, it's women's work."

"Eileen, you're worse than they are. Nothing is woman's work and nothing is man's work. It's just habit."

"I couldn't leave. I wouldn't know where to go. Never had a job till this, till you came. I'm not fit for owt."

"Of course you are. You just need confidence."

And was I the person to give it to her? Hardly. She trudged into the kitchen and began the laborious preparations for making soup while I went into my bedroom and changed into my working clothes. I still felt ill but I was not going to go back to bed. I was going to go into that barn and force myself to overcome the deep repugnance that I felt at ever entering it again. I was going to clean out the loft and then begin firing the kiln and making some pots. Before the day was done, I swore I would have had a trial run, no matter how appalling the results. But my steps were slow. I fiddled about uselessly washing large rubber buckets that did not need to be clean – they were only going to have clay and water in them – before I could bring myself to enter the barn. Even with the big double doors open, and the side door, and even with Eileen on call, I felt extremely nervous. Going up into the loft was torture and I quickly persuaded myself that I felt sick. The mattress stared up at me offensively and I found it hard to touch it at all. But bit by bit I carted down all the stuff until the loft was quite empty and then I dispersed the contents round all the various outhouses not in use. The only thing I could not lift was the big cabin trunk, and I went to get Eileen.

She was reluctant to lift the brute even an inch. "Me hands," she said, aggrieved. I told her that, if she kept her precious gloves on, her hands would not be affected. All I needed her to do was to help me lever the thing down the steps – I could drag it the rest of the way by myself. "Wasn't in the way up there," Eileen said crossly, "doing no harm." I said I wanted the loft empty to give me more room but she knew I already had more than enough. It was painful, bumping the trunk down, and I winced several times as the weight on my sore wrists hurt dreadfully. "Oooh," Eileen said suddenly, as we reached the bottom, "what've you done to your wrists?" She was staring at them, horrified. I looked at them too. I could think of no possible explanation. "I don't know," I said, "I just woke up and they were like that. It must be a rash," and I hid them quickly by pulling down the sleeves of my sweater.

I sent Eileen back to the cottage and her soup and told her to tell me before she left. Then I dug out a length of chain and fastened Rufus near to the bench where I was going to work. He did not want to come into the barn at all but I forced him in. Although he had proved useless as a guard dog, I felt he would at least bark if any stranger approached, and bark twice as hard if it was a stranger he recognised. Rufus, after all, was the only one who had seen whoever came the day before. Then I unpacked the two consignments of clay that had been stored in damp polythene since they had arrived from Acme Marls Ltd in Stoke-on-Trent and tested them. If clay is to be used for throwing, it must be plastic enough to form easily and to hold its shape after forming. It should not be so plastic that it is slippery and difficult to control, neither should it shrink too much or crack during drying. Testing it involved rolling some of it into coils, about half an inch in diameter and three inches long, and then bending it round to form rings. I was lucky. The clay formed well and when it was dried out there were no cracks to split when fired. To be doubly certain I would fire these first and inspect them for glaze reaction.

The clays I was going to use were white – the colour of clay can only be changed by making it darker and since I wanted the palest dove grey I had to begin with white. There are several manufacturers of "body stains", which can be used to colour clays, and to get the grey I wanted meant experimenting with proportions of these metal oxides. This took me over an hour and then I had to allow for adding the glaze and the effect of the firing process. I knew it would be a matter of trial and error and that if I were to obtain the exact colour I wanted in the finished pot I must be prepared to be patient. It also required patience to be absolutely methodical in what I was doing. All clay with colouring added has to be kept separate from the original clay to avoid contamination, which meant working it in one distinct area. Plastic bins for storing the uncoloured and coloured clay have to be kept rigorously apart and no foreign matter must be allowed anywhere near it.

The discipline involved in all this kept my mind from wandering over unpleasant subjects. I quickly became absorbed, particularly when I was applying the glazes to each batch of coils. Hygiene is very important at this stage, and so is precision. I used a small scoop to fish out samples of glazes and had to concentrate hard to make sure only the smallest amount went where I intended it to go. At every stage I wrote down the mixture I had used, otherwise it would be quite easy to achieve a desirable end result and not know how it had been reached. When Eileen came to tell me she was leaving, she was clearly disappointed not to see several hundred plates lying in rows on the racks I had shown her. "Haven't you done nothing?" she said. "Plenty," I said, "but you won't see anything for a week." She went off looking scornful, doubtless ticking off in her head the immensely satisfying jobs she had herself done while I was messing about. A small part of me was looking forward to impressing the unimpressed Eileen – I wanted to see her face when I was properly in production, with scores of pots completed and beautiful. Then, perhaps, she would rate my work as work.

My kiln was oil burning, situated near to a huge storage tank behind the barn. It was of the trolley hearth type – that is, it could be pulled out on rails for easier loading. Mr Rigg had built a reinforced concrete floor to take the weight. He had also fitted controllers to regulate the heat in the kiln and to switch it off, and it was these I was nervous of. I hate all mechanical devices and find them almost impossible to understand. The senior in the art department had always looked after the controllers on the college kiln, and I had never bothered to learn how it was done. The written instructions left to me baffled my lazy brain. I wished passionately I had attended when the inspector from the local authority had come to pass the kiln – he had asked me if I understood how to set it and I had said, airily, that of course I did. But I did not. I sat staring at the bloody thing and fiddling with the knobs and poring helplessly over the closely drawn Figure 1 etc in the diagrams on the leaflet. I saw myself having to crawl down to the nearby Greenrigg pottery and saying, "Excuse me, but I can't make my kiln work" – what would they think then?

I had to leave it. Kilns are too dangerous to meddle with if you do not understand them. Once my kiln was in operation I would have no problem – I was extremely familiar with working a kiln once it was functioning – but I had to admit defeat over starting it up. There was plenty to occupy me otherwise so I hardly wasted time but over everything I did hung the knowledge that at some point I must fire the kiln. A man's work, Eileen would say, triumphantly, but it was not. It was simply a weakness in me that must be overcome – but I doubt whether I would have been able to overcome it without Casper. He came home from school to find me bad temperedly poring yet again over the wretched instructions. Quietly, he took them out of my hand, smoothed them out, and carefully started to press switches and turn knobs in rotation, hardly a pause in between. "Are you sure you know what you are doing?" I said anxiously, but as the kiln started to heat up and all the noises sounded like the right noises, the noises I was used to, I acclaimed him as a genius.

"I don't know where you get it from," I said, "it's so unexpected, this facility with mechanical things." Casper said nothing. We both knew Gerald had been useless, totally un-handy, and Antonia, though artistic, not practical. "You don't have to inherit everything," Casper said, after a long pause. "Everybody has something that's their own." He sounded so world weary I almost mocked him and laughed at him openly but stepped back from that abyss just in time. He wandered about the barn, looking at the not very exciting results of my day's work, while I hovered near the kiln, still not trusting the controllers which would stabilise the temperature after it had reached the level I wanted. "There's nothing much to look at," I called after him. "I've just been getting ready today. I won't be throwing on the wheel until tomorrow." I thought about asking him if he would like to learn but feared the offer would come out too patronisingly. Better just to let him watch and ask himself.

Once Casper had convinced me the kiln was not going to explode, I left it to do its work. I had already packed it with the testing coils, supported on stilts, a job that has to be done with great care, and did not need to surpervise the kiln again until the soaking period was reached. Too long a soak makes the glaze become liquid, or even makes it glossy instead of matt, and I wanted to experiment on the length of time to prolong the soak. I also wanted to be sure the cooling process took place at 100°C per hour and, at some yet undetermined point, I would have to ease the kiln door open, so that the glaze and clay would not receive a thermal shock when coming into contact with air at normal room temperature. But there was time to have my first proper break of the day and I went with Casper back to the cottage to eat Eileen's inevitable soup.

We lit the fire and the orange lamp and I was soothed by the cheerfulness of the room. I wanted to ask Casper about school but not directly and while I supped the soup I was trying to ease myself into a natural way of asking the direct questions I dared not attempt. "Rehearsal much good?" I asked eventually, not knowing what the rehearsal had been of.

"Not bad."

"When's the real performance?"

"End of term. I'm doing the lights. They asked me."

I held back from too much enthusiasm. "Lucky you went – for them, I mean. Isn't doing lights boring?"

"No."

"What's the play?"

"Something by someone called Stoppard, about an Inspector."

"Oh, I saw it when it opened – *The Real Inspector Hound* – how ambitious, for a little country school, I mean."

"It's a big country school," Casper said, scathingly.

"Yes, but I meant obscure – compared to Highgate – I just meant it's adventurous of them. We used to do Shakespeare or terrible morality plays like *Everyman* – never anything modern. Did you ever go to the theatre in London?"

"No."

"Except at Christmas. I took you to *Peter Pan* myself, when you were four. You wouldn't leave the theatre after it had finished, in case it started again."

"I can't remember. I don't like the theatre anyway. Films are better. Or tele."

"Would you like to have a tele?"

There seemed a struggle going on inside him – I knew he wanted to shrug and say that he didn't mind, I knew he wanted to remain consistent in his not-caring attitude, but, on the other hand, his very real longing for a tele fought this.

"Yes," he said.

"I'll get one, then. Perhaps a portable. Your room isn't big enough for anything else and I don't want it in here. You should have said you wanted one, Casper – how am I to know these things, if you don't say?"

"I just like the films on tele."

"I don't. I like going to the real cinema but I don't like films on television – it kills them – don't know why. God, I'd like to be going to a film or the theatre tonight – I'd like to walk out of that door and pick up a cab and rush down to the West End and see what's on in Leicester Square." I closed my eyes, dramatically, and groaned. "What on earth am I doing, stuck up here in this Godforsaken dump?" I opened my eyes. Casper was ignoring me, head bent over his soup bowl, not a flicker of expression on his face. "Do you think we should give up before we've really begun, Casper?" I asked. "Go back to London, I mean."

"No."

"Why not?"

"We're here. I don't like moving. We've just got settled."

"I don't feel settled. I feel very unsettled. There's no point in clinging on to a mistake."

"What mistake?"

"Me rushing up here, thinking it would solve anything. It was stupid. We would get on better in London, after all."

"*I* wouldn't."

"I think I'm bored with it, already."

"Typical."

"How do you know what is typical for me?"

"Edward said. He said running away from London was typical. He said you were always unstable. Mum used to say it too – said you never settled to anything for five minutes – you were always restless. It's disgusting, thinking about giving up already. Why did you come, if you weren't going to like it? You knew what it would be like, it wasn't as if you hadn't been here before. Why did you bother coming? All that fuss. And that pottery – all that effort, for nothing. I think it's awful, awful."

For Casper, it was a spectacular outburst. I stared at him in astonishment. Normally so taciturn and withdrawn, it was a shock to witness such vitality. These rare outbursts revealed a depth of passion which almost scared me – I imagined all this pent up energy churning around inside him behind the self-contained façade, and it was painful to think of it so suppressed.

"Well, then," I said, as lightly as possible, "we'll stay. But I'm not going to pretend everything is working out as I had hoped, and you're not going to make me ashamed of being disappointed. I can't help it if these surroundings and – and other things make me feel depressed. Perhaps when I'm in full production with the pots I'll feel better. I'll have to go and look at the kiln now. Can you come with me? I still worry about how it works."

"There's nothing to worry about," Casper said impatiently, "it's all completely automatic, now it's set. You don't even seem to know what you've bought – what you've paid all that money to get." But he got to his feet.

It was pitch black outside, quite impenetrably dark, except for our own lights. Without Casper, I would have been afraid to return to the barn, but I hoped he would not realise it. The light we had left on in the barn was hidden by the thickness of the walls and since it was near none of the small slit windows it cast no glow outside. Already, the smell inside was familiar – that close, thick atmosphere of clay and heat and dust which stifled upon entering. The kiln was operating beautifully, the cooling process well advanced. Casper showed me how to turn it off in two hours' time, and how I could leave it set at a low temperature if I wished. Under his guidance I thought I might quickly get the hang of it. I would return on my own – a test of will and ability – before I went to bed.

We walked back to the cottage, guided on our return journey by our own lights. Without Casper noticing, I had locked the small barn door (the big double ones were already bolted and barred at dusk). Nobody could possibly get into that barn now. It could withstand a siege, let alone a single man's attempts to penetrate it. "You go to bed," I said to Casper, "I can manage on my own next time." I thought he might protest it was too early, but he went at once and I sat down to wait until it was time to rescue my coils from the kiln, determined to be bold and resolute about going across that black stretch of ground to the gloomy barn.

Thirteen

A great and welcome calm seemed to settle upon me during that next week and I look back on it, even now, with pleasure, as an interlude before the storm – or if not a storm, a series of difficulties. So much had gone wrong since my hurried departure from London that I had almost come to believe I must face up to continuing disaster. But from the evening Casper fired the kiln successfully I enjoyed a week free from scares or depressions and I am glad to see, when I look back, that I made the most of it.

The test coils showed I had not got the glazing quite right and I spent another day re-running a further batch, until the finished objects had a smooth and beautiful pearl-grey sheen, and then I set to and produced a dozen plates, a dozen bowls and a dozen jugs. I worked from first light until well after dark and I hardly stopped for food or drink. Eileen was astonished out of her habitual apathy when she arrived at nine o'clock to find me bent over the potter's wheel with clay up to my elbows. She stood quite fascinated, watching a jug arise from my busy hands, and said, "Didn't know that was how it were done." All morning she came backwards and forwards on one pretext or another, just to peep, and when I gave her little jobs to do she was clearly glad to be around. Twice I had to throw away a less than perfect bowl when it came off the wheel, and she winced as I hurled the ruined lump of clay into the bin at my side – it hurt her to see it end there. I wondered if I would discover Eileen had untapped artistic resources – that her hands were shaped so finely because in them resided a completely unsuspected delicacy and skill. Evenutally I planned to let her have a go, to teach her a little, but first I wanted to make a batch of pottery I could begin to sell.

In the evening I was tired and made Casper prepare the supper, which he did clumsily but without resentment. Eating had become once more something I needed to do but did not really wish to be bothered with. I knew I would lose weight and was glad of it. I despise women who are forever slimming but equally I am contemptuous of those who allow their bodies to grow fat and slack. I was in no danger, as yet, of that, but I did not like to see even the smallest roll of excess weight beginning to appear. I had eaten too much for several weeks, partly out of discontent and partly, in a feeble way, to keep Casper company. This absurdity – eating because the person one is with is eating – had rarely happened to me before. Edward was the only other person I had lived with for any length of time and his eating habits had been as erratic as my own, so I had never faced the tyranny of being obliged to feast in order to appear companionable.

I let Casper do almost everything. He cleared the dishes away (but left them for Eileen to wash in the morning) and looked after the fire and then disappeared to watch the television I had made time to go and buy immediately. Vague stirrings of guilt troubled me as I sat by the fire – was it right to be so unfriendly that a child of thirteen had to go up to a small attic and watch television, for want of any human fellowship? But I observed Casper closely and saw that he was in no way pathetic in his television watching – he loved it, it made him entirely happy and it would have been foolish of me to sneer at his taste and berate him for not reading books instead. It left me in possession of our small living-room and I was glad of it. There was no point at all in my regretting that I had failed to establish with Casper any degree of closeness. I saw that our relationship would flourish better if we kept to our separate compartments and respected each other's individuality.

It happened that the weather was also kind, that memorable week. Nothing dramatic, but a series of fine days with a good deal of sun in the middle of the day. I had the barn door open, of course, and several times, as I looked out onto the fell, I was caught by the strange beauty of the landscape. It was a three dimensional feeling – the stillness and emptiness, the way the dark green-grey grass rose steeply to the horizon, without interruption of tree or bush, created an atmosphere of being suspended in air. I would look, and feel part of it, feel disembodied and far off, and I would have to detach myself once more and pin mesmerised eyes on the spinning of the wheel. The sheep came right to the door, great dirty shaggy things with twisted, curled horns, and added to the roughness of the image. There was nothing pretty in what I saw, nothing that could have made anyone exclaim with delight, nothing really that could be called a "view". It was more that I became drawn into the land – it contained me and physically pushed powerfully against me.

And so it turned out that when David Garibaldi called on the Thursday, as he had said he would, I was happy, and that happiness influenced me in what followed. Other women may seek love-making as a consolation – they may look to it for reassurance, or something to lift them out of a depression – but I am not like that. I have never made love to anyone in my life except through joy or excitement. Indeed, I cannot imagine anything more obscene than allowing my body to be made use of, and I suppose that is one of the many things I dread about marriage. How, one million times over, could desire be maintained? I saw myself having lust inflicted upon me – conjugal rights, if you like – and hated the idea. Edward was of the opinion that sex did not always need to be a star studded occasion but I did not agree. I would not let him touch me unless I felt like being touched – persuasion against my inclination was repugnant to me. And this hurt him. He was in a permanent state of lust his entire life, it seemed to me, and he expected me to be sympathetic to this need. He said if we waited until I felt like making love we would sometimes wait weeks. Yes, I said, and this is how it ought to be. It was he who accepted anything less than rapture, rather than have nothing. I would not. It was a vital difference that went through our whole life together, every facet of it. Edward would drink cheap, disgusting instant coffee if he could not get good stuff;

he would go to a poor film if the queue for the one he wished to see was too long; he would buy a coat he did not really like because he was tired of looking for one that he *did* like. Edward was perfectly happy to accept second best all the time, whereas I was uncompromising. It made Edward a wonderfully warm, easy person, and myself a rather hard one.

I suppose happiness in fact pre-disposed me towards my gentleman caller before he ever appeared. I was stacking the kiln about midday when I heard Rufus bark and the sound of a man's voice – a perfectly pleasant man's voice – saying, "Good boy, down boy," and so I was prepared for David to find me. I did not go out to meet him – the stilt I was using to support my jugs made stacking a precarious business, not easily deserted. I had my back to him, but heard him walk in and I said, "Sorry not to turn round – if I let go of this saddle, the stilt underneath will fall down."

"Can I help?"

"Yes – if you just hold this – like that – great. There, that's the lot."

"Looks impressive. You've been busy."

"I have rather."

"You look much better – perfectly all right again."

He looked at me critically, his stare excused by his previous concern over my health. I looked back just as searchingly, for different, less justifiable reasons. Was he attractive or was he not? I wiped my hands on my filthy smock and said, "I was just going to have something to eat. Would you like something or are you rushing?"

"No," he said slowly, "I'm not rushing. I never rush. I just let things take their course."

He followed me to the cottage and stood in the doorway while I got beer out of the fridge and bread and cheese. "Nothing much," I said, but not in the least apologetic. I knew perfectly well what was going to happen – what I wanted to happen – and one half of me was already congratulating myself on the fact that Eileen had gone and Casper was staying late for his precious lighting rehearsal. I took the food and drink outside to where there was a bench against the wall and said, "We might as well sit in the sun while it's here. I expect you'll predict rain before dark."

"No," he said, "not today. Today will go on being a lovely day right up to the end, don't you worry."

"I'm not," I said, giving him a very cheeky and bold smile. "I'm not in the least worried."

He took his time. We drank the beer, to the last drop. We ate the bread and cheese. With sweaters and jackets on, the sun felt warm and we leaned our heads against the stone wall behind us and raised our faces to the sun. It went on so long, this basking, that I feared he would make no move at all without encouragement. I was perfectly prepared to give it, but hesitated, knowing most men dislike any positive lead from the woman, and I was not, on the other hand, prepared to resort to the accepted feminine tricks and wiles. But how he was wasting time, sitting there, and how impatient I became, how weary of waiting for an arm about my shoulder or a hand on my knee.

"You are a very modern young lady," he said at last, "so I don't have to pretend I'm falling in love with you, do I?"

"No," I said, and laughed. He sounded like an echo of myself.

"That's good. I'm married."

"Now you're a very old fashioned man," I said, "thinking you had to confess to that. I don't care if you're married or not. It isn't of the slightest interest to me."

"I thought it might not be, but I didn't want any misunderstandings to spoil things." He stood up. "Shall we go inside?" he said.

I led the way. He stood aside at the door and made a mocking bow and I nodded and brushed past him and went straight upstairs. He followed and with perfect poise entered my bedroom and looked about him, hands in his pockets. There was no unseemly rush to the bed, nor did he try to pull my clothes off me. He had his back to the window as he watched, quietly, while I took them off myself. It is not something I have ever found hard to do. My mother, who was brought up in a very prudish household, was always determined that Antonia and I should never think our bodies something to be ashamed of. I don't know whether she would have been as successful if we had not been blessed with bodies we were unlikely to be ashamed of anyway, but the result of her attitude was certainly a complete lack of embarrassment about nakedness. I took my sweater off first, and then my skirt, quite happy that David Garibaldi should see me, and then I stepped out of my trousers and with great care placed them on the stool near the door. I put my hands up to my hair and undid the pins holding it up out of my way while I worked. It fell heavily onto my shoulders and I shook it out, the only conscious gesture of coquetry I made. "Well?" I said. He was still fully clothed. "I'm not going to get on that bed and lie there like a sacrificial lamb," I said. "You're very beautiful," he said, "I'm quite transfixed." But he began, very slowly, to take his clothes off too. I liked the slowness. I hate men who fumble out of their clothes, or keep half of them on, looking ludicrous. Men do not seem to appreciate that women can find looking at the male body as pleasurably erotic as they find looking at the female. I like to look before I feel.

We were either side of the bed in that small room, facing each other like protagonists. "Come on, then," he said, his arms wide open. I walked round the bed and faced him again, knowing that once we touched all control would go. I like to savour that moment, to prolong the delicious anticipation. He moved towards me first and clasped me to him and a great current of lust set every nerve end in my body singing. I suppose we had both reached orgasm within two minutes, with no time to find out about each other's bodies at all. It reminded me – the suddenness, the near violence of it – of my lovemaking with Edward, at the very beginning. But, then, love had ignited us and not mere physical attraction. Now, my body was satiated but the accompanying stirring of the soul I had experienced with Edward was not there. I felt quite earthly, not moved to tears or laughter, no visions of heavenly secrets vouchsafed to me.

But I enjoyed it. We lay in bed afterwards and congratulated ourselves without hypocrisy. "I was always a good judge," David said, "though it wasn't hard with you. You have every man for miles around half insane with lust."

"How horrible."

"It isn't horrible at all. It's entirely natural. I'm one of them, so I know. I haven't had you out of my head for six weeks, ever since I saw you."

"I'm afraid I can't say the same about you."

"Arrogant bitch. I didn't think you could. But you wanted someone, didn't you?"
"Is that a sneer?"
"No, why should it be?"
"You sound as if you were talking about a dog – as though you wanted to say something very crude, about me panting for 'it'. I hate that. I just happen to like sex, at the right time, in the right mood."
"So it could have been anyone, and you don't want me to flatter myself."
"Not at all. It couldn't have been anyone – that's what I'm trying to say. I'm not a nymphomaniac."
"A pity."
I laughed and he began to caress me, all over, expertly and yet with every semblance of feeling. I loved it. Long before he had finished I was clutching him and wanting to consummate our passion and when he finally thrust into me I moaned with pleasure and was dizzy with gratification. Afterwards I was, this time, a little shaken. I did not like being so clearly revealed as less lacking in control than David – I did not like to be the one begging for more.
"You're very cool," I said, slightly resentfully.
"All good lovers are cool," he said, calmly, his arms behind his head and his face turned away from me. "Making love well needs a lot of self-discipline. Most women never get it."
"You mean they don't receive it, or they don't employ it?"
"Both. Women expect so little and this encourages men to give it to them. They aren't really interested in sex as an art."
"But of course *you* are."
"Naturally. It's worth practising, and practising well."
"And what about love – where does love come into this marvellous philosophy?"
"It doesn't. I know nothing about love."
There was an unmistakable sadness about him as he said this, without glibness or any boastful leer. I lay and thought about it. If he knew nothing about love, it would explain that abstracted air he so often had, that absence of any Edward-like enthusiasm. Love consumes the lover and leaves its mark and there was no mark on David. "And you?" he said, suddenly turning to look at me. "Do you know about love?"

"Oh yes," I said, lightly, "I'm an experienced veteran."
"Who do you love?"
"A man called Edward – it really doesn't matter who he is – he's in South America."
"And when will he come home and live with you happily ever after?"
"He won't. I don't want to live with him. I love him but it doesn't seem to mean I want to live with him."
"What a pity my wife doesn't think like that. It would have been much better for both of us."
"If you're going to start talking about your wife," I said, "I'll get up and make some coffee."
I was quite clear on one thing – I did not want to know David's history. Since I am a naturally curious person this would entail a great deal of self-control but I was determined to exercise it. It was vital that I should. I did not want to know about his wife or his children, if he had any; I did not want to know about his likes and dislikes; I did not want to know any more than I already knew about his life. What I wanted was a purely physical relationship and if you think that makes me little better than a prostitute then you are quite wrong. I did not sell myself. I did not regard this sexual coupling as mechanical, something to be gone through with my mind on other things. I felt a great attraction towards David – you know that I did – and it was that attraction alone which bound me to him. It was an attraction dependent on a certain element of mystery – on not being properly acquainted – and it stood in danger of disappearing if he made himself too familiar. I liked his lean, olive skinned body and his dark good looks – I did not want to know what lay behind them.
It can often be strained, that drinking-coffee-afterwards part. I can think of several lovers who I only wanted to see the back of. There are too many men who, the job done, want to preen themselves and be told how wonderful they were. They think they have suddenly earned rights over your mind as well as your body and cannot believe you have finished with them for the time being. But with David the aftermath was comfortable. He took no liberties, he stayed true to himself, and as we drank the coffee we chatted in a desultory fashion – the mention of his wife was not repeated – I began to see he could

perhaps understand the unspoken rules. When he looked at his watch and said he must go I was glad that he also added, "I hope I can come again? Without you thinking that means I expect the same reception?"

"Where did you get your formal manners?" I said.

"From my Italian forebears, lady."

He said he would call in the following Tuesday, that perhaps I would like to go to a sale with him and have lunch, if I could spare the time. I thought by the following Tuesday I would have earned a break and said I would love to. I walked with him down to his van. He looked around as he walked, thoughtfully. "You're very isolated here," he said. "Lucky you've got a big dog." It was on the tip of my tongue to tell him Rufus was no bloody good as a guard dog but I restrained myself – not that I feared David knowing this but I would then have had to launch into the unpleasant saga of my mysterious visitor and I simply did not want to, not then. It could wait. I could treat David as my confidant later.

As he got into his van, Geoff Crosthwaite's tractor appeared over the horizon in the top field, half a mile away. "Oh God," I said, "Geoff will have seen you."

"Does it matter?"

"Not in *that* way – but yes, it matters. You know perfectly well what it's like, living in a place like this. They know absolutely everything everybody does and says and they make you suffer for it, in an odd sort of way. Geoff is just a neighbour, he means absolutely nothing to me, I'm not beholden to him except that I've made use of him in a trivial matter – lugging those wretched crates into the barn – but because of being so set apart up here I can't avoid him. He's becoming a damned nuisance with his censorious attitudes – I'm not supposed to talk to any man except him, even though I've given him no encouragement at all. Now he'll see you and be furious."

David smiled. "Well," he said, climbing into his van, "you can hardly blame him. The thought of you must drive him mad. He's a frustrated fellow anyway – they make a pair, he and that sister of his. You're not afraid of him, are you? I'm sure he wouldn't hurt a fly – all talk, all brawn and no brain."

"Of course I'm not afraid of him," I said crossly.

"Good. That was a very enjoyable afternoon, Miss Grove."

He said it quite solemnly but we both burst out laughing. I couldn't help wondering if the sound of the smug laughter would carry across the fell and be heard by Geoff, above the noise of his tractor. After David had driven off, I stood for a few minutes looking down the track, reluctant to go back either to the cottage or barn. In spite of saying I wasn't afraid of Geoff, I began to feel just a little fear – or not exactly fear so much as a deep sense of unease. I did not want a jealous neighbour. Jealousy might make blundering old Geoff violent and it was nonsense to say, as David had said, that he wouldn't hurt a fly when he repeatedly hurt Eileen. Knowing David Garibaldi came and went, as he was bound to get to know, Geoff would become convinced that he too could enjoy me. If I had kept really to myself, if I had had no truck with any men at all, then he might have respected my solitary state. But knowing David Garibaldi was receiving my favours would be enough to make Geoff turn to the chase with a vengeance, and the idea appalled me.

I heard the sound of a car behind me as I slowly retraced my steps, back to my work. Turning in surprise, I saw Roger Markham's jeep bumping over the ruts and coming to a halt where the thicker mud began. He got out and waved and though (after Geoff) he was the last person I wished to see, I had no alternative but to stop and wait for him to catch me up. He would, of course, have passed David's van on the bottom road.

"Afternoon, ma'am," he said cheerfully. I thought his look very insolent but I was ready to imagine anything. "And what have you been a-doing with your fair self, this lovely day?"

I was irritated enough to want to reply that I had just been having a good fuck, thank you, but said, "I've been working."

"In production at last, eh? Can I see?"

There aren't many choices in the country. I could hardly say no, with few excuses to hand. Rather annoyed, I took him to the barn and showed him the first set of plates. Though I was heavily prejudiced against him, I must say that his enthusiasm pleased me and I warmed a little towards him, just as I had done before. Enthusiasm was an Edward-quality I loved –

those who have not got it can never simulate it, no matter how hard they try. David had *admired* the plates but Roger glowed over them and asked a string of pertinent questions I enjoyed answering. He asked me where I intended to sell them and I said I had absolutely no idea, I had not got that far. He suggested that when I thought I was ready I should ring him up – he fished a card out of his pocket – and come over at some arranged time to show them to the Earl himself. I must have looked scornful, as though I thought I was being patronised, because he said quite sharply that there was a point to this – the Earl's stately home was open to the public in the summer and there was a tea-room where he liked to use locally produced goods. He might buy a great deal of pottery if it was to his taste, and not only would that be a good sale in itself, but the stuff would be seen by others and inquired about and more orders would come in.

"Thank you," I was obliged to say, "it's a very good opportunity. I'll ring you, perhaps straight after Christmas."

"Will you be here for Christmas?"

"Yes."

"Then you must join in our festivities at the Hall – would you come to the party if I invited you?"

"I don't know. I'll think about it when you invite me."

We were out in the open again, watching the mist begin to gather in the folds, high up on the top fell. Soon, at dusk, it would come creeping down, softly infiltrating itself into the darkness.

"I must get on," Roger said. "I'm going to look at Miss Cowdie's tree. Apparently the storm last Monday blew a branch across her roof – John Armstrong rang me about it."

"Who is John Armstrong?"

"He's a shepherd, from Dash Farm way, haven't you come across him?"

"No."

"Nice man, been at it over twenty years. He sees everything going on. He thought the branch might be resting on the broken tiles – said he couldn't be sure, looking at it from high up – so I thought I'd better check up. Did it scare her?"

"I don't know," I said, "I haven't seen her this week. I've been so busy."

"You mean with work?" He looked at me with raised eyebrows and an unpleasant twist to his ever smiling mouth.

"Just what do you mean?" I said angrily. Roger Markham was not Geoff Crosthwaite – I need have no inhibitions.

"I saw Garibaldi's van coming from this direction. I assumed you must have been – entertaining."

"It's none of your bloody business what I do."

"Quite. But I don't like to think of a nice independent girl like you getting caught up by a rat like Garibaldi."

"Shut up," I said, fiercely. "All anyone up here ever does, it seems to me, is condemn other people. You're all the same – whisper, whisper, – why can't you leave each other alone? If David is a rat, I'll find out, won't I? I only think less of you for telling me."

"You know he's married?"

"Oh for *God's* sake," I said, exasperated. "This is ridiculous – yes, as a matter of fact, of course I know he is married. It was about the first thing he told me. What difference is it supposed to make? Aren't men up here allowed to talk to another woman if they're married?"

"Oh yes, they're allowed to *talk*."

"But not to fuck?"

He looked pained. The smile went from his face and without it there was no attraction. He looked straight ahead and said, "I hope you aren't going to be as direct with other people."

"Why not? Why shouldn't I be direct? I loathe the furtive way people carry on. I'm not in the least ashamed of what I do with David Garibaldi, so why should I pretend that I am?"

"You might be misunderstood. Your honesty could be dangerous – to you. And it isn't necessary."

"What rubbish. You provoked me into telling you anyway – that leer as you asked if I was preoccupied with work – I can't stand that kind of thing."

"You haven't got the slightest idea what you're doing, have you?" he said. "You'll end up raped and you'll only have yourself to blame. However, before you remind me, it isn't any of my business and you're a liberated lady who is going to do what she damn well likes. So I'll trot off, and wish you luck."

He was gone before I could think of a suitably cutting reply.

Rage made me incapable of moving for several minutes – time to watch Roger disappear completely round the hill. What upset me was the edge of contempt in his voice – or rather, I was upset that I should be upset by it. He had shown himself at our first meeting to be a traditional male, the type whose views I totally disregarded, and yet, when he gave expression to them, as he had just done, I was irrationally disturbed. Why should I be? I did not want the so-called "respect" of the Roger Markhams of this world – dull, boring, prudish little men with a Victorian image of women. But on the other hand I did not want him to draw wrong conclusions from what he had discovered about my behaviour and I supposed that was what upset me. He had deduced I was a slut without standards or morals. I wanted to prove to him that my approach to sex was not what he had taken it to be – I wanted to show him his inferences were mistaken. He had gone off convinced he had made me ashamed of myself, and nothing could be further from the truth. He had made my afternoon with David seem dirty and sordid and grubby, whereas in fact it had been glorious. Then, as I at last turned and went into the barn, I had a new thought – could Roger Markham be merely jealous, as jealous as Geoff Crosthwaite certainly would be? It seemed hardly likely – nothing he had said or done had shown he was in the least attracted to me – but the way in which he had called David a rat suddenly struck a familiar note.

I did no more work that day. I removed the fired pots from the kiln and put them on racks and then I cleared up, a long and tedious business in the daily life of every pottery. Eileen would have made a better job than I – slow brushing and endless washing and scraping was more in her line than mine – but she was never there in the afternoon. It would make more sense, I reflected, if she did come late afternoon, and I resolved to suggest to her, but I had an idea she might refuse. My view that Eileen's days were long and empty, except for the couple of hours she did for me, was not shared by Eileen herself. She saw onerous tasks, revolving round the making of meals for Geoff and John, as entirely filling what looked to me like empty hours. The preparations and clearing up weighed heavily upon her and I knew the mere mention of perhaps coming at four o'clock, when the men were coming in from the fields, would horrify her. There would be potatoes to peel and mince to stir and all manner of trivial, utterly moveable tasks to attend to. But I would encourage her to be daring and think about walking out on them.

I thought I would see Roger returning to his jeep – he could not fail to pass me – but somehow I missed him, and did not have the chance to show him how I had thrown off my bad temper. I had wanted to arrest him with some casual, off-hand greeting, to show him I was now amused by his scorn. He must have deliberately gone down by the beck from Miss Cowdie's cottage, a very long and awkward detour indeed, to avoid passing my cottage and barn. The sound of his jeep starting up was the first indication I had that he had done this and I could not help pondering the significance. He did not want to see me. Was he disgusted with me; did he want, quite literally, to shun me? Yet why go to such lengths if, as had seemed obvious, he felt himself to be in the right and perfectly confident in what he was saying? It did not really make sense.

There is no possibility in those kind of isolated situations of ever quickly getting over anything – there are no external distractions to take the mind off the one track. In London, brooding was for me an almost unheard of activity (if anything so negative can be called an activity), simply because I was surrounded by so many opportunities for action. The times when I found myself bugged were easily dealt with – I lifted the telephone, contacted friends, went somewhere, and before very long had successfully shaken off whatever it was that threatened to drive me half mad. But up on the fells I could not do that. The demon of my own current obsession had to be faced, head on. I swept the floor, washed the tools, busied myself grimly – but my head went round and round with silly conversations I would have with Roger Markham. I longed for Casper to return to break the relentless continuity of my thoughts and was ready to herald his arrival extravagantly, but there was another hour before he was due. I thought about going to meet him, on the excuse that it was going to be dark and misty, since he was returning home so late, but he would not like it. He was looking forward to the excitement of using his lights, of cutting swathes with them through the utter blackness of the country roads, and would not be pleased to be robbed of the thrill. It was no use at all my encouraging Casper to be fearless if, at the first sign of him developing this happy tendency, I acted towards him like his dead mother. The stifling dependency she had fostered was only just beginning to lift – I must not allow it to return.

So I waited, unhappily. I fidgeted around the cottage after I had securely locked the barn. I made the bed David and I had disturbed and set the table for the evening meal I would have later with Casper and I examined the casserole Eileen had left in the oven. Still I was restless. It was by now half past four and dark in our part of the world. I stood gloomily at the window, watching for Casper's lights coming up the track. I felt faintly worried about him cycling all the way from Wigton and could not entirely suppress my nervousness as absurd. He was a big boy, and strong and sensible, but he was not used to negotiating country roads in winter. As yet, there was no ice, but rain frequently made stretches of the less used roads slippery and I imagined him coming off his bicycle and being miles from help. I saw how easy it was to be a clucking mother, forever anxious over safety, always convinced danger threatened.

It was the need to put a stop to this kind of foolish ruminating which drove me to put Rufus on a lead and set off to meet Casper. I thought, when I met him, that I would say Rufus needed the exercise, and thereby cover up my real motives, which were in any case mixed. It was not just concern for Casper that drove me out, nor even impatience at that concern, but the same claustrophobia that overcame me every time it was dark or dreary and I was alone in that wretched cottage. I could not bear to be in it when I was so jumpy – I imagined faces at the window or footsteps on the path and had a constant urge to lock and bolt the door. As soon as I was outside, such feelings miraculously lifted, even if it was dark and the wind was howling. The blackness stretching around me, the vast void of black air, frightened me less than my own home, where comforting lights were lit.

I stood still for a moment until my eyes were used to the gloom and then I set off, Rufus straining at the lead. I was not in the least afraid or hesitant, even though it was hard to see anything at all. My own cottage lights created a well of illumination, only six feet or so in depth, and after that there was nothing to pierce the inky blackness. But I quickly grew accustomed to the dark and did not need to use the torch I had slipped into my pocket. The stars were not yet out, nor had the moon risen, but the sky was a dark grey, quite distinct from the ground, and before I had reached the point where the made-up track began I was able to differentiate shapes quite well. I saw sheep that had been invisible five minutes before and rocks that had so completely melded into the ground that nobody could have guessed they were massive outcrops. The thick tufts of grass where the track was boggy no longer made me stumble – I picked my way quite daintily round them and felt triumphant that I reached the gravel and hard-core track without once falling.

From then on it was even easier. I saw the lights of the Crosthwaites' farm to the left – duller and less dramatic than mine, but then I supposed all the many curtains and shutters were already closed, whereas I had left mine open – and further down the cottages and farms at Greenrigg looked like fireflies clustered together. The hillside down which Casper would travel, some two miles off, had more lighted houses on it than I would have thought possible and I saw that his way was not as perilous as I had falsely remembered. I had no intention of going further than the bridge at Greenrigg, where the B road swept round to join the Uldale one. That was far enough. Until that point I was still on the fell, and the track along which I walked was used only by the few people who lived along it, but once I joined the proper road a surprising number of cars would pass me. I thought about letting Rufus off the lead but was afraid I would never be able to get him back onto it and so I continued as I was.

We went along very silently until we reached the tiny bridge I had set as my target and then we turned and began to walk back, with me looking over my shoulder frequently, trying to spot the solitary lamp that would be on the front of Casper's bike. I did not really want to go home without him but there was a limit to how long I could take over walking back in the cold and dark. Passing the end of the Crosthwaites' lane again, I thought briefly of dropping in, but dismissed the notion for the foolish thing it was. Dropping in was not something one did at the Crosthwaites'. Doing so would not even be recognised as such – it would be thought outrageous to call without a specific request and I had none. Total consternation would greet me and it was not worth provoking it when the idle chat I required would not be forthcoming.

My cottage beamed forth as I turned the last corner and I thought how stupid I was to have left it. There was nothing so attractive on the whole fell. Resolving to go inside and settle down to wait for Casper by reading a book or writing a letter, I hurried across the ground we called a garden and searched in my pocket for my key. And then I saw there was a figure standing at the door.

Fourteen

Instinctively, I tightened my hold on Rufus's lead, winding the chain round and round my hand until the poor animal could not move. For a moment, so great was my fear, I thought of turning and running away, but there was nowhere to run to and I would only fall and hurt myself. Afterwards, I thought how clearly this showed the jumpy state I was in – quite silly and unlikely behaviour for me – and I could hardly credit that the mere sight of a figure on my doorstep, a figure standing quietly and in no way threatening me, had produced such strong symptoms of terror. My body seemed to have a reaction of its own, not prompted by anything I was thinking – a great thrill of horror swept through me, through every limb, as though I had been struck by lightning. It left me weak and trembling and even before Miss Cowdie spoke I was incapable of moving.

She had been standing at the door, knocking on it and listening intently, but she had made no move to open it. I watched her knock twice and then wait, and then knock again and turn her head to the left so that her ear was almost against the door. It was then that she saw me, though I don't know how – I was frozen in my tracks some twenty yards away and not lit, I was sure, by the light from the cottage windows. I might have been standing at the other end of a sitting room for all the surprise I gave Miss Cowdie. She clapped her hands together and said, "Oh, Miss Grove! Do forgive me! *Quite* out of tea!" I felt incredibly stupid. Legs still shaking, I let go of Rufus – I had wound the chain so short and tight that my wrist hurt when I released him – and hurried forward, not knowing what to say. "Sorry to keep you waiting," I mumbled and Miss Cowdie said, "Not at all," and it was as though we were acting out some elegant comedy of manners and not freezing outside a fellside cottage.

She came into the cottage looking very pleased with herself. Relief and shame were both making me feel giddy and I had to put a hand out to steady myself as I went through the tiny living room and into the kitchen. I got down two packets of tea and held them out to Miss Cowdie, who stood in front of the fire gazing around her in something resembling awe. "Enchanting!" she cooed, "quite, quite enchanting." Her leathery face was creased into a smile that took in every feature – her eyes almost disappeared with the force of that mighty smile. She took the tea and quickly slipped it into the pockets of her battered man's raincoat. "Until I shop," she said, "only a loan, you know," and she nodded significantly. "Please," I said, "you're welcome to the tea. Don't think of returning it."

"Oh yes, I must – never a borrower or a lender be, my mother used to say, and she was quite right, quite right, but then, she lived in a street, you know, and there was temptation, whereas for us it is different – if one runs out of something here, it is an emergency and borrowing is not at all the same."

"No, it isn't."

"I would *always* wish you to avail yourself of my nearness," Miss Cowdie went on, nodding her head earnestly. "I am here to help – always remember that, my dear Miss Grove."

"Alexandra," I said, "and will you have a drink? A small sherry, perhaps, if it is not too early in the evening?"

God knows what I thought I was doing, playing her game, but I could no longer go on standing there, stiff with embarrassment – I had to do something to ease my own dismay. I told myself, as I poured the sherry, that this was what I had envisaged when first I set out to conquer Miss Cowdie, but now that she had appeared in my cottage and was so perfectly at home I foresaw all sorts of complications. I still did not know how to treat her, that was the trouble – all the time I kept forgetting her madness and falling inadvertently into the habit of talking to her as though there was no impediment to a beautiful friendship, but at the back of my mind lurked the memory of the dead rabbit and the sheep's head.

She was blissfully happy, drinking the sherry. Without undoing her frightful coat or her headscarf, she sat down on the chair nearest the fire, legs neatly crossed, back ramrod straight, and sipped from the glass I had given her. "So reviving," she murmured, "so civilised." She seemed to be in an ecstatic trance – her head, between sips, was thrown back and her eyes were closed. "Of course," she said suddenly, quite sharply, and with her eyes now wide open and fixed intelligently upon me, "I was not always a tramp, living as I do. You must not think that. Once, I drank a small sherry every night about six, before dinner, every night – I am accustomed to sherry, you know. Sometimes it is very hard when I look back and think what I gave up for love, very hard." She paused, and yet again, as in all my few conversations with her, I wondered at the wisdom of questioning her, but before I could make even the smallest enquiry she was off again. "I drank sherry with him the night before, you know," she said, turning to look into the fire, "just the two of us, a small celebration before the big day. I remember how he looked at me – with such feeling – there was not an inkling, not an inkling. All the preparations were made. It was not to be a big wedding, you know – only twenty guests, because of course neither of us had any family left to speak of and we were among strangers. We had a few friends, very select, that was all. And we drank a toast, in sherry." Miss Cowdie raised her glass. "To our wedding day, we said." She seemed to shudder and I half rose, expecting another dramatic weeping fit, but within seconds she had collected herself and turned back towards me. I saw at once that the expression in her eyes was different. "The Earl," she said, much too brightly, "prefers Scotch, but he will have no objection if I drink sherry. You will come to our wedding tomorrow, will you not, Miss Grove?"

"Yes," I said crossly, irritated beyond caring about offending her.

"I will throw you my bouquet," she said with an awful roguish air, "and *you* may be next."

I jumped up, afraid I would say something I should not, and took refuge in filling our glasses again.

"Is your roof safe?" I asked. "I hear a tree blew down across it."

"Mr Markham assures me no damage is done," she said, quite agreeably. "He is a very dependable young man. I trust him." She shot me a funny, shrewd little glance. "Do you like him, now you have met?"

"No."

"Indeed. Why not?"

I shrugged. "We don't agree on things," I said. "We have too many different opinions to get on."

"But I meant *as a man*," Miss Cowdie said impatiently. I was disgusted with her but managed to reply, "No, not even as a man."

"Of course, he is *not* tall. I did tell you he was not tall. He likes you," she said, simpering, "he told me so. He said he thought you were quite beautiful. There. He did – he told me himself."

"I do not care what Roger Markham said about me," I said.

I knew I ought to laugh out loud – it was an absurd, schoolgirlish conversation of a type I had not heard in years. Antonia and I used sometimes to gossip like that – "I know he likes you" – "No he doesn't" – "Yes he does" – but never for long. Even then, it made us feel too much like cattle and we stopped, shamefaced, before we had properly started. But Miss Cowdie clearly imagined I needed the solace of being assured I was liked. There was no possible way of showing her she was wrong.

"But," she said, leaning forwards and narrowing her eyes, "you prefer him to Geoffrey Crosthwaite, surely? Surely you do?"

"I haven't thought about it," I said. "It has never entered my head to make any comparison. Why should I?"

"They are both eligible," Miss Cowdie said, pronouncing the last word very distinctly. "One must take account of all those who are eligible, at least. The field is small up here, you know – one cannot pick and choose. I have the Earl, of course, and there are not many others. You must not be too proud, my dear, or you will – pardon me – end up on the shelf. I have seen it happen, even to lovely girls like yourself. They have waited to be swept off their feet and nothing has happened. You should not rule out Roger Markham. He *is* small, I did say he was small, but he is kind. Very. Now Geoffrey Crosthwaite is a peasant, like his father. I am not, I hope, a snob but I know a peasant when I see one. He is a peasant in looks and in ways. He is a brute. I have seen him kick dogs. I do not trust him, nor his evil sister. You must not be misled by his strength. Strength in a man is attractive – his father was also strong – but you must resist it."

I was about to repeat, very loudly, what I had said to her the time before – that I was not interested in her nineteenth century ideas on marriage – when Rufus suddenly barked and rushed for the door. I opened it so that he could go to greet Casper, whose bicycle lamp I could see wobbling along the track some hundred yards away. "It's my nephew," I said, over my shoulder, "coming home from school. I don't think you've met him. He will be so pleased to see you." It was a stupid thing to say and a little gasp of laughter at my own crassness escaped me as I stood at the door, waiting for Casper. He would be completely nonplussed at the sight of Miss Cowdie. Lacking any social graces whatsoever, he would be bewildered by the polite interchange of quite meaningless phrases between us. And in any case, finding a half mad tramp of a stranger sitting in the cottage drinking sherry was not exactly the welcome any boy would look for on returning from a four mile bike ride in the freezing cold of a dark November evening.

I tried to mouth at him who was there but ought to have realised he could not see my lips moving in the darkness and only wondered why I was barring his way. "Miss Cowdie is here," I whispered, and then stood aside to let him in. "Miss Cowdie, this is Casper," I said. I hoped Casper's Highgate School training would be sufficient to enable him to at least say "good evening" with some semblance of interest, but he just nodded and moved awkwardly to the fire, where he warmed his hands.

"Are you very cold?" I asked him. Another nod. "Was the rehearsal good – I mean, did it go off all right?"

He grunted "yeh" and turning from the fire crossed the

room diagonally, as far away as possible from our visitor, and went into the kitchen, muttering key words about washing his hands and changing his clothes, which were covered in mud from the splashes he had thrown up on the track. Normally, he did neither and I never asked him to, but I was glad to condone his escape. It was not fair to inflict Miss Cowdie on Casper.

"I'm afraid I must make Casper's supper," I said. I was relieved to find Miss Cowdie knew her cue. She finished her sherry off at once and jumped up.

"I will not detain you," she said cheerfully, and then, finger to her lips, she came very close to me and gesturing towards the kitchen, where Casper had gone, she whispered, "Beware!" and nodded significantly. I found myself whispering back, "I beg your pardon?" "The young man," she said softly, "beware – he will be much sought after – a beautiful face – and so tall already – he will be pursued." I smiled and said I would watch Casper carefully, and then I walked a little way across the garden with her. She thanked me for the tea, which she promised to return, and then off she went, walking purposefully into the utter blackness of the fell, as confident as if she were marching along a well lit street.

Casper was sitting at the table, eating a slice of bread he had cut for himself. I was quick to bring out Eileen's casserole and the baked potatoes that had been in the oven several hours. I was still smiling as I sat down to eat with him. He did not ask what the joke was. "Won't be coming home tomorrow," he said, after he had helped himself. "It's a late rehearsal. Doesn't start till six. Doesn't end till ten. I'm staying the night with a boy." I didn't dare let my pleasure show. Casper, I was sure, had never in his young life stayed the night with anyone – such deprivation was all part of his pathos.

"Fine," I said, "who is the boy?"

"Morton. He does lights too."

"Where does he live?"

"Don't know. His dad keeps a pub in Wigton somewhere."

"You're sure you've really been invited – that his mother knows?"

"Yeh," Casper frowned irritably. "I wouldn't ask myself, would I?"

"It's very kind of this Morton. Is that his first name or his second?"

"His second," Casper said wearily. "Mike Morton. He's only asked me 'cos of the lights – he can't manage them himself and he's scared I wouldn't be able to go, 'cos of getting back here, and he'd muck it up. I'm only his assistant but I know more than him. He isn't a particular friend or anything." We ate in silence for a while. Casper was ravenously hungry but I only picked at the meat and carrots. Suddenly he blurted out, "I need a white polo necked sweater." I looked up, startled. "White?" I said. "Yeh. I just need one. I haven't any money." He looked faintly defiant, as well as embarrassed. "Look," he said, "*have* I any money – for now, I mean, not when I'm twenty one?"

"I can give you some," I said. "I ought to have thought about it. I can make you an allowance."

"But is it *my* money?"

"It could be. I'm your guardian. I could sanction an allowance, if that's what you want."

"It is."

"Your grandmother would object but I suppose she needn't know. She wants you to have your inheritance intact."

"Will I be rich?"

"Depends what you call rich. You will have about eighty thousand pounds. It's invested for you, so by the time you're of age it might even be doubled." He looked very pleased. "I'll give you an allowance of ten pounds a week," I said, "but if it isn't enough you can prove it and have more. You're bound to have expenses, now you're growing up."

I spent the rest of the evening contemplating how much Casper had indeed grown up. Miss Cowdie's romantic notions no longer seemed so out of place. In the three months he had lived with me he had not only grown another two inches at least but his frame had begun to fill out. Perhaps it was all the exercise he now got, but he had muscles in his arms and that stooped shoulder look had gone – he might even end up heavy in build, like my father. I thought, looking at him furtively, that there was now a prospect at least of him ending up reasonably attractive and I was unreasonably glad. A white polo necked sweater indeed – what had put that idea into his head? I could not imagine that white sweaters were *de rigeur* at Nelson Thomlinson school. I longed to tease him about it but resisted the temptation. Let him have the sweater and the money in his pocket.

He went off the next morning in extremely good spirits, whistling all the way. Before he left he had taken Rufus for a run, so that I should not be obliged to, while he was away for the night, and I heard him talking to the animal, explaining that he would be back soon and Alexandra would still be here and that this was "OK". I noticed he had combed his hair carefully – pointless, considering he was cycling, and the work of art would be destroyed before he had gone a hundred yards. He took a bag with overnight things – I didn't inspect it or fuss over clean pyjamas or anything so falsely (to me) motherly. But I did wonder whether I ought to instruct him in saying thank you – something he was not very good at, at the best of times – and did manage a slight reminder. He even smiled and said, "See you tomorrow, then," before he went off and I said, "Have a good time," and tried to keep the amusement I felt out of my expression.

Eileen met him on the way up. I don't think they exchanged any words – both were as bad as each other – but her beady eyes noticed the bag slung on his back, as well as the usual bike bag full of school things, and she said to me as soon as she came in, "Casper had a bag on his back," as though I might not know. She didn't, being Eileen, ask for any direct information but I gave it to her without a struggle. "He's got a late rehearsal at the school," I said, "he's staying overnight with another boy." "Morton," Eileen said, impassively. "How did you know, Eileen?" I said, genuinely astonished. She smirked – little triumphs of that nature were the staff of life to Eileen. "Seen them," she said, "seen them last week in Crown Street. Outside Pig and Duck." "Well, you're right," I said, and I could not resist adding, "What is this Morton like, then?"

"Quiet," Eileen said, tying on her pinny. "Serious. Not like his sister. I was at school wi' Madge. She's a devil. Gets if from her dad – he were wild till he married. Grace Morton is my mother's cousin."

"Does your mother ever see her?"

"Sometimes. Not regular."

"Well, when she next sees her, could you get her to pass on my thanks? Casper didn't want me to write or anything formal like that."

I noticed, rather late, that something shone in Eileen's ears. She stood at the sink and seemed to have trouble with her hair, pushing it back constantly and fiddling with the dreadful clip she wore – and then I saw the dangling ear-rings. They were bright, lurid blue, tear drops of cheap coloured glass hanging from a gilt ring in each ear. "Eileen," I said, "you've had your ears pierced – how daring."

"Carlisle Market," she said. "Two pound, just. Did it with your first money. Just had the sleepers out – first day I've got these in."

"You've got a lovely neck," (and she had) I said, "you suit them."

"Going to get my hair permed," she said, a little spot of colour coming into each pale cheek. "Our Geoff says I'll look a tart and he'll kill me but I don't care. Alus wanted me hair permed. And dyed. I'd like black curly hair – alus did. Hate this pale thin stuff. Alus have. I'd like curls.

Half way into the baggy dungarees I was going to wear over my other clothes to work in, I stopped. The vision of Eileen with a mass of black curls literally halted me in my movements. Slowly, I sorted out the straps and began to button them up. "Eileen," I said, carefully, "do you think black curls will suit you? You're so fair skinned. It might look very odd. And what about your eyebrows? They're almost white. If you dye your hair, it will look so strange. I'd think about it, if I were you."

"I have," Eileen said, defiantly, "I've thought and thought. I'm going to have it done, for the Christmas Dance. I'm going to go to Binns in Carlisle and have it done properly with your money. Never could before – never had any money. And I'm going to buy a taffeta dress – red, with a low neck – and gold sandals wi' very high heels."

I left her day-dreaming, slopping dishes through the soapy water and visions of her transformed self through her head. It troubled me that I was the instrument of Eileen's liberation. With my money she would dress herself up and what would it lead to? Perhaps a dance. In Eileen's mind it led to the altar. The red taffeta would be exchanged for white organza, and the black curls crowned with orange blossom. Eileen had no other ambition in life, her expectations could not be lower, and unwittingly I was aiding and abetting her in this self-destruction. As I worked, cold and shivering at first in the freezing barn, I thanked God for my independence. Bending over the wheel, my breath coming in misty patches into the chill air, I imagined what it must be like to have one's horizons fixed on hair-dyeing in Binns, and then, my hands warming to the friction of the wet clay, as I shaped and turned it, I rebuked myself for my condescension. What were my own aims? Recently I had reclaimed some ambition but it was puny and limited enough. I was making pots, good pots. I would sell them. I would have proved I could make a life for myself, by myself, without the support of anyone.

But I cheated. Already, I looked forward to David's visit the following Tuesday. I was scheming in my mind, wondering if Casper might happily have a lighting rehearsal that day, if he would stay with the Mortons, if David could come back with me and spend the night . . . I was *not* existing on my own, nor was my own head as empty of Eileen's sort of fantasies as I liked to think. I too thought of clothes. For two months I had existed in jeans and sweaters and I was tired of them – I wanted my bit of glamour. Worse, I wanted David, and even Roger Markham, to see my bit of glamour. I wanted to subtly perfume myself and wear silk next to my skin and have my legs bare and smooth beneath a dress. It was only different in degree from Eileen's longings. I had always persuaded myself that I dressed up for my own benefit – that the impulse was purely narcissistic – but I was not even sure this was true. I *did* dress for myself, but it depended upon what that self was going to do, whom it would be seen by. No matter which way I looked at it, glamour was for going out and displaying myself.

Eileen was supposed to bring me some tea at ten o'clock, and again at eleven thirty, before she went home. I had taught her how to make it as I liked it – weak and very hot – and to carry it to me in a particular mug that kept the liquid at the temperature I liked it. She appeared at ten minutes to ten with a face disturbed out of its usual blankness, a great furrow of unaccustomed anxiety across her brow. "Tea's gone," she said, wiping her hands on her pinny over and over again. "Caddy's empty – none in the cupboard either." It flashed through my mind that perhaps she thought I would accuse her of stealing it. "Well, make coffee then," I said, "proper coffee – thin and black." She hesitated. "Don't fret about the tea," I said, "Miss Cowdie borrowed it last night. I'll get some more tomorrow." Eileen's face relaxed instantly and she sighed with relief before going off. I did not like this evidence that there was an element of fear in our relationship. Who had put it there? Had I been haughty or brusque with Eileen? Had I given her any cause to fear me? I thought not, and yet I had glimpsed the smallest shade of terror. She brought the coffee a few minutes later, visibly anxious that it was as I liked it. Coffee, to Eileen, as I had quickly discovered, meant a dash of the cheapest instant stuff, thrown into a sea of heated condensed milk – I was physically sick when first she made me "coffee". She agonised over ground coffee to a ridiculous extent. I had shown her how to use the little electric grinder, how to measure the beans and then the resulting powder, how to stir the finished brew and how to scoop the grounds off the top and strain the stuff into a cup. But she found the whole process difficult and her expression, when engaged in the job she found so laborious, was distasteful.

"Thanks," I said, stopping a moment to appreciate her efforts truly. I tasted the coffee. "Delicious," I said, and smiled. "Have some yourself." Eileen shook her head, but she did not go. "Shouldn't lend anything to Miss Cowdie," she said at last, her arms crossed in front of her and her whole stance accusing. "She'll come again, now she knows."

"I don't mind," I said. "Someone should make friends with her. I quite like her."

"She does funny things," Eileen said, slyly.

"I know," I said, calmly. "But I don't think she'll do them to me any more."

"She has turns," Eileen persisted. "She could have one any minute. She gets violent. She could just turn against you and you'd never have a chance."

"I'll risk it," I said, and then I thought a bit. "Doesn't she ever see a doctor?"

"No. Hates doctors."

"Doesn't anyone else ever mention her to a doctor? She must have had one once."

"Dr Teasdale at High Ireby, but she won't go near him, won't let him in either. She remembers him from the wedding day – he took her home and that. Wouldn't look at him again, never. Won't have his name mentioned."

"Is that your doctor?"

"Everyone's doctor."

I made a mental note of that, as Eileen trailed off with my cup. I had not registered with a doctor and ought to have done. I could do so, and have a chat with the knowledgeable but ostracised Dr Teasdale. "Eileen," I shouted after her, "when is Dr Teasdale's surgery open?" She came back looking self-important and told me the times, and said she was going herself that afternoon, about her hand. I could see nothing wrong with the hand she produced so tenderly out of her rubber glove. "Getting a wart," she said confidently, and pointed. I could see nothing and wondered if Dr Teasdale would. "Don't want anything on me hands," Eileen said, "specially not at Christmas, with the dance." Twice she had mentioned the precious dance, so I asked her when it was to be and she told me the date and time and place with some excitement. Everyone, she said, went – all the young folk from miles around. It was a good do. There was beer and cider and food – Christmas food, mince pies and brandy cake and cold turkey with all the trimmings. It went on until four in the morning and there was no other event like it.

Again, I cautioned myself against being patronising about Eileen's pleasures. Was I not feeling a little bleak about the prospect of a party-less Christmas myself? Since Mrs Matlock's letter, I had been steadily refusing to look Christmas in the face, and yet it was only a month off. Nor had I forgotten that the day after Christmas, Boxing Day, was Casper's fourteenth birthday. Something would have to be done and as I returned to work I thought hard about the whole problem. Clearly, we would stay where we were – tonight I would write to Mrs Matlock myself and compel Casper to add a note upon his return. I would make a great effort to buy exciting presents and fill the cottage with unaccustomed luxuries. But obviously the spectacle of Casper and me on our own was bound to be a little sad. We needed company, and there lay the rub. I could invite Miss Cowdie, but I quailed at the thought. I could perhaps invite David Garibaldi, though I was sure he would be committed elsewhere – he had a wife, perhaps children. I could invite the Crosthwaites, for a drink at least, but in our tiny cottage so many people presented problems. Perhaps Casper would by Christmas have made a friend he could invite – but that was ridiculous, for all "friends" would be in their own homes over the crucial period. It was really very difficult and I tired quickly of trying to work anything out.

By the end of that day I had achieved my first objective. Packed into the kiln was the last selection of cups and saucers, and when they had been fired (assuming they were perfect) I was ready to display my wares. I would pack the lot into my car and begin the slightly unpleasant job of touting them around. I did not relish the prospect, though it was not because I was in any way embarrassed by, or ashamed of my product, which I knew to be original and good. Rather, I dreaded the human contact. I am not in the least shy but I have nothing of the salesman about me. I hated the idea of trying to sell my stuff – the mechanics of it, the driving up to some hotel or restaurant and asking to see the manager and explaining why I had come. The more I thought about it, the more I saw how impossible the whole thing was. I had simply not thought this part of my plan through. Better, by far, to write or ring up and make appointments.

I caught Eileen just before she left and asked if I could come and use her telephone that afternoon. She said she was going into Carlisle with her mam but the door would be open and I could just walk in. I said I would get the operator to tell me the cost and leave the correct money. But I doubted, even as I asked the favour of Eileen, or of her parents through her, the wisdom of it. They were perfectly generous and had themselves offered the use of their telephone, realising before I did how important it would be, and I had certainly not taken advantage, but all the same it made me a trifle uneasy. In the country, the whole basis of good relationships with neighbours rests on mutual exchanging of services, and I had nothing to offer. I employed Eileen, who had not otherwise been employed, but she served me and I paid her – it was not at all the same thing. I did nothing freely for the Crosthwaites. I took but did not give, and I saw that if this was to continue it would be bad.

It seemed sensible to start with Roger Markham. Before I went down to the Crosthwaites', I looked out the telephone number he had given me. He would be expecting me to call – I had said I would not be ready until much later – and I did not relish appearing to hustle him. Indeed, I felt uncomfortable about ringing him at all when I had been so dismissive about the contact he had offered me. How would I phrase my request? I did not want him to get any hint of embarrassment on my part but I was afraid it would come through if I did not rehearse myself very carefully. All the way to the Crosthwaites' I was going over in my head what I should say and cursing myself for this silly nervousness. I could not imagine how commercial travellers managed. Often, in book shops particularly – which had always surprised me – I had cringed on behalf of the salesmen, who were treated with such a lack of courtesy, and I had watched them, obliged to stand humbly by, and wondered how they could bear it. Because they had to, I supposed. Because it was their living and they had no choice. But I had a choice. Never at any time had I pretended I must earn my living by selling pots – it would be an advantage but not a necessity. I did not have to subject myself to this selling process that I found abhorrent, but in some strange way it seemed important to me that I should. It was part of the deal with myself. I could not just fool about in the barn making pottery for my own amusement – it was not good enough. I had to carry the thing through. I had to be professional or forfeit my own self-respect.

These rambling thoughts carried me to the door of the Crosthwaites' farm. I was so preoccupied on the way that I observed nothing of my surroundings, something that I had noticed happened more and more. At first I had been unable to go outside my own cottage without being intensely aware, both of the landscape and the weather. I had noticed each change of colour in the earth, each shift of cloud in the sky. I had constantly been aware of the emptiness, the stillness, the openness around me. But that had stopped. I seemed to have absorbed my surroundings and no longer mentally commented on them to myself. Only the weather still raised my level of consciousness – like everyone else, I hung on whether it was wet or dry, on whether the cold wind blew harshly or softly.

The farmhouse looked quite deserted, but then, it always did. The yard at the back and to the left was filthy with manure and full of broken bits of farm machinery. The Crosthwaites seemed to me so tidy on their land – their fields clear of thistles, their fences in good repair – but about their own homestead there was always this air of neglect, which I found hard to understand. I had been told by Eileen to go to the side door – the front, as I had originally suspected, was simply never opened and never would be, Eileen said in her delightfully morbid way, until a coffin went out of it – and I picked my way carefully round a particularly vicious piece of old threshing machinery to get to it. I knocked, for form's sake, though I knew nobody would be in, and then, after a decent pause, I entered the house. Just inside the door there was a line of Wellingtons, so I took mine off too and left them there and then padded rather self-consciously, though there was no one to see me, through the kitchen into the dark hall and settled myself at the telephone on a stool I took from beside the kitchen table.

It was quite dark in that little corner, but the darkness was due to the situation, rather than the lack of much strong daylight outside. I did not attempt to put a light on but crouched uncomfortably over the small rickety table, holding the telephone, and peered at the dial. My hand shook slightly as I lifted the receiver, which annoyed me – I could not account for the sense of extreme anxiety which was forever gripping me these days. I found myself looking over my shoulder up the dingy staircase, imagining shadows in the large patterns of the heavily embossed black and brown wallpaper. There were none. I turned back to the telephone and cleared my throat. The number Roger Markham had given me was ringing. Eventually, a woman's voice answered and I asked for Roger. "Roger isn't in, I'm afraid," the woman said, "can I take a message?"

"Yes," I said, feeling rather happy and relieved, "could you tell Roger that Alexandra Grove rang, and that I'm ready earlier than I thought, and would like to take him up on his kind offer?"

"Couldn't you ring him when he comes in, after six?" the woman said, crossly, I thought.

"No, not really. I haven't a telephone – I'm at a neighbour's and I really don't want to bother them again. I'd be terribly grateful if you would give him that message. Shall I repeat it?"

I repeated it twice more. I thought it was a perfectly simple message, easily remembered, but the woman insisted on writing it down and seemed to find it very difficult. It transpired she was Roger's mother and that she found taking the many messages he seemed to get very tiresome – particularly, she said with emphasis, those from girls. But at last she had it down and I thanked her and only after I had put the receiver down wondered if perhaps I should have strained her patience further by making some arrangement to meet Roger at the place he had mentioned – that is, the café that was part of the tourist attraction at the Hall. Perhaps he would get the unfortunate impression that I was summoning him, an idea I did not like. But it was too late – I could not possibly ring Mrs Markham back. I left some money beside the telephone and then went into the kitchen and put my boots on and left the house.

I noticed as soon as I stepped out how cold it had become – quite bitingly cold. I shivered and turned up the collar of my jacket, glad that Casper did not have to brave another ride in this arctic wind. In London, I had never had a proper heavy coat – there never seemed any need – but I realised then that winter up here was going to be a more serious business, and both Casper and I would need much more adequate clothing than we had yet collected together.

I lit the fire as soon as I got home and made sure I had enough wood in for the long evening. The kiln had turned itself off and I hung about the barn, keeping myself warm by brushing the floor, until the cooling process was complete. The last batch of pots was beautiful, and I felt very proud of them. I lined them up with the others I had completed over the last few hectic weeks and admired them. No one with an ounce of taste could fail to like them. The grey was a master stroke – subtle, but dramatic, with the faint black markings I had so delicately drawn. I put the light out quite reluctantly. Tomorrow, I would have to get down to the miserable business of costing, aware that the price would be the first thing any prospective buyer would want to know. It would, I thought, give me an appalling headache working it out and I hoped Casper would come home early to help me with his calculator.

Fifteen

The knock, when it came, was quite soft. I thought at first that I was hearing things. I had had a bath and afterwards sat in front of the fire in my towelling robe, writing to Mrs Matlock and drinking wine. Without Casper, I had felt less constrained – I hated to say it again, for it was an unpleasant realisation, but if Casper sat with me instead of watching his beloved television I always felt less relaxed. To be totally on my own gave me such pleasure, and I was not in the least nervous. But when the knock came I instantly was. It brought me sharply into the world around me – I had a sudden image, from above, of my tiny, well lit cottage with smoke coming from the roof and, all around, blackness. The terror I had felt in the barn returned to me as though it had never been absent and I could not believe that in the interval between that attack and this knock in the night I had done nothing to safeguard myself.

But of course the door was locked. I took a deep breath as I reassured myself – the door *was* locked. I had locked it as soon as I came in, at half past four, the very minute it was dark. And I had put across it the bar Mr Rigg had made for it. It could not be more secure. The door itself was heavy, made up of oak, Mr Rigg had said, and there was no prospect whatsoever of anyone being able to break it down easily. The windows all round me were shuttered – I thanked God I had kept those shutters. They all fitted properly and were secure. My cottage was as fortified as a little castle and the thought gave me courage. When the third rap came, a little louder, common sense returned to me. There was no need to suppose my visitor was the attacker in the barn – it was more likely to be Miss Cowdie, in search of tea and company. She had knocked just like that. Though I had not been in the cottage and had not heard the knock from inside, I had seen how timidly she held her hand, and how gently she rapped with her bunched fist. Almost certainly it was Miss Cowdie, but though the guess made me happier it still presented me with a problem – not so scaring, but equally pressing. I did not want to let Miss Cowdie in. This time, no Casper was coming home to give me the perfect excuse to turf her out. I was not afraid of her – I did not fear that, as Eileen predicted, she would have a fit on my doorstep – but I did not want to sit for hours and hours with her rambling on. Perhaps it was cruel of me to deny her the relief, but I did not care. Offering a certain amount of casual friendship to Miss Cowdie was one thing, but becoming her support was another. If friendship became, in her mind at least, intimacy, then I was lost. I would never be able to escape her.

My wrist-watch was lying on the table, a few feet away. Taking care to disturb nothing that would make a noise, I got up and retrieved it, and almost laughed out loud when I saw the time. It was only eight o'clock. My long, lazy evening had started so early I had deluded myself into thinking it was midnight at least. For some reason this newly discovered earliness of the hour made me more cheerful. I stood and thought. Then suddenly I remembered Miss Cowdie herself, leaning out of her top window, and I realised that was the perfect solution. I could not open the door without letting her in, but if I leant out of the bedroom window, or, better still, Casper's attic window, then inspiration might come to me to fend her off. I could say I was in bed, feeling ill with a cold – I could say I would see her in the morning without giving unnecessary offence, and if she had come about something specific, which was unlikely, I might be able to deal with it there and then.

But as I went up the few stairs in my bare feet, the stone striking ice cold, a slight hesitation remained. If it was *not*

Miss Cowdie, though only the smallest doubt remained in my mind, then I would be revealing myself as what I was – a woman on her own, and vulnerable. Rufus had stood up when the knock came but then he had lain down and had not moved since. I knew already he would not defend me – he was a worse coward than I. Perhaps if Casper was threatened he might retaliate, but he would not do so for me. But then I reminded myself that the visitor need not know I was alone – if he or she knew anything about me, if they were local, then they would expect Casper to be with me, and if it was a total stranger I could pretend there was someone with me.

I went past my own room, up to Casper's attic. There was no shutter on the attic window, which was set at a slight angle in the roof. I had fixed up curtains but Casper had taken them down – he said he didn't need them, that he preferred the bareness. Without putting on the light, I crossed to the window and, keeping well to the wall, tried to see below. I could see nothing. The window was in fact set slightly back and I would not only have to open it to see who was below, I would have to lean right out. If whoever it was stood close up to the door, I would not be able to see them even then. I thought of returning to my own bedroom but I had closed both shutters and curtains there earlier because it had seemed so cold and in opening them I feared I would attract attention, which I did not want to do – I wanted to see who it was before they saw me. If I could get a good view, I was considering the possibility of sitting tight until the person knocking gave up and I could watch their retreat.

Gently, I took hold of the latch which fastened the four paned window and eased it out of the hole it was fixed on. Like every other fitting, it had been newly made in the original style, and was smooth to open and shut. I pushed the window out, holding it firmly with one hand so that it would not blow back against the frame in the wind. The rush of freezing air took me by surprise and I clutched at the neck of my robe. I shivered and thought about going to put my clothes on but at that moment a firmer knock came and I changed my mind. Cautiously, I leaned out of the window and looked down, quite expecting to see nothing, but as if to assist me the moon came out from behind thick black cloud for a brief instant and brilliantly illuminated in its pale ghostly light the unmistakable figure of a man. I withdrew at once. Heart thudding, I closed the window and sank on Casper's bed, wrapping my arms round myself to calm my shaking body. I had been so sure it was Miss Cowdie – the shock of seeing the large figure numbed me. I could not think. I simply sat there, listening to the growing volume of the knocking, and did nothing. I did not know whether to stick to my intention and open a conversation from the window or whether to hide. I had a hysterical image of myself dropping out of the landing window at the back of the cottage and running away, but I could run nowhere while my legs shook.

Then Rufus barked and growled, and made the need to act imperative. I could not open the door – that was the one certainty – but I could open the window again, if I forced myself, and take a cooler look. But this time, as I leant out, with the ledge digging into my stomach, there was no moon to help me. I could see only a shape, quite indistinct. There was a tremendous hammering on the door and a sudden exasperated shout of "Come on – open up," and I realised that this was no stranger. It was Geoffrey Crosthwaite.

Relief was my undoing. I flew down the stairs, all fear gone, not a thought of any possible consequences in my head, and unbarred the door and unlocked it. I even said, "Geoff – I'm so sorry – I was in the bath with the radio on and only just heard you – come in." Rufus gave a small growl that quickly changed to a whimper and slunk out of the room – he was not fond of Geoff, who treated his own dogs abominably. I never allowed for the effect it would have on Geoff to see me standing in front of him with only a white robe round me and my hair in wild disarray. I think I actually put out my hand and touched his, urging him to come in, welcoming him as a deliverer from my own fear. I know I was carefree and chattered happily and it was not until he was standing with his back against the door and I saw him lock it and put the key into his own pocket that I felt any apprehension. It was much too late. The return of that awful sense of foreboding exhausted me. "Well," I said, weakly, half sitting on a chair at the table, "did Eileen send you?" I suppose I hoped that by mentioning Eileen I would remind him of his situation. "Did your mother want something?" I said, in another pathetic attempt to warn him that there would be a reckoning for any act of his. He shook his head and smiled. "Were you frightened?" he said. "All on yer own here, and somebody knocking on the door? Not even that soft lad to keep you company tonight, eh?"

"No," I said, "I wasn't frightened. There isn't anything to be frightened of. And if I was frightened, I could always come to your kind family, couldn't I? You would always help me, I know, so you see I don't worry."

He went on standing there with that idiotic smile fixed on his lips, though his eyes were narrow with quite another expression – of malice, of calculation, I thought. He was considering how to proceed and I rapidly tried to seize the advantage I had lost. I whirled round and went into the kitchen, saying loudly that we might as well have some coffee. I quite expected him to follow me – my back grew tense with the strain of waiting for his hands upon it – but when he made no move I grew more confident. I could be up the stairs and into my bedroom in a trice, and there I could bar the door by dragging the chest of drawers across it, and I doubted if even the strength of Geoffrey Crosthwaite could get past that. Then I would sit the night out, knowing he must at some point slink home or be found out. But Geoff stayed where he was. When I came back into the living room, a steaming mug in each hand, he had not moved from the door. "Really," I said briskly, adopting my best schoolmistressy tone, "are you going to stand there forever? Have some coffee – you must be frozen, standing outside all that time." Reluctantly he came across to the table and sat down, awkwardly, not sure where to put his legs, which would not fit underneath. Uneasily, he swivelled round, sitting sideways on, half into the fireplace. "Take your jacket off," I ordered, "you'll roast in it, if you sit too near the fire." He shrugged himself out of the huge garment and hung it on the chair and I marked the pocket which held the key. "Is this a social call, Geoff?" I said, primly, my hands round the coffee, which, I was busy reflecting, would make an excellent weapon if aimed at anybody's face – quite enough time, while the boiling hot liquid splashed into the eyes, to kick where it hurt and get upstairs.

"Ay," Geoff said, slowly. "I thought I'd drop in. Everybody else does."

"Really?" I said politely. "I'm surprised you think so. I don't have many callers."

"You have that Garibaldi."

"True."

"And that Roger Markham."

"No," I said, carefully. "No, Mr Markham has never been in this cottage. I've only spoken to him outside the barn, as he was on his way to Miss Cowdie's."

"But you're expecting him, eh? You're waiting for him next."

"No, I'm not. Where did you get that idea?"

"Little bird telt me. You're waiting for him to come, you're ready for him to come. Ready for everyone except me, eh?"

Of course, Geoff had been in the house – I had not imagined a shadow on the stairs. He had heard my message to Mrs Markham and misinterpreted it accordingly. I considered confronting him with his eavesdropping but thought better of it. Geoff was stupid. Better to let him go on thinking he had been clever.

"Well, I don't know what your little bird is talking about," I said, "but I assure you I am *not* waiting for Roger Markham. I detest him. I'm only sorry that I have to meet him to sell my pottery to his employer – I'd rather have nothing to do with him, but it's too good an opportunity to miss."

"You don't like him?" Geoff said, suspicious, the effort of trying to work out what I meant contorting his features.

"No. I hate him."

"Get away!"

"I do. He is the all time male chauvinist pig."

"Eh?"

"Women are just decorations to him. He likes to wear them. A bit like you."

"I don't want to wear them," Geoff said.

"No, but you're not interested in a woman as a person at all."

"I am," Geoff said, leaning earnestly on the table. "I'm interested in you. I think about you all the time – honest."

"But *what* do you think about?" I said, before I could stop myself. Geoff's eyes glazed over. "I think," he said, his voice thick and hoarse, "I think about you in here, in your bed, with no clothes on. I come and stand outside sometimes, at night, and I look up at your window and I think – I think – "

He could not stop himself. He got up as though in a dream, and I rose too, in self-defence, and when I threw the coffee he did not even blink, just went on advancing, and I retreating, and at the foot of the stairs, towards which I had been backing, he caught me and held me so tightly I could not move. A great bear hug it was, pinioning my arms and shoulders, and yet there was nothing horrific about it, nothing against which, after the first shock, I tried to struggle. He did not try to kiss me, or to explore my body, but simply held me, groaning, his own limbs quite still, and we remained there, locked into a perfectly chaste but suffocating embrace for several minutes. My head came beneath his chin – he seemed to have his neck arched back – and my face was pushed against his chest. I could feel his heart thudding wildly and gradually this violent beating calmed my own pulse. Geoff was incapable of rape. He had so tortured himself with visions of carnal lust that now he had me in his grasp he could not go on. Instead of being driven to overpowering me and having his way, he had become ensnared in his own dreams of perfection. For now, he was content to hold me – desire had made him weak, not violent. I stood and waited, quite passive. When I felt his grip relax slightly, I freed my arms and put them round his neck. Pity made me tender. "Geoff," I said softly, "carry me upstairs."

He was crying. As he lifted me, so easily I might have weighed nothing, and as we went upstairs, his tears fell onto my robe and I shut my own eyes so as not to be a witness to them. The awful truth was that poor Geoff's distress had awakened in me a need to console him. If he had tried to ravish me I should have screamed and struggled, and my hatred would have inspired me to reject his advance totally, but his simple-minded ecstasy melted my hostility. It did more. It made me want to make him happy by giving him what he wanted, not in any cold blooded, altruistic way, but to make him see sex as something as beautiful as he had always imagined. I would initiate Geoff. He was a blundering fool and did not deserve his luck, but I could not bear to see his frightful need and to do nothing about it. There was nothing cheap about my sudden decision – I did not see it as selling myself, like any streetwalker. There was no element of self-sacrifice in my bargain with myself – I wanted to make love to Geoff, then. With David, it had been a meeting between two equals, no emotion other than lust present, but Geoff called forth a kind of pity I did not know I possessed.

He put me on the bed and stood looking down at me. "I'd better go," he said, not bothering to wipe away his tears.

"Stay," I said. "Get into bed with me. You don't have to make me a prisoner to get what you want. I'll give it to you freely." He was speechless, and I laughed. "It isn't so terrible, Geoff," I said, "you don't have to be so frightened. And you don't have to think of me as a whore." He sat down on the edge of the bed and put his head in his hands. Gently, I stroked his back, and when he lay down beside me, still fully clothed, I put my arms round him and kissed him. "It's nothing to be ashamed of," I said. But he was so ashamed. His beautiful strong body was full of shame – he could hardly bear to take his clothes off and when finally he had done so he seemed terrified. "I love you," he kept saying, and then moaning with anguish. His excitement was awful – his body had taken him over and he was no longer in charge of it. The pleasure for me was minimal and I was bored long before Geoff was satisfied. He lay on top of me, spent and exhausted, his hair damp with exertion and his whole torso suddenly dead. I extricated myself as painlessly as possible, wondering if I had gone quite crazy. I had given in to an impulse and there was no excusing it.

Naturally, he could hardly bear to look at me. He came downstairs, scarlet in the face and tongue-tied – if one thing was certain, it was that sex had been no liberation. But at least he did not strut, nor try to pretend he had covered himself with glory. "There you are, Geoff," I said, handing him his jacket, from which I had already taken the key, and I unlocked the door. "You'd better go home." The more boldly I looked at him, the deeper his blush became. "You won't need to hang about any more outside," I said, I suppose sarcastically, "your dream has come true. But it won't come true again, understand? That was to finish it."

"But –" he began.

"I don't want to discuss it," I said abruptly. "There is no need ever to mention it again. It was a favour." I could not keep the contempt out of my voice, and Geoff was not to know it was for myself and not him.

I sent him out into the night with every appearance of a man shell-shocked. He literally stumbled out of the door and appeared not to know which way he was going. There was such desperate confusion on his face that I did not like to look at it, nor to think of the consequences of what I had done. Let Geoff sort himself out. I was determined to exorcise the whole incident from my mind – it was to be nothing to me, merely an annoying mistake which would not be wiped out by brooding over it.

But of course I did brood. It was a very long time since I had so let myself down. Once, it had been my way of life – to act on the spur of the moment, to follow some unconventional path, assuring myself I knew where it led and did not care – but I had thought all that was behind me, once I had left London. Living in this remote spot was supposed to give my character the stability it lacked – I was supposed to have finished with erratic patterns of behaviour.

And yet, do not mistake me – I did not regret the impulse itself, the urge to give Geoff what he wanted. At the time, it seemed right. It was certainly what I wanted to do and my remorse had nothing whatsoever to do with the act. What troubled me was my failure to weigh against that act the forseeable consequences, and to see that they ought to have formed an insuperable barrier against it. I had been brought up to look at all decisions like this. From my earliest days, I remember my father, sitting with the tips of his fingers pressed to each other in an attitude of prayer (though he never prayed in his life), telling me that in all important acts of will there was always a moment of balance when "I want" became "I will", and that if I was to find happiness I must learn to fuse the two without shame. He said that they were at either end of a see-saw and that the fulcrum was the question of whether one could proceed to "I will" without tripping over "I ought not". Naturally, I hardly listened to him, though he would ponderously have debated the matter all night. I never saw, either in him or my mother, any straightforward enthusiasm for anything, and despised them for their humming and hawing. I was going to follow the dictates of my heart forever, and I did, for years and years, until I was compelled to admit the pleasure was ruined by what this did, not to myself but to *other* people.

Miserable and worried, I sat by the fire, thinking about Geoff Crosthwaite. I had no doubt that he had never made love in his life before – the taunts of Roger Markham, repeated by Eileen, had been true. That fine body had not known how to function until it was shown. Geoff would lie all night, remembering my too expert ministrations, and I did not know how he would feel. Would embarrassment turn to horror, horror directed towards me? Or would it slowly burn into passion, into a belief that, next time, he would be able to show what he was made of? Would he avoid me, or seek me out? Had I quelled forever that boundless lust, which had so inflamed him, or had I kindled a greater fire, which would attempt to consume me? I did not know, nor did I know whether Geoff had seen in my love-making the tenderness and pity I had felt. Do gentle hands convey sympathy, or were they to him all part of a seducer's art? Did he hear in my whisperings the compassion that prompted them, or only the honeyed, meaningless mutterings of a seducer?

It was an awful mess, and gloom filled my mind. I longed for my earlier life and the comfort of relationships that were understood for what they were. And I longed for Edward, who would have laughed at me and scolded me and obliterated guilt with kisses. He had not, this time, sought me out. Safe on the other side of the world, not even knowing my exact whereabouts, he would surely by now have found consolation in the willing arms of some other woman. I must reconcile myself to the inevitable, which I had brought about. I was alone, at last. Neither David Garibaldi nor Geoff Crosthwaite could ever give me what I found I needed, and yet I could not survive without some close companionship with a man. Like Miss Cowdie, I would go mad, bereft of sex and love and a kindred spirit. Work brought happiness of a kind but it was not nearly enough. Suddenly, the whole of the last few months seemed merely a preparation for this humiliating discovery, and I went to bed finally as depressed as I had ever been.

In the morning, it snowed, and with the snow came that physical sense of cleanliness that can heal all manner of internal wounds. I looked out of my bedroom window in amazement at the transformation – the bleakness gone, everywhere sparkling brilliantly as an Alpine sun caught the crushy white surface. Eileen, arriving earlier, assured me it was mostly hard frost with just a sprinkling of snow, but she could not kill my joy in the beauty of it. Half the morning I just stood and looked while she brought out one dire warning after another – the roads would be treacherous, the water would freeze in the pipes, the hens would not lay. She told me that if it really snowed I would soon get sick of it, I would soon lose my taste for it when I had been marooned for a week in the kind of giant drifts that so quickly built up in this part of the world. Snow, Eileen said, was a damned nuisance to a farmer, especially in the New Year, when the first lambs were about to arrive. She warned me not to say to anyone that I hoped it snowed more – nothing worse to a farmer, she assured me. On and on she went, but I persisted in my cheerfulness. Until, with a final flourish of her broom on the living-room floor, she said that, as if this awful weather wasn't enough, Geoff wasn't well.

"Didn't get up this morning," Eileen said. "Mam went and shouted but he couldn't get up – said he hadn't the strength of a kitten. Never happened before. Mam says he must be sickening for something bad. He's never spent a day in bed in his life, our Geoff, strong as a horse. Nobody to help Dad, and there's a lot of extra work." I kept very quiet. "He were out last night," Eileen droned on, "don't know where – went off about eight, not in the car, don't know where he went, and came back at ten, looking as if he'd seen a ghost. 'Have you seen a ghost?' Mam said, he were that white. He just sat there wi' his eyes closed, couldn't get any sense out of him. Dad said he'd been on the drink but he hadn't, not a whiff of anything, and our Geoff'd never *walk* to the pub. Mam said perhaps he'd come off his bike but I don't think he was on his bike, he hates bikes, it's horses or cars for Geoff. Didn't have any supper. Just sat there till the tele news was over and then he went to bed, not a word out of him." She paused, as though some comment was expected from me. "Poor Geoff," I said calmly, "I hope he'll be better tomorrow." "He'd better be," Eileen said darkly, "farmers can't be ill, not our sort of farmer."

As if to underline the contrast between her world and that of the gentlemen farmers, Roger Markham's jeep bounced to a halt at the end of the track as she finished speaking. We both saw him jump out, muffled up in a sheepskin coat for once, and hurry over towards us. I opened the door and went out to greet him, not pausing to put anything extra on in my haste to have any conversation with him out of Eileen's range.

"Got your message," he said, slapping his hands together to keep them warm. "My God, you'll freeze, coming out like that – get back in."

"I'm on my way to the barn," I said, teeth chattering. "I've been warming it up since seven this morning. Come, and I'll show you my stuff."

We ran to the barn, which was only marginally warmer than an igloo, in spite of the two large Super-sers blazing away. Roger examined my collection while I thanked him for coming so promptly. "Well," he said, "that's splendid. Let's get it into your car and you can follow me back."

"What, now?"

"That's why I came. Howard's keen to see it and there's no time like the present – he's stuck at home with a foul cold and you're not likely to have him in one place and all attention again – it was very lucky you rang. Go and get some proper clothes on and I'll start packing."

I suppose excitement banished all thoughts of caution. I rushed inside and put my very warmest trousers and polo necked sweater on, and bundled myself into the only jacket I possessed – a fur thing, totally unsuitable – and ran back again, shouting to Eileen as I went that she could lock up and go when she had finished, that I was off to the Earl of Cumberland's to try to sell my pottery. She would have seen me anyway, going backwards and forwards loading the car with Roger. We had to take care not to slip and there was a good deal of childish shrieking and laughing as we slithered about with our precious cargoes. I suppose it looked as though we were enjoying ourselves hugely, and I ought to have guessed Eileen would go home and tell Geoff what a good time I had been having with Roger Markham, how happy I had been, how we had seemed such good friends. I ought to have found time to make some sort of remark that would have put the matter in a different light – though how I could have done that, I don't know.

Driving down the icy little road to Greenhead was terrifying and if I had not been following the bold Roger I should certainly have turned back. The Range Rover was solid and steady enough but nevertheless I twice went into a short skid and had trouble correcting it. When we got to Greenhead bridge and the road leading round to Uldale, Roger stopped and got out, leaving his engine running. "Look," he said, appearing at my window, "go *with* the skid – never brake in a skid. Women always put the brakes on and it's fatal." I found it hard to excuse the tone of absolute superiority with which he addressed me. I did not reply. Smiling, he went back to his jeep and I forced myself to follow him. Luckily, once we were on the Keswick road, the surfaces had been gritted and my confidence returned. I followed Roger without difficulty, keeping up a steady speed, even though the road twisted and turned and plunged up and down hill alarmingly.

We came out, after twenty minutes or so, at High Side and I expected Roger to turn left along the A591 to Keswick, but instead he turned right, doubling back on himself, and we drove round the northern end of Bassenthwaite Lake. The road was easier for a while and I did not need to concentrate so grimly. Behind us, I could see Skiddaw in my driving mirror, white and spiky with snow, and below it the lesser fells in that range, all greyly dipping in a dizzy line against the too blue sky. Tucked away in the bleaker folds of the most northern part of the mountains, hidden in the last hills before the Solway plain began, I rarely saw such extravagant beauty. The power and sweep of those Lake District peaks was concealed from me, the sudden lushness of so much vegetation a secret. Our fells were barren and smooth, their interior valleys silent. There was no rock to dominate the landscape, no ridges to attract the eye. Our land was one giant sheep pasture, without obstruction, and though I had gradually come to love the peculiar attraction of those empty uplands, I could not help but wonder that I had wilfully shut myself away from this other, more spectacular vision. There was colour here, even in the snow, and the lake gave a depth of texture lacking in our waterless settlement. It shone in the sun and flashed its blueness back to the sky and even in the icy conditions gave to the surrounding hills a warmth. I felt excited by it, I craned constantly to see the views all round, and was sorry when Roger led us away from this pretty scene and began to climb, on the other side of Bassenthwaite, along the road that led to Hithop Hall. He had told me, and Eileen had told me, where the Earl of Cumberland lived but I had not paid much attention. Somehow I had got the impression that his estate was near Keswick and had imagined a baronial mansion standing majestically above Derwent Water. But I saw, as we once more followed endless curves, and I worried again about skidding, that I could not have been more mistaken. Already more fells closed round us, in the way so familiar to me, and the lake with all its splendour was lost to view.

Nor was the Hall either baronial or majestic in situation. Hidden under Ling Fell and overshadowed by Thornthwaite Forest, it was a grim and gloomy place, built of granite and slate, imposing in size but little else. Double fronted, with large windows, it could have been any country house, built not earlier than the mid-eighteenth century, if it had not been for the two towers, incongruously attached on either side, and the line of chunky battlements that ran along the house façade at the top. I disliked it intensely on sight and wondered why anyone should want to live there. The grounds were extensive – we drove at least a mile from main gate to the front door – but had an air of having been carved out of the forest. Near the house there were some magnificent oak trees and a copse of silver birches, but they could not take from it that forbidding look of severity. I saw, as I got out, that Hithop Hall was well maintained. The paintwork was fresh, the windows clean, the giant urns at the foot of the main steps filled with fresh greenery, partly hidden under the weight of the snow. Holly bushes, blazing with heavily clustered berries, stood sentinel along the path leading to the steps. In the windows, I saw flowers and a glimpse of thickly embroidered tapestry curtains. The double front door had a shining brass knocker in the shape of an eagle's head and a bell push, similarly glowing.

We went round to the side and under an arch, which led to a courtyard. All round the yard were doors, tidily labelled

"TEA-ROOM", "GIFTSHOP", and so on. Roger pushed open the door marked "ESTATE OFFICE" and stood aside to let me in. There was a small log fire burning in an old fashioned grate surrounded by dark green tiles with pale pink roses painted on them. I went to warm myself and exclaimed at their design. "It's very snug," I said, admiring the huge roll-top desk and the filing cabinets made of varnished wood that filled one wall. "A very un-office office."

"We're very un-office sort of people," Roger said, "and we make very un-office coffee, freshly ground and complete with a lacing of whisky on such a morning." Amused at his pride, and genuinely impressed by the luxury of it, I watched him prepare the coffee. "Only one thing wrong," I said, holding up my mug when he had handed it to me, filled with the delicious brew, "frightful pottery." We laughed, and were still enjoying the joke when Howard came in, gum booted and sheepskin coated, like Roger.

Now I am not the sort of person who is either overawed by, or even interested in aristocracy. There were plenty of them round Oxford and I felt totally at home with the breed. It caused me no embarrassment to be introduced to an Earl, nor did I find myself particularly curious about his station in life, but all the same I confess to an inquisitive streak about this particular scion of a noble house. He was, after all, Miss Cowdie's prospective bridegroom. A small smile still hung about my lips at the thought, which I hoped would be excused as part of the atmosphere when he came in. "Alexandra doesn't like our pottery," Roger said. "What are we going to do about it?" "Buy hers, I should think," Howard said, and at once I liked him – not for saying so quickly and graciously that he would buy my pottery without seeing it, but for the relaxed, friendly way in which he nodded at me and enjoyed our company. We all three chatted for a while and then we went out to my car and carried in my samples. Howard would not let me help. Roger told him sarcastically that I was a liberated woman, and strong with it, but he firmly insisted I should stay in the warmth of the office. He let me unpack the cups and saucers and plates and jugs and bowls and mugs – the whole lot, seventy two pieces in all, and then he simply said, "Lovely. When can you treble the order?"

I don't suppose anyone has ever done business so swiftly or painlessly, and it would be silly to pretend I was not absolutely delighted. The price was agreed – though I noticed Howard speedily spotted a mistake in my calculations – and a cheque made out, there and then, for the goods received. I promised to deliver three times as much before the season opened on March 20th. Howard said that, for such a large order, he would expect a deduction in rates and, rather more to my surprise, and slight concern, he also insisted, as part of the bargain, that I would not make this particular design for anyone else. That, I thought, was going a little too far, but I did not want to spoil my own elation and so I agreed, assuring myself it would be more of a challenge to evolve something completely different after this initial run. (But a little voice at the back of my mind piped up to say agreeing to such a condition was folly.)

We went down to the Pheasant Inn near Bassenthwaite for lunch, Howard very much in command and Roger undoubtedly in his shadow. I thought, as I watched him during that hour, that he seemed the most contented man I had met for a long time. Everything about him showed confidence – in himself, in what he was doing, in what he was saying – and yet he was not arrogant. I wondered privately about his wife – was she part of his happiness? I saw that though he was interested in me there was no deeper gleam in his eye – he was not attracted to me. This was a relief, and yet there automatically arose in me a desire to make him attracted to me, a perverseness on my part that I had noticed before. I wanted men to like me as a person and not a woman only, but the minute they did I regretted their celibate taste. Roger, listening to me, must have observed how I put myself out to be entertaining and I thought I saw some secret amusement in his face. "You're coming to the party, of course," Howard said, as we got up to go. "Roger has invited you, I hope." "I've invited her but she hasn't agreed," Roger said. "We'll take it for granted then," Howard said, "December 21st, and you'd better stay the night as you're so far away, Jennifer will expect it."

I drove to Wigton, a little drunk with the unaccustomed civilised company and with the success of my pottery. I was going to pick Casper up from school, knowing he could not possibly manage to cycle in this weather, and while there I would stock up with provisions, in case, as Eileen predicted, we were to be cut off. Dreamily, I thought of Hithop Hall and the Christmas party, and knew I could not pretend I was not looking forward to it every bit as much as Eileen was looking forward to the village dance.

Sixteen

The snow did not last. Next day, there was evidence of another severe frost – I was glad it was Saturday and Casper did not have to face the perilous journey to school – but then all the whiteness disappeared. I was disappointed and so was Casper. We had had visions of sledging among the fells – naïve souls that we were – and of skating on Bassenthwaite. Eileen said we would learn soon enough not to wish for snow, when she arrived on Monday morning, and repeated her litany of prospective disasters. She said the weather forecast was good, if you could trust it, and for the time being there was no anxiety about the weather. But now we were into December we must be prepared and expect the worst, and Geoff and her father had that morning gone off to bring the sheep down from the higher reaches of the neighbouring fells. If there was heavy snow, Eileen said, the sheep got drowned in it – literally stuck in the drifts and only able to breathe if they had huddled up against a dry stone wall and had an air passage through to the other side. It was better to have them nearer the farm and then, in the event of a blizzard, there was some chance of getting them near shelter.

"Geoff's recovered, then," I said, as casually as possible, not wanting to display any undue interest to Eileen, who, I was sure, relayed every word I said to her family.

"He's up and out," Eileen said, "but he hasn't a word for

anyone. Says nothing. Nice change, anyway. In a dream, he is, all day long, but he leaves me alone. Didn't go out on Saturday night – never moved. Mam says she doubts he hasn't shaken it off yet, whatever it is." "Well, these things take time," I muttered, glad that Geoff was safely up on the hills and well out of the way.

There was a great deal of work to be done and I felt a slight sense of panic at having to make such a large repeat order. To start with, I had not enough materials, and was uncertain whether I could have deliveries guaranteed within three or four weeks. I sat down and made a list of everything I would need and then wondered where I could phone through the order. I did not want to use the Crosthwaites' telephone, nor could I sensibly use a call-box – the calls I wished to make would be too long and complicated to be able to cope with money in the slot and all that nonsense. The difficulty of finding a telephone almost made me resort to writing instead, but that would be foolish, in view of the urgency. I had to know whether what I wanted was in stock and I had to arrange there and then for immediate despatch. The only solution I could think of was Roger Markham's office. After all, it was in a way estate business – the pottery was for him.

I left Eileen in charge of preparing the last quantity of clay I had – she was good at measuring, with laborious slowness, the different proportions of materials – and went down into Caldbeck to the telephone outside the post office. Roger agreed straight away that I could come and spend half an hour in his office but said, quite tartly, that I had better put in an application for a telephone of my own immediately, if I was to be a business woman. When I finally got there, he said the same thing again before he left me alone. "I can't imagine why you don't want one anyway," he said, "it's plain silly to me." "Then there isn't much point in trying to explain," I said, crossly. "Look, if I could just make those calls, and I'll get the operator to ring back with the cost." "Yes," he said, easily, "do that. Howard is fussy about details." "So am I," I said, sharply. I sat down and started looking up code numbers in the directories, hoping Roger was not going to go on standing there, staring at me. "How's that boy, Casper?" he said suddenly. I flushed. "Casper's very happy, I think," I said, "he likes the school. He seems to like the life too." I did not ask him why he had particularly inquired after Casper. "The head of the maths department there is an old girl friend of mine," Roger said. "She was talking about him the other day. Says he's clever." "He is," I said, "at some things." I was irritated by Roger's continued presence, but it was, after all, his office. "I've got to go now," he said next, to my relief. "You'll have gone when I get back, I expect, but I'll pop in on you tomorrow – I'm coming up to see Miss Cowdie, last quarter's rent to deal with. She won't have it, but Howard likes me to go through the motions." "I might not be there," I said, lifting the telephone receiver and looking busy. He stopped at the door. "I'm going to a sale with David Garibaldi," I said. "I'm not sure when we will be back."

There was no need for me to give this piece of information but I wanted to. I was not ashamed of my friendship with David and I had no wish to conceal it from Roger, but on the other hand I did not want him around when David was there. Should I bring David home, which I thought quite likely, I did not want to be fretting all the time about Roger arriving. Better, I thought, to tell him the truth and then he would keep away. But the effect of my news made me regret I had ever given it. Swiftly, Roger crossed back from the door to his desk and, taking the receiver out of my hand, banged it down. His face was scarlet with anger. "I can't believe it," he said, "you can't have got yourself really involved with scum like that – not to the extent of being seen around with him. For God's sake, I could tell you things about Garibaldi that would make your hair stand on end. Do you know that – "

"No," I shouted back, equally loudly, "I do not know and I do not want to know. I like David and I'm not concerned with what he has or hasn't done. It is no concern of mine – I don't care about his past."

"Just about whether he's good in bed when you're feeling randy?"

I gathered up my things quickly and put on my coat. "I'm sorry to have disturbed you," I said, "I won't do so again." He caught at my arm as I turned to go. "Don't be stupid," he said, "I'm only telling you for your own good. Everyone knows David Garibaldi is – "

"Shut up," I said, "I don't want to hear your vulgar tittle-tattle and I don't want to have anything more to do with you. I'll deliver the pottery when it is ready – there is no need for you to contact me until then." His grip on my arm tightened. "Get off," I said, pulling away from him but unable to loosen his vicious grip. Harder and harder he dug his fingers into the sleeve of my jacket until even through that thickness he began to hurt me. Our faces were very close and it was difficult to avert my eyes from his frenzied expression. I tried to push him away but he only held my other arm and forced me to look at him. "You're going to listen, whether you want to or not," he said. "David Garibaldi is a brute. He's been convicted twice of causing his wife grievous bodily harm – I won't go into the disgusting details. He isn't safe to have in the house, certainly not in your lonely house. He's the sort of man who would rape his grandmother, if he got the chance. You take your life in your hands every time you go out with him. He's been had up for interfering with young girls – there's no sexual crime they couldn't pin on him. You'll end up murdered."

"I don't believe a word of it," I said, raising my voice to drown his instant assurances that he could prove he was right, "and I don't care what you tell me – I like David Garibaldi. Until he does something to change my mind, I'll go on liking him. I think you're simply sick with jealousy."

He let me go, quite suddenly. Mustering up a look he clearly thought was contempt he said, "And what would I be jealous of? Sleeping with you? My dear girl, I wouldn't touch you with a barge pole. You're little better than a prostitute. I don't have anything to do with ladies of easy virtue, thank you very much." I suppose he thought I would be insulted and hurt, so my unforced laughter unnerved him. "I'm glad you find it so funny," he said, stiffly, "but you might end up regretting your amusement. I only hope you have the decency to make sure that child of yours is out of the way when you're cavorting with Garibaldi." I stopped laughing and opened the door. "My nephew," I said distinctly, "is a perfectly healthy adolescent. Unfortunately, you obviously had something nasty happen to you at his age to make you see the world and everyone in it the way you do. Goodbye."

I slammed the door shut with satisfaction and began walking

back to my car, not at all sorry to have ended that encounter and more than a little triumphant because I thought I had come off best. My head was full of plans to do my telephoning from the Pheasant Inn on the way home and I did not at first notice Howard Lowther coming from the other direction. When I did, I was disconcerted. I feared Roger would come running after me and would hurl abuse in front of his employer, which would lead to embarrassment all round and leave me at a disadvantage. I waved and tried to hurry into my car, hoping he would not think me rude, but he called out, "Hold on!" and I was obliged to stop. It would be inexcusable to get in and drive off. "Morning," he said, with a nice smile, "I was just wondering if I could persuade you to come and meet Jennifer? She rather thinks she's an old friend of yours – wanted to meet you, at any rate, and was awfully cross I hadn't brought you in the other day. Do come in and have some coffee – or a sherry or something." I hesitated and said, "I'm not sure I should," and I looked over my shoulder to see if Roger, who had been about to leave before I did so myself, had yet come out of his estate office. "I've just offended Roger," I said, "I think perhaps I'd better get off the premises as quickly as possible. Perhaps some other time?"

"Oh, I wouldn't worry about Roger," Howard said, "but we can go this way if you like – if you don't want a head-on collision." He seemed amused by my reluctance to face Roger Markham, and yet strangely unsurprised. As we walked towards the left of the house, away from the courtyard holding all the various offices, he said "You have to make allowances you know – chaps in love are awfully touchy."

"Chaps in love?" I echoed, thinking I must surely have misunderstood his drift.

"Roger, you know," he said, smiling even more broadly. "Potty about you – don't say you didn't know. We've heard nothing but how marvellous you are, ever since he first saw you."

"But he *hates* me," I burst out, stopping dead in my tracks. "He's never given me the least sign he even likes me – I'm sure you're quite mistaken."

"No, I'm not. It's just his jolly old pride. He doesn't like people knowing what he wants. Jennifer always said that when Roger stopped being a philanderer it would be because he'd set his sights on someone unattainable. Like you."

We were by this time in the house, walking along a passage carpeted in sisal matting. I felt utterly confused. There was Howard, talking with such confidence about Roger loving me when he had just told me he would not – what was the charming phrase? – would not touch me with a barge pole, and there was I, immediately softened by this news I knew to be demonstrably false. In the semi-gloom of the long passage I tried in vain to see Howard's face, to see if he was perhaps enjoying a complicated joke at my expense, but I could see nothing. "But Roger hates my sort of woman," I said eventually, just as we rounded a corner and came into a square hall. "He likes dutiful feminine types, who will look up at him and adore him and be absolutely conventional." Howard laughed out loud and started to climb the broad polished wooden stairs in a corner of the hall. I was just behind him, panting slightly to keep up – his pace was very fast and he knew where he was going – still trying to puzzle out the conundrum. There was no time to challenge Howard further before he opened a door at the top of the short flight of stairs into a crowded little sitting room full of toys and junk and books. "Come and meet Jennifer," he said.

I recognised her instantly. Ten years had left little mark upon her – I knew the changes to be all in myself, and wished I had realised who I was going to meet and could, out of sheer vanity, have prepared myself better. My hair felt unkempt, my face raw, my body heavy and clumsily dressed. Jennifer, even at midday, was perfection. She stood near the window – I thought she must have been watching Howard and me the whole length of our walk from the car – smiling, her hand outstretched. "Alexandra!" she said, and I found myself stumbling over obediently and being kissed. The perfume was the same – stephanotis, faint and unbelievably fragrant – and if I had ever known the colour of her lipstick I was sure that was the same too. Small and slender, with a delicate pointed face, the only thing that had never been a cliché about Jennifer was her hair. To be truly in type, it ought to have been blonde and carefully coiffeured into a debutante style, grown to shoulder length and flicked up. Instead, she had always worn it extremely short, a cap of closely cropped curls, shining like the palest of moons. Everything about her, except the red, almost purple, mouth, was pale and fragile, and her clothes, always dresses in fine, soft fabrics, were always dark – browns, greys, black. It made one afraid to touch her, afraid to disturb the composition. She was truly elegant and lovely, the sort of woman who makes her own sex despair.

I am rarely tongue-tied, but I was then. I could not think what to say. My mind still churned on about Roger and could not cope with this new shock. I felt stupid and I'm sure looked it. Jennifer went on smiling, her hands daintily clasped in front of her, like a shy child's, while Howard delved into a cupboard and produced glasses and a bottle of sherry. He was beaming too. "Orders not to tell you," he said, seeing my dazed expression. "Jennifer thought you'd be surprised, eh?" Wildly, my thoughts went off on a tangent – instead of concentrating on how I was going to react to my old enemy, I found myself obsessed with trying to imagine by what extraordinary means Howard had come to capture such a woman. I have described Howard sufficiently – tall, yes, and pleasant enough, but ordinary, all the same, like any number of country gentry. The only thing that was attractive about him was his relaxed, confident manner, and the only thing impressive, the fact of his title and wealth. But Jennifer would not have married for that. She, like me, had her principles. Whatever else I might say about her, I would never accuse her of being either mercenary or a snob. And Jennifer liked London and society even more than I did – a party every night was very much her line. To live in a house like Hithop Hall and lead the life Roger had described her as leading must have been hell for her. Yet there she stood, bandbox fresh and apparently thrilled with herself.

I took the sherry, grateful for the distraction, and, as I sipped it, managed to exchange preliminary pleasantries while I collected myself. My heart beat a little faster. It was just possible . . . "Well, Jennifer," I said loudly. "I'm astonished. I had no idea you had married Howard, or that you had ever left London, for that matter."

"It was *quite* a big wedding," Jennifer murmured, batting her eyelids at me, "but I think you were in America. You must have missed it." She fingered her necklace, a classic pearl effort. "And of course I couldn't invite Edward *and* you, so I thought – as you were in America – didn't he ever mention it?" I was tempted to say her name had never crossed Edward's lips since – since the whole affair was over but I smiled and said instead, playing her at her own game, "No, he didn't. How odd. But then he always was odd, wasn't he?"

"Down to old flames already," Howard said, pleased. "Look, I think I'll push off and leave you two together."

I would much rather he had stayed, as a chaperon if you like, but Jennifer waved him away graciously. Her attitude changed as soon as he had gone. She sat down in a big, battered wing chair – I worried at once over whether it was clean enough for her – and said, "I hear you're on your own up here," with a new hardness in her voice.

"Yes," I said brightly, "one of the brave new frontier women."

"You were always brave."

I stared at her and said warily, "Oh yes?"

"Knowing what you wanted, I mean, and making sure you got it. Not giving in to pressures on you – putting yourself first."

"It doesn't sound like bravery to me."

"Aren't you lonely?"

"No."

"Roger says you have a boy?"

"Antonia and Gerald's son," I said. "Didn't you read about the crash? I'm his guardian."

"Yes, I read about it. Of course, I was sorry. Is he like his father?"

"Hard to tell," I said, sitting bolt upright and alert, "he's changed a great deal lately. He's only thirteen – fourteen at Christmas."

"Ah yes," Jennifer said softly, "Boxing Day, wasn't it?"

I kept quite still. Let her take the lead, and I would follow, adapting myself as I went. Suddenly, she stood up and went over to the small log fire, burning noisily in the black grate, and with her back to me, as she made a pretence of warming her hands, she said, "I did love him, you know."

"I'm sure you did," I said, deliberately choosing to misunderstand, "he's a very nice man, I can see that, very sweet, I'm sure you're very happy, though I admit – "

"Oh stop it!" she said, quite fiercely. "You know perfectly well who I mean. I loved Edward, you've no idea how much. I was absolutely passionate about him. I couldn't keep away – it wasn't spite, I wasn't after a conquest. I couldn't believe my luck – that you'd thrown him over. He was so hurt and upset – you don't know what you did to him, you were such a fool – but I told myself why should I care, why shouldn't I just jump in and have him? So I did. And of course it was no good. I was only a stop-gap. He never loved anyone except you. But when you rang that time – when I answered the telephone and said he wasn't there – I never thought for one minute of the consequences – I thought you'd telephone again, or write – I didn't see myself as keeping him away from you. I didn't tell him because I thought I had such a short time left, I wanted to hold onto it, I knew he would go back to you and I would have to leave. I didn't realise the significance of your call – on that day – at that time. It did me no good anyway, did it? He didn't stay with me. He went back to you. But once I knew why you'd rung – why you'd tried to get him through me – I've felt guilty ever since."

I did not believe for one minute in Jennifer's guilt. She was not the sort of person ever to be haunted by such an emotion and no amount of persuasion could ever make me think she had felt anything except triumph when Edward and I remained apart. Jennifer had always been a schemer, always calculated cause and effect. She was the sort of woman other women call a bitch. They kept away from her – she had no female friends – and were frightened of her capacity to hurt. Men, on the other hand, found her gentle and undemanding. Edward had told me how soothing he found his affair with her, at that particular time in his life, and though I could see nothing whatsoever that was sympathetic about her I had to believe him. But why had Jennifer Dawson – now the Countess of Cumberland – brought herself so forcibly back into my life? Her whole attitude seemed to me threatening, in spite of the great effort she was making to disarm me by her frank confession. I only wanted to be rid of her.

"Really, Jennifer," I said, as casually as I could manage,

"there isn't the slightest reason for you to feel guilty. Even if I had spoken to Edward then, it wouldn't have made the slightest difference. I'd already decided what I was going to do and nothing would have stopped me."

"You wouldn't have told him?"

"No."

"And Antonia and Gerald are dead," Jennifer said. "How cruel the world grows." I knew she did not mean that at all. She meant me to understand what she had so recently understood – that only she and I knew the secret. I suddenly wondered if she had told Roger Markham, and as if divining my thoughts she said, "We must be friends, Alexandra – only the two of us left who know."

"I don't see that is a basis for friendship," I said. "After all, we never had much in common, did we?"

"Only an attitude to life," Jennifer said, "and a similar taste in men, don't you think?"

"Was my attitude yours – is it?"

"We didn't want cosy homes and slippers by the fire for hubby and squawling kids around our necks."

"No. But you wanted a man. A man was part of your plan. You hated the idea of being on your own. You weren't really a loner, as I was. As I am."

"Are you?"

"I don't have to convince you. You know the facts. You know my history. You know what I am doing now. The situation speaks for itself. Whereas you – you've given up everything you loved to come up to this Godforsaken place for the sake of a man. What happened?"

She lit a cigarette, smiling, and crossed one smooth silk leg over the other. "Do you find Roger Markham attractive?" she said.

"No."

"A pity. He finds you very attractive, but then, they all do – all the men. Of course, up here there isn't much competition. I suppose he told you we are lovers?"

"No."

"It isn't like the old days, is it?"

"I don't really remember them."

"You don't? I don't know how you could forget. Those

three years gave me everything I've ever wanted in life – it's never been the same since. I experience the most sickening nostalgia every time I walk down Goodge Street. I really wanted it to go on forever – one long art course with all those people around me and all those parties and theatres and – just all that activity. I used to pray it would never end – please God, let me not have to make decisions, let me not have to choose between one man and another. I wanted not to be pinned down."

"I was never pinned down. You didn't need to be. I'm still not pinned down. I don't know what you were afraid of."

"I was tired." She said it so simply that I felt a new curiosity. "Tired?" I echoed.

"Yes. I was almost thirty – twenty eight two days after I married Howard – and I was tired. My job bored me. I saw I was never going to be the kind of designer I wanted, never really make the grade, and I was too proud to enjoy being an also-ran. I was tired of affairs. After Edward there were a couple of others I was serious about, but it never came to anything. In between I found myself sleeping with men I didn't even particularly like. I wanted stability. And I wanted to be looked after – properly – so as I should never have to think about anything again. Howard offered this. I liked him, I even found him attractive. I felt the most enormous relief the minute I accepted his proposal."

"Well, that's fine, then," I said, "all's well that ends well. Hithop Hall seems a small price to pay for the security you wanted, especially with a lover thrown in."

"We have a flat in London," Jennifer said, "very pleasant. I go there whenever I like. Howard doesn't mind."

"Perfect arrangement."

She had by now smoked half of her cigarette, still smiling mysteriously. I realised, as I watched her, that she was very tense, and knew that she had not yet done with me. All this stilted reminiscing about our art college days – which I remembered quite differently, of course – was a ruse to suggest an intimacy that had never existed and I did not doubt that she intended to move on and exploit it. I sat and waited quite patiently, thinking how much I detested women like Jennifer, women to whom all relationships with men were carnal bargains. She never gave herself freely, never followed any instinct but that of self-aggrandisement. There flashed into my head an image of Miss Cowdie, humble and adoring before the concept of marriage, and I looked at Jennifer with barely concealed disgust.

"Alexandra," Jennifer said, "I am bored. I am so bored I feel I could go mad."

"How sad."

"My days are empty. And now Howard wants me to have a child – an heir for all this."

"That's understandable."

"I can't bear the thought. I pretend we are trying and all the time I go on taking the pill without his knowing."

"Jennifer, I would really much rather not know all this," I said, exasperated. "I'm not suited to the role of confidante."

"Does Edward write to you?" Jennifer said, standing up as I did.

"No. At least, he may do – he doesn't know where I am. There may be letters at Carlisle GPO. He sent a card a while ago, from South America. I don't really care whether he writes or not."

"But you are still, in a manner of speaking, attached?"

"No. Not really. We are both quite free."

"Except you have a child to care for. How strange, that it should turn out like this, a sort of poetic justice, don't you think?"

"If you like to see it like that – yes."

"These curious quirks of fate."

I said goodbye very firmly, but Jennifer was abstracted, gazing into the distance with a vacant expression on her neat features. She irritated me immensely and my heart sank when she said she would pop in on me sometime soon. I did not want her anywhere near me, carrying with her that faint air of blackmail. I said I was very busy, that I didn't have much time for visitors, that I would not like her to have a wasted journey, but she would not be put off. All the way home I brooded on the inevitable visit she would make and when I got back I was irritable with poor Eileen, simply because she said she would not be coming the next day. She was going to Carlisle to have her hair done. I ought to have shown more interest – I do not like to think how brusque I was. After she had trudged off I thought how much having her hair done mattered and I regretted my disinterest. I did not need anyone to tell me – that is, if anyone had existed – that Eileen now set great store by anything I said. I was an influence in her narrow life, and I ought to have watched my words.

I was not pleased, the following morning, to find I had a very early morning caller. Casper had just set off for school and I was getting myself ready to forestall David's visit by driving into Caldbeck and ringing him to say I would rather postpone it when Roger Markham's jeep appeared at the end of the track. He could, of course, merely be visiting Miss Cowdie, but I knew at once that he was coming instead to see me. Somehow I had expected it. I had intended to spend the whole day out, simply to thwart this event, but I had delayed a little too long. I was caught. Resigned, I watched him walk doggedly towards the cottage, head down, hands in his pockets. I wished Eileen was there to give me moral support and to relay to Geoff later how quickly I had sent Mr Markham packing, with what finality I had dismissed him.

I opened the door before he knocked – it was foolish to try to hide. I was not in the mood for games. Roger stood there with a smile on his face so unconvincing that it looked as though it was purely a nervous contortion of the features.

"Good morning," he said, "I've come to apologise. I'm sorry I was so rude yesterday."

"Apology accepted," I said. I did not see why I should ask him in and so I stood there, in the doorway, barring his way.

"Accepted but not believed, by the look of it," he said.

"I really can't be bothered to think about it. It doesn't matter enough."

"It matters to me. I feel I'll never get in your good books again."

"You weren't in them anyway."

"Thanks."

"I'm going out, actually."

"So I see. I'll walk to your car with you, if you don't mind."

"There isn't anything to mind. My car is only twenty yards away – it isn't much of a walk."

I finished buttoning up my coat and pulling on my gloves –

gloves were suddenly essential items of clothing in my wardrobe, so great was the cold – and we walked to the shed where the car was garaged. I was determined not to offer anything in the way of conversation, nor to respond to any such overtures from Roger – but how shabby one always feels in such circumstances, how mean and unpleasant. Even though I was perfectly in the right, I disliked myself for being so unrelenting. He had, after all, come in person to say he was sorry, a difficult matter for someone as proud as Roger. I could not have done it. I find it almost impossible ever to say I am sorry – I can *act* sorry, I can demonstrate regret by some gesture or token, but the words "I apologise" I find hard to come out with, especially at those times when they are really needed. I sensed the act of repentance was equally difficult for Roger Markham.

Roger noticed the tyres before I did. They were slashed, all four of them – gouged with a sharp knife, a very sharp, thick knife, driven with enormous force into each one. Naturally, they were completely flat. "Well," Roger said, down on his knees examining them, "we can't pretend that was an accident, can we? Somebody clearly doesn't want you to drive your car." I found it hard to speak. My fury was so great I was literally choking with it, and anger made me stupid. "I can't have this," I said, and other silly comments. "This is the absolute end. She *is* raving mad, it's no good pretending any more."

"Who?" Roger asked, turning to look at me.

"Miss Cowdie, of course – it's typical, exactly the sort of spiteful thing she does."

"Don't be ridiculous," Roger said, quite sharply. "Miss Cowdie couldn't cut this sort of rubber – look, these tyres are tough – you would need tremendous strength to make that sort of cut – try yourself – go on, you can't make it any worse now the damage is done," and he took out of his pocket a clasp knife, which he opened out and handed to me. I refused it. "Oh, what does it matter?" I said crossly. "If it wasn't Miss Cowdie it was some other maniac – it's pointless thinking about it."

"I wouldn't say that. Surely you want the culprit caught?"

"All I want is to be able to drive my car."

"You won't just forget about it?" Roger said. He seemed

more shocked by my attitude than by the tyre slashing. "You can't do that. I'll drive you into Caldbeck and you can talk to the constable. You must at least report it."

It was on the tip of my tongue to tell him I had not reported far worse occurrences, but I stopped myself in time. I did not want Roger to know too much. Gloomily, I got into his jeep and drove down to Caldbeck with him and made telephone calls. David was immensely helpful. When I told him what had happened, he said he would bring new tyres out for me. If they were in stock he would bring them the next day. If not, he would order them and bring them as soon as they arrived. I rang the garage next and they said they had three in stock, which, with my spare, was enough.

I came out of the call box smiling. "David Garibaldi is bringing spare tyres out for me tomorrow," I said. "He's so kind."

Roger flushed a deep red at once. "I better hadn't make any comment," he said.

"No, you better hadn't."

"I'll drive you back."

"That's all right, I'll walk. I'll enjoy it."

"I'll take you to the police house."

"I know where it is – I saw it on the green. Thanks for your help."

"It doesn't sound as if you need it."

There is no doubt I felt guilty as he jumped into the driving seat and roared off. I had rather slapped him in the face with David's goodness – I suppose I'd looked smug that my troubles were so easily resolved, and by someone else. There had been no need to be quite so triumphant. I pondered my own cruelty as, for form's sake, I walked back across the green, past the police house – I had no intention of reporting the tyres – and down through the village. Roger Markham irritated me. I could not honestly say that I disliked him – it was his attitudes I disliked. He was the sort of man with whom I could never have a superficial relationship – it would be all or nothing. I would have to know about him, to become involved, before we could make any progress. The investment in time and trouble was not one I was willing to make. Increasingly, that was true of me – I shied away from discovering people's souls.

I was sure there was a good deal about Roger worth knowing, that I would enjoy becoming intimate with his mind, but I would not allow myself to consider it. Roger Markham was forbidden territory. He represented trouble of a kind I had done with – there was no place in my new life for him.

I was therefore extremely put out to find his jeep outside my cottage when eventually, after an hour's steady walking, I reached it. I saw him sitting in it and thought, "Oh *really*." "Nice walk?" he asked, getting out.

"Yes, thank you."

"What are you going to do now?"

I struggled with a desire to say, "None of your business," and said instead, "Do some work."

"I thought you might like lunch somewhere – to cheer you up."

"I don't need cheering up, thank you."

"You look as if you do."

"I can't help my looks."

"No, luckily. That long walk has given you a lovely colour. Very becoming. David Garibaldi is a lucky fellow."

"Please, not that again."

"I'm jealous, of course. I admit it. I don't really see why he should be more fortunate than I."

"This is very embarrassing. I do wish you would go away."

"Jennifer said you were implacable."

"Then take her advice. Don't waste your breath."

"She seems to know a lot about you."

"She knows nothing."

We had walked across the rough garden grass to my door during this interchange and, now that we had reached it, I had had enough. "I'm going in now," I said, "so you'd better go home."

"You didn't report the tyre business, did you?"

"No."

"Why not?"

"I didn't want to."

"Because the police might ask questions you didn't want to answer? About who could have done it?"

"No. Because it doesn't really matter – I told you – the damage is done."

"But it means somebody – some man – has a grudge against you – he could be dangerous – next time it could be you and not the tyres."

"I'll take the risk."

"You aren't safe to be left on your own."

"Don't be absurd."

I had the door open. I turned to face Roger, who was glaring at me angrily, his lips pressed grimly together in a thin line and his brow furrowed in an anxious frown. "Goodbye," I said, and, stepping inside firmly, shut the heavy door in his face.

Seventeen

I thought that what I should like to do was to pack a bag, take a train to London and never come back to Lowther Fell again. I have no doubt that if it had not been for Casper and my tyreless car I should have done just that, so great was my desire to be gone from all those people. There was no one I wanted to see, so I took Rufus for a walk to console myself.

When I got back, Casper was just putting away his bicycle. "I've been on the most amazing walk," I said, "right up Longlands on to the top of Knott and down Roughton Gill waterfall." He nodded, but said nothing, and we walked towards the cottage from the bicycle shed, Rufus barking and jumping up to lick Casper's hand. "Have you been there?" I asked, directly, wanting a definite response. "Think so," he said, "I don't know the names. I've been up a waterfall near the old mines, if you mean that." "Yes, that's it. I was terrified." He made no comment. Suddenly, he began to smile and I thought he was laughing at my terror. "It wasn't funny," I said, though quite glad he should take even that much interest, but then his smile deepened and he began to laugh openly and to shake his head. "No," he said, "nothing to do with you – I saw Eileen just now. Her hair – she looks like a gollywog." He spluttered into the coffee I had given him until he was scarlet in the face – I had never seen him laugh like that, with all of himself (Edward used to do it), and found it so infectious I was laughing too, without really appreciating the joke. "It's for the dance," I said at last, "Eileen's big event of the year. She's had her hair dyed and permed in Carlisle. Oh dear, is it dreadful?" Casper nodded, still incapable.

My heart sank at the thought of having to call forth the enthusiasm Eileen would want, but I need not have feared. When she arrived in the morning she was so thrilled with herself she hardly noticed my expression. She had a headscarf carefully arranged over her head and took it off with a flourish. Underneath, her pale lank hair had been frizzed out into an extraordinary creation of waves and curls – I could not imagine where the hairdresser had found the sheer volume of hair on Eileen's sparsely covered head – and then dyed a deep, dead, lacklustre black. The effect was startling. Eileen's wan face shone out of this fierce halo like a ghostly apparition – it could not cope with the weight and the thickness. Her features could not fight their new dramatic surroundings and so sank into a blob of white. And yet in Eileen herself – in her personality – there was a change, overwhelmingly for the good. Whatever she had seen in her mirror, it was nothing ludicrous. She held her new head erect, proudly, instead of ducking it all the time, and there was a new spring to her step. "Eileen!" I said admiringly. "You actually went and did it."

"Said I would," Eileen said, "said I would and I did. Nobody believed me. Was only growing it to have this done. Now it's done." She gave a great sigh of satisfaction.

"And what about your parents? What about Geoff?" I said. She shrugged.

"Don't care," she said, complacently, not sullenly. "Can think what they like."

"Yes, but what *did* they think?"

"Dad laughed. Said I were done up like a dog's dinner. Said I ought to have more sense. Mam said it made a change. Geoff didn't say nowt. Just looked. Don't care if he *is* mad at me anyway – he doesn't own me. Nowt to do wi' him if I dye my hair. He has funny ideas." She paused a minute and then looked at me slyly. "He hangs about here, you know, at night," she said, watching to see how I would take the news. "Goes off by himself. We know he comes here. Just hangs about. Dad says he should grow up, behaving like that. Geoff says he does no harm." She paused again. "Don't let on I telt you, eh?"

"No," I said, "I won't."

She told me more about the dance during the morning, while we both used the very last of the clay to make a final set of jugs – I had chosen jugs so that, if I could not absolutely match the glaze next time, the jugs would be less noticeable. Eileen sat opposite me, watching while I shaped the clay on the wheel, and I let her try for herself with the discarded bits I threw into the bin. She made quite a creditable attempt at a small jug, once she had got used to the feeling of power under her hands and had learned how to control it, though of course she had trouble with the handle and the lip, both hard for beginners. Little spots of colour appeared high in her pale, flat cheeks and her eyes, normally so wary, grew round with excitement. It pleased me to think of the pleasure I was giving her and I vowed to keep my resolution to teach her more and take her into partnership eventually. When we had finished the small batch, it was Eileen who packed it into the kiln, supervised by me, and Eileen who anxiously set the controls. Her sense of pride when the firing was under way was amusing and touching to behold. "We must celebrate, Eileen," I said, and when we went back to the cottage for her to collect her things I opened a bottle of the sweetest sherry I had and poured her a glass. "To your future as a potter," I said. She looked pleased but uncertain. "Don't drink really," she said, "it goes to my head. I get tiddly on nowt." But before I could say that in that case she must certainly not drink it she had downed it at a swallow and was beaming at me. "Glad you come up here," she blurted out.

"That's nice," I said, alarmed at the thought of such a demonstration of affection.

"Made all the difference. Not just the money – not just getting the work. I like you."

I was deeply embarrassed and at a loss as to how to respond. "And I like you," I managed to say.

"You shouldn't," Eileen said, "not after what I did."

"What did you do?"

But at that moment, as we stood there on a cold December morning, with glasses still in our hands, both with red faces at the intimacy of our situation, there was a knock on the door. The door was not even properly closed – we had rushed in, warm with our exertions, and had not closed it – and as I went to open it wider it was pushed open and I saw Eileen's father standing there. Eileen at once put down her glass, looking horribly guilty and uncomfortable, and rushed to get her coat. We both jumped to the conclusion that she was late, that the men had come for their dinners and found it not out on their plates as it ought to be, gravy steaming from it at just the right temperature, ready to be gulped without the hindrance of having to be cooled. But even as I looked at the clock and saw Eileen was not late in leaving Mr Crosthwaite said, "I've got your lad in the truck. Found him collapsed, top of Faulds."

"Casper?" I said, startled.

"Ay. Not an accident, like – seems he felt poorly at school and they said he could come home. Offered to drive him but he were stubborn, like, I expect. Anyway, nearly got here and his legs gave way. Had to get off and rest and reckons he must have passed out. So I was passing and saw him and bob's your uncle. He'll be all right."

I hurried out to the truck and helped a shockingly white faced Casper out. He staggered on his feet and needed Mr Crosthwaite's support on one side and mine on the other. Indeed, he was so unsteady that without Mr Crosthwaite's help I doubt if I could have got Casper up to his bed – he was taller now than I and much heavier and quite impossible for me to carry. Once in his room, we laid him on the bed and I said, "I suppose I ought to get a doctor. Trouble is, I've never actually registered with one."

"Don't you worry," Mr Crosthwaite said, "Dr Teasdale at High Ireby'll come out. He'll go anywhere. He won't bother about any registering – turns out all weathers. I'll ring him for you and give a message. If he can't come I'll send Eileen down with the reason, so as you'll know what's what." Grateful for such forethought and true kindness, I was fulsome in my appreciation, but I did not miss the intonation in Mr Crosthwaite's voice as he dismissed my thanks with, "About time we helped, I should think."

It was hard to decide exactly what he meant. He did not seem to me the sort of man who had any over-developed sense of good neighbourliness – it was his wife who was friendly, in her own scared way. And he knew that he *had* helped me in all sorts of small ways. I thought I read into his brief statement some admission that he knew how Geoff bothered me, or was bothering me, and regretted he had not done anything about it. John Crosthwaite was a powerful father – both Geoff and Eileen were afraid of him, and had an Old Testament respect for him as their father. If John had said "stop" to Geoff, Geoff would have stopped. It was not just his womenfolk he ruled. Eileen had told me that when he was younger he had had a terrible temper, that he had been wild until her mother quietened him down. She had painted a picture of her father as a desperate character – "a lad wi' the girls – not like Geoff" – but I had found it hard to reconcile with what I knew of the middle-aged man. He never looked at me straight. He was never at ease with me. And yet, suddenly, as we came down from Casper's room, there had been that flash of insight.

I went straight back to Casper as soon as Eileen had scurried off with her father and was relieved to find his eyes open and a perfectly sensible look in them. "Well," I said, gently, "poor Casper." His eyes filled with tears. Alarmed, I patted his hand – awkwardly, I know – and said, "Don't worry, darling, you'll soon feel better." I suppose it was the first time I had ever called him darling, and I was ashamed to realise it. Shame made me brisk. "The doctor is going to come and look at you, this afternoon I hope. Why don't we get you into bed properly and I'll give you a hot water bottle and perhaps you'll sleep?" He sat up, wincing, saying he had a terrible pain in his head and a sore throat and that what he most wanted was a drink. I went to get it and though I was very quick he had got into his pyjamas by the time I came back and was huddled under the blankets. I put the mug of hot orange juice down on his bedside table, where his stamp album lay open at South America, but he displayed no interest in it. I felt his brow, which was burning hot, and told him to take the two aspirins I had brought with the drink. He groaned and protested but I was persistent and he finally managed to swallow them both, with about half the drink. Then I left him, checking the radiator was on. The room did not seem obviously warm but then, when it was very cold, as it was that day, the heating did often seem inadequate.

I cannot say that I felt worried – it seemed to me that Casper's symptoms were consistent with influenza of some sort. I remember thinking he might miss the school play, which was in three days' time, and what a pity it would be when he had worked so hard to help with it. Never having seen him ill before, I had no idea how quickly he recovered from bouts of flu and colds – I did not know his history as a patient, and wished I did. Nor did I know his medical history, which any doctor would be sure to ask me. Had he had measles, chicken pox, mumps? I wasn't at all sure. Somewhere in the back of my mind I had a vision of a very small Casper sitting up in bed, covered with red spots, when I visited him, but I could not remember what the spots signified. Antonia always took those childhood diseases so seriously – her solemnity bored me. She had a theory that Casper was "chesty", which gave her an excuse for further coddling, and put it down to his premature birth. That was all I knew about Casper – the only medical detail I could offer. He was born at three in the morning on Boxing Day, not my most favourite day of the year, and only weighed 4lbs 10oz. But he was only in an incubator for forty-eight hours and gave no cause for anxiety afterwards. I remember he did not look as scrawny and terrifying as I had imagined when I first saw him – I never doubted he would survive, having come so far against such unspeakable odds.

I fiddled about with the thermostat on the boiler, trying to get it set at the maximum, and then I ate a solitary lunch, noticing the intense cold of the draught, snaking through the thinnest of cracks in the window. Perhaps it would snow again and this time lie, keeping us prisoner. I checked our food supplies and thought I must go to Wigton and do another big shopping trip just as soon as Eileen came the following morning. It would not do to be caught out. Hardly had I finished inspecting the cupboard and making a list before I saw a strange man coming up the track, carrying the standard black bag of a doctor, though his clothes were those of a farmer. I hurried to open the door and saw the first flakes of snow beginning to fall. "How kind," I said. "I didn't expect you so soon – Dr Teasdale, isn't it? I hope I haven't dragged you out unnecessarily, especially when I'm not officially a patient," and I ushered him in from the Siberian cold.

Dr Teasdale was in no hurry to see his patient. I could not but contrast his leisurely, friendly air – his positive inquisitiveness, too – with the rushed, uninterested attitude of those medical practitioners I had had brief dealings with in London. This was more like it had been in my Oxford childhood – the doctor treated as a friend and responding as one. Dr Teasdale looked round the living-room of the cottage with the greatest curiosity, exclaiming at the transformation, asking where I had got the lovely table, stroking the wood with his hand, and then he gazed frankly and fearlessly at me and asked as many questions – did I like it here, what exactly was I doing, did I know many people, how did I find the climate? And yet there was no impertinence in his inquisition – the questions came quite slowly and respectfully, and he weighed each answer carefully, his head on one side and a kindly, humorous look on his face. He reminded me of the illustration in a book I had loved as a child – *The Night Before Christmas* – in which Father Christmas was depicted as "a right jolly old elf". I wished very much that I had gone to make his acquaintance before he had come to me.

It was fully twenty minutes before we climbed the stairs to Casper's room. We went in quietly. I was glad Dr Teasdale's eagerness did not extend to heartiness in front of the sick – he went round to the side of the bed where he could see Casper's face and stood and looked at him for a minute and then very gently peeled back the blankets and took hold of his wrist. He said hello to Casper but seemed unworried about the lack of any response and continued with an examination of his chest and all the usual other parts – ears, throat, eyes. Though Casper did not speak, and for the most part had his eyes closed, he was obedient enough. At the end Dr Teasdale patted his hand and tucked him up and said not to worry, it was just the beastly flu that was going about and at least he would be better for Christmas.

Downstairs, I offered Dr Teasdale some coffee, which I thought he would refuse, but he accepted at once. "I feel guilty calling you out just for flu," I said.

"Flu isn't to be despised. It can be very nasty, particularly this strain we've got this year."

"What do I do? Just keep him in bed?"

"Yes. Hot drinks and aspirin every four hours, and if he doesn't seem any better in a couple of days, give me a ring." He looked about him again, thoughtfully. "I used to come here a lot, you know. The people before you had a baby here – died, unfortunately – and before them there was an old couple, oh, I came out scores of times to see Mrs Clegg, she had a heart condition and every time she crossed swords with her neighbour her husband would think she'd had a heart attack and call me out. I couldn't persuade him it was psychological in origin and if he just kept her and dear Miss Cowdie from meeting all would be well."

"You know Miss Cowdie?"

"I should think I do." He shook his head and pursed his lips.

"I suppose I can't ask you to talk about her, as she's a patient of yours."

"She isn't a patient. I'm *persona non grata* in her opinion, I'm afraid. She said she never wants to see me again and I'm dreadfully afraid she means it."

"But wouldn't you be sent for, if she was ill?"

"By whom?"

"Well – I don't know – suppose Roger Markham found her collapsed, wouldn't he send for you?"

"He might. But I would send an ambulance and have her into Carlisle Infirmary for treatment. She wouldn't be a home nursing case, whatever was wrong."

"I feel so sorry for her."

"We all do."

"But nobody does anything."

Dr Teasdale took his spectacles off, blew on them, cleaned them, and replaced them. "Elfrida Cowdie isn't mad," he said, firmly, "she is simply suffering from one delusion, which doesn't prevent her functioning in most other respects. Perhaps you think she ought to be forcibly shipped off to some mental hospital but in that case half the local population ought to be in one. In the country we tend to let the slightly deranged live side by side with the totally sane, if there is such a thing, until they can't manage any more or until their mental condition deteriorates. I don't see anything wrong with that. What Elfrida needs is love and kindness, a happy marriage if possible, and those things aren't prescribed on the National Health."

I felt I had been delivered a lecture, though Dr Teasdale smiled throughout. Suddenly he got up and handed me back his cup. "I must go," he said, "measles at Todhunter's Farm." I walked to the door with him and as I opened it we both saw Miss Cowdie trailing slowly past up the track to her home. We stood still and watched till she was out of sight. "That damned bonnet," Dr Teasdale murmured, "but how pretty it looked on the day, an absolute picture."

"You were at the wedding?"

"I was in the church. The prospective bridegroom had looked me up as a friend of his father's. He and Elfrida were new here, you know, hadn't many friends and few relations, so I suppose we were invited to swell the numbers. She looked so pretty with that bonnet on, and a pretty dress too, though not white, I think – I would have to ask my wife." He stepped out into the thin snow and put his collar up, but I could not bear to let him go at that point. "I'll walk to your car," I said, "just for some air," and I snatched my jacket off the peg. Together we walked across the grass, which was already lightly covered with dry powdery snow. "Why do you think he jilted her?"

Dr Teasdale shrugged. "How can one ever be sure? He never came back. Nobody ever heard from him again."

"But you must have had a theory?"

"My wife thought he'd been trapped into the marriage in the first place – she reckoned he'd tried to back out long before but Elfrida wouldn't have it. She's a very determined lady. The only way he could cope with her was to go along with her wishes and then run at the last minute, as if the finality of the ceremony gave him Dutch courage."

"But that's your wife's theory, not yours? You don't agree?"

"Well, not entirely."

"What do you think happened?"

"There was a rumour at the time that he *did* break it off because he saw her with – " and here he hesitated and shot me a quick suspicious look, "another man, just once, and that she went on with the wedding plans, even though she knew she'd disgraced herself in his eyes and that he would never marry her. She was a very – *sensual* person, if I may use the phrase. He wasn't. I think he thought he would never be passionate enough for her. That one lapse – it may have been quite harmless – convinced him. I think he was the sort of man she wanted to marry in her head – a good, sober, hardworking, Godfearing citizen – but she was actually attracted to – " and again there was a pause, "quite a different sort of man, and she loathed herself for it. I think the breakdown began long before that wedding day. I always felt she deliberately put herself through that ordeal as a punishment." He stopped a moment. "Of course, there was a lot of speculation about who that man had been." "Was he local?" I asked. Dr Teasdale looked uncomfortable. "Oh yes," he said "yes, I'm afraid he was – local."

We were at his car, a battered but beautiful Riley. "Lovely car," I said, automatically. "Yes, it was Elfrida's, you know," he said, absently, "her pride and joy. I bought it from her, the week before the wedding – the money was going towards her honeymoon. She said she wouldn't need a car when she was married, they would share his. Quite a self-sacrifice, really – his was an awful Ford Escort. I offered to sell this back to her afterwards but she said she didn't know what I was talking about. Too painful, I suppose."

"It makes me feel worse than ever," I said.

"Don't let it. Get back to that young man and get him on fluids."

David came soon after Dr Teasdale left, bringing the tyres with him. I didn't even try to pretend that I did not care whether he fixed them for me or not, for of course I could not have managed it myself. I suppose Casper could have made a pretty good shot at it, but otherwise I would have had to ask Mr Crosthwaite or Geoff. I did not want to do that. I had a strong suspicion it was Geoff who had slashed the tyres in the first place – I could think of no one else – and part of my reluctance to report the incident had been because of this unprovable but strong feeling that I was right. Nor did I want to ask Mr Crosthwaite himself. I did not know why, but I was never easy with him. Even after seeing him practically every day for two months I was not comfortable in his presence, nor he in mine. I think I was a little afraid of him, though he had never been anything but polite and helpful. My fear arose from suspecting he held himself in all the time from expressing his real thoughts – he had a heavy, ponderous way of looking at me from underneath his thick blond eyebrows – frowning, almost, in concentration – that I disliked. I felt he was an unknown quantity, dangerous, in his own quiet manner. His wife looked drained by him and nervous at his side. She was not much older than I was, but had an aged, worn out look to her that had not, I was sure, come from hard work alone. I felt she suffered and that John Crosthwaite was somehow the cause of her suffering.

I made coffee while David worked in the freezing cold shed and as soon as he had finished – it took him more than an hour, which made me feel very guilty – he came inside to drink it. I had not yet mentioned Casper upstairs. When he had drunk two cups and was warm enough at last to remove his coat I said, "My nephew is ill, in bed." I was ashamed to find I was blushing – I had announced Casper's illness in such a way that David could not fail to understand my meaning, which was that we could not go to bed. "Poor chap," David said, quite easily, and I was grateful he had ignored the crude message. "Flu, probably," he said, "there's a lot of it about." I nodded, and said I hoped it would not last long.

"You don't like being shut in, do you?" he said.

"No."

"You should go back to London. You don't belong here."

"I've thought that myself."

"You're too exotic for here."

"What about you? I can't see you fit in either. Why don't you go south?"

He stared at me very hard, an odd little smile on his face. "No questions, remember?" he said. "We didn't want to know each other."

"I'm sorry."

"They were your rules. I'd be very happy to break them, but you might not like what you'd hear."

"No, I don't want to hear anything at all."

"It isn't natural, you know – it never works." He got up as he spoke and began putting his coat back on. "You can't just be a body, not really. But we'll have another try sometime shall we?"

"Yes."

"I'll drop in next week, before Christmas. I'm going away on Christmas Eve – for a month, abroad. I'll come before I go – say goodbye until later."

"Thanks for your help, I can't tell you – "

"A pleasure. But don't leave your door unlocked, will you? You've obviously got an enemy."

"Only one?"

He laughed. "Well, anyway," he said, "you haven't got as many as I have – not yet. You'll have to work hard to catch up on me, I can tell you. It makes a nice change not to be the only source of salacious gossip around here."

It began to snow in earnest about five that evening, when it was dark. I ought to have gone to the barn to take the last pots out of the kiln, but I thought I would give Eileen the thrill in the morning of unloading her own first attempts. They would come to no harm overnight – the kiln would have switched itself off automatically. For a long time after dark I kept the shutters open to watch the falling snow. It was impossible not to be mesmerised by it. I shivered, though with the fire on the cottage was now perfectly warm, and thought of the sheep, huddled against the walls of the Crosthwaites' farm. Nobody would be out on the fells tonight, not even the shepherd Roger had told me of. The top of Knott would be submerged in snow and I felt a thrill of excitement at the thought of being up there in the dark and in a swirling blizzard. Part of me wanted to wrap up and go out and wander around, just to experience the full force of the winter elements, but I chided myself for such affectation. Nobody would go out tonight. Every farm and cottage in the fells would be battened down against the snow. I shut the shutters at last and barred the door and put another huge log on the fire before I went upstairs to sit with Casper for a while.

I do not think he particularly wanted me to sit with him but I gave him no choice in the matter – it was too heart-breaking to think of him lying in that tiny room feeling wretched. He was not asleep, but neither was he fully awake. His eyes were open in his flushed face and he turned his head restlessly and plucked at the bedclothes continually. I put my hand lightly on his forehead to find it burning hot and dry – there was no relieving perspiration. With some persuasion, he drank another glass of water and took another dose of aspirin but resisted all suggestions about eating anything. I made myself comfortable in the one chair that fitted into the corner of his room, sitting in it with my feet resting on the end of the bed. I had brought a novel with me but wished instead that I could knit or sew – it would have been more soothing for Casper, less like a guard on duty.

The novel would normally have gripped me. I am a great reader of contemporary fiction and find it easy to lose myself in the imaginary plights of others. And it was a particularly good novel I had chosen, a paperback version of V.S. Naipaul's *A House for Mr Biswas*, which I was enjoying – but I could not concentrate on the West Indies when I was so aware that I sat in a sickroom on a lonely fellside. The effort of the imagination, in the circumstances, was too great for me to make. I found myself alternately staring out of the still uncurtained window, against which the snow flickered and stuck and then slid away, and at Casper, lying so uncomfortably against his blue pillow. I could not tell if he also looked at me. His eyes did not meet mine and the light was not good enough to make out any subtleties of expression. The atmosphere was intimate and hushed, the deep silence both within and without broken only by his occasional cough and the creak of the wooden chair as I moved my position.

I wanted badly to talk. My whole being strained towards communicating with Casper. I felt that never again would I be presented with so natural an opportunity to tell him so many of those momentous things part of me wanted him to know. The deception I had practised his whole life had never worried me while Antonia was alive. She had said I would be haunted by it but the truth was I had hardly even thought of it. I had cut it out of my experience, just like that. But these last months it had begun to prey on my mind. I could no longer live with it. I felt guilty and nervous. This feeling was at the root of my relationship with Casper – so long as my sin went unconfessed, his nearness would accuse me. Yet still I was held back by that other half, that more rational half, that told me I ought to leave well alone, that my sudden wish to tell all might help me but it would not help Casper. His life was just beginning to straighten out, he was on an even keel again, and there was I, tempted to shatter his new found peace.

The lamp flickered and then went out. "Don't worry," I said to Casper, "it will be an electricity cut. The snow must have been too heavy for a cable or something. I'll get candles." The darkness without the lamps on was so complete I had difficulty finding my way downstairs, where Rufus alternately growled and whimpered. The fire gave a welcome glow to the living room and helped me find the box of candles in the cupboard, where they had remained since we first arrived. I fitted them into empty bottles and took two upstairs. One I put on the window sill and the other on Casper's bedside table. I could not help seeing by its flickering yellow light that he had tears in his eyes, and a kind of panic gripped me at the sight of them. I could not bear him to cry. Edward had cried once, once only, when I told him that night, the last night we spent together, at the end of the summer, that I was leaving him and never wanted to see him again. His eyes, in an implacable face, so implacable it frightened me, had also filled with tears, and the anguish I felt had frozen further words in my throat. His tears were never shed. He did not even wipe them away.

"Does your head hurt, Casper?" I asked. He turned away without answering. How could I go on and ask if it was rather his heart? "Don't be sad," I said, "it's just the fever."

"I'm not sad," he said, his voice croaky and deep. I couldn't ask why, in that case, his eyes were full of tears. Helpless, scorning my own uselessness, I walked up and down the tiny space in the room – three steps to the window, three back. Suddenly he blurted out, "I'm frightened," and his voice rose in a wail of distress. My relief was so great I almost laughed out loud. I sat on his bed and found his hand and held it and said, "Frightened? Oh, Casper – there's nothing to be frightened of. You're quite safe – you're not even very ill – what are you frightened of?" From under the blankets I heard him say, "Geoff."

"*Geoff*?" I echoed, disbelieving, "but why Geoff? Geoff wouldn't hurt you."

"He says he's going to kill you. He says he comes every night and waits and he's going to come and kill you."

"When did he say this?"

"Yesterday. He met me at the top of Faulds. He got off his tractor and stopped my bike – he just stood over the front wheel and held the handlebars – and he said, 'tell that Alexandra I'm going to kill her before long,' and he laughed."

"Well, that's nonsense. If you weren't ill you would know it was nonsense. Did you tell his father when he picked you up?"

"No."

"Geoff is unbalanced, that's all. He's always threatening to kill or maim people. It's only his horrid way. Eileen gets threatened very week."

"But the rabbit – and when we were in the tent – that prowler – "

"That was Miss Cowdie. All that is over. She was just a slightly deranged woman, who thought I was her enemy – we're friends now."

But even before I thought of the slashed tyres, I remembered my terror in the barn. Had it been Geoff? I went on holding Casper's hand and looking into the candle flame and wondered. Was that why Rufus avoided him, why the usually friendly dog slunk away at the sound of his voice?

"Nobody will be out there tonight anyway, Casper," I said confidently, "it's snowing heavily. There is no need for you to worry. Tomorrow I'll go to see Geoff and have this out with him – no, don't worry – it won't rebound on you. I wish you'd told me sooner, the minute you came in. Never keep secrets like that. Now try and think of something cheerful – think of Eileen at the dance tomorrow. She'll have to go, whatever the weather. The snow is thick up here but I expect the roads will still be clear. She will cover her beautiful hair with a scarf and off she will trip, looking for her Prince Charming."

He cheered up considerably. I could not afford to let him see how shaken I was, both by his actual story and by this reminder that he was still a young boy and not the half-man he had begun to look. He had another drink, cold, because of course the electric kettle and cooker no longer worked, and we even played a game of Scrabble, in which the highest score was five.

When it got to ten o'clock, with the electricity still off, I bedded him down for the night and dropped a swift kiss on his cheek, and then I banked up the fire to keep some warmth going during the night and went to bed myself, after a last look out into the swirling whiteness.

Eighteen

The snow was still falling when I woke up, though without much force. The snowflakes whirled about helplessly, as though they did not quite know which way to go, and they took a long time to reach the ground. I could see, looking from my bedroom window, that the snow had drifted deeply against the barn wall and the walls of the sheds, but it seemed powdery and soft – a wind, a gentle wind, whipped the surface up into a mild froth and I suspected there was no hard crust on top. The sky was dull grey and the only light came from the snow itself.

I was impatient for Eileen to arrive, so that I could perhaps go to Wigton and do a mammoth shopping. The electricity had come on during the night but I intended to buy a calor gas heater immediately and fuel for the paraffin lamps, which until now I had foolishly kept only as pretty ornaments. The thought of driving in these conditions terrified me but it had to be done, especially with Casper ill and in need of warmth and nourishing food. He seemed a little better, not quite so flushed, but when he got out of bed to go to the bathroom he was sick and had to be helped back to bed, where he pulled the blankets over his head and curled up like an animal. I gave him a hot water bottle and then left him to try to sleep.

I stood at the window in the living room for half an hour, staring out, willing Eileen to appear on the track. The track was no longer visible – every muddy rut and hole was covered in snow and no one could know what lay underneath. I worried about the depth of the snow – was it above knee level on the track? It struck me that I ought to be clearing my own paths, and the idea of such activity relieved me. I dressed in my warmest clothes – though it did not seem so cold, now the snow had fallen – and set to with a broom and shovel. It was quite easy to clear the path round the house – there was no need to dig, the snow yielded to the broom and I made splendid progress. I was half way to the garden gate when I saw Eileen plodding slowly along the track, lifting one Wellington booted foot above another with difficulty, each leg shrinking almost to the knee with each step. I waved and shouted and Eileen waved back. With enormous vigour I completed my brushing, so that by the time she got to the gate the path to the cottage was roughly cleared.

"Thank heaven you've come," I said. "I couldn't leave Casper, and I must go and get a million things in Wigton."

"You'll have to wait," Eileen said, "you'll not get onto the road yet. Can't drive on the track till Dad's cleared it. Said he'd do it for you in half an hour."

"Couldn't I drive through it? The car's got big wheels."

"Dad says you can't," Eileen said firmly.

I had a strong desire to challenge Dad but did not want to anger him, or, even worse, fail to manage the drive and be compelled to rely on him to get me out, so I contented myself with getting the Range Rover out of its shed and running the engine until all was in readiness. Eileen had brought me four chains, which Dad had sent instructions should be put round the wheels and by the time I had done this I heard the roar of Geoff's tractor and saw Mr Crosthwaite slowly advancing, pushing the snow aside with a makeshift snow-plough. As he reached my car he stopped and got out. "Going out?" he said, inspecting the chains critically and tightening two.

"Yes – I must – I must stock up."

"You'd best be quick, then, and keep to the main roads. More snow's on the way, and a gale for good measure. You'd best get off now and be back in the hour."

I felt nervous and even excited as I got into the driver's seat and followed the tractor down to the tarmac. Mr Crosthwaite had cleared that all the way down to Greenhead but, even so, there were several parts where a hole had got completely filled with snow and was veiled by the treacherous smooth white, and my wheels would slump alarmingly into it. But each time we came out and when we got to Greenhead Mr Crosthwaite took the chains off and said the road was all right, that the snow was quite soft and easy on it and there was no cause for alarm. He wished me good luck and told me again to make haste, so I fairly zoomed into Wigton, once I had tested the surface and found he spoke the truth. The roads were like the black, fine lines of a web, stretched across the white landscape, and I swung from one to another, marvelling at the grace of the pattern.

There was no snow on the streets in Wigton. I parked in front of the church and tore through the High Street, buying huge stocks of the best quality tinned foods I could find. I had thought everyone would have had the same idea about paraffin and calor gas heaters but I had no difficulty obtaining both – clearly, Wigton was used to real winter and not taken by surprise, as I was. Last of all, I rushed into the little bookshop in Westmorland Lane and alarmed the lady there by sweeping twenty pounds' worth of paperbacks off her shelves – I needed food and warmth for the mind, if I was going to be besieged, as well as for the body. I thought Casper too old for colouring books and so forth but, on a sudden impulse, bought some felt pens and paints and a big block of cartridge paper.

The car was heavily and untidily loaded by the time I set off – I had just thrown everything in, in my hurry. The snow had begun to fall straighter and thicker as I reached Red Dial and I felt a little anxious as I saw the black road disappearing ahead. An hour, Mr Crosthwaite had said, and I was well within the limit, but he could not have forecast the speed with which the wind suddenly increased and the snow ceased to become something pretty and harmless and became instead vicious and dangerous. My windscreen wipers, even at slow speed, could not cope with the weight of the snow driven now against it and soon I was compelled to drive almost blind, depending on my wing mirrors for traffic behind, and on luck for any ahead.

It was not quite noon by the time I got to Greenhead, almost sobbing with relief. Out I got, to struggle with the chains, but I could not get the front two on. I huddled against the wheel, covered in stinging snow that was half hailstones, and fiddled about, but it was no good – I could not get the damned things fastened. Swearing, I got back in and turned onto the tarmac track – I could, I was sure, get at least to the end of the tarmac without disaster and then if necessary I could abandon the car and ferry the goods painfully on foot. But only a few yards up the hill my two front wheels slipped into a drift of snow I had not even suspected was there – I was not, in fact, squarely in the centre of the track – and that was it. I was a mile and a half from my cottage and stuck. The wheels whirled helplessly and I sat there, pointlessy revving the engine and telling myself to keep calm, I was almost home and could walk on and get Mr Crosthwaite's help. Reluctant to admit defeat, I at last got out again and stood looking at the wheels. I kicked them, and grovelled about in the snow, trying to determine where the drift began and ended. There was a sudden blast from the horn of a car and I turned to find Howard waving at me from his army style truck. I held my arms out in a spontaneous gesture of appeal and he stopped as I went back the ten yards I had come until I was standing beside his window.

"Filthy weather," he said cheerfully. "You stuck?"

"Yes, I am. And Casper is at home ill – I'm absolutely desperate to get back."

"Want a tow, then?"

"Yes, please. Or even a straightforward lift with my stuff – anything to get back. I don't care about the bloody car."

"Oh, you can't leave your car abandoned – jolly bad for it. Come on, we'll manage with a bit of heave-ho."

Gallantly, Howard inched his truck past my car, taking care first of all to be sure where the hard ground was, and then he got out a towing rope and tied it on and within seconds had me out. I was willing to go on by myself but he insisted on taking me the whole way and I was of course more than a little glad. When we were as near to my cottage as we could get he jumped out and insisted on carrying the two heaters I had bought across the garden to the door – a further kindness I begged him not to do me, fearing that by delaying longer he would get into difficulties himself, but he said there would be a lull in a minute and not to worry, he was storm proof in his truck. It was as he returned to his truck, refusing to come and have coffee, that the worst thing that could have happened happened, and I did not even appreciate the true magnitude of the disaster until afterwards.

Howard was standing at the door of the truck, one hand already on the handle, and foot already on the step. I was standing beside him, saying for the third time, "Well, thank you very, very much – I cannot tell you how grateful I am." And at that moment Miss Cowdie passed us – or rather, she came out from behind the end of the truck, head bowed, shoulders completely covered in snow and her poor feet in the cracked boots wringing wet. Without thinking I said, "Oh, Miss Cowdie – you gave me a fright," and indeed she had, emerging like that so silently, so unexpectedly, and then looking so wretched and forlorn, as she always did on her return journeys. She stopped and looked up at me, eyes quite blank, and because I was distressed by her apathy I said, "Howard, I don't think you've ever met your tenant – Miss Elfrida Cowdie." Howard took his foot off the ridge of the car and politely held out his hand. "How do you do, Miss Cowdie, delighted to meet you," he said. We both smiled. Miss Cowdie, however, remained perfectly expressionless. "Howard just rescued me from the snow," I said, thinking some explanation might bring her out of her trance-like state. She ignored me. Slowly, she trudged off and was soon in thick snow, leaving behind the track Mr Crosthwaite had roughly cleaned, floundering about knee-deep in it, both arms outstretched to keep her balance. On and on she struggled, a small black figure only just rising out of the white hill, and neither of us said anything.

After Howard had gone, with another re-issue of the invitation to his party, I went back inside to sort out all the things I had bought. As Howard had predicted, there was a sudden lull in the snowstorm. The sky was still dark grey but the air was clear and the wind blew only a few forlorn flakes in our direction. "More on the way," Eileen said when I commented on the slackening of the weather, and for once sounded anxious, rather than complacent. The dance, of course, was on her mind. Every five minutes she peered out of the door, looking towards the west, where she assured me the weather came from, and I grew quite cross with her for letting the precious heat escape. Briskly, I told her to stop fretting about the roads being blocked and to go instead to the barn to unload the kiln. I wanted the barn cleared and locked up until the new materials arrived. While it was so cold we could not have worked there anyway, and I did not want to have to worry about it being left open if we were shut up in the cottage. Carefully arranging a thick scarf over her wonderful locks, Eileen put her Wellingtons and coat back on and obediently went off across the garden.

I realised, as I went up the stairs to see Casper, that I had not yet spoken to Eileen about Geoff, nor had I thought about whether I should or not. I dreaded tackling Geoff himself and in any case seeking him out would be no easy task in this weather. If I went up to the farm I would have to tell Eileen because of Casper – I would not want her to leave until I returned. I considered the idea that a hint dropped to Eileen might be the most effective way of dealing with Geoff and his silly threats, but I could not be sure. I was not myself in the least perturbed but I wanted to be able to reassure Casper, to demonstrate how swiftly I had acted. I knew he would not mention his fear again, unless it returned at night time, but I wanted to mention it for him and dispel it.

But I said nothing. Instead, I sat on his bed and described the outside conditions and how I had got stuck and I gave him the paper and pens. He showed no interest in them, but I left them on the bedside table. Again, he was flushed and restless and complained of a headache, and my heart sank at the thought of yet another day cooped up in that tiny room when we both ought to have been sledging in the snow. Antonia, I swear, had loved running a sickroom but I hated it. I was a dreadful nurse – impatient, bored and hardly able to disguise my conviction that the sick person could instantly become well if only they tried hard enough. Trying to hide my irritation from Casper, I went to the window and looked out for inspiration. I saw Eileen running – lumbering – across the garden, without her protective headscarf, without her warm coat.

Before I had got down the stairs she had burst into the room. "Smashed!" she shouted at me, "Smashed! All of it, in smithereens! Come and look." Pausing only to put on my boots, I hurried after her, gasping at the cold. The barn was icy. Eileen pointed dramatically to the area in front of the kiln where the drying rack stood. The kiln door was open and the floor in front covered with a mound of glistening broken pots – a heap of multi-coloured fragments, the sharp edges sticking up like teeth. Beside the pile lay a hammer, my own hammer, to prove, if there had been any doubt, how the work of destruction had been done. "I just come in," Eileen was saying, "and I saw it – smashed, deliberate like, all taken out and belted wi' the hammer. Look, all them little pieces not even broke in half – in smithereens! And look – " and she pointed to the shelves holding all the various tools of my trade. Someone had swept each one clean and at the end of each one was a pile of debris. The last of the cement had been scattered everywhere and the sand bags emptied all over the floor. My potter's wheel lay on its side and there were large dents in the boards holding it. "I've never seen owt like it," Eileen said, tremendously excited rather than horrified. "Who could have done it?"

My thoughts naturally flew to Geoff – it fitted in so well with his promise to Casper. And yet I could not believe it – why should Geoff destroy my work? I had no idea why he should have turned so violently against me, when I thought I had made him so happy and settled his frustrated soul, but if Casper was right and he was full of hate, then this act of violence would make sense. Then I thought of Miss Cowdie. She had not recognised me that morning. She had not been near me for several weeks and in the dark December days, trapped in her cottage by the snow, she could well have returned to her former state of aggressiveness towards me. Smashing the pots was little different from leaving the dead rabbit and sheep's head. It needed no strength. The hammer was there, the barn door unlocked, the pots obvious and fragile. "Who do you think might have done it?" I said slowly to Eileen. "It snowed all last night. It must have been someone near at hand. There aren't any wanderers on the fells in snowstorms."

"Eh, I don't know," Eileen said, "it doesn't make sense. It weren't me – my own pots smashed. I wouldn't smash my own pots."

"Eileen, I never for one minute thought it *could* be you – for goodness sake." But she looked frightened. I thought she worried I suspected Geoff. "Don't tell Casper," was all I said. "Let's clean up, anyway, and lock the place."

It took us an hour, both working hard at the dismal job. Even then, we did not leave the place as immaculate as I would have liked it to be, but the water was frozen in the pipes and we had to be content with sweeping and dusting – nothing could be washed. Eileen kept muttering, "It's a damned shame, a bloody damned shame," and she handled the pieces of her own broken pots tenderly – in fact, I saw her slip the larger fragments into her pocket. She was far more upset in the end than I was. When we got back into the cottage, she proclaimed herself too churned up to consider drinking any coffee, and said the discovery of such chaos had completely spoiled her day. "Don't let it upset you any more, Eileen," I said, "just think of the dance tonight."

"I won't enjoy it, not now."

"Yes, you will. You'll wear your new dress and have a lovely time." I saw her face soften. "How will you get there?"

"Dad'll run me in."

"Not Geoff?"

"Won't go. Pig-headed. Hasn't even asked Mildred – says he doesn't want to go."

"How will you get back?"

"Oh, a lift." She smiled slyly. "Depends, really," she said, and I saw the whole thrill of the evening lay in who gave you a lift home.

"Well, take care," I said, "have a good time. I'll look forward to hearing all about it."

Eileen put her pinny in her bag and was ready to go, but hesitated. "Seems a shame," she said, "leaving you here, me going to the dance. Doesn't seem fair."

I laughed. "Don't give it a thought," I said, "I've been to millions of parties and had millions of lifts home. I'm perfectly happy to be without them now."

I believed what I said but all the same I watched her go with some regret. Life did seem bleak, especially in the light of Eileen's anticipation of a happy evening. Slightly mournful, I prepared a hot lemon drink for Casper and took it up to him and supervised his swallowing of it and gave him more dope and then, when he immediately buried himself in the blankets again and either slept or feigned sleep, I came back downstairs and looked with some resentment at the clock. It was only just after noon. I stared at the clock quite stupidly. There was no doubt that it was ticking. The sound was gratingly loud. There was so little that I could do. Work was impossible without materials and in these weather conditions. There was nothing Eileen had not done in the way of cleaning and cooking, and though sitting down to read in the middle of the day ought to have been a desirable luxury, it simply did not appeal. I did not want to read, I did not want to do anything except get out, and that I could not do. I had had my outing for the day.

Standing yet again at the window, staring out, I told myself to be consoled by the beauty of the snow, but beauty is never comforting. It did not make me feel any more content to see the broad sweeping plains of pure white, rising to a crest against the dark grey sky. The contours of the fellside were softened and shaped into unaccustomed dips and hollows but though I admired the pattern it did not cheer me. The old feeling of being trapped persisted. I felt as claustrophobic as I would have done in a lift, sinking through the earth to a coalmine. Images distorted my vision as I gazed dully out – images of a man swinging a hammer in the barn, of Geoff's contorted face as he threatened Casper, of Miss Cowdie's brave figure, fighting the snow. She, of course, was as trapped as I, but she was used to it. She would have a thing or two to teach me about long days and nights spent shut up, at the mercy of the elements, daydreaming and woolgathering. I had not acquired the knack. Some tranquility of spirit was lacking in me.

Somehow, I put in the afternoon, and at dusk drew the curtains and closed the shutters with relief. I let Rufus bound around outside first and stood at the door watching him. The wind had risen again and was pushing the snow against the walls, picking up the loose stuff on top and driving it inwards. It had not snowed again but I could feel the cold in the wind and it did not need Eileen to tell me another storm was on the way. Everything bolted and barred, with Rufus inside and fed, I built up the fire and prayed there would be no electricity cuts. Warmth and light were the two things that made my imprisonment bearable and without them I would give in and go to bed and crouch there until summer. I told Casper he was in the very best place but then, in the next breath, I was encouraging him to get up for a little while, anything to bring his recovery forward. He refused. He said his head still ached and his throat was sore and when I took his temperature I was obliged to admit getting up would be a bad idea. Indeed, I was secretly alarmed. His temperature was 104°. He had been ill for two days and instead of improving he was getting worse – aspirin and fluids and rest had not yet done the trick.

I wished passionately that Dr Teasdale was at the end of a telephone, though even if he had been I could not have made him come out on such a night except in the most dire emergency. I cautioned myself against displaying my alarm to Casper and tried to be reassuring. But as I sat with him, bored out of my mind, he tossed and turned and even began to mutter to himself. His eyes were wild and his arms went up in front of his face instinctively, as though to ward off something or someone. "Casper," I said, loudly, trying to break into his dream. He seemed to start at my voice and then to doze but within a few minutes he was hallucinating again. I ran to the bathroom and returned with a bowl of icy water and a sponge and towel, and then I sat cooling him down with frequent cold applications on his forehead. It seemed to work. His eyes stopped rolling and flickering and I was even relieved rather than upset when he burst into tears and said, "I dreamt of my mother – there she was, standing in front of me – it was really her, I could touch her." He cried in my arms and I held him and said nothing. "I don't want her dead," he said, his voice muffled in the material of my sweater. "No," I said, "I know you don't. But she *is* dead, Casper, and you've got me instead. It may seem a bad bargain, but I love you too. You're not without some sort of mother. And it will get better, I promise you. Everything does, with time. Everything."

Should I have told him then? Probably. But he went off to sleep even while I was considering it and that was the last chance I had that evening. I tucked him up and for the next few hours looked in on him every ten minutes, listening anxiously to the rasping breathing. I had a bath and sat by the fire, writing to Edward, pouring out my heart to him, knowing that I would never post the letter. I admitted my mistakes and outlined for him the mess I had got myself into. And then, half doped with whisky, I went to bed, leaving my door open wide, so that I would hear Casper. His breathing was noisy enough for me to hear it clearly and I was sure that if there was any change in it I would automatically waken. Naturally, when the crying began, I thought it was him. I woke in the night to hear this sobbing, quite loud and insistent, a continuous noisy wailing. I was on my feet and into my dressing-gown in seconds, fully awake and concerned. Lightly I tiptoed up the little staircase to Casper's attic, only to find him deeply asleep. I stood still, at his side, and looked down upon his silence while the sobbing continued – one long, keening note. Rufus was growling softly when I went into the living room. I put on the lamp but it merely clicked – once more there was an electricity cut. As I found and lit a candle and then, by its light, a paraffin lamp I had set up in readiness, I wondered if it might be an animal – a fox or a stray dog – but it sounded so human I could not believe it. I stood hesitating at the door. So suspicious had I become, I was considering whether it was a decoy, whether, if I opened the door of my own volition, I should regret it. Yet the heart-broken crying could not be ignored.

I took the precaution of opening the door on the chain Mr Rigg had provided, which I had never before bothered to use, and in my other hand I held a poker, though God knows what I thought I could do with it. Through the nine inch gap I could see nothing whatsoever. It was totally black outside, except for falling snow, and even that appeared murky grey and not white. I waited and called out, "Is anyone there? Is anyone hurt?" The crying, if anything, redoubled in volume, but there was no reply. Growing bolder, I opened the door properly and held the lamp high in my hand. I looked to the left and to the right, shivering in my thin nightdress and gown, but I could see nothing. Behind me, Rufus padded out and it was only when he trotted over to a mound of snow near the corner of the cottage wall and began sniffing and barking and wagging his tail that I realised the crying was coming from there. Not pausing to put on boots, I went over, plunging into the snow, which sent shock waves sweeping up my legs, and bent down and peered at what looked like a bundle of old clothes, thrown anyhow on the ground and long since covered with snowflakes.

"Who is it?" I said, scared at what I should see. "What has happened?" I bent down further and put out my hand to lift the corner of cloth I could see but as I did so it was gripped by another hand, which shot out, and I screamed at the sudden contact and tried to snatch my own hand away but instead I was pulled down and ended up staring terrified into the tear washed face of Eileen Crosthwaite.

I got her into my cottage only by dragging her. She would not come. There she lay, in the snow, soaked to the skin and chilled literally to the bone but she refused to come in. She wanted me to lie with her there until death from exposure carried us both away. I had to use my other hand to free my first by brutally prising her fingers off with my nails, and then I shouted at her and ordered her inside and, when she went on with that awful sobbing and shook her head, I took hold of her by her shoulders and with tremendous force pulled her upright. "Eileen!" I yelled, "whatever is the matter, we can't stay out here," and I gave her a great shove in the back and bundled her towards the door and when she sank down on the threshold I took hold of her hands and drew her into the room, the last few feet. Thankfully, almost sobbing myself with the effort, I again closed the door, without pausing either to lock or bolt it. Even before I looked at Eileen, I staggered up the stairs, trembling in my sodden clothes, and ripped them off and pulled on my jeans and jumper, and then I went into the kitchen and put the kettle on, before I remembered it would not work. No hot drinks. Cursing, I tried to find the brandy but failed, and then I went back to Eileen and gave her my attention, warm enough at last for compassion.

She lay just inside the door, on her side, her knees drawn up and her arms round them. The light from the dying embers of the fire showed me her poor face. It was a pitiful and ugly sight. Her customary pallor was replaced by a mottled, blotchy purple and down the left-hand side, from ear to jaw, was a bright red line. Her narrow eyes, never dominant in her face at the best of times, were almost closed with weeping. At first I thought she had developed bruises under them overnight, but then I saw the blackness was merely mascara which had run. Her expression was one of utter misery, every muscle contorted into a painful grimace. I touched her gently and said, "Eileen, whatever has happened?" She moaned and shook off my hand and tried to bury herself yet deeper in her wet coat. So I sat there with her, noticing some new mark of disaster with every minute. The famous hair-do was devastated. Wringing wet, the waves and curls were plastered to her head, the whole edifice collapsed, and instead of framing her face her hair now clung to it, streaked across in flat black clumps. I saw that on one foot she had a cheap gilt shoe, the stiletto heel twisted round and almost snapped off, and on the other she had nothing. Beneath the coat – a kind of cape I had never seen her wear before – I caught glimpses of red taffeta, torn and spoiled, and in one hand she clutched a necklace of pearls, half of them gone from the string.

"Come on, Eileen," I said after a long time, "you'll feel better if you tell me." I put some more wood on the fire and when it blazed up I crouched down near the light and warmth and spread out my hands in front of it. The crying had stopped. Eileen sniffled and groaned a little, but she no longer wailed. I turned to look at her. Her eyes were open and she was staring at the fire. "Take off your wet things," I said, "you'll feel better." She shook her head but I went upstairs again and found my bathrobe and a towel and came back. "Put these on," I said, "I'll help you. You'll get pneumonia if you keep those on much longer."

"*Want* pneumonia," she suddenly burst out, "want to die," and she was off again, sobbing noisily, though with such depleted strength the volume was nothing like it had been. I got down on my knees and held her face in my hands, and said, "Eileen, Eileen, nothing can be that bad. Come on, off with this coat." I managed to push away her feebly protesting hands and to get the cape, heavy with melted snow, off her back. I flung it on to the stone floor near the door and turned my attentions to the dress. Eileen had closed her eyes again and looked agonised. She had her arms crossed over her chest and when I uncrossed them I saw her dress had been ripped from neck to hem – one mighty pull which had split the thin, shoddy material, instantly exposing Eileen's curious underwear. She wore a strapless brassière of a kind I had not seen for decades – boned and stiffened, encasing her small sweet breasts in a constricting mesh of pink net and satin. She turned her head away and said, "No, no," but I was determined to have her warm and dry and with great briskness wrapped the towel round her and rubbed her wet limbs and then forced the robe on and belted it round her. It was like trying to dress a rag doll – the arms were floppy and hard to push through the sleeves and when I lifted her back to get the robe round her, the head flopped forward.

The fire was now burning well and lit the whole room. I put a cushion under Eileen's head and found it easier to look at her, now that she was out of those awful clothes. It was beginning to enter my head that she had been raped and that the trauma had sent her plunging through the snow to me because she was afraid to go home, and I did not relish being confronted with the evidence. I did not want to hear her story and share her ordeal and yet I felt I could not leave things as they were. Should I prompt her, by voicing my suspicions, or should I go on sitting there, hoping she would eventually talk? I studied her carefully. She was much calmer. I went over and put my arm round her and tried hard to give her some affection.

"You went to the dance and . . ." I said, letting my voice tail off. The tears began again, but quietly. "You danced with lots of boys – did you, Eileen? You had a lovely time, and someone said they would run you home?"

"Didn't know him," Eileen said, covering her eyes, "from Carlisle, he was. Don't know how he come to be there, him and his mates. Said he was called Pete. He – he was nice." Her shoulders shook. "Said he'd drive me home. Got to Greenhead and he stopped the car and kissed me. Said he'd ring me next week, works at Metal Box. He was nice." She stopped and I said, "And you got out of the car?" She nodded. "Did he get out?" She nodded again. "And then he tried to make love to you?"

"Oh *no*," she said violently. "It were just *kissing* – we were just stood there, kissing, he was *nice* – and then – then – our Geoff – oh – "

I saw the picture at once. Geoff wandering about, even in the snow, locked into God knows what kind of mad world of his own, hating all women, and me in particular, and there he sees Eileen, embracing a man, and at once his savage loathing for her entire species drives him to knock them apart and assault his sister. Of course, it would be Geoff who would rip a dress like that, Geoff who would batter and beat a girl, not the innocent Pete.

"The brute," I said, and held Eileen tightly with real compassion at last.

"He knocked Pete out," Eileen gasped, "clouted him in the face and he went down and then he screams at me, 'you filthy little slut,' and takes hold of me and hits me, and then he tore my cape off and his horrible hands got hold of my new dress and he tore it and – "

"Don't, Eileen," I said, "that's enough. I can see it all. Don't talk any more. You're quite safe here and Geoff can't get you. In the morning I'll go and see him, and your parents."

"They won't believe me," Eileen sobbed, "alus on his side. He'll say I was letting a stranger do owt he liked, and he was teaching me a lesson. Mam and Dad'll believe him – alus do."

"But he hit you – they won't approve of that."

Eileen nodded. "They will. They know he hits me. And Mam will ask if I was kissing, and I can't deny it, and she'll hit me too. She'll say I'm wicked, disgusting – she will. And Pete won't ever ring – the first boy I've ever had – he won't come near."

"He will," I said, without convincing myself, never mind Eileen.

"He won't." Eileen clenched her fists and beat them against each other. "Oh, I wish I'd done it with him, in his car – I wish I had – I wish he'd given me a baby – I do – they couldn't take that away – they'd have to let me go to him, turn me out. I'll never get another chance. I'll end up like Miss Cowdie. I'll never get a baby."

There was no point at all in trying to argue with Eileen. She was much too emotionally and physically exhausted to be able to listen to sense. I felt that what she most needed was sleep, and so I coaxed her onto the sofa and covered her with blankets and gave her aspirins and the brandy I had finally located. She fell into a deep sleep almost immediately. I banked the fire up and bolted the door and went to bed, after a last look at Casper. I could not think what I ought to do. Everything Eileen said was probably true – Geoff would be believed. She was fortunate to have escaped him before he did her further damage – I will not confess the other fates that crossed my mind – and lucky that he had not followed her, guided by the crying to where she had lain for so long against my cottage wall. I lay in the absolute darkness, thinking how much deeper the real tragedy was – not a matter of a sister beaten by a brother, but of a girl desperate for affection and a man determined to see that she did not get it. Eileen's absurd fantasy of marriage and babies with the youth she'd known half an evening lay at the heart of her distress. She could take being knocked about by Geoff – she had taken it endless times before – but what she could not take was the collapse of her dreams. That night, she had been Cinderella, for whom a Prince Charming had finally materialised. Now she was back in her rags, with little idea of how empty her ideal future might have been. Marriage and a baby, a wedding and a christening – those were the magic spells to banish misery forever. She did not for one minute see that the transformation must come from within herself.

Nineteen

Casper's coughing woke me at six in the morning. My first thought as I got up was that the electricity was still off – the bedroom was freezing cold, so I knew the boiler had not clocked on and therefore the automatic electric clock was not working. I pulled on the same warm clothes I had had on the night before but they did not feel in the least warm – they felt wet as well as cold, but it was just with lying so long on the floor, where I had carelessly thrown them in my exhaustion. Casper's room was even colder and real alarm gripped me when I saw his flushed face, warmed by his own temperature and nothing else. I said good morning to him and tried to be cheerful but failed. My first priority must be to get one of the heaters into his room and my next to find some way of heating water and milk for him to drink.

Downstairs, Eileen still slept. Thankfully, I threw another blanket over her – at least we were not short of bedding – and carried up a paraffin heater to Casper's room. I was pleased with myself when I managed to get it working efficiently at once. I had less luck with heating water. The only method I could think of was using the fire, and that would be slow and not particularly easy. The embers were still hot, so I crouched there, putting on little bits of kindling and waiting until it was thoroughly burning before I added some more, increasing the size of the sticks bit by bit until I had a couple of sizeable logs blazing away. Then I selected the heaviest pan I had, filled it with water and carefully set it on the fire. Immediately the logs collapsed, and it was my cursing that woke Eileen.

She made no reference to how she came to be there. At her most phlegmatic, she got up and came over to me and silently pushed me aside. She rebuilt the fire much more cleverly, using a different shape of log, and then she had the brilliant idea of taking one of the grids from the oven and setting it over the firegrate, which it fitted almost exactly. The pan was then quite stable. Eileen said it would be ruined, that only iron pans were any good for the fire, but I replied sharply that beggars could not be choosers and that if I didn't have some sort of coffee soon I would faint.

I loaned Eileen some clothes. She looked at them with distaste – for some ridiculous reason, Eileen never wore trousers – but in fact when she had them on she looked better than I had ever seen her, or at least her body did. The black cord jeans showed her slim hips off to great advantage and the scarlet polo neck made her look bright and neat. But clothes could not transform her battered face, nor restore her hair to its former glory. I saw her steal a look in the mirror above the mantelpiece, and her hands flew up to her head and then fell down listlessly. There was nothing she could do to make it look better and, as if she knew this, she did not even attempt to brush it with the brush I held out. She shook her head and I put it away.

Until this point I had not opened the shutters, thinking they must help a little to keep the room warm, but now I opened the first pair and got a new shock. No light came in. I gasped and did not at first realise that what I was looking into was a snow drift. The snow had come to the top of the ground floor windows and was stacked against them. I opened all the other shutters and found that on the right-hand side the drift only came up to the top of the second pane. Through the remaining top row, I looked out on to a pure white sea that stretched for unbroken miles. I asked Eileen if she thought we could try the door but she shook her head and said we would find the biggest drift of all there and if we opened it an avalanche would engulf us. She did not seem in the least perturbed and I felt irritated by her apathy. She said she had seen it all before and when I questioned her about how long it would last she said once they had been holed up a week and that even then they – the Crosthwaites – were better off than I was because they were further down the valley. I was at exactly the worst point for drifts, Eileen said. The wind came straight off the fell and swept the snow in my direction. Even Miss Cowdie, protected by the lee of the hill, was better off.

The water took an hour to boil. I made some coffee and drank it as though I had been dying of thirst for a week, and then I took some to Casper, who seemed oblivious of the comfort it had given me. I sat on his bed and told him about the drifts and urged him to look from his window at the spectacular snowfields. He did at least look, and agreed it was like looking out of an aeroplane window on to miles of puffy white clouds, but then he slumped back and coughed and was worn out by the effort. He took a thin slice of brown bread and honey and then gave up the struggle to sit up. In the kitchen, Eileen prepared soup on my directions – I knew it would take all day to cook on the fire and could not get it on soon enough. She did not speak. I counted the logs, piled high on either side of the fireplace, all brought in providentially the day before, and worried about how long they would last, at the rate we were using them. Not a week, at any rate.

I would much rather have been completely on my own with Casper than doomed to share Eileen's miserable and depressing company. All the optimism she had increasingly shown over the last few weeks, with the consequent flowering of the little personality she had, seemed to have vanished. Though knowing the reasons for this ought to have made me sympathetic, it did not. I felt resentful that she had reverted so quickly to type.

"Eileen," I said, after a morning of her brooding silence, "don't you think your father will come to get you?"

She shrugged. "Could he get through drifts like this?" I persisted.

"Don't know."

"Will he try?"

"Don't know."

"But do you *think* he will?"

"Maybe."

"Won't he be worried about you? Will he guess you came here last night?"

"Don't know."

I gave up and went back to staring out at the snow on the least blocked side.

"If I open the door," I said, "how do you know the snow will fall in?"

"Alus does."

"But you haven't been in this cottage in a snowdrift."

"Faces north, like ours. Just the same."

"So what do you do – don't you open the door?"

"Yes. Dad and Geoff dig us out. Have to, to get to the animals."

"Well then," I said triumphantly, "we can dig ourselves out."

"Where to?" Eileen said, her voice remaining perfectly flat and level.

She was right, of course, and I ought to have listened to her. We could not possibly dig ourselves to anywhere useful. Even clearing a fairly small amount of snow the day before, to the wall, had merely brought me out to the track and the real problem. Without the Crosthwaites' home-made snow-plough I would not have been able to make much progress – certainly, I would not have been able to use the car, which was what I really wanted to do. This time, digging through a drift would only bring me to bigger drifts. Any attempt to rescue us must come from the other direction, and whether it would be made depended on how great was the general anxiety about Eileen. Had Geoff seen the direction she had taken? Would he tell his parents she was quite safe? I had no idea how they would react.

Opening the door was a very silly thing to do. Everything happened as Eileen predicted. Even as I inched the door open the snow began to fall in and because I was so furious I let it, pretending it was all part of my plan. The door was not quite six feet high. The drift was not quite five. Four and a half feet of loosely packed snow fell straight into our living room and had to be hurled out with a shovel. It took me half an hour simply to clear the floor and then I started on the drift itself. As I stood on the threshold it came over my waist and, every step forward I tried to take, it closed round me. I seemed to make no progress at all, to be forever hurling shovels of snow to right and left, only to find more fell back in its place. Eileen said not a word. I did not ask her to help. I knew she was behind me, watching with her deadpan expression, and I did not turn round once. Once more I was soaked to the skin, and hating the icy trickle the snow turned into when it worked its way through my clothes, but I was determined to get at least to the woodshed to justify my foolishness. The woodshed was fifty yards from the cottage door. After twenty yards, and two hours' constant shovelling, I prepared to give up.

I stood with tears of self-pity in my eyes, staring over the crisp white hummocks of snow, down towards the invisible track. The light was beginning to fade already, at three o'clock, and as I turned my face up to the sky I thought I could feel the first snowflakes upon it, even though I could not see them. Nobody would come to rescue us – they would not think it worth the effort, knowing we had plenty of food and wood for the fire. This was not Siberia, or even Canada – they knew the weather would change in a day or two, that a thaw would quickly release us. And I knew it too. Slowly, I trudged back along the channel I had so laboriously dug with Rufus, stupid Rufus, barking and wagging his tail so vigorously he knocked down more snow into the cleared pathway. Now that I had stopped shovelling I was quickly cold and when I thought I could not even have a hot bath the tears no longer stayed in my eyes but trickled down my cheeks.

I dashed them away before I went in to Eileen. She was sitting on a stool, very close to the fire, watching the precious soup, in case it boiled over. With her awful ruined hair and bruised face she looked like a witch over a cauldron, every bit as intense and ferocious. All afternoon she had sat there, feeding the fire with sticks of exactly the right size to fuel it without putting it out or making it too powerful for the pan to survive. It was a job that suited her perfectly. The smell which filled the little room was appetising and though I was cross with her for her abject attitude I was grateful for the results. I said that tomorrow I would get as far as the woodshed, as long as no more heavy snow fell, and asked if she had heard the weather forecast on the radio. She said she had tried to put it on but the battery was flat and she did not know where the new ones were, or how to put them in. Of course, I had forgotten new batteries.

Sharing that living room with Eileen was twice as bad as it had been with Casper. I thought I would go mad with irritation. We had our soup at the table and then Eileen washed up while I went to give some to Casper, who ate hardly any. His temperature was still high, his cough bad, but at least he was no longer hallucinating. All he wanted to do was sleep. Choosing whether to sit and watch Casper toss and turn or watch Eileen sit and stare was like choosing between the devil and the deep blue sea. I only chose Eileen because the living room was warmer and I still had not managed to get really warm again.

At first, I read and ignored her, but after an hour she began to get on my nerves.

"Eileen," I said, "*do* something. Read – I'll find you a book."

"Don't like reading. Haven't me glasses."

"I didn't know you wore them."

"For reading, and watching tele."

"Would you like to play cards, or chess or something?"

"Can't play anything."

"I'd teach you."

"Don't want to."

"You can't just sit all night. It isn't as if you're quite happy just sitting, is it? You're just thinking about last night, aren't you? Aren't you?"

My tone was hectoring and Eileen did not know that my bullying was simply a measure of my own frustration. She got up and said, "Shall I close the shutters? Getting dark," and I sighed and said I supposed so. She seemed to stand a long time at the first window, the one looking north, the one from which the track could not be seen, when she said, without excitement, "Somebody coming." I thought she was playing a sick joke. "Oh, Eileen," I said, exasperated, "how can there be?" but I got up, stirrings of hope spurring me on. If only the

Crosthwaites would come and take Eileen away and telephone Dr Teasdale for me, how happy I should be.

But it was not Mr Crosthwaite, nor Geoff. It was Miss Cowdie. Both Eileen and I stood mesmerised at the strange sight before us. Clad in an amazing assortment of garments – I suspected she had put on every article of clothing she possessed, plus a blanket or two – Miss Cowdie was coming towards us, down the hillside, sitting on a makeshift sledge, which stopped and started every few yards. She had a bag in front of her, between her feet, and some sort of stick in each hand, with which she was propelling herself. She would swoop a little way, quite fast, and then she would stop and have great difficulty guiding herself to the next slope. Sometimes her sticks sank completely into the snow but she always rescued them. As I watched, I saw her progress was not as haphazard as it seemed. In my mind's eye, I saw the path to her cottage, which followed close to the rocky part at the bottom of the fell, high above the stream and yet below the spongy turf where the sheep normally fed. Miss Cowdie, by trial and error, was following it. The drifts were well to her left and the danger not as great as it appeared.

"Come down to us one time," Eileen murmured. "Five year ago. Slept in the kitchen, couple of nights. Said she was dying – nowt we could do. Went back when the thaw come. She niver said thanks neither."

"Maybe she's on her way to you now," I said. "Maybe we could rig up a sledge and get down too. I'd never thought of it."

"Hard, mekking a sledge," Eileen said severely, and then she looked critically at Miss Cowdie. "Anyways, she's coming here – not taking the right direction for our farm, she's too high. Shall I open the door?"

There was no question of saying that she could not. The door unbolted, Eileen stood there waiting for Miss Cowdie to slip and slither the last few yards, the light from our paraffin lamps making an orange path of its own, across the darkening snow. I was numb with misery. In the background, I stood by the table, dreading the entry of my neighbour, seeing ahead a whole night of unbelievable tedium – three of us round the fire, three solitary women, unused to each other's company and totally incompatible. But Miss Cowdie came in smiling, that death mask grimace that had no humour in it at all, carrying her bag and apologising for some delay that existed only in her own mind. "I am so sorry," she kept saying, "I *did* try to get here sooner, but events conspired. However, I am not too late, I hope."

"I don't think you're late for anything that I know of," I said, a little grimly.

"Oh, good. No harm done. I couldn't risk getting cut off completely, in view of tomorrow, but I left it as late as possible. Now, shall I change in the bedroom? Perhaps you would show me the way?"

I hesitated. Eileen smiled, a smile as unpleasant and sinister as Miss Cowdie's. She, at least, was enjoying herself. Miss Cowdie, bag in hand, waited, face falsely expectant.

"Is there any need to change?" I said slowly. "I have not changed. It's more comfortable, this weather, to stay in the same clothes."

"But I think he will expect some show," Miss Cowdie said indignantly. "We are not very elegant, are we?"

"No. But why should we be elegant?"

"Oh really," Miss Cowdie said, eyes raised heavenwards. "Well then – I shall use the bathroom. Which way, please?"

The bathroom was preferable to my bedroom, which was somehow too intimate to allow Miss Cowdie into – I would never, afterwards, feel comfortable there, with the memory of her presence. I showed her the bathroom and with great dignity she entered. I did not want to go back, leaving her there with the unsuspecting Casper only a few steps up the staircase in his attic, but I knew I would hear every movement she made and did not have to fear that she would go up without my hearing, so I left her and returned to Eileen, who was busy closing the shutters. "No," I said, on a sudden impulse, "don't close them. Leave them. I prefer them open, for a little while anyway." Obediently, Eileen undid the ones she had already closed and left the rest. I could not explain, even to myself, why I wanted the windows unbarred.

"What do you think she has come for?" I whispered to Eileen, who shrugged and shook her head. We were not left long in doubt. Down Miss Cowdie came, wearing her wedding dress and carrying in her hand a white prayer book, encased in polythene. The dress was grossly distorted on her greatly changed frame. I had only ever before seen the bedraggled inches of net peeping out from underneath her coat but now that I saw it in its full glory I realised how grotesque she must always have looked. It was not a wedding dress, any more than Eileen's red taffeta frock. I had imagined her, pale and slim, in a simple white satin gown. Instead, she had evidently decked herself out in a parody of a ball gown, low necked and full skirted, the pink ruched silk of the bodice covered with net, and the bunched skirts huge with net flounces, decorated with artificial flowers. Even with youth on her side, she could never have looked anything but ridiculous. Now, with ten years of neglect against her, she was a frightening apparition. The fact that she held herself so regally made the sight of her worse, not better. She could have been pathetic but instead was macabre. My eyes were drawn to her filthy bosom, where a white cloth gardenia hung drunkenly between sagging breasts, and to her arms, all bone, with pads of flesh loosely dripping from shoulder to elbow, as though they no longer had the energy to cleave to the muscles.

"Well," she said, with a small exclamation of content, as she turned, so that we could have the full effect of her costume. "I am ready." And she stood still, in front of the window, and went on standing still while Eileen and I moved away. We expected some outburst, but none came.

"Do sit down, Miss Cowdie," I said. "While you're waiting you could be resting."

"I need no rest," she said, haughtily, raising her chin high. "I have rested enough. I am ready."

Deliberately, I sat down and took up my book. Eileen resumed her position by the fire, though there was now no soup to watch. It is impossible to over-emphasise the depth of the silence in the room – the logs crackled faintly, Casper's cough floated, muffled, from above, and otherwise there was only the clock ticking and our breathing and an occasional sniff from Rufus to disturb the peace. Except it was not peaceful. The room was quiet, but not peaceful. Miss Cowdie stood rigid, at attention, her whole body taut with anticipation. Eileen crouched low, nursing her bitterness and resentment, hatred making her limbs stiff and hard. And I was so tense I could not turn a page of my book without trembling. I sensed in Miss Cowdie a real madness, a final surrendering of her will to the forces of disorder in her mind, and I felt sure that after an hour or so, when her bridegroom failed yet again to come, that violence would break forth. I tried, as I sat there, to make some sort of plan for the emergency I envisaged, but I doubted my own strength. Whatever she did, Miss Cowdie would need restraining, and I knew she would have a manic energy I would find it difficult to match. For the first time, I was glad to have Eileen.

We sat there for two hours, from five until seven, and Miss Cowdie never moved. I got up twice to go to Casper, relieved to find him asleep, and she ignored the interruption. Eileen went once to the lavatory and the cistern roared through the quiet like an express train but Miss Cowdie did not flinch. The longer she stood there, the easier it became to be lulled into a false sense of security. I began to think that instead of rage her disappointment might take the form of grief and be much simpler to deal with. I thought I was sensitive to the slightest change in her expression but when she whirled round from the window I was completely unprepared. "You!" she shouted, pointing to me. "You! You took him, you wicked, wicked girl." She advanced upon me and I jumped to my feet, swinging the chair I had been sitting on in front of me, to form a barrier between us. "Miss Cowdie," I said, my voice shaking, "calm down. I have taken nobody from you."

"I saw you – oh yes, I saw you," she screamed, "yesterday – you had him here – you had the wickedness to introduce him to me – to *me*, his fiancée – oh, how did you dare, you wicked, wicked – " and she lifted up her hand to strike me, her mouth distorted with the terrible effort of forming words at all, her whole face bearing down upon me, suffused with anger. I stayed her hand. As I instinctively put up my arm to stop hers, I was astonished to find myself by far the stronger – her own hand simply fell away at my touch and this gave me more confidence than I felt. But though her blow had not met its target, this by no means diminished her fury. "You took the Earl," she shouted at me. "You took him, you stole him from me, he had come for me and you, *you* took him."

"I did not take him," I said, equally forcefully.

"It *was* Howard, Earl of Cumberland – you said so – I recognised him, of course I did – "

"Yes, it was the Earl, but he had only come to help me home when I got stuck in the snow."

"That was a trick – a trap – "

"It was not. He left at once, he never came into this cottage, you saw him leave."

"But he returned – you have hidden him from me – I saw him come, searching for me – and you have hidden him."

"I have not."

"I will find him – you cannot keep him from me – I know he is here, waiting – " and she whirled round again and with frantic movements began searching the room. There was nowhere anyone could hide, but she flung open the cupboard doors and looked behind the curtains and even went on all fours beneath the table, quite out of control. She rushed headlong into the kitchen, snatching ridiculously at stupid things, and then, before I could get there first, she was up the stairs and into my bedroom, hurling clothes from the rail and emptying the drawers and looking under the bed. "Miss Cowdie, there is nobody here," I said firmly, and at that moment Casper again coughed. Her face lit up and she raised one finger in an appeal for silence. He coughed yet again. "There!" she whispered, "it is he."

"It is Casper, my nephew," I said, "he is ill," – but she was hardly listening to me. Stealthily as a cat, she crept towards the attic stairs, but this time I was there before her and barred her way. "I cannot let you go up," I said, "he is ill – you will frighten him."

"You are hiding him from me," she said, her voice rising again, shrill and piercing.

"It is *not* the Earl," I said.

"Then let me look."

"You must not speak – you may peep round the door, and that is all."

There was no other way to keep her quiet or to resolve the matter. She followed me up the stairs. The door of Casper's room was open so that I might always hear him and I merely had to push it wider for her to look in. He was lying on his side, his face fortunately clearly visible, and his eyes were closed. "There," I whispered, "you see?" But whatever she saw, it was not Casper. She went down on her knees and pressed her hands together in an attitude of prayer. Alarmed, I tried to close the door but at once she said, "No," so loudly that I hastily took my hand away from the doorknob. I dreaded Casper waking up. "It is *not* the Earl," I whispered in her ear. "It is my nephew, we must not disturb him – he is ill."

At that moment there was a piercing scream from below, a scream of such horror and desperation that I automatically ran downstairs, deserting Casper. "For God's sake," I shouted as I ran, "what has happened, Eileen?" I burst into the living room and saw Geoff Crosthwaite, with one arm round his sister's throat and the other holding a shotgun at her head. "Geoff!" I gasped.

"Weren't expecting me, eh?" he said, grinning. "Took a long time coming, didn't I? But I got here in the end."

"Put that gun down."

"Put that gun down," he mimicked. "And who says? Lady of the Manor, eh? Think you can tell anybody to do owt and get away wi' it. Made a monkey out of me, didn't you? Encouraged her, didn't you? Egged her on, taught her your little ways. No wonder she come here."

"I don't know what you're talking about."

"Hoity-toity, does what she likes. You don't do what you like wi' me, nor my sister. She's coming home to a good thrashing or I'll shoot her, here and now. I'll show her who's boss. Get moving."

He released his arm from Eileen's neck and with one swift movement switched the point of the shotgun to between her shoulder blades. He gave her a jab and she began to stumble towards the door, which stood wide open, the snow and wind rushing inwards with such force that the curtains billowed out in the gale and the mirror lifted on the wall. "She has nothing on her feet," I protested. "Let her have my boots – look, they are there, behind the door," and I made to get them. Alarmed, thinking I was going to grab Eileen, Geoff gave me a great whack on the side of the head and I went down on to the floor. I lay there, dizzy and sick, remembering all of a sudden that Casper too was in peril. My hand went up to the side of my head where I had fallen and came away covered in blood. Eileen was crying, the same awful sound I had heard the night before. There was no point in denying to myself that I was frightened of Geoff – bravery seemed out of the question. I simply wanted him to get out, even at the cost of Eileen's safety. "That'll teach you to meddle," he said. "Someone should've done that to you a long time ago. You've been asking for it and now you've bloody well got it. Mind your own business in future, like we do, keep your filthy tricks to yourself."

There were so many things I wanted to have the nerve to say, and I said none of them. I wanted to curse him for his brutality. I wanted to expose him as the prowler in the barn, as the madman who had smashed the pottery. I wanted to lash him with my tongue for his cruelty to Eileen and to Rufus and to Casper and to all things weaker than himself. I wanted to scorn him for his base ingratitude, to ask if this was just reward for giving him my body so freely. I wanted most of all to attack his twisted thinking and mercilessly straighten it out for him, to demonstrate to him beyond any doubt that his ways were filthier and more despicable than any of mine. I wanted desperately to defend myself against his base charges, to be proud of my own conduct. But I lay on the floor, at his feet, hurt and terrified, willing myself to keep still and not incur his wrath. It was the situation of all women, faced with a man stronger and in a position of power. No fine words could get over it, no liberation free me from that fact of nature. I dreaded the next kick from his heavy boot, inches from my bleeding face, and I concentrated on making myself small and insignificant, to escape his attention.

None of us heard Miss Cowdie come down the stairs. Just as Eileen was about to be propelled into the freezing night, she crept round the corner of the staircase and stood behind Geoff, without him even being aware of her. I saw the hem of her tattered dress – it flirted across my vision as I lay on the floor – and I looked up and saw her softly steal behind him. "That'll learn you," Geoff was saying again, "now don't meddle again. Go on, you – out – you won't melt – follow the path." He had relaxed his hold on his sister, once he realised she was utterly subdued, and the shotgun hung down from his right hand in a less menacing fashion. I did not dare call out but I prayed that Miss Cowdie would just let them go and that she would not do anything foolish when we were so nearly rid of the monster. I tried to signal to her but she was staring at the back of Geoff's head, standing exactly behind him like a shadow, and suddenly, with a speed I would never have thought her capable of, she had wrenched the gun from his hand. Geoff roared and slammed the door shut as he turned, and Eileen vanished like a frightened kitten under the table.

"Good Christ!" he shouted when he saw Miss Cowdie, back up against the wall, holding his gun. "Good God Almighty – what the hell – good God, give me that gun, you silly bitch." He advanced quite confidently, hand held out, and at once Miss Cowdie fired straight at his hand, and he screamed and backed away, clutching it to himself, the blood pouring down his trousers. "You maniac – you bloody bitch – " he yelled, but did not go nearer. He sank on to his knees and looked in terror at his mangled hand. I had moved almost as quickly as Eileen at the first shot, but in the direction of the staircase, and I could not see in the dim light what damage had been done, but Geoff did not faint, nor did the blood continue to pour out, and I saw him examine himself and seem relieved, in spite of the pain. "Get back," Miss Cowdie said, and I noticed at once that her voice was quite steady and clear. "Get back against that door, but do not try to open it or I will shoot you. Do you understand? I mean it. I will kill you if you open the door or move towards me. Is that understood?" Geoff did not reply, but he backed against the door, nursing his injured hand. "You are a brute," Miss Cowdie said, "a brute and a bully. I've watched you since you were a child, and you have lied and cheated and pushed your way through life. You're an animal, not a man."

"And you're a bloody madwoman," Geoff muttered, "a nutcase."

Miss Cowdie smiled. "If I am," she said, "thank your father."

"Bloody mad as a hatter," Geoff said, and moved just a fraction away from the door. Miss Cowdie raised the shotgun instantly above her shoulder and her finger moved to the trigger. Geoff shouted out and once more went on to his knees.

"I said I would shoot," Miss Cowdie said, "and I will. I don't care in the least if I kill you."

"When my dad hears of this he'll – he'll . . ." Geoff said, his voice thick with a strange combination of fear and rage, first one uppermost and then the other.

"He will do nothing," Miss Cowdie said.

"He'll brain you – "

"He will not. He is afraid of me. He is afraid I will tell everyone what I know. Your father, Geoffrey Crosthwaite, is nothing better than a common seducer. He seduced me, on the eve of my wedding to Arthur Armstrong. Then he told Arthur, boasted of his achievement, and that is why I was jilted. My madness stemmed from that. I was guilty, you see. I let him take me. I could not resist the attraction he had for me, though I loved Arthur. I wasn't any longer worthy to be his bride, but I pretended nothing had happened. Every time I see you, I remember your father's attraction. Like you, he was handsome. Like you, he was strong. Like you, he was a brute and a bully. Like you, he despised women and abused them."

"Bloody *mad*," Geoff said desperately.

But Miss Cowdie was not mad. For the first time, there was no mention of the Earl, or of a wedding tomorrow. She was perfectly sane and I believed every word she said. "I am going to kill you," she said to Geoff, "but only when you have apologised to your poor sister. Get up." Geoff struggled up. It was just beginning to dawn on him that all this was in earnest and his square, deceptively open, honest face was a map upon which could be read every developing emotion. "Say you are sorry to her," Miss Cowdie said. "Eileen, come out. He cannot hurt you. Stand here, beside me. Come." Eileen crawled out, shaking with nerves, and stood beside Miss Cowdie, head bent, hands twisting continually together. "Say, 'I am sorry for all the misery I have caused you.' "

"I am sorry for all the misery I have caused you," Geoff said, at lightning speed. Miss Cowdie raised the shotgun and seemed about to take aim. Even before Geoff could protest I had shouted, "Don't shoot him!" Miss Cowdie lowered the gun, but kept it trained on Geoff.

"Why not?" she asked. "I am putting down vermin."

"You're committing murder," I said, "cold blooded murder. It's wrong."

She smiled, but did not take her eyes off Geoff. "I will enjoy committing murder," she said, "and when I have murdered him, I will commit another murder. I will shoot that dear young boy upstairs, so that he will never grow up to be a man. I will save him from himself."

The room swam before my eyes – the soft colours of lamps and fire merged together into one swirling orange glow, the faces of Miss Cowdie and Eileen turned and turned, the window panes swivelled and changed position – and I could feel myself weightless, a roaring in my ears. I came to with Eileen supporting my head and I heard Miss Cowdie say, "A cold damp cloth on her forehead, Eileen. She is naturally shocked." Eileen got the cloth and bent down to apply it. I saw her pupils were dilated and fixed and though I knew she was almost concussed herself with terror I whispered, "Go behind her – knock the gun out of her hands," into her ear as she bent over me. "Stay where you are, Eileen," Miss Cowdie said. "It will soon be over."

"Don't!" Geoff pleaded. I could not see him but I could sense the tears. "I haven't done nothing to you – it isn't my fault – it was her that started it – playing around wi' me – didn't know what I was doing – couldn't think of anything else, night and day – she was wicked, wicked, and she started Eileen off the same way – it was for her own good I hit Eileen – before she got as bad – " but Miss Cowdie went on pointing the shotgun while Geoff poured out his gibberish defence. I knew she was going to shoot and that I must stop her, but as I got unsteadily to my feet the appalling roar of the gun exploded again and Eileen screamed and Geoff fell and at the bottom of the stairs appeared Casper, like a sleepwalker, clutching his pyjamas and open mouthed with bewilderment.

I rushed over to him while Miss Cowdie struggled to re-load

her gun, a task which took all her strength. She took the cartridges confidently from Geoff's pocket, as though she had known they would be there. I clutched Casper to me, and pushed him back against the staircase wall and spread myself across his warm body. "Get out of the way," Miss Cowdie said, "or I will shoot through you."

"Then you will have to shoot through me," I said, "he is my son. He was born out of that same passion with a man that you succumbed to – the same crime you shot Geoff for. I've denied his birth all my life, but now I am quite happy to die with him." I felt Casper's intake of breath and then his arms came round me slowly from behind and held me tightly. An insane happiness filled me and I even smiled and said, "I didn't marry the man I loved either, Miss Cowdie, but unlike you, I jilted him. You wanted to serve your lover, I dreaded serving anyone. I wanted freedom – I wanted only to consider myself – I didn't want to be either a wife or a mother. I wanted the passion you despised in yourself . . ."

All the time I was talking I could of course see Eileen crawling towards Miss Cowdie's feet. Her intervention could only be disastrous but I hoped she had heard what I had said earlier. Miss Cowdie's finger was permanently on the trigger – I did not know how many of her shots had been by design and how many by accident – and to touch her would surely make her fire. The gun pointed straight at us both, as it had done at Geoff, but it was nearer. What could Eileen possibly do? When she was next to Miss Cowdie's feet I saw her stop, but I could not see what she was doing, and I feared Miss Cowdie's reflex reaction. Eileen's sobbing interrupted my flow of rambling confession. "Eileen," Miss Cowdie said, still with the gun pointing at us, "Eileen, my child, there is no need for you to be afraid. He is dead. I'm not going to touch you." Eileen's crying became louder and more insistent. "Look," she wailed, "look what he done to me," and she held out her arm. Miss Cowdie, for the merest wisp of a second, looked, and I knocked the barrel of the gun upwards at the precise moment Eileen lunged and brought her down. The gun went off, there was a scream, Casper collapsed behind me and I fell upon the tangled mass of bodies below me, screaming myself and shouting, "Eileen! Eileen!" my eyes tight shut against the sight of the blood I knew there must be, and my hands shrinking from feeling the warmth of it, and my ears straining to hear the gun again, and Miss Cowdie triumphant.

All I heard, as confusion overwhelmed me, was the blissful noise of Eileen's sobbing, and nothing else.

Epilogue

I have just let myself in to my cottage, afloat on a black squelchy sea of mud, and I am sitting at the table, quite calm, about to make my decision. Now that you have heard all this, you may think there is no question about it – I will of course return to London and that life which suited me so well. I cannot possibly want to stay on Lowther Fell, can I? Not after such a tragedy, not after Miss Cowdie's death. She fell on the gun and blew her own poor addled brains out (except I still say that, for that hour or two, they were not addled, but the verdict at the inquest showed otherwise). Geoff is still in Carlisle, in the Cumberland Infirmary, seriously ill, but with a complete recovery ahead. The bullet went between his ribs, to the right of his heart, where it ruptured his spleen and did little other real damage. He will be as good as new, ready to work as hard as ever, in two or three months. His father was not too stunned to complain he would be short-handed at lambing time. I cannot bear even to see him at a distance since Miss Cowdie made her accusation, which, needless to say, nobody has mentioned since.

Eileen still comes. She said she would stay until I left – everyone, you see, assumes I will leave. They are surprised I am still here, a month later. There is very little to do, now that I have not the heart to do any pottery, now that there is only me, and I neither eat much nor make any mess for Eileen to clear up. But she has become quite devoted to me and likes to see me each day. She saved my life but persists in acting as though I saved hers. Her own little confession lies heavily upon her – it was Eileen who put the rabbit carcase and the sheep's head in the cottage, not Miss Cowdie. She said she did it "for fun", and wept at the thought. It was no use asking how it could be fun – she only became more upset and trying to get to the bottom of the mystery was not worth the effort. I am determined not to make too much of it, now that it is long since in the past. Eileen is happy – yes, happy. She knows Geoff will never molest her again, even when he is well. She feels she has gained power over him and told me he had "done himself in". She had known, of course, that Geoff was the intruder in the barn and that, too, had lain on her conscience. And Pete, the boy Geoff struck, the boy who brought her home from the dance, rang up. He saw the story of Miss Cowdie's death in the *Cumberland News* and then read all the lurid details in *The Sun*. He recognised Eileen and rang her up, and he has come out and taken her into Carlisle to the pictures, twice. She is talking of getting a room there and having a job where he works at Metal Box. It is not exactly the kind of break for freedom I would have liked to see her make, but it is better than being shut up on this fellside for the rest of her life. At least she will be able to get her hair done regularly.

I must take Rufus to the vet. Though we have just been for that long walk, he lies on the hearthrug, listless and sad. I know he pines for Casper but I think it is more than that – he hardly runs at all and droops along with his tail between his legs at all times. I pat him and talk to him but of course he wants Casper. I expect Casper wants him, however good a time he is having with Edward, with his father. Casper had measles, not flu – the spots came out the morning after that terrible night – but the moment he recovered I drove him to Manchester and put him on a plane to South America. He was so thrilled he could not contain his excitement, and I was afraid he would be ill all over again. The news that Edward was his father astounded and stunned him – he simply could not believe it. He asked me over and over again just to tell him if it was true, really true, and when I assured him it was, he had no interest in my explanations. In one bound he transferred his affections from the dead Gerald – who, perhaps, he had never liked – to his hero, Edward. He did not seem to care that this meant Antonia had not been his mother, or that in letting him believe this we had both practised a gross deception. I was perfectly prepared to tell him everything – indeed, I wanted to – but his mind wandered, the moment I launched on the explanation. I wanted to tell, but he did not want to know anything, except that Edward was – is – his father.

I spoke to Edward on the telephone from Howard's house – I had found the address on the back of Casper's railway stamp envelope. I sat in a room on my own – they were very discreet, very thoughtful – waiting for the pre-arranged call, twisting my sodden handkerchief over and over, applying it again and again to eyes that would not stop watering. When I heard his voice, astonishingly clear, I had to exercise the most tremendous will power not to break down and waste the opportunity I had, for such a short time. I told him to listen carefully, that he must not interrupt, and then I began at the end, outlining the details of Miss Cowdie's insanity and her death, and the situation I had found myself in. Then I told him what I had told Casper. There was a continued silence. When I asked if he was still there, he said he was, and could he now speak? He told me Geraldine, his sister, had told him – he too had had a letter, written from her death bed. He had let me keep my secret because it was so important to me and because he did not want to blackmail me. If I would not tell Casper I was his mother, then he could not tell him he was his father. I said I loved him, and wept at last. He told me he was coming home instantly, but at that I collected myself – no, I begged, not yet. I asked him to wait a month, and it was then that he suggested sending Casper to him. They will both return together, father and son, and then we can sort our future out.

I wonder if we can? Edward is so sensible – he can be relied on to think clearly. I do not imagine he will want to hear the full story of why I gave birth to Casper in such secrecy, and why Antonia and I pretended it was hers, even to Gerald. It was the most spectacular coup. The moment I was pregnant I thought of it. Antonia longed and longed for a child. After only a year of marriage, she had had repeated tests and had found herself proved almost certainly sterile. I, on the other hand, became pregnant by accident. I did not want an abortion – I could not bear the idea – but I did not want a child. I feared the consequences too much, I did not see how I could maintain my independence, and I was afraid that if I told Edward he would convince me we must marry. I lied to him. I told him I no longer loved him and that I thought I loved someone else and that I did not want to see him again. I thought the shock and the blow to his pride would make him go away, and it did. My horrible ruse was successful. I went off, on my own, and when I had thought everything out I went to see Antonia and presented her with my plan. Her only doubts were practical, not moral, ones. Did she have the nerve to carry it off? Could I go through with it? I convinced her it was possible. I took a job in Gloucestershire (not, of course, knowing that Edward's sister Geraldine was a nurse in the maternity hospital of the town I chose), and meanwhile Antonia told Gerald she was pregnant. She pretended she had booked in for the birth at University College Hospital, and became fat enough to pass for pregnant in loose maternity clothes. None of this would have worked if Gerald had not been sent abroad for three months – a fact we knew from the start. He was due to go to the Middle East at the end of October. The baby was due the end of January. Antonia planned to spend Christmas with me, which Gerald approved of, and then she intended to stay on, pleading influenza, until Gerald returned at the beginning of February, by which time the baby would be born, with me as guardian angel. Our anxiety hinged on the possibility of Gerald returning early for the birth, so Antonia wrote frequently, stressing that the doctors thought she had her dates wrong and the baby was more likely to be born mid February. In the event, Casper was a month premature and fitted into our plans beautifully. Gerald flew home two days later, to Antonia in bed with the infant and me standing beside her, able to say with feeling, "I think I feel worse than she does." Gerald didn't even notice my ashen face.

It was then, while Gerald was with Antonia, who was in my hospital bed, that I rang Edward, and Jennifer answered. I don't know what I had been going to say, nor how much difference it made that Edward was not at home at that precise moment. If I had heard his voice – if he had asked why I was ringing, after such a long silence – would I have burst into tears and told him I had borne his son, two days ago? I suppose I might – I had little self-control at the time. I felt so low and lonely, and desperately needed comfort. But Jennifer answered and her cool, clipped voice restored my resolution. I did not even leave a message, nor give a telephone number where I could be reached. And Jennifer never told Edward I had rung.

Gerald had to return to work in forty eight hours, a happy man, and by the time he came back for good Antonia was installed back home, a mother to her fingertips, while I had disappeared to America. The only person we had not fooled during those days I switched places with Antonia was Geraldine, who never even revealed her identity.

She had met Antonia briefly, all those years ago in Ullswater, but she had never met me, though of course Edward must have talked of me often. She certainly knew we were identical twins. I suppose I must have seen her, without knowing it, on the ward, and I suppose Antonia also saw her during her brief stay in my bed, but did not recognise her. All that matters is that Geraldine knew what had happened and kept her own counsel, and then spent the rest of her life wondering if she had done the right thing. She had not a shred of responsibility for the subterfuge, but she seems to have been haunted by a feeling that if she had either told me she had guessed the truth, or alternatively had relayed her suspicions to Edward, then everything would have been different.

I did not return for a year. I suppose during that year I had some sort of concealed breakdown. I worked (in a New York art gallery, restoring pictures), and I functioned perfectly well on the outside, but I hardly knew what I was doing. I was numb and miserable. I dreamed of babies every night. I wanted Edward. I did not know whether I was mad or not. Every time I thought of what I had done, in the name of freedom, I could only weep at my stupidity. Yet I came out of it. I had a love affair with a nice American, and this gave me back some of my confidence, and then I came home and began to enjoy myself again, and finally I laid the ghost of my baby by visiting Casper and finding him Antonia's baby, a perfect stranger, to whom I felt no attachment. I met Edward again and we began a different, more sporadic relationship. After five years, I knew I had done the right thing. I had escaped the chains of motherhood and the servitude of marriage. I was my own person.

But now I reckon the cost, and not just to myself. Fate killed Antonia and Gerald, and exposed Casper to misery, but I compounded the felony, a felony which need never have happened. Babies are not gifts to be gracefully donated. Casper was my son, he was Edward's son. I made him a cuckoo in a nest – a very comfortable, loving nest, but not his rightful home. I betrayed him. I ought either never to have had him or to have stood by him. The sort of adoption I arranged for him was wicked. Antonia shared his blood, but that was a cheat. My guilt is enormous. It is hardly less towards Edward. What I made him suffer is unspeakable. To be so afraid of his love, so unwilling to surrender to it . . . The world is full of women, of Eileens and Miss Cowdies, who hunger for it and never find it, and there was I, blessed a hundredfold, throwing the precious stuff in life's face, trampling upon it, destroying it, saying I did not want it.

This cottage shares my distress. Out there, on the fell, I no longer feel alien. Though I am unhappy, I have no wish to flee. I feel as if I have at last come home, and that those truths about myself for which I searched are finally revealed. I know them. I can face them, and accept them. The lessons are learned. No man is an island, nor any woman either. I have admitted it. All that remains is for me to admit it to others.

FICTION

CRIME/ADVENTURE/SUSPENSE

☐ The Killing In The Market	John Ball with Bevan Smith	£1.00
☐ In the Heat of the Night	John Ball	£1.00
☐ Johnny Get Your Gun	John Ball	£1.00
☐ The Cool Cottontail	John Ball	£1.00
☐ The Megawind Cancellation	Bernard Boucher	£1.25
☐ Slow Burn	Peter Cave	£1.50
☐ Tunnel	Hal Friedman	£1.35
☐ Barracuda	Irving A. Greenfield	£1.25
☐ Tagget	Irving A. Greenfield	£1.25
☐ Don't be no Hero	Leonard Harris	£1.25
☐ The Blunderer	Patricia Highsmith	£1.25
☐ A Game for the Living	Patricia Highsmith	£1.25
☐ Those who Walk Away	Patricia Highsmith	£1.25
☐ The Tremor of Forgery	Patricia Highsmith	£1.25
☐ The Two Faces of January	Patricia Highsmith	£1.25
☐ Labyrinth	Eric Mackenzie-Lamb	£1.25
☐ The Hunted	Elmore Leonard	£1.25
☐ Confess, Fletch	Gregory Mcdonald	90p
☐ Fletch	Gregory Mcdonald	90p
☐ Fletch's Fortune	Gregory Mcdonald	£1.25
☐ Flynn	Gregory Mcdonald	95p
☐ All the Queen's Men	Guiy de Montfort	£1.25
☐ Pandora Man	Kerry Newcomb and Frank Schaefer	£1.25
☐ Sigmet Active	Thomas Page	£1.10
☐ Crash Landing	Mark Regan	£1.25
☐ The Last Prisoner	James Robson	£1.50
☐ The Croesus Conspiracy	Ben Stein	£1.25
☐ Deadline in Jakarta	Ian Stewart	£1.25
☐ An H-Bomb for Alice	Ian Stewart	£1.50
☐ The Peking Payoff	Ian Stewart	90p
☐ The Seizing of Singapore	Ian Stewart	£1.00
☐ Winter Stalk	James L. Stowe	£1.25
☐ Rough Deal	Walter Winward	£1.10

HISTORICAL ROMANCE/ROMANCE/SAGA

☐ Hawksmoor	Aileen Armitage	£1.75
☐ Blaze of Passion	Stephanie Blake	£1.25
☐ Daughter of Destiny	Stephanie Blake	£1.25
☐ Flowers of Fire	Stephanie Blake	£1.50
☐ So Wicked My Desire	Stephanie Blake	£1.50
☐ Wicked is My Flesh	Stephanie Blake	£1.50
☐ Lovers and Dancers	Michael Feeney Callan	£1.50
☐ The Lofty Banners	Brenda Clarke	£1.75
☐ The Enchanted Land	Jude Deveraux	£1.50
☐ My Love, My Land	Judy Gardiner	£1.25
☐ Walburga's Eve	Elizabeth Hann	£1.35
☐ Lily of the Sun	Sandra Heath	95p
☐ Strangers' Forest	Pamela Hill	£1.00
☐ Royal Mistress	Patricia Campbell Horton	£1.50
☐ The Rebel Heart	Anna James	£1.25
☐ Gentlemen Callers	Nancy Lamb	£1.50
☐ Fires of Winter	Johanna Lindsey	£1.50
☐ A Pirate's Love	Johanna Lindsey	£1.25
☐ Trade Imperial	Alan Lloyd	£1.35
☐ Dance Barefoot	Margaret Maddocks	95p
☐ The Open Door	Margaret Maddocks	£1.25
☐ All We Know of Heaven	Dore Mullen	£1.25
☐ The Far Side of Destiny	Dore Mullen	£1.50
☐ New Year's Eve	Jeannie Sakol	£1.50
☐ The Pride	Judith Saxton	£1.50
☐ Heir to Trevayan	Juliet Sefton	£1.25
☐ Never Trust a Handsome Man	Marlene Fanta Shyer	£1.25
☐ Shadow of an Unknown Woman	Daoma Winston	£1.00
☐ Call the Darkness Light	Nancy Zaroulis	£1.95

FICTION

GENERAL

Title	Author	Price
☐ Chains	Justin Adams	£1.25
☐ Secrets	F. Lee Bailey	£1.25
☐ Skyship	John Brosnan	£1.65
☐ The Memoirs of Maria Brown	John Cleland	£1.25
☐ The Last Liberator	John Clive	£1.25
☐ A Forgotten Season	Kathleen Conlon	£1.10
☐ My Father's House	Kathleen Conlon	£1.25
☐ Wyndward Fury	Norman Daniels	£1.50
☐ Ladies in Waiting	Gwen Davis	£1.50
☐ The Money Wolves	Paul Erikson	£1.50
☐ Rich Little Poor Girl	Terence Feely	£1.50
☐ Fever Pitch	Betty Ferm	£1.50
☐ Abingdon's	Michael French	£1.50
☐ Rhythms	Michael French	£1.50
☐ A Sea Change	Lois Gould	80p
☐ Forced Feedings	Maxine Herman	£1.50
☐ Love Among the Mashed Potatoes	Gregory Mcdonald	£1.10
☐ Gossip	Marc Olden	£1.25
☐ The Red Raven	Lilli Palmer	£1.25
☐ Summer Lightning	Judith Richards	£1.25
☐ The Hamptons	Charles Rigdon	£1.35
☐ The Dream Makers	John Sherlock	£1.50
☐ The Affair of Nina B.	Simmel	95p
☐ The Berlin Connection	Simmel	£1.50
☐ The Cain Conspiracy	Simmel	£1.20
☐ Double Agent — Triple Cross	Simmel	£1.35
☐ Celestial Navigation	Anne Tyler	£1.00
☐ Earthly Possessions	Anne Tyler	95p
☐ Searching for Caleb	Anne Tyler	£1.00

WESTERN — BLADE SERIES by Matt Chisholm

☐ No. 1 The Indian Incident	75p
☐ No. 2 The Tucson Conspiracy	75p
☐ No. 3 The Laredo Assignment	75p
☐ No. 4 The Pecos Manhunt	75p
☐ No. 5 The Colorado Virgins	85p
☐ No. 6 The Mexican Proposition	85p
☐ No. 7 The Arizona Climax	85p
☐ No. 8 The Nevada Mustang	85p
☐ No. 9 The Montana Deadlock	85p
☐ No. 10 The Cheyenne Trap	95p
☐ No. 11 The Navaho Trail	95p
☐ No. 12 The Last Act	95p

SCIENCE FICTION

Title	Author	Price
☐ Times Without Number	John Brunner	£1.10
☐ Drinking Sapphire Wine	Tanith Lee	£1.25
☐ Watchtower	Elizabeth A. Lynn	£1.10

WAR

Title	Author	Price
☐ The Anderson Assault	Peter Leslie	£1.25
☐ Killers under a Cruel Sky	Peter Leslie	£1.25
☐ The Serbian Triangle	Peter Saunders	£1.10
☐ Jenny's War	Jack Stoneley	£1.25

NAVAL HISTORICAL

Title	Author	Price
☐ The Mary Celeste	John Maxwell	£1.00
☐ The Baltic Convoy	Showell Styles	95p